MACHIAVELLIAN

GANGSTERS OF NEW YORK, BOOK 1

BELLA DI CORTE

Bella Di Corte

Editing by: Alisa Carter

Cover Designed by: Najla Qamber Designs

To all the Mariposas of the world.
11:11 belongs to you.
Make a wish...

"Men judge generally more by the eye than by the hand, for everyone can see and few can feel. Every one sees what you appear to be, few really know what you are."

— Niccolò Machiavelli

FOREWARD

Dear Reader,

This journey began with the Fausti famiglia. (You'll meet them soon in the pages of Mac.)

When I first started writing the Fausti saga, I had no idea *what* kind of story I was (truly) writing until Book 2. Once I hit my stride, I couldn't stop. The Faustis opened a door to a world that I was instantly taken with, and before long, they took over *my* world.

By the time their saga was complete, I couldn't wait to start writing spin-off stories. There are so many worlds connected to that one that have captured my attention, which is why, after I realized how many branches there were, I decided to dedicate an entire name to my criminal worlds only.

From this point forward, all of my criminal-world books will be in one place, and most of the stories will connect in some way. The Faustis have long-reaching arms, they rule *that* world, and in some way, you'll probably reconnect with one or two of them in each book, even if it's set in a different criminal world.

Enter Machiavellian.

This story, like most of my others, completely captivated me. I had other books planned, books that revolved around some of the main men in the Fausti *famiglia*, but Capo & Mari had other plans for me. It was a wonderful change of pace to step into a similar but different world with them. And even though some of the Faustis make an appearance in Machiavellian, you do not have to read the Fausti saga before you read Mac (or any of the Gangsters of New York books). If you decide to, Mac's timeline fits after Book 5 and before Book 6 of the Fausti saga.

That being said, I put together a list of names for each family and how they belong so that it might be easier to keep track.

Machiavellian has such a special place in my heart. It's unlike anything I've ever written before. And now, given the unprecedented times we're facing, I think we need more stories like this one. Stories that open a door to a new world and invite us in for a while. I've only said this about the Fausti saga—there are some books that feel like coming home.

Machiavellian is one of those books for me. May it be the same for you.

Much love,
    Bella

P.S. All (3) books in the Gangsters of New York series are standalones, but each are set in the same world. Read on to find out who will be next!

THE
FAUSTI
FAMILY

Faustis who are either mentioned or make an appearance in **Machiavellian:**

Marzio Fausti (deceased) was the head of the infamous Fausti *famiglia* in Italy. He has five sons: **Luca, Ettore, Lothario, Osvaldo,** and **Niccolo.**

Luca Fausti (incarcerated) is the eldest son of Marzio Fausti and he has four sons: **Brando, Rocco, Dario,** and **Romeo.**

Brando Fausti is married to **Scarlett Rose Fausti.**

Rocco Fausti is married to **Rosaria Caffi.**

Tito Sala, MD is connected to the Faustis by marriage. He is married to **Lola Fausti.**

Donato:
Head Soldier

Guido:
Soldier

———

There's a drawn-out feud between the Faustis and the Stones in the **Fausti Family Saga.** It's not truly explored in **Mac,** but it is worth mentioning because one of the **Stones (Scott)** makes an appearance in **Mac**— he'll also be in **Book 2** of the **Gangsters of New York series** in a more centralized way.

IL LUPO

SCARPONE

Arturo Lupo Scarpone:

He is the head of the Scarpone family; one of the five families of New York.

He has two sons: **Vittorio Lupo Scarpone** (mother, **Noemi**) and **Achille Scarpone** (mother, **Bambi**).

Vittorio Lupo Scarpone:

He is the son of **Arturo** and **Noemi**.

His maternal grandfather, **Pasquale Ranieri**, was a world renown poet and novelist from Sicily. He had five daughters (who all, but Noemi, live in Italy): **Noemi Ranieri Scarpone, Stella, Eloisa, Candelora,** and **Veronica.**

He has one brother: **Achille Scarpone**

Achille Scarpone:

He is the son of **Arturo** and **Bambi.**

He has four sons: **Armino, Justo, Gino, and Vito** (Only **Armino** and **Vito** are mentioned by name in Mac.)

He has one brother: **Vittorio Lupo Scarpone**

Tito Sala (married to **Lola Fausti**) is **Pasquale Ranieri's** first cousin.

MACHIAVELLIAN

adjective

1. cunning, scheming, and unscrupulous, especially in politics.

noun

1. a person who schemes in a Machiavellian way.

PROLOGUE

VITTORIO

We were once the rulers of the world. Side by side, my father and I reigned over what I assumed would be mine one day: a kingdom of misfits and a throne built on fear and respect. Soon enough, though, I'd find out that ruling the world was only one reality.

Reality differs from person to person, soul to soul, perspective to perspective.

For instance, my father saw life as a game to be won—to be precise, a chess game. Move for ruthless move, he had become the king of New York by being brutal and cunning. No matter what he did, or what move he made, he did so with one objective in mind: *win all, no matter who gets trumped in the end.* Strategies, forethought, take no prisoners and show no mercy, not even to those closest to you—these were the three codes he religiously lived by.

He made the right connections, married the perfect girl, worked all the lavish parties and schmoozed or killed numerous people from all walks of life. He proved to the reality we created, *the world we ruled over*, how competent he was and how vicious he could be. Even those who ruled the streets feared his name.

Arturo Lupo Scarpone, the King of New York.

No one could trump his moves. No one could get close to him. Not even his own flesh and blood. His son.

Vittorio Lupo Scarpone, the Pretty-Boy Prince.

Arturo stripped me of the reality, *that name,* and banished me from the kingdom he had so savagely prepared me for, and then, *and then,* he wrote me off as dead.

There was a reason his men called him *il re lupo. The king wolf.* He'd kill his own offspring if it meant more power.

There's an old saying: *Dead men tell no tales.* I didn't have tales to tell. I only had one gruesome story.

This time the man who created me was going to pay. Because if I was already dead in his eyes, how could he see me coming?

Boo, motherfucker. You called me The Prince. I'm back to rule your world as King.

1

16 Years Ago

Arranged marriages were not uncommon in our culture. I'd always known that someday I'd marry Angelina Zamboni. Her father was connected, and apart from mine, he was one of the most powerful men in New York. Angelo Zamboni, Angelina's father, was in politics.

Mine dealt more in fear and bloodshed, though hers didn't shy away from that either. Angelo's hands were clean even if his conscience was filthy. Arturo Scarpone was born without a conscience and grew into a man with palms full of blood— most people in our circle both admired and feared that about him. Angelo craved that sort of ruthless backing, so he agreed to the marriage before his daughter had a say.

We were the couple that everyone admired and praised. *We made a beautiful couple. We would make beautiful babies. We would make a beautiful life together,* even if the shady parts of my life were hidden behind the seemingly perfect life we lived. When the day came for me to rule this ruthless kingdom my father left me, she'd be the queen next to me on this throne built on bloodshed.

Angelina would also be my very own *omertà*. She'd be my vow of silence through thick and thin, good times and bad, sickness and health, through the most trying police interviews and adversaries attempting to put the fear of God into her.

Loyalty was even more powerful than love in this life. It was imperative to know your enemies better than your friends. But I had learned early on that no one was truly your friend. Loyalty all depended on how much they depended on you, and you on them.

Angelina grinned and then nudged me as we walked the streets of New York, bringing me out of my thoughts. It was dark out, but the many lights around us lit up her face.

Her hair was the color of soft caramel, her skin tan, and her eyes brown. My brother once said she had wicked eyes. They were. When she wanted revenge, they narrowed to daggers and showed no mercy. She wasn't taller than me even with heels, but she was tall for a woman. Her legs were long enough to wrap around me and pull me closer when we fucked.

In a month's time, I'd call her my wife—*Mrs. Vittorio Scarpone*—and years' worth of business dealings between my father and hers would come to fruition. Arturo liked telling Angelo that the two families shared an olive tree. Angelo brought the tree from the old country. Arturo planted it in New York soil. To kingdom come, both families would enjoy the golden oil.

"You've been quiet," she said, her eyes glistening as she glanced up at me.

"Can't get much talking in during a Broadway show." The breath rushed out of my mouth in a cloud of smoke.

"I can't read your mood." She stopped walking. I did, too. She backed up a pace so we could really see each other. Her eyes narrowed. "Have you been having second thoughts?"

Snow twirled between us. White specks landed on the dark

material of my jacket. They collected for a few seconds, even on my lashes, before I spoke. "I'm returning the question."

She smiled a little at that. She shook her head. "This is a done deal."

In our world, it was always about the art of the deal, and making sure you paid for your sins if you went against the king. "Only God could sever this arrangement," I said.

"God or your father." She stuck her long, elegant fingers inside the pockets of her expensive jacket.

A man in a suit passed us, one hand on his briefcase and a phone stuck to his ear. I didn't miss his eyes, though. They roamed over Angelina as he hustled to get out of the cold. It didn't trouble me. What bothered me was the cold hand that seemed to touch my neck—and it wasn't the weather.

Angelina had been used as a pawn in this game before she could even string two words together. I was at her side since we were kids. We both understood that love had nothing to do with this arrangement, but I wanted this to be a great union, a powerful one, and I knew it'd be easier if we both held mutual feelings for each other. I expected the kind of respect from her that had its foundation in loyalty.

Lately, though, I could sense something from her that felt off. It wasn't the first time the cold hand seemed to touch my neck and make my instincts prickle.

"You really are a beautiful man, Vittorio. You should have taken your father's offer when you had the chance."

My eyes narrowed, as if I could see her better. *See straight through her.* These sorts of remarks didn't sit right with me. Not one to mince words, she was getting better at the art of subtlety. I didn't fucking like it. Especially when she started throwing words around that she had no business bringing out into the open.

She was right. My father had once given me an out. A chance to live my life the way I saw fit while still doing his dirty work. Instead of being an integral part of the business, he wanted me to be the face of it. I'd own all of the fancy restaurants and grease high society to get them closer to his pocket. He said my looks and charisma would charm them. My brother, Achille, was better suited to be his right-hand man.

It was the only choice my father had ever given me. However, it wasn't truly a choice. It was a dare. Let my younger brother, who he called The Joker, control the kingdom with him, and what did that make me? A pussy that he'd have no use for. I'd be lower than the ten-dollar guys he hired to clean his tables.

Angelina seemed to know that my father would never let me live it down. Once he found a weakness, he'd stick his finger in the soft spot until the sore refused to heal. Until it healed around him, so he could reopen it anytime he wanted.

My father knew my mother was my only weakness. He still made asinine wisecracks about how beautiful I was, just like her family in Italy, just like she was.

Arturo would never say it to their faces, though. My mother had ties to the powerful Faustis, and unless my father had an immediate death wish, he respected them. The last thing he wanted was for them to come sniffing around. They didn't, unless you included them in your affairs. Even though Arturo was the King of New York, he couldn't touch the Faustis. They ruled his world.

After I told my father that I'd rather be dead than let Achille have what was rightfully mine, he laughed like lunatics do and then went to the room he shared with his wife Bambi. Not my mother. Bambi was Achille's mother.

My father always felt that Achille was better suited for the ruthless part of the business. He was harder in the face, but that was about it. I had proved my worth, despite the reflection that stared back at me in the mirror. My blood and heart was made from the same flesh and bone. I killed just as savagely as he did.

Angelina had never spoken about it before. I had never shared it with her. *How the fuck did she know?*

"Achille is giving you private information now." I took a step forward and she held her ground. "Why is that, *la mia promessa?*"

She laughed, the breath coming out of her mouth in a cold fog. "That's all you ever call me. *Your promised.*"

"Would you like me to call you something different? In a month, I'll call you my wife."

"It doesn't matter." Her teeth clenched and her jaw tightened. "All that matters is, I'm yours. I belong to you. You *own* me."

"Your point?"

She laughed even harder and then sighed. "I'm pregnant, Vittorio."

"Good," I said. "That pleases me." It seemed the warnings about protection not being a hundred percent were spot on. I'd always protected myself with her. But there were a few times we were rough and things got shady.

"If my father finds out that I had—"

"He won't touch you." If her father found out that I had sex with his daughter before marriage, it could cause some tension. Angelo had a bad temper. He'd go as far as pulling down her pants and whipping her ass with a belt if he found out that she had disgraced him. She was only eighteen, but as the old saying goes, *age is just a number*. She was mature beyond her years. She had to be.

Her phone rang and she turned from me, searching in her purse. A moment later, the phone was up to her ear and she was talking quietly. Whoever she was talking to, they were talking about where we were headed.

My maternal grandfather's first cousin, Tito Sala, was in

town, and we were supposed to meet at the restaurant Angelina and I planned on going to. While she was busy changing our plans, I sent a quick text to Tito letting him know where he could meet me. Earlier, he said he had something to discuss with me, and it was important. He was married to Lola, a Fausti by blood.

My phone was back in my pocket before she turned around.

"Change of plans," she said, telling me something I already knew. "Mamma ate at Rosa's tonight, and not only was it packed, but Ray ran out of veal. I want veal *parmigiana*." She touched her stomach. "We'll go to Dolce instead."

I nodded but said nothing else. I refused to move. She knew why, so she went on to explain.

"What I repeated to you, I overheard in a private conversation, Vittorio. Your father and Achille were having dinner, and as I passed the dining room, I overheard. You never told me that before." She shrugged. "It made me curious."

"It's none of your business," I said.

"Right." She turned from me again. "Let's just go to dinner. I'm hungry and cold."

"Angelina," I said.

Before she turned to face me, a cloud of breath drifted from her mouth. She was almost too eager to get to the restaurant.

"You know the rules. You'll be my wife, but what happens in my family is my business. Unless I tell you what's going on, you'll stick to your business, understood?" There was a reason why I knew her as a child, protected her even. I was molding her to be my wife. She had to have rules, or this life would slay the both of us.

"Perfectly," she said, more than a bite to her tone. "But my business is yours." The words were said underneath her breath. I didn't bother contradicting them because she spoke the truth.

We walked next to one another in silence until I cleared my

throat. "We'll tell the family about the pregnancy when we get back from our honeymoon."

"Fine," she said. "At least I'll be out of his house and away from him by then."

She loved her father, but she feared him more. For her, an arranged marriage meant freedom. An arranged marriage for me meant that I'd be in even deeper, so deep that I'd never find a way out, unless it was in a body bag.

By the time we made it to the restaurant, the breath was coming faster from her mouth, and her feet showed no sign of slowing. Again, she was almost too eager. I went to put my hand on her lower back and usher her into the restaurant, but she shook her head.

"Let's go through the back," she said. "Gabriella and Bobby are having dinner. Mamma told me. I don't feel like catching the gossip train tonight. Patrizio has our private table reserved."

Bobby worked for my father, and Gabriella was one of Angelina's many cousins. Every time we saw her out—or at family gatherings, or passing her in the hall—she had nothing to talk about but the wedding. *Waa. Waa. Waa.* The woman could talk for days without needing a glass of water.

As we turned the corner, entering into the dark and damp alleyway that ran parallel to the restaurant, the zippy sounds of Louis Prima met us, along with the smell of boiling pasta, roasting garlic, stewing tomatoes, and tonight's already freezing trash from the dumpster.

Instead of stopping to let me open the door for her, as usual, she stood in front of it, staring at the metal handle. A second later her eyes darted up to meet mine before they returned to the cold brass.

"You're stalling," I said, calling her out on her odd behavior.

Louis Prima sang out "Angelina" from behind the door, and her eyes flew up, her body tense. When the realization washed over her that no one had called her name, she visibly relaxed, but I knew better. She was wound tight.

"You're being foolish, Vittorio."

"Am I, Princess?"

She whirled on me, and I caught her wrist before she slapped me across the face. "Fuck. You," she spat at me.

"Touched a nerve?" Her father called her Princess, and she hated it. She hated it so much that during our private meeting to discuss the terms of our marriage—*"this is what I expect from you,"* I'd demanded; *"this is what I expect from you,"* she'd countered —she requested that I never call her that. But something was off tonight, and whatever she had locked down on her tongue, she needed to get it off of her fucking chest. It was unlike her to keep quiet.

She yanked her wrist out of my hold. "You know you did! You know exactly what you're doing. At all times! You're so cold. So..." She paused, like she was trying to collect her thoughts. "It doesn't matter. There is no changing you! It's useless to even waste my time and breath."

I lifted my arm, making my jacket fall back, exposing my wrist. My expensive watch lit up the darkness and the wolf on my hand. "Time." I motioned toward the Panerai. "Speak now or forever hold your peace."

She narrowed her eyes at me when I spoke those last words. "What do you know—"

Before she could finish, two big goons I didn't recognize stepped out of Dolce. Patrizio ran it, but it was just a front for the Scarpones. One of the goons smoked a cigarette. The other one had his hands stuffed into the pockets of his leather jacket, collar pulled up to his ears. Each man took a spot next to Angelina.

"I'll only say this once," I said.

"Say what?" Cigarette said. His Irish accent was light, but I caught it.

"Move."

"Or?" Leather Jacket said. He was Italian, but not a man I knew.

I said nothing, staring at them, giving them the chance to retreat without me having to use violence.

"The baby's not yours," Angelina blurted.

It took me a moment to break eye contact with the two goons and concentrate on her.

"I can't marry a man who doesn't love me," she continued, and I could see how the two fuckers standing next to her made her feel brave. *Confident.* "I hate that we have to part on these terms, but I promise to bring you flowers. It's the least I can do."

My eyes moved with the two fuckers next to her, who were moving closer—not to me but to her.

"After all these years you didn't learn a fucking thing from me, did you?" I said.

"I learned enough to know that you're not capable of love. You're too fucked up to even attempt to feel it. Noemi—"

"Keep her name out of your mouth," I almost growled.

Even with the two next to her, she knew she had gone too far, so she changed course, cutting right to another quick. "Do you honestly think I'd have a child from you? I want the Scarpone blood, but not from you."

"You're stupider than I gave you credit for," I said.

She went to take a step toward me, no doubt to land the slap that she couldn't before, but my brother took a step outside, wrapping an arm around her waist.

"Come now, sweetheart," he said. "Don't you think my brother's having a rough night as it is? Go easy on him."

"Achille," I said. "I hear congratulations are in order. You're going to be a father." The pieces easily fell into place—her confession and his presence.

His smile came slow, turning up the corners of his mouth like the fucking Joker. "She told you?"

"In not so many words." I returned the smile.

He shrugged. "We both know it doesn't really matter."

Angelina looked between the two of us, confusion warring with the stoicism on her face. I saw her throat bob when she swallowed hard. "Why didn't you just kill her, Vittorio?" A brief show of remorse joined the battlefield of emotions she tried to hide.

"Yeah, why didn't you kill her, Pretty Prince Vittorio?" Achille mocked. "Not that this would've turned out any differently, but you made it so, so easy to convince Pop that one of us had to go. He was all set on giving you the kingdom one day—beautiful wife, beautiful home, beautiful offspring to carry on the family name, and all that belonged to him—and there you go, fucking it all up by betraying him."

"We both know it doesn't really matter," I said, repeating Achille's words. It summed up everything so perfectly. All I needed was a bow to wrap things up.

Achille tucked his nose deep into Angelina's hair, breathing her in, his eyes shut tight. "Thank you, Angel," he said. "For everything, but it seems your loyalty to my side was unneeded. In the end, my brother put the nail in his own coffin. You just gave him one more thing to regret. Who needs a woman like you when a man is better off in the bed of a viper? Treachery is an unforgivable sin, sweetheart, no matter who in my family you cross."

Her eyes froze and her breath came faster as he slid his nose up higher, along the skin of her face, placing a soft kiss on her cheek. He whispered something in her ear, and she closed her eyes, a lone tear falling. The light of the restaurant caught its slow track.

Achille finally opened his eyes, gave me a wide smile, and then shoulder checked me on the way out. The two goons next to Angelina took her by the arms; at the same time, four men came up behind me, one holding a knife to my throat. Angelina started fighting, screaming at Achille to come back—"*How could you do this to me!*"—before she started screaming for me to help her.

You want to scream for me now, Princess? After you set me up to be slaughtered? The words were on the tip of my tongue, but they'd fall on deaf ears. Instead of screaming for me, she should scream for God, the only force strong enough to stop this. No one was getting out of this alive. Not if the king wolf had ordered it and there was no angel to stop it.

2

MARIPOSA

Present Day

Only the truly poor know the difference between being hungry and being starved. My stomach made an obnoxious noise, reminding me of how starved I was. *How long had it been since I last ate? One day? Two?* I had scraps here and there, crackers from some fast food restaurant that they left out with the ketchup and other condiments sealed in plastic, but that was about it.

My stomach made an even louder noise, and I mentally told it to shut up. It should've been used to the neglect.

It wasn't easy making it in a city that easily chewed you up and spit you out. I'd never lived anywhere other than New York. Dreamed about it, but I never had the means to leave. Funds meant freedom, and I was not free by any means.

Even sadder than the state of my growling stomach was the fact that once I faded from this place called earth (or for some of us, hell), there would be nothing of me to truly leave behind.

"What is this, Mari?" I said to myself. "A pity-fuck day? This is your own fault, and you know it. You shouldn't be standing here."

I couldn't help myself, though. As poor as the streets of New York could be, there was another side to it that was every bit the definition of opulent. It was hard to overlook the draw, the richness, the sheer absurdity of it all. How some people were barely making it, eating week-old bread and wearing someone else's (too small) shoes to keep their feet clean, hustling for their next dollar, while others were wasting thousands of dollars on ass implants and clothes they'd never wear.

It wasn't that I begrudged them these things—*who am I kidding? I do fucking begrudge them these things.* Especially the ass implants when my stomach hosted a pack of hungry wolves howling to be fed.

Yeah, New York had chewed me up, but it had yet to spit me out. There was no doubt, though, that I was close to becoming dumpster trash one of these days. I'd probably end up with the wasted food I'd love to eat.

I sighed, long and hard, fogging up the glass window of Macchiavello's. The name was done in gold and looked elegant. It was the kind of restaurant that you probably needed to make a reservation for months in advance. On the opposite side of the shiny glass, expensive suits and fancy dresses dined, most of them getting the steak. They usually did.

My mouth watered. "If we make it out of this alive, we'll be getting the steak, too."

It was good to dream, right? I could put it down in my dream journal. I once saw this woman with a mega-watt smile and hair extensions say that I, too, could live the dream, *my best life,* if only I had one of these journals. I should list all of the things I was thankful for on a daily basis, even things I didn't have, things that seemed so far beyond my grasp that sometimes I called myself foolish for even thinking about them. The idea was to project all that my heart desired onto my life.

Will it to be true.

My entire journal was made up of *I am's.*

I am thankful that I am no longer poor.

I am thankful that I am a millionaire who wants for nothing.

I am thankful that I am a world traveler.

And the one that I'd rather die than let anyone see. *I am thankful to be loved beyond measure by someone special.*

I made a mental note to add *I am thankful for the steak I had at a ritzy restaurant* to the top of my list. Maybe I needed to get more specific more often. Come to think of it, I think the happiness guru mentioned doing just that. I was at work at the time, so maybe some of the details got lost in translation a bit.

This happiness guru never gave a time limit on when these things were supposed to start happening. I sure as fuck hoped it would be soon. That steak looked so good. If one of the people behind the glass needed a kidney, I'd trade mine for the steak. As far as I knew, both of mine were in pretty good shape.

Besides, why keep two when you only need one? In light of the prospect, I wasn't a gluttonous person, and if someone needed my assistance in return for a good meal—just once in my life—I was there for it. *Yesterday.*

"Hey!"

I turned around at the sound of the voice, holding tighter to the straps of my old leather backpack. Normally I wouldn't have turned around, but the voice was close and the reflection in the glass seemed to be staring right at me.

"You talkin' to me?" I said.

"Yeah," he said. "Get the fuck away from here. You're scaring our customers. Staring in the glass like some wide-eyed bug that needs to be squashed."

Even though his words stung me to my core, because I knew that he knew I was dreaming of the food behind the glass and had no means to even enjoy a burger from some fast-food joint, much less this five-star restaurant, I squared my shoulders and narrowed my eyes against his. "You and what army are going to make me?"

"You don't move along, I'm going to have security escort you to a place you might find more your speed. The dumpsters."

If I had any fucks left to give, I would've certainly given one to that underhanded crack. "I'm doing nothing wrong! I'm trying to decide if I want to come in for a bite or not." *Lie.* "But seeing as your restaurant is probably full of rodents like yourself, I think *I'll* pass."

And to think I was willing to give a kidney for one of his crummy steaks. I needed to up my standards some before thoughts like that took hold and appeared in my journal. Who knew when that shit was going to come true? I'd probably end up owing this asshole a kidney for a steak.

He doubled over and belly laughed. Then he stopped suddenly and pointed behind me. "I'm not going to tell you again, Dumpster Princess. Get the fuck out of here or—"

The words died in his throat as an expensive black car drove up to the restaurant and parked in front of it like he owned the place. Like he was king of the world. I couldn't tell if the driver was a he or a she, but something about the entire scene screamed male. Followed by *dominance.*

I thought about walking before the mysterious man stepped out, but since he had silenced Smart Mouth, I waited to see how this was going to play out.

Smart Mouth almost ran to the fancy car and greeted the man—*he was a man.* Smart Mouth's voice was eager to please, the exact opposite of how he'd spoken to me.

Smart Mouth chattered on as the man stepped onto the sidewalk and headed straight to the door of the restaurant. I wasn't aware of many men, but this one... Not going to lie, I couldn't look away from.

Under what was no doubt a custom-made suit, he probably had more muscles than I could count. He was tall with wide shoulders, jet-black hair, and golden skin. His nose was angular, as was the shape of his face. His lips were full. I wished I could see his eyes, but they were hidden underneath a pair of sunglasses that were probably worth more than I'd see in more than three years.

I could smell his cologne—citrus and a hint of sandalwood —and it seemed like a breath of fresh air in this city full of too many people and too many dumpsters. He smelled the way I imagined the ocean did, an exotic place to get lost in. He walked with so much swagger, I was convinced that he was the owner of the restaurant. Maybe even the sidewalk.

Smart Mouth opened the door to the restaurant for the man in the suit, and before they both stepped inside, the man in the suit stopped. Two women in expensive dresses slid past him and Smart Mouth, who greeted them with a huge smile on his face and a hand welcoming them inside.

One. Two. Three. Four. Five seconds after the women had gone in to be seated, the man in the suit turned to me, and I released a breath I didn't realize I'd been holding.

Fucka me. He was even more attractive from that angle—full frontal. The only words that came to mind were *head-on collision with a massive wave out of nowhere.* He'd take me out with a tide I couldn't fight, since I had no idea how to swim, and then wreck me, his power enough to slam me up against a rock.

Not that it was hard. I hardly had anything left to wreck.

Smart Mouth sucked in a breath when he realized who the man in the suit was staring at. His face turned a shade of red reserved for raw meat. Maybe because of my reaction to Smart Mouth giving me a death stare, the man in the suit looked between us.

"I apologize, sir," Smart Mouth said. "I'm about to get—"

The man in the suit lifted his hand and silenced Smart Mouth before he could utter another word. I couldn't stand the intense way the man in the suit studied me from behind his glasses. I knew he was studying me by the way my body reacted. It had been years since I felt...small in the presence of someone.

Judged. Sentenced. Ridiculed. Banished.

I looked down, playing with the straps of my backpack, feeling even worse when my eyes caught sight of my tennis shoes. They were two sizes too small. My toes pressed against the fabric, close to breaking through, and some days I thought, *what a relief that will be,* because they hurt. Blood stained them in spots from the wear and tear on my flesh. Then again, if I didn't have these shoes, I had close to nothing. I didn't have the money to buy a used pair, much less a new set.

I am thankful to have shoes that fit—an entire closet full.

I'd fill in the details later, once I was home and could put some thought into the ones I liked the best.

I am also thankful that this baseball jersey matches the damned shoes. I'm not mismatched today.

It was all I had to hold on to in the moment, something completely mine and true.

Oh, right, back to the guy in the suit. I wanted to lift my eyes, to defy him, daring him to judge me so I could give him the *"see how much I care about your opinion"* look—*zilch*—but I couldn't bring myself to meet his eyes again. My cheeks felt hotter than the pits of Hades. A bead of sweat rolled down my chest, between my breasts, and I was suddenly highly aware of my body. How anxious I felt.

Spur of the moment, I lifted my eyes, pretending like the way he looked at me didn't make me feel like running and keeping still at the same time. Even a little of that went a long way, so I turned then, preparing to walk away.

I stopped after two steps, turning back. "Who needs your crappy restaurant anyway?" I shouted. "The steak is probably not even worth the kidney!" Then I sent them both an aggressive chin flick.

At first the man's dark eyebrows drew down, but then...was that a grin tugging at his lips? It was hard to tell. It seemed foreign. Like he hadn't used the muscles in a while. It didn't matter. I disappeared into the bustling crowd before I could get another look. I was just another body in the midst of millions.

3

"Come on, Caspar! Give me another chance! Cut me some slack."

"You're late again. Fired. Fired. *Fired*."

"You don't mean that! You really don't."

"I do. And if you'd like me to lend you my dictionary so you can truly understand the meaning behind the word, I have one in my office for days like this one."

"Today is the wrong day to fire me! I have my shit together. I really do this time. I made some changes. Thought some things out. It won't happen again!"

He slapped the rag he was using to polish the counter down. "You want me to cut you some slack?"

I nodded, eager, biting my bottom lip. *Shit!* Why did I spend so much time contemplating trading kidneys for steaks and staring at a man who was probably a trust-fund baby? His biggest worry was probably what car he should drive to match his tie.

And what about those *eyes*? He hadn't even revealed those mysterious eyes... A multitude of colors played across my mind —green, hazel, brown, blue? Light like the ocean in Greece when the sun hits the surface, or dark like the sea during a reckless storm? I mentally tried them on his face, one after another.

"Listen carefully to the word of the day, Mari."

I blinked, bringing Caspar back to central focus.

"Are you listening, Mariposa?"

I narrowed my eyes at him, trying not to be snarky but hating it whenever anyone called me by my full name. Caspar was privy to that information because he had hired me. "Ya— Yeah, I am."

"*Fired.* Definition: dismiss (an employee) from a job. Let me use it in a sentence. Mari*posa* Flores is fired." He said fired like FI-*YERED.* "Got it?"

"How is that cutting me some slack, Caspar?"

"You didn't have to walk to my office to get the dictionary."

"Oh, come on! *Really?*"

"*Really.* You walked right into that one. When you signed on to work here, that was one of my rules. You get fired. You read the word from the dictionary out loud. It might save you from making the same mistake twice." He paused. "Maybe you should read it out loud."

The backpack in my hand dropped to the floor, and I fell into a chair with a dramatic "umph!" As soon as my ass hit the wood, I slumped over and hid my face under my arms, my hair fanning out, my forehead pressed against a wrinkled newspaper. "This is so effed up, Caspar," I mumbled, my voice muffled. "So effed up. I thought we had something good going here." I motioned between the two of us.

Even though I had screwed up a couple of times, I really enjoyed working at Home Run. It was a baseball-themed shop that specialized in rare baseball memorabilia, and it also catered to those who wanted personalized items made. After the baseball business took off, Caspar and his wife, Arev, opened up a small coffee shop inside the establishment.

It wasn't big, but it brought in enough customers who enjoyed being surrounded by twenty-four/seven baseball games (or sports channels) and news. All walks of life came in, but our loyal clientele were over forty-five, and most of them came in for a good cup of coffee and a newspaper.

Retract. *Caspar's clientele*. He'd fucking sacked me.

I knew more of Caspar's verbal lashing was coming since I sat down and didn't leave, but before he could really get started, the chime on the door alerted us that a customer had entered. Even without the chime, the scents that drifted in would have alerted me. Rose and...lavender. Both of them were subtle but distinct.

Peeking through my self-made solitude, I watched Caspar greet two women from behind the counter. One of them had auburn hair and the other blonde. Both of them declined his offer for coffee before the woman with the darker hair gave her name.

"Scarlett Fausti. I called a couple of months ago about having a framed jersey and hat done for my husband. My friend here has been keeping tabs on things. Violet." Scarlett nodded to the blonde. "We were told it was ready."

I was positive she, Scarlett, was the one who smelled like rose petals and the other one, Violet, lavender. For whatever reason—maybe it was Scarlett's auburn hair and fair skin, or how gracious she seemed—but it was hard not to smell roses and think of someone like her.

Caspar struggled to remember the order, but what struck me as odd was, at the mention of her last name, Caspar's demeanor seemed to change. I had seen him deal with celebrities before, or someone he felt was important, and he stood taller, pride evident in his stance.

I lifted my face, blowing straggling pieces of hair out of my eyes. "I took the order," I said. "It's in the back. It came out really nice. Your husband will love it."

Scarlett had ordered her husband's baseball jersey and matching hat to be framed. Apparently he had played high-school ball.

As Caspar limped into the back to retrieve the frame, the two women turned to me.

"Did I speak to you?" Scarlett asked.

I nodded. "When you first placed the order."

"Mari, right?"

"That's me," I said.

She nodded but didn't say anything else. Instead, she seemed to stare into my soul. Her eyes were a piercing green, and they seemed to know too much. And after what had happened to me earlier—the fuck I gave when the guy in the suit scrutinized me—I didn't feel like being judged again. Though I couldn't completely confirm that was what she was doing to me. It was like she was feeling me out.

"Scarlett." Violet nudged her.

"Hmm?"

Scarlett seemed lost in space. Violet nudged her again when Caspar came from the back room holding the frame. Scarlett turned at the sound of his voice, but she seemed reluctant to.

What was going on in the world today? Was it "judge Mari" day? The entire world, except for a couple of people, had no clue that I even existed. Then all of a sudden I was the central focus, like a bug on a platter.

I let my head fall to the newspaper again as the three in the background chattered on.

Scarlett: *"Oh, my husband is going to love this! He played in high school and was granted scholarships. The big league wanted him, but he decided to join the Coast Guard instead."*

Violet: *"Brando Fausti will smile when he sees this, and somewhere in the world a woman will get her wings."*

Caspar made small talk with them while he wrapped Scarlett's frame in brown paper. After he was done, another chime came at the door, and when I turned my head to look, it was a man in a suit. He had come to retrieve the package for the two women. Scarlett called him Guido. He spoke to her in Italian. Dark hair. Dark eyes. If he had a theme, it would've been dark. Honestly, beside the man in the suit from earlier, I'd never seen a man so attractive. He was built, too. His muscles filled out his expensive suit perfectly.

What the hell was in my tap water this morning? Too much iron? I was attracting crazy shit today.

Guido might be ridiculously good-looking, but compared to the man in the suit...I blew out a breath of hot air. There was no comparison. The man in the suit had made me feel something, which made me feel uncomfortable. *Vulnerable.* Therefore judged. I felt nothing when I looked at Guido. He was attractive to the eye only. No big surprise there, though. I rarely felt anything for anyone. How had one of my foster people described me? *Emotionally dead.*

Guido hauled the framed jersey outside, followed by Violet, who held the door open. Scarlett stopped when she came to me. It seemed like she wanted to say something, but she hesitated. Violet called her name, and after biting her lip for a second, she thanked me for my help and left. I could've sworn she said something like "*see you soon,*" though.

After they'd gone, I waited for Caspar to put me out, but after a minute or so, he took the seat next to me, a cup of coffee in his hand. "Have you read this?" He tapped on the edge of the newspaper probably staining my forehead.

Sighing, I sat up and glanced at the headline. *Huh. A murderer in New York City. How about that? Maybe he'll do me a favor and visit me next.* I was full of sarcasm today, but since it was getting me nowhere, I decided to bite my tongue.

"Fausti," he said. "Do you recognize the name?"

I was about to ask what the name Fausti had to do with the

headline, but I kept quiet. I didn't have the energy for small talk. My world was imploding all around me, and I was waiting for one small spark to set me on fire, since it seemed gasoline ran through my veins instead of blood. Random chitchat felt like watching in slow motion as it edged its way toward me. I felt like running to save my life, but the problem was, I had nowhere to run to.

"They think it's someone in the mob committing the murders. Or one mob targeting another." Caspar sighed. "Not that the sweet girl who just left has anything to do with this. She's a famous ballerina, but her husband's people rule that world. It made me think."

"Don't strain yourself," I said.

Caspar laughed. For the most part, he got my sense of humor. "You know this isn't personal," he said, his voice sincere. He pushed the cup closer to me.

When I looked in the cup, it held four ten-dollar bills. I stared at them, not sure what to say.

"Consider it commission for taking the Fausti order." He became silent for a minute or two and then cleared his throat. "I can't depend on you, Mari. Arev, she is sick. You know this. I have to be with her now. The chemo..." He didn't finish the thought. "My son is coming to take over the business for me soon. I can't hand him a business with a flaky worker. It would not be fair."

Standing, I tapped Caspar on the head, not having the energy to feed him poor excuses. True, I had been late today because of the mysterious guy in the suit, and that damn steak, but for the past couple of months I'd been attending community college. My school schedule didn't always match up to my work schedule.

I wanted to make something of myself, but I was too chicken to tell anyone. If I failed, I'd hide it in my metaphorical closet full of skeletons. Which was exactly what I was going to do—leave the secret there. There was no way that I could keep going.

What was the point?

Hitting rock bottom didn't always make you go up like people claimed. Sometimes it weighed you down and buried you under ashes. Hopelessness was a burden that refused to let me move.

After collecting my bag, I stood at the door, coffee cup in hand. I was so in the negative that not even this small ray of kindness could put me in the positive. "I hope Arev gets better," I said and then left, the door chiming behind me.

No, no, no, *no!* I flung my backpack to the ground, breathing heavy. My heart felt like it was about to burst.

Shit! The locks to the crummy apartment I rented had been changed.

Apartment stretched the description, though. It had a cot in the kitchen, which consisted of a rusty stove and an even rustier fridge, and a bathroom that was probably built when indoor plumbing was first a thing. It wasn't much, but it was *mine*.

Mine meant that I wouldn't be out on the street all night. *Mine* meant that I wouldn't be bouncing from one all-night establishment to another, hoping my money wouldn't run out before the sun came up, coffee cup after coffee cup to keep me rooted instead of roaming. *Mine* meant that I was safe, for the most part. This wasn't the best part of town, but I kept my head down, my backpack close, and the shitty shoes on my feet while I kept forward, minding my business. And now?

Out. On. The. Street.

Whoever said the devil strikes in threes, they fucking meant it. I was convinced the guy from the five-star restaurant (not the guy in the suit, but the other one) was the devil himself and had kicked off this day straight from hell.

Reality took a nice swipe at me then and made my problems entirely too real. I couldn't breathe. The heat of the day felt like it swarmed around me, alive with a buzzing sound. My oxygen was low to nonexistent. My vision faded in and out. Sweat poured out of me and soaked my clothes. My stupid baseball jersey and the ratty jeans and the too-tight shoes were going to stink even worse after this.

Could shoes that were too tight make you dizzy? Cut off the oxygen to your brain? Or was New York on fire?

"Crazy thoughts, Mari," I said. "Stop thinking insane thoughts."

When I looked down, I had somehow slipped to the floor in front of my apartment, all of my energy gone. Gone. Gone. *Gone.*

I was sick of always being only one step ahead of the devil that chased me. I was sick of fighting for one more day only to be touched by this hell. What felt like so many years and so much running...and what good had it done? Nothing. It had caught up to me anyway.

Opening my bag, I dug around, looking for my journal.

No, no, no!

My fingers frantically pulled and set aside, knowing that I'd never leave it behind. *Butterfly clip, a new pack of colors, a coloring book, gum, a pen.* It had to be here. It was gone, though! Another thing of mine gone! My sacred place to keep all of my dreams and wishes and things to be thankful for was *gone!*

It was stupid, I knew, but it was something to hold on to...it was mine. Like the mediocre job and the too-tight shoes and the ratty place currently keeping me upright.

Think, Mari! When did you have it last? I mentally pulled it forward, trying to remember the last time I wrote in it. *This morning. Before I left for Home Run. Shit!* I'd left it next to Vera in the "apartment."

It was like fate knew my life was going to implode today and was saying, *Leave your book of good behind, kid. Less painful when you have to watch your dreams burn to ashes with the rest of your life.*

I had no idea why I was so attached to the stupid thing. The same went for Vera. It wasn't like I ever had anything good in my life to call mine, *for good*, but once upon a time, I felt like I could. The possibility for something better was there. It was the chance that something great could happen to me, or I could make it for myself, if only I could get two steps ahead.

The day the idea took root, it had all felt so kismet.

During one of my evening shifts at Home Run, the happiness guru appeared on the television, claiming that she'd written in her journal for years. She wrote down all she was thankful for, even if she didn't have it yet. She claimed that being thankful for a life you didn't have prepared you for a life you would have. She had compared it to having enough faith to build train tracks before the train even had the route.

It all sounded so...true...and doable.

It didn't take a lot of money to give it a try. All I needed was a journal. So, after work, I ventured to a part of town known for sidewalk vendors, looking for something I could afford. It would put a dent in my stash, but one day it would be worth it. I'd look back on that journal and have proof. I'd changed the course of destiny. I had earned an ocean to put out that fire consuming me.

I found two things that day: a purple journal and an aloe vera plant.

The plant had been sitting on top of the journal, real artsy looking, and the vendor sold me two for one. Five bucks for both. I named the plant Vera and the journal Journey. From that day forward, Vera Journey was born. When I needed a confidante, I talked to Vera. When I needed to feel not so broken, I wrote in Journey. Needless to say, Vera was doing pretty well with all of our chats, and Journey was almost full of notes.

Both of them were right beyond my reach. My hands tingled, like I hung on to the highest mountain and my fingers and palms were just too slippery. I was falling.

"Just my luck," I mumbled.

The panic attack passed and suddenly I felt so tired. Like I could sit on that shitty floor and sleep for eons. I lifted my head, turned my eyes to the ceiling, and then closed them. Wishing. Hoping. Wanting something so different.

I *needed*. I needed a safe place to land for once in my life.

I didn't even have the energy to open my eyes when the tip of a boot touched my leg. "I changed the locks," Merv said. "You didn't pay your rent. I'm not running a charity here."

"Get lost, Merv," I said. "I wasn't *that* late."

"Over a month, and not for the first time. I forgot about the late fees, didn't I?"

"You ever heard of cutting someone some slack? It's not like this is the royal palace. You let the rats live here rent-free. A huge-ass family lived with me the entire time. Bastards stole my food, when I had it, and then shit all over the place!"

He was quiet long enough that I forced my eyes open. He hadn't left, I knew, because his cheap-ass cologne kept assaulting my nose. I never got a good feeling about him, so I usually kept my distance, and the feeling was as strong as ever. There was something about his eyes that reminded me of a diseased rat. I always assumed he was their leader.

I used my knees to push up the wall, keeping the straps of my bag clutched in my palms, sliding down a little bit, but he bulldozed over the space between us and came close to my face. "I could forget this month." He shrugged. "If you'd do something for me."

Before he even told me what that something was, I'd started shaking my head. I knew what that something was, and there was no way *in fucking* hell. This wasn't the first time he'd insinuated sex for payment, but this time, something had changed. He felt more like a predator.

Get. Out. A voice screamed in my head. It came from my gut.

"Go fuck yourself, Merv," I said, and I meant it literally. "I need two minutes to get my things and then I'm gone."

He shook his head. "You owe me. You want your things? You have to do something for me first."

"When hell freezes over," I whispered, hoping the low tone of my voice would hide the hint of fear. "You'd have to kill me first."

I might have jumped from house to house, place to place, throughout my life, but I hadn't gotten to the point where my hunger and fear were worth more than my body, my strength to keep putting one foot in front of the other on *my* own terms.

Tiredness might have made it to my bones, but the thought of him made me cringe to the point where acid burned the back of my throat. I'd rather pick up a seedy stranger in a dark alley than to see him in the light of day. He had ass crack for days, and it didn't always look like dark hair back there.

"You'll be back!" he yelled toward me, leaning one beefy shoulder against the wall while I hauled ass to get out of there. A door across from mine opened and two people spilled out. "And the cost will go up when you do!"

SINCE I LIVED on the third floor, I sometimes left the window cracked. Call me foolishly hopeful or truly insane, but I always wished for a stray cat to slip through so he could take care of my rat problem. I couldn't afford anything else, and getting anyone to listen in this city (a complaint against the landlord) was harder than talking a brick wall into moving by itself.

What was even more insane than hoping for a cat hero was plotting to get my journal and plant back from Merv the creepy landlord. I refused to let him have my hopes and my dreams— and my plant. I might have hit rock bottom, but I'd be damned if the last memories of me went to *him*.

I slapped my palm to my forehead. Again, the guy in the suit from this morning seemed to scramble my thoughts, and all common sense seemed to slip through the cracks. I had left the window open in case of this exact scenario. Not being able to make rent and getting put out.

On a normal day, I would've had Journey with me, but Vera always stayed home. I mean, who carries a plant around? In case things got shady, I purposely left the window open so I could snatch her from the ledge.

With nothing but time on my side, I waited in the extreme heat, too far away to be seen, until night fell and I was sure Merv was probably watching porn for the rest of the night.

After securing my backpack, I climbed the fire escape as quietly as possible.

It was old, and with each step, rust fell to the street from my weight. My toes had a pulse and my stomach felt like it had an acid sandwich for lunch. No matter what people say, no matter how little you eat, you never get used to feeling hunger. There was a big difference between a growl and a roar. Or maybe there was a big difference between choosing not to eat and not being able to.

I had to stop halfway up to the second floor. My head became dizzy, and everything seemed to swim out before it righted itself again. I looked up, remembering why I had to do this.

Journey. Vera. My things. *Mine. All that will be left of me.*

Once I reached the third floor, my apartment, I peeked

inside, not seeing anyone. Vera was on the ledge and Journey was underneath. That was right. I was trying to be artsy today.

Maybe I can sneak in and get my two shirts and one pair of shorts. My only pair of flip-flops. I even had a bottle of water in the fridge. It didn't really keep things cold but cool. *That will do me some good when I'm ratting the hot streets tonight. Maybe Merv won't even know that I spent the night. That'll give me an extra day to try and make some other kind of arrangement. It's too late to get into a shelter for the night.* I didn't like staying there, either. I always felt trapped.

My eyes narrowed when one of the rats took his time walking across the floor. Yeah, they weren't afraid. Most of them could take on a small cat, but dealing with rats was better than dealing with humanity.

Taking a deep breath, I fully lifted the window and climbed inside, feeling somewhat ahead. I never felt settled, not since I was ten, but "somewhat ahead" had become my normal.

A searing pain ran from my scalp to my neck. My hair was caught in a tight-fisted grip, and my head pulled back at an awkward angle. "I knew you'd be back," Merv sneered in my ear. "And what did I tell you? The cost is going to be so much higher. You're going to meet Big Merv tonight. Mari and Big Merv, sitting on that bed, K-I-S-S-I-N-G." He sang the last part childishly.

My heart raced, my palms tingled, and my mind worked overtime. The son of a bitch had been waiting for me! I had nothing in this nasty-ass place to even defend myself with.

He pulled my head back further, and I looked at him from the side of my eye. "You're not all that pretty—*that* nose—but there's something about you..." He licked a wet trail from my chin to my ear, and I had to stifle the urge to vomit. His spit stunk. "Your body, though. I'll have some fun breaking it in."

Words. They kept soaring through my thoughts. I wanted to threaten him, to tell him that if he touched me, I would kill him. But in the moment, they were meaningless, flying because they held no weight.

He was right about one thing, though.

My body.

It was going to fight, even if this was the last fight we'd ever know. I started fighting him then, not caring what I did, but doing it anyway. We seemed to hit one wall, the stove, and then he rammed my head into another wall, this one closest to the window.

He let go for a second, breathing heavy (the lazy prick probably couldn't even climb a flight of stairs without wheezing), and we did a sort of bob and weave dance around each other. I was hell bent on making it to the door. Screaming wouldn't help, but it was a chance to outrun him. I had him *there,* but he had me *here.* Caged like an animal.

He came at me again, and I tried to go around, but tripped over my flip-flops. As soon as I went down, he grabbed me by the legs and pulled me further away from the door. He wheezed from the struggle, and I made some smartass remark about him not having to usually fight for his food. The girls down the hall paid him in sex all of the time, but they were more like corpses after they had hits of drugs.

Snot dripped out of his nose. His cheeks were bright red. His palms were hot, burning through my jeans, and his white tank was full of stinky, unhealthy sweat. I was able to get one leg loose and kicked out at him. I hit his knee and he groaned. My toes came completely through one shoe from the impact, but I was able to rise and make it to the door. Just as my hand went to turn the knob, he grabbed me by my hair again, yanking me back.

He swung me around, wild with anger, and put my head through the wall. Before I could even recover, he spun me around again and then slapped the shit out of me. He made direct contact with my nose before he went in for my eye. I barely registered the pain, only that I needed to get out.

I knew death was coming for me soon, but not like this. Not with this asshole taking me apart before he decided to kill me for the rats to have. That was probably how he fed them. I clawed and kicked and made noises that sounded inhuman, trying to muster the energy to continue to fight. I knew from the outside it probably sounded like we were having wild sex, because he was making nasty noises, too.

Somehow we made it to the window, and I had a feeling he was going to put my head through it. Maybe he decided fighting with me was not worth it. He'd just end my life and be done with it.

"All right!" I shouted, hardly recognizing the sound of my own voice. It was full of grit, but sounded so worn down. "All right! I'll do it." He stopped the motion, but his hold didn't lessen. "I'll...I'll do whatever you want me to."

The apartment was scalding—no air conditioning—and the only awareness I had of my injuries were the stings from sweat slipping into them. His hot breath flowed over me, like the heat of a million fires blistering my skin.

Slowly, without any struggle, I let him turn me to face him. He let my arms go, and as his mouth came against mine, the sweat from his hair splashing across my face, I reached behind me and grabbed Vera from the windowsill.

I hit him with as much strength as I could, smashing her small pot against his head. The pottery held together against his temple until I moved my hand and pieces of it crumbled to the floor. I was dimly aware of the stunned look on his face before snatching Journey, a piece of the terra-cotta pottery, and my flip-flops, and running as fast I could to the anonymity of the overcrowded streets.

4

MARIPOSA

As the sun came up, I gave the waitress a slim tip at the all-night diner I sat at. She was nice enough to let me stay the night, continually filling my cup, so I didn't have to sleep on the street. She even brought me a piece of apple pie that tasted like it was over two weeks old, but since I hadn't had anything for a while, it was the best thing in the world.

Maybe she felt sorry for me because I was all busted up. Bloody nose, puffy eye and lip, pieces of wall stuck in my hair. A bruise would soon come up on my forehead. It was sore to the touch and swollen. Even though it would only draw more attention, I set my hair back with the butterfly clip in my bag to get it off of my face.

Vera. She had saved my life. The thought made my eyes water, but I sniffed up the emotions, refusing to let a tear fall. Crying got you nowhere. It helped nothing.

After stepping outside, I stuck my tennis shoes in my bag and slipped on my dollar pair of flip-flops. The size of these were perfect, but I didn't wear them often because, *one*, I didn't want to ruin them, and *two*, they caused severe blisters between my big and second toe. But they protected my feet and I was glad to have them.

I was glad to have Journey back, too. I spent most of the night writing things down between the pages. I even drew a picture of Vera and her pot to remember her by. The rest of the time I colored in my children's coloring book. There was something really relaxing about coloring all of those princesses and bringing them to life.

A guy walking down the street bumped me and pushed me back a step. He had earphones in and wasn't paying attention, but the hit made me feel the fight from last night.

It was going to be a long day.

Not having anywhere to go, or anyone to see, I let my feet take me in whatever direction they wanted to go. I took the ferry to Staten Island, and after walking around for a bit, I made my way back. A few markets/a stroll by Broadway/getting lost in the crowds at Time Square-later, I was back at the five-star restaurant, Macchiavello's.

Dinner rush. There must've been a dress code, because not one person was dressed in jeans. Rich perfumes and fine colognes lingered from down the street. It sort of masked the fact that New York was scalding and the dumpsters were baking. Sweat coated my skin, and I felt crusted in it. Hopefully, the rich scents would mask my scent, too.

This time I didn't stare in the window but kept my distance. I leaned against the wall, watching as people came and went. I was bored out of my mind, so I toyed with the idea of going to the library. Sometimes I hung out there and read all day. But my feet were hurting (all of me was, actually), and the thought of sitting down for a bit and coloring seemed more appealing. Then I'd go to the shelter before they ran out of beds.

After taking out my supplies, I started to color a picture of a young girl with a cloak on talking to a mean wolf. Some time passed by, because the weather started to feel a little cooler.

Setting my blue color down to dab at an itchy spot on my injured nose, I happened to look up.

My eyes narrowed on the same scenario from the day before. Smart Mouth hustled to open the door to the restaurant for the guy in the suit, but instead of going in, he watched me. I lifted one eye, not able to open the other the entire way.

It was hard to look away. When he looked at me, I felt trapped, cornered, not able to move an inch. But in an odd way, it didn't bother me as much as it should. I realized then that I didn't feel judged by him because *he* was judging me, but because I was judging *myself* in his presence, wondering how I measured up.

Merv was right. I wasn't the prettiest thing to grace the earth. My hair was a dull brown, my eyes hazel—my DNA couldn't decide between gold, green, and brown—and my nose...well, I was told by a kid in the old neighborhood that I had what his mother called a "whopper schnozzola."

Jocelyn had told me not to worry about what the kid had said. He didn't know shit, just like his mom didn't know if his dad was the barman or her husband.

Jocelyn had said that I had an aquiline nose, or sometimes people called it a "Roman nose." It was beautiful and it fit my face, she had said. She went as far as calling my profile "regal." She even brought me to the library to look at pictures. I had to admit that, compared to some, I had a good Roman nose, one that seemed right for my face, but it was still different.

At least my skin was clear. Well, when it wasn't bruised.

What does the guy in the suit think about my nose? After a second, I blinked, bringing myself back to the moment. Unconsciously, I had been stroking the bridge of it, calling attention to my thoughts.

What in the hell was going on with me? Why would I even think about it, or much less care?

I still didn't look away, though, and neither did he. Not until something made him turn to look. An unmarked car cruised down the street. It seemed like it was heading toward the restaurant. A second later, the man in the suit disappeared behind the door with Smart Mouth on his heels. I got the strangest feeling then that maybe the man in the suit hadn't wanted to leave, but had to.

Was he going to talk to me? I couldn't even explain why I thought that.

Then I started to laugh. I laughed while I packed up my things, preparing to go to the shelter. It was so ridiculous, *him* coming to talk to *me*. He was probably assessing me, trying to figure out if I was going to become a problem. If he even remembered me. Maybe he was trying to place me.

My fingers stilled when I noticed the piece of pottery at the bottom of my bag. I turned it over in my hand for a second, admiring the butterfly I'd drawn. I had wanted to up Vera's living space and had drawn a few things on her pot. The butterfly was my favorite. I always admired things that had to struggle to find beauty in life.

If only we all could be so lucky to find our beauty, our peace, our purpose before we left this earth.

The piece landed at the bottom of my bag again, and after zipping up, I stood, brushing some dirt from my hands on my jeans.

A tall man in another pricey-looking suit came out of the restaurant's door, going straight for the unmarked car. Two detectives got out, and the man met them before they made it to the door.

I could hear snippets of the conversation, but not much. The tall man had a strong Italian accent. It sounded like he was explaining to the detectives that the man they'd asked to see wasn't there, and if they had any more questions, they should contact his lawyer first.

For a minute, I thought that maybe they'd called the cops

on me, but common sense kicked in. I doubted detectives would be called out for someone who sat against the building and colored most of the evening.

Not wanting to get caught up in any kind of trouble, because I was already in my own kind of hell, I decided to leave.

"Hey!" a man's voice shouted from behind me. "Hey, wait! You with the backpack!"

I stopped, turning around. A young guy weaved around foot traffic to get to me. He carried an ice pack in his hand. When he got close to me, he held it out, and I took it.

"Mr. Mac wanted me to give you that. And this." He dug in his back pocket, coming out with a gift card. "He said come in whenever you want. Just use that card."

It took me a moment to find my voice. "Mr. Mac, your boss? The guy who got out of that car?" I nodded toward the expensive one. The young guy nodded and I went on. "Does he always hand out these cards to the needy?" I held it up.

The guy squinted at me for a moment before his features relaxed. "No."

"What about women?"

"Uh, no."

"What about the other guy, the one who rushes out to meet Mr. Mac? Will he give me any trouble?"

"Bruno?" His nose scrunched up. "No. Whatever Mr. Mac wants, Mr. Mac gets."

I nodded, he nodded, and then he hustled back inside. I stood there for a moment staring at the card. If there was one thing I had learned throughout my life, it was that nothing was ever free. Everything came at a price. I didn't mind Mr. Mac looking at me, for whatever reason, but this—no matter how nice—made me feel like a charity case.

Yeah, okay, I was a charity case, but for some reason, coming from him, I couldn't stand it.

Maybe because I wished that I was on steady ground with him. I wished, for once in my life, to be a woman who could compete with his...everything. Even if I wasn't poor, I doubted he would've been interested in me. Not with the models that came and went from the restaurant he either owned or frequented. If anything, he noticed me because I was poor. It was no secret when you looked at me.

Jocelyn once told me that a woman should never want to be treated as a man's equal. She should demand to be treated better. Our doors should be held, along with receiving the same pay and opportunities, that sort of thing. And she also said that if a man truly loved you, he'd treat you as though he didn't deserve you, but hell if another man could do better.

My feelings and thoughts were not truly lining up, but for whatever reason, one somehow fed the other. Either way, I gave the card for Macchiavello's to a woman and her daughter on the subway. The mother had cancer. She had a scarf wrapped around her head, no hair underneath, and dark circles underneath her eyes. Maybe a nice dinner would get their minds off things, even if for a short amount of time.

I was too late arriving at the shelter. So I walked the streets the entire night, thinking of the man in the suit, Mr. Mac, and why he'd been so kind to me. If I couldn't accept his kindness, maybe thoughts of him would ward off any evil until daylight brightened the darkness.

5

MARIPOSA

"**S**hit! Mari! What in the hell happened to you?"

Keely grabbed me and pulled me so hard into her that I winced. She was a hugger, but since she had been my best friend since we wore kiddie underwear, and I considered her family, I didn't mind.

Keely Ryan and her family had lived next to mine on Staten Island. Her parents were Irish/Scottish immigrants who had seven mouths to feed. Keely had four brothers. But after the kids were old enough to fend for themselves, her parents decided to move back to Scotland. Keely and two of her brothers stayed in New York. The rest of the boys followed their parents.

We stayed close even after I'd been put into foster care at ten.

She released me so suddenly that I almost stumbled back. She was a whirlwind. Her hair was fiery red with countless ringlets. Her skin was pale with freckles. She had the purest blue eyes, and she was at least five foot ten inches tall. The volume of her hair probably put her closer to six.

"I called Caspar and he told me what happened." She

planted her hands on her hips. "I've been looking all over for you. Why didn't you come see me sooner? Why are you just standing there not answering my questions?"

"If you'd give me a second," I said, adjusting my backpack, "I would."

"What happened to your face?"

"It seems Merv had a difference of opinion with it, due to the fact that my body refused to screw him in return for rent."

"That bastard! He did this to you?" She reached out and I moved my face.

"Yeah." I didn't like how her kindness made me feel, and I didn't want her to worry. She'd want me to stay with her, and because her roommate was a certified bitch and possibly a psychopath, I didn't want to have to refuse her offer.

Keely struggled to make ends meet, too. She'd been trying for years to land a major role on Broadway but hadn't yet. She sounded like a jazzy bird when she sang, and she had the Irish's flair for theatrics to go along with it. She took as many jobs as she could to keep her head above water.

To keep afloat, she had to share rent with someone. Sierra was her third roommate over the years, but one that she could, so far, depend on. But Sierra didn't like me. I had accidentally eaten her eggs one day when Keely told me I could help myself to whatever I wanted in the fridge.

Sierra had walked in and caught me. She took a knife out of the kitchen drawer and held it up to my face. She threatened to "cut a bitch" if she ever found me eating her stash of food again. Keely and Sierra didn't share food, and her stuff was off limits.

I tried to explain that it was a misunderstanding, but Sierra wasn't the type to stand around listening to excuses. She refused to leave until I said the magical words. "*It won't happen again.*"

"It better not," she had said. She lifted the knife up to me once more and then walked out of the kitchen. She counted her things on the regular and probably twice after I left. I made it a point to stay away from her.

There was just something about her that didn't sit right with me. That was why I never came to stay the night. I worried that she'd harm me in my sleep. I never told Keely because they got along fine. Sierra had an aversion to me, and Keely needed her to keep up her share of the rent.

Keely's mother had once warned me about what happens to two drowning people. One always takes the other under for good. Keely didn't need me dragging her down, so I always downplayed my situation when she asked about things. This time, I couldn't. She had called and found out that I had been fired.

She had gotten me the job at Home Run after she had quit to work someplace else for more money. She knew about Merv, too, since I had to tell her. Besides, Keely could smell shit from a mile away, so I could downplay but never tell a full-out fib. Which meant...

"You're back on the street, Mari?"

She looked so disappointed in me that I had a hard time keeping my lip from trembling. "A little," I said.

"A little," she repeated, sighing afterward. She opened the door wider and told me to come in.

"Is Sierra here?" I asked.

"Yeah, she's getting ready to go out."

Finally, something going my way for once.

"She's not so bad, Mari," Keely said. "Everyone has a story. Whatever hers is, it seems like a dark one. Who knows what she's gone through to get where she is?"

"Where is she, *exactly*?"

Keely laughed a little at that. "Last I checked, in the bathroom." Her humor faded as soon as she looked me over again. "You really look like shit, sis."

"You got anything new to tell me, Kee?"

"No, but I do have some bread, butter, and cheese. Sit." She pointed to her tiny kitchen table. "I'm going to make you something to eat and then you're going to tell me what the hell is going on."

"Who bought it?" I asked as I took a seat. "You or Sierra?"

Her eyes narrowed. "Does it matter? If I borrow something from her, I always give it back."

I shook my head. "I don't feel comfortable eating other people's food."

"It's mine," she said. "I swear."

I hated how she scrutinized me, digging for the truth, so I tried to put her suspicions at ease. "I know she struggles, too. I don't want to take what isn't mine. I'm not even that hungry. I had bread earlier." I patted my backpack. "Caspar gave me a little money after he fired me."

"I'm still making you a grilled cheese sandwich. And Mam sent over some bread from scratch. Try it. It's in the bag on the counter."

As Keely made our grilled cheese sandwiches, I was honest about what had happened. Bruno. Caspar. Merv. The only thing I left out, or *who*, was the man in the suit. For some reason I wasn't ready to share that yet. I had spent the entire night thinking about him and his kindness, and I didn't want her to pick my feelings apart. I usually didn't have those toward men.

Feelings.

I was twenty-one and I'd never had a relationship, serious or not. I had no time for that when all of my time was spent surviving. It was who I had become. *Merely-Surviving Mari.* I had no idea what living really felt like. Besides, it was ridiculous to even think about him in that way. The man was probably a millionaire, and to top it off, he looked like a model.

Keely slid a plate toward me, the smell overwhelming my

senses for a moment. I rubbed my hands together, licking my lips. She laughed and I looked up before I took a bite.

She smiled at me, the corners of her eyes crinkling. Then she took a seat next to me, grabbing my hand. "I'm so sorry, Mari." She squeezed. "I wish." She closed her eyes for a moment, taking a deep breath. "I wish—God, I wish there was more I could do."

A tear slipped down her cheek and I winced. I hated that she took my problems and made them her own. Keely was a fixer, it was what she did for her brothers, and I refused to do the same thing to her.

It made sense what her Mam had told me.

We all had our own hells to survive. Some of us felt like we were drowning. Others were in a burning room with no way out. Even though I felt the fires of hell, Keely was close to drowning. Barely keeping her head above water. My problems would only bring her down.

"Keely," I said, putting down the sandwich. I squeezed her hand. "This. Just you being here, in my life, that's more than enough. That's worth more than all of the gold in the world."

"Ha!" She barked out a laugh, but it didn't sound all that funny. "True, but money helps."

"Yeah." I smiled. "I'm sure it would."

"You need to call the police on Merv, Mari. He can't get away with this. I might—I might just kill him myself for putting his hands on you!"

I stood from the table, walking over to the sink. I took out a glass from the cabinet and filled it with water from the tap. Sierra couldn't cut a bitch for that.

"Have you seen yourself, Mari? You need to do this. You have to put him behind bars."

"How long will he stay there, Kee? Not long. And when he gets out? I don't need some animal coming after me. He has my scent. He'll hunt me down."

"I won't let him. I'll get the boys involved."

"No!" I regretted snapping at her as soon as I did. "No." I brought my voice down. "I don't mean to snap, but no."

She came up from behind me and hugged my shoulders. "I know, sis," she said. "I just can't stand the thought of him getting away with this. And if you want, I'll talk to Caspar. He has a soft spot for me. Maybe we can get your job back."

Choosing to change the subject, I took a step to the side and then turned around to face her. "I wanted to say this when I first got here, but you didn't give me the chance. This is serious now, Kee. What in *the* hell are you wearing? And *why*?"

We stared at each other a moment before we both exploded with laughter. She had some type of costume on. I knew it had something to do with her heritage. The green velvet dress was long, touching the floor, and the sleeves flared out. Her hair was tamed underneath some kind of hair covering, and a crown sat on top.

She laughed a little more and then wiped her eyes. "I have a job in Upstate New York. Some kind of Scotland meets medieval-times fair, and they needed an old-fashioned maiden to walk around and greet guests. Lachlan nearly shit a brick when he saw me earlier. He took a photo and sent it to *everyone*."

Lachlan was one of her brothers. And he would. If I had a phone, there was no doubt I would've gotten it, too. Most of Keely's brothers had a great sense of humor, all but her brother Harrison. Her family called him Grumpy Indiana Jones behind his back. Though he didn't look grumpy. All of her brothers had dark hair, light eyes, and golden skin. Keely was the fire in their darkness. Jocelyn used to say that one day the Ryan boys would be easy on the eyes. She was right.

"I bet your parents are proud." I wiped my eyes.

"Mam was praising the Lord! She's hoping that I'll find a suitable man while I'm there. One I can bring home with me."

Our laughter tapered when a knock came at the door. A second or two later, Sierra emerged from wherever she had been in the apartment. Her platinum blonde hair flowed down her back in perfect waves. Her top was long enough to cover her really short shorts. She looked like she'd been working on her appearance all day, when in reality, she'd probably just woken up. Whatever work she did, she did at night.

Keely raised her eyebrows and we both became quiet as Sierra opened the front door. She'd had a string of boyfriends since she'd lived with Keely, but the one knocking had been around the longest. So we were both surprised when he started cursing.

Apparently, she had broken up with him. A second later, his voice still demanding to know why—"*Is it the rich fucker at the club?*"—she slammed the door in his face. His voice was still high but muffled when she came into the kitchen.

Sierra gave me a death glare when she noticed me. Her eyebrows were much darker than her hair, which made her brown eyes more intense. *Mean.* She had wicked eyes to go with her wicked personality. "Going somewhere?" she asked Keely, eyeing the sandwich Keely had made me still on the table.

"Work," Keely said. "I'll be back late."

"You, Mari?" Sierra chucked her chin in my direction.

I hated how she said my name. Instead of Mar-ee, like most people pronounced it, she said, Marry. Except she made it sound like Murry. She didn't really care where I went, but she didn't trust me alone in their apartment. Maybe she thought I'd steal something since I ate one of her eggs. "I—"

"Mari is spending the day with me," Keely cut me off. "I'm taking her to the fair after she eats the sandwich I made for her and she takes a shower."

"I'll be back late, too," Sierra said.

"Work?" Keely asked.

"You know how it goes. Things to see and people to do." She

grinned. "Don't worry about Armino. He'll get sick of complaining at the door soon. When he needs a drink. So I'd appreciate it if neither of you answer him."

Keely nodded. "No worries. I won't answer and neither will Mari."

Sierra took one last, longer look at the sandwich on the table and slowly left the kitchen. I could tell she wanted to count her slices of cheese before she did, but instead, she slammed the door to her room a few seconds later.

HARRISON PICKED US UP. Keely didn't tell me he was coming. Not that I usually minded, but he was always really sweet to me. I appreciated the thought, but I hated refusing him when he always tried to give me gifts. He had gone to law school, but because of the economy and other factors, he was in the same situation as Keely: barely treading water.

Keely told me on the way to the car that he had recently gotten a good job, though, and was doing better. The vintage sports car he drove testified to that.

He was nice enough during the drive, but I kept catching him staring at my face. His jaw clenched and his hands tightened around the wheel. Keely must have warned him ahead of time not to make a big deal about it.

Once we arrived at the fair, and I refused to allow him to buy me food and things, he stuck his hands in the pockets of his jeans, refusing to look at me. After Keely asked me if I wanted to help out a booth that was short a person, he walked off without even saying he'd see us later.

Working the fair gave me some extra money, and food for the day was included. The only drawback was that I had to wear some kind of medieval getup. When Harrison finally came back and saw me, he grinned. He snapped my picture to send to his brothers, I was sure. They'd get a good laugh at my expense.

The ride back was quiet. I was thankful. My nerves were on edge. The day brought temporary relief from all of my problems, but the closer we came to the city, the more dread hung over my head. I was never one to keep thinking, *What am I going to do?* I just did, even if my options were scattered in the wind.

This time, though, life felt like it had brutally trumped me. I had no money but the measly few bucks in my bag, and no food except a loaf of bread. I had no job. No prospects. No home, and possibly, a crazed man with terra cotta pottery sticking out of his temple on the hunt for me.

I sighed long and hard as Harrison pulled up to Keely's place.

"I'm coming in for a sec," Harrison said, shutting off the car. "Give me a minute."

Keely gave him a narrow look, but she got out, waiting for me to get out before she walked up to her door. I breathed a sigh of relief when I realized Sierra wasn't home. She must've left in a rush, because the door to her room was cracked open. Maybe she did that when it was only her and Keely, but whenever I came over, it was always closed.

"I'm going to get out of these clothes," Keely said, going for her room. "Don't even think about leaving, Mari!" she yelled over her shoulder. "We need to work on a plan. We need to get your shit together before you disappear on me. If you do, no fucking joke, *I'm* going to hunt you down."

I took a seat on their second-hand sofa, sinking into the comfort of it. I lifted my feet, dirty from walking the dusty fair, and noticed blood spots between my toes. They'd burned like hell earlier when I took a shower—the cuts on my face, too. I thought about taking out the cold pack in my bag and sticking it in the freezer but was too tired to get up.

"Mari?"

"Hmm?" I looked up to find Harrison standing in the doorway, watching me. He held a wrapped gift in his hand.

"Your birthday," he said. "I know it's coming up soon."

I almost groaned. Why? Why? Why! Why did he have to be so nice when he really wasn't? There was a reason his siblings called him Grumpy Indiana Jones. He wasn't the nice one, but in his own way, he was kind to me, even though he knew gifts made me uncomfortable. And my birthday wasn't until October. It was early April.

I never accepted anything from anyone, not unless I paid or worked for it. No exceptions. Besides, his mother, Catriona, would blow an important vein if she knew how he always tried to buy me things. The woman didn't hate me, but she didn't like me either. The only reason she made an effort to find me after I was put into foster care was because Keely refused to eat unless she did. After the third time she passed out, Catriona made the effort and found me.

"Why do you always get that look on your face when I try to do nice things for you, Strings?"

Harrison had given me the nickname Strings when we were kids.

"Harrison..." I bit into my lip, feeling it split again. "I've told you before. I just don't like gifts."

"Humor me. You can donate it after you open it."

Fucka me. I rubbed my temple for a minute and then, meeting his eyes again, nodded. To make the situation even more awkward, he sat next to me, watching as I opened it. I held it up, not sure what else to do. "You bought me a cellphone?"

"Yeah. That way you can keep in touch with Keely. Or... whoever. I told Kee I wouldn't say anything, but I can't keep quiet. That fucker is going to get his day after what he did to you."

His eyes were hard to meet, so I looked at the phone. It was the first time in a long time that I had a hard time resisting kindness. He gave me this out of a place of worry. Still. My rule was worth more than his thoughtfulness.

"You didn't have to do this," I said quietly. Then I picked my bag up, dug around, and handed him two bucks. "For the phone. I can't take it unless you take the money."

He hated to, but he did. He slipped the two bucks in his pocket.

"What did you do?"

I startled, not realizing Keely had come back into the room. I sat up straighter, almost feeling like we had been caught doing something wrong. Harrison stood from the sofa, sticking his hands in his pockets.

"Nothing, Kee," he said. "I gave Mari a gift for her birthday, sort of."

"Her birthday isn't until October," she said, pointing out the obvious.

He shrugged. "I hate being late."

She opened her mouth to respond, but a loud knock came at the door. I looked at Keely, Harrison looked at me, and Keely looked toward the door.

"Expecting someone?" Harrison asked.

Keely shook her head. "No, Sierra said she was going to be home late."

"I'll get it," he said.

I stood, standing beside Keely, while we listened to Harrison talk to someone on the other side of the door. A minute later, he came in, followed by two men in suits. It was the same two lawmen from Macchiavello's.

"Keely," Harrison said. "This is Detective Scott Stone and Detective Paul Marinetti."

The younger of the two, Detective Stone, stepped up first, offering his hand. The older man offered his second.

"Ms. Ryan," Detective Stone said, a serious look on his face. "I regret to have to inform you that your roommate, Sierra Andruzzi, was found dead. We've been trying to get in touch with you, but this is the first time we've been able to."

Keely stumbled back, clearly in shock. She took a seat on the sofa after Harrison and I helped her sit. "She..." Keely shook her head. "She told me she wouldn't be back until later. Her ex-boyfriend. Armino. He was at our door earlier. Mad. She broke up with him. Did he..."

"From what we've pieced together, Ms. Andruzzi ran to the store earlier, and that's when she was assaulted and then murdered. It seems like she was headed back here. As of right now, we can't say for sure. That's why we're here. To piece the time together."

"I—I mean—" Keely struggled.

"We hate to ask you to do this, Ms. Ryan, but would you mind coming with us to identify the body? We cannot find a next of kin for Ms. Andruzzi."

"No," Keely said. "She was a foster kid."

"My sister is not—"

"No," Keely said, cutting Harrison off. "I'll do it. It's the least I can do for her." She was visibly pulling herself together, using a reserve of strength to stand. "Let me grab my things."

Detective Stone pulled out a business card and wrote the address to the place where Sierra's body was being held on the back. He handed it to Harrison, who told him they'd be there shortly. I stood in the middle of the room, not sure what to do. I didn't like Sierra, but no one deserved to be murdered.

Shit. Was it Armino?

Before Detective Stone left, he warned us that Armino might be lurking. Armino's last name was Scarpone. He need not say any more. They were one of the meanest crime families around.

"Mari?"

I turned at the sound of Harrison's voice. Keely stood next to him. "Come with us."

"No," I said. "I'd rather not."

"You can't disappear," Keely said, and the pleading in her voice hit me straight in the center of my heart. "I need to know where you are. After what happened to you...and now tonight." She sniffed, even though she wasn't crying. Then she barreled into me, almost knocking the wind from my lungs.

"Can I stay here?" I said, barely able to take a breath. I wasn't good with affection, but I wasn't sure how to remove myself from her embrace without making a deal of it.

"Sierra's old man." Harrison shook his head. "It might not be—"

"He's not coming back here." I took a step back. "He's probably long gone."

Keely released me fully, nodding. "Yeah, he's probably gone. Just make sure to lock the doors."

"I will," I said.

"Use the cellphone—" Harrison nodded toward the sofa "—to call me if you need anything. My number's programmed in."

After they left, I set the locks, checked them twice, and then scooted Keely's old desk against the door.

———

THE DOOR to Sierra's room was still cracked. There was no reason why it shouldn't be, but still, it felt odd to think that she'd never close it again.

Where had she been going? What had she been going to do? She had just run out to buy something, the detective had said.

I knew it was probably the wrong thing to do, but I couldn't seem to help myself. Opening her door the entire way, I was shocked to see that her room was impeccable. Her bed was made. No clothes on the floor. And it still smelled like her. Like maybe she had spritzed some perfume on before she left.

The only odd thing, compared to the rest of the place, were the things she had left out on her bed—a fancy black dress, a gold card with writing on it, and a few gold boxes. Shoes to match the dress sat on the floor.

I stepped in and paused. I waited. And waited. I expected her to jump out at me and scream, "*I'm gonna cut you, bitch, for being in here!*" The scare never came, but I was still on edge. Goosebumps puckered my arms.

The fear wasn't enough to stop me from looking around, though. The dead were not the ones to fear. It was the living.

The black dress was classy. The top reminded me of wings, while the rest seemed to be form fitting. The fabric felt expensive. I took the card from beside the dress. It seemed like an invitation. It had the date (*today*), the time (*11:11 P.M.*), and the place (*The Club, New York, New York*) in regal-looking black script. It stood out against the gold. At the bottom, in smaller writing, it noted that no entry would be allowed without the card.

Interesting.

On the way to the fair, Keely had mentioned that Sierra was excited about a new job prospect. Sierra had told Keely that if she got the job, she'd be moving out, able to afford more than what she'd been swinging.

All of her problems will be solved, for good, Keely had said.

I wondered if she was going to be a high-priced call girl. I didn't voice the thought aloud, though, because I wouldn't want to just assume something like that, but I couldn't figure out what else she could do that would solve all of her problems *for good.* She was a foster kid just like me.

The gold boxes were filled with perfumes from Brazil. I opened them, sniffing. Vanilla and caramel stood out right away, and I could pick up on hints of pistachio, almond, jasmine petals, and sandalwood after I read the description on the box. I inhaled again, almost intoxicated by the exotic smell. It was a hell of a long way from the salty smell that usually followed me around. I opened the cream, rubbing a little bit on my arm. It smelled even better on the skin. Sierra even had the body wash to match.

Taking a seat on her bed, I set the lotion down and picked up the invitation again, twirling it between my fingers. The shoes were next to my bare feet. Sierra's feet were a size or two bigger than mine.

How fitting, I thought, *either too big or too small*. Nothing ever fit me.

Because you can't afford anything made for you.

Then a bunch of voices seemed to come at me at once:

Take the opportunity, Mari. You have the dress. The shoes, even if they're too big. Perfume. The invitation. Sierra can't make it. But. You. Can.

Even the princess you color in the books had a fairy godmother. This is your chance to have one.

You have no place to go, no money, nothing.

This might be your last opportunity.

Things are bad.

So bad.

It would be nice to have a pair of shoes that fit. A phone I can afford on my own. Bread and cheese. A warm place to sleep when it's cold out and a cool place when it's hot. No rats. No Merv.

Security.

The other side of the glass.

What if it means trading your body?

Could you even do something like that with a face like yours?

It's worth the shot to survive. To live. This might be your last chance, a once in a lifetime opportunity to solve all of your problems. For good.

Can you trade what's solely yours and no one else's for worldly goods?

It's not going to be offered out of kindness. It'll be a business deal. I'll work for it.

Was the protection of my body, my honor, more precious than things only money could buy?

It took me only a second to answer.

Not anymore.

I made my choice.

To live.

I took the body wash and headed into the bathroom, prepared to make myself look as tempting as possible.

6

MARIPOSA

The heels slipped comically as I stepped out of the cab and onto the sidewalk. I had used the last of my money to splurge on a cab. In New York, a cab was the equivalent of a magical carriage.

Even though the cabbie took my money and his meter ran, he watched with humor in his eyes as I tried to navigate my way from his ride to the front of the building. It wasn't far, but far enough when my shoes constantly slipped because my feet were too small. I wasn't sure what was worse. Shoes that made my toes curl in or shoes that made me waddle like a duck to find a natural rhythm.

Besides, I'd never worn heels in my life. Add that to two sizes too big, and what do you have? A natural disaster on legs.

I hoped that whoever would be checking me out tonight, *if* that was the case, wouldn't check the bottoms of my feet. I'd taken the heels off while walking to the cab, and my pads were stained black.

A whistle from behind made me turn to look. Two guys dressed in nice clothes walked past, smiling at me.

"Hey, Beautiful," one of them said, and then he winked at

me. "You smell as good as heaven. You wanna try to be my sin tonight?"

I looked behind to make sure it was me he was talking to. It was. Heat crept up my cheeks and I turned, trying to hide my smile. It was the first time I'd smiled in a long time. And not because he called me beautiful or even attempted to flirt. It was because he said I *smelled* good.

The heat from outside made the golden-boxed perfume even stronger, but it wasn't too overbearing. It made my head float in the clouds. I wanted to bathe in the body wash twice a day and slather the cream on myself morning, noon, and night.

"Dude!" The other guy said, shoving him. "What kind of pick-up line was that? Horrible. We need to work on your skills."

As soon as the two guys passed, I remembered why I was here, and my nerves attacked again. With shaking hands, I pulled out the gold invitation from my backpack. The card shimmered in the glow of the lights from The Club.

The Club was massive, and it seemed exclusive. Streams of beautiful people were able to walk straight in, but others were not so lucky. The line wrapped around the building, regular people like me anticipating their turn in the swanky nightclub. Music blared from inside, thumping with bass, and every so often I could smell alcohol on the slight breeze.

Taking a deep breath in, I stuck the card under my arm, and then pulled out the cellphone Harrison had let me buy for two bucks. I sent a text to Kee. Harrison had programmed her number and his into the phone.

Me: How's it going?

A second later the phone lit up.

Kee: Who is this?

Me: Me.

Kee: Me who?

I realized my mistake.

Me: Mari

Kee: I'm so glad you have a phone now. And things are going as expected. I can't stop seeing, you know? How are you? What are you doing?

Me: I'm going out for a bit.

Kee: ...?

Me: Don't worry. I won't be home too late, Mam. If I am, I'll keep in touch.

A few seconds went by and she hadn't responded. Then the phone dinged in my hand and I jumped a little, not expecting it.

Kee: I figured out why Grumpy Indiana Jones is so pissed all of the time.

Before I could type back, her response came lightning fast.

Kee: He's in love with you.

The phone fell out of my hands. It clanged against the concrete and I scrambled to pick it up. Kee had already sent another text before I could respond.

Kee: You don't have to respond. After tonight, I realize how short life can be. Nothing hits home like this. So I must speak on his behalf. He's too stubborn to admit it, but after he gave you the phone, I knew. Some people can't say the words. Some people have to *do*. They do things like give you a phone to make sure you're okay. Love is not only in one language—it speaks in more than just words alone.

Another ding from my phone came a second later.

Kee: I love you, Sis. Be safe. *XoXo.*

Me: Love you back, Kee Kee. *XoXo.*

I didn't have time to consider what she had told me. It was eleven o'clock and the invitation stated 11:11 PM.

Be prompt.

I had no idea if I had to stand in the miles-long line or do something else. I was fucking clueless. Spotting a man who worked a door off to the side, I duck waddled toward him, afraid my knees would give in and I'd tumble over.

All the king's horses and all the king's men couldn't put Mari back together again...

"You need help?" the humongous guy said when I walked up. He was clearly Italian. He had a heavy accent.

I wasn't sure what to say, and not wanting to say the wrong thing, I flashed the card at him. His eyebrows rose when he realized what I held. He spoke into the earpiece he wore, the words in quick Italian. Then, without a word, he took me by the arm, pulling me to the side of the building. He slowed down when he noticed how hard of a time I was having keeping up. Baby steps were needed for this adult.

Finally, we made it to a side entrance. It was private. Two more Italians stood at the door. I assumed they were, anyway. They all spoke the same language. Then one of them asked for my ticket in English.

I handed it over. He scanned it with his eyes before he used some kind of contraption to scan the card. It beeped a second later and he nodded.

"Ms. Andruzzi, identification. And I need to check your bag as well."

He was all business. And I started to sweat. I had hoped that the ticket would be all that I needed, but just in case, I'd taken Sierra's identification card from her dresser. We looked nothing alike, but one of the foster kids I once lived with had told me that bouncers never really looked at the picture, just the date. But somehow I knew that something...*different* was going on here. If he busted me, I was in real trouble.

I had no money, zero, and nothing else to hang my hopes on. I figured this would be a long shot, but I at least hoped to get through the door before getting buried a little deeper.

Taking a deep breath, I dug in my bag, handing him the I.D. If he turned me away, there was no reason to check my bag.

He studied the picture, shined a light on my face, and then did it once more. A second later, he spoke into his earpiece, again, speaking a language I didn't have.

Then, not even recognizing my own voice, I lifted a hand to a man who had breezed past the security without even stopping. "Guido," I said to the man at the door. "You can ask Guido...Fausti," I tried at his last name, but it sounded like I was putting two different ones together in case his last name was not, in fact, Fausti. "Ask him to identify me, if you don't believe me."

Guido was the Italian man with Scarlett Fausti at Home Run. He had showed up at The Club, and everyone seemed to move out of his way. It was clear to see he had pull.

The Faustis. They were basically Italian royalty, among other things.

What the hell did I get myself into?

The guy with Sierra's ID stood still for a moment. Maybe he was listening to his earpiece, but he watched me the entire time. Then he nodded once. "You're clear. Now your bag, Ms. Andruzzi." He held out his big hand.

I released a breath I hadn't realized I'd been holding and handed it over. He took it inside, and I bit my lip, hoping it wouldn't bust again. I had used Sierra's makeup to cover up the bruises the best that I could. I wasn't skilled in makeup application, so the results were...iffy. I had thought of it as coloring in one of my books, making the princess more appealing with color.

The other guard watched me but turned his eyes in a different direction when the other guy who had my bag came back out.

"Where's my stuff?" I said with bite.

He handed me a ticket in its place. "Checked in. All bags stay with us until you leave."

"Bullshit." I felt territorial over my bag. It was all I had. Everything that was *mine* was in there.

He lowered his eyes. "You read the rules?"

Trick question, I could tell.

"Yeah," I said. I tried honesty. "I did. It's—it's all that I have."

He had no reaction. He stepped to the side and held his arm out. "Enter."

Another guard met me at the door. He told me to follow him. The first thing I noticed was the smell in the air. Chocolate. It seemed to be coming from...candles. They were lit from one end of the hall to another, and the sweet scent seemed to be coming from them.

At the end of the hallway, we took stairs to a second level. If I had to guess, The Club was an old warehouse that had been redone into the space it had become.

Opulence. The word came right after *chocolate.* The Club meant to play on all of the senses.

Squeaky-clean glass stretched the entire second level, and I could see from one end of the club to the next. Below, hundreds of people danced and mingled. Upstairs, people only mingled. Men and women in fine attire circulated the room. Some lounged on dark blue velvet sofas or chairs, a drink in hand, smiles on their faces. Crystal and gold touches enhanced the crushed texture of the velvet. Candlelight softened the atmosphere to a warm glow. Everything shimmered.

This had to be the VIP area, where all of the gorgeous people hung out. These people were a step above beautiful.

As soon as my feet touched the floor, I recognized two wildly popular actresses, two actors, three singers, a couple of famous baseball players, and a few high-powered businessmen that I'd seen on the television at Home Run. They'd give their opinions on stocks and things like that. One thing I noticed they all had in common, apart from being famous enough to recognize, was that they were all young. If I had to guess, they were all around my age, early to mid-twenties.

Except for one man.

He stood out because of his age. He had to be in his late sixties, at least, though his olive complexion seemed to cover his true age. He wore an old-time suit with suspenders and nice shoes. He sat in the corner with a drink in his hand, watching, almost studying.

"Ms. Andruzzi." The guard who had led me in captured my attention by using Sierra's last name. "Make yourself comfortable." He pointed to a room that was hard to see through the crowd. "Food and refreshments can be found in there. If you would like a drink, there are servers passing that can take your order. Whatever you wish for, do not hesitate to ask." He paused for a second. "Do not worry about your bag. If you lose your ticket to claim it, just remember that your number is eleven."

Then he left me.

Eleven. My number. *Fucka me.* Did that mean when my number was called that it was time for me to...what? Screw someone in this room? My stomach took a dive and acid bit the back of my throat. I needed a drink.

I slowly headed toward the room that offered food and *refreshments.* Luckily, it wasn't as packed as the rest of the place. It was mostly filled with women who were lingering around the different stations of food. Lobster. Shrimp. Caviar. Varieties of rich, creamy soups. A station with meat that a man carved with a knife. Hundreds of desserts and chocolates. Coffee. Tea. If you wished for it, this place seemed to have it.

I slapped my forehead with enough momentum that a loud *whap!* sounded. Then I sucked in a gust of air, remembering after the fact that I had a bruise there.

Shit!

A while back, Keely had invited me over on a Sunday, a rare

day off for her, and made me watch a movie with her. It was about a girl who switched places with her younger sister so the little girl wouldn't have to become a human sacrifice. The girl had to fight to survive while the entire country watched. I had remarked that it was no different than surviving New York, but the thought suddenly hit me.

What if this was some kind of sick game?

Whoever the host was held nothing back, money wise. I couldn't even fathom the kind of money it would take to host a party of this magnitude. And then after we ate and drank until we had our fill—then what? We'd have to fight for the important things in the huge-ass cornucopia to help win our survival?

That was straight up Keely's avenue. She was a master with a bow and arrow. My sister from an entirely different mister and mam was kick-ass.

Me? I didn't even have my measly piece of pottery to use in defense.

Accepting a glass of amber liquid, I sipped on it while I studied the women in the room. None of them were speaking to one another. Glances. Polite smiles. But sometimes, when one or the other wasn't paying attention, eyes would linger. Judging. Wondering who wore it better. Every woman was dressed for this. We, meaning the girls in the room and me, looked like we belonged here.

Something was missing, though. *We* didn't belong here. Not on a regular day.

It was the vibe. None of the people outside of this room ventured in here. *Of course not. If you're not starving, you're not worried about being hungry.* I didn't think any of these girls were homeless, but something told me they were all only a step ahead of the devil, too.

They were starved. They were in a constant state of fight or flight. They only existed.

Just like me.

Fucka me.

An insane urge to ask someone what was going on weighed on my tongue, but the weight kept me from speaking. There seemed to be unspoken rules floating through the richly scented air. *No speaking. No questions. You read the rules. You accepted them. Now. Shh. Be quiet.*

I hadn't read the rules, which put me at a severe disadvantage. I had no idea what I was here for, or what was going to happen to me. All I knew was that desperation was a nasty bitch, and when she clawed with poison-tipped nails, you listened. No matter what, I'd separate my body from my mind, *my emotions*, and get on with it.

In a way, this was the survival of the fittest. Wherever the cornucopia was, whatever it held, I was ready to battle for it. The only problem was, these women were gorgeous, in all different ways. It was going to be a bloody war.

If there was no competition and we were all herded like animals to sell to the highest bidder...well, I didn't feel so alone. We were all here for the same purpose, living and not surviving. *For good.*

Only time would tell what side we stood on—unity or battle.

A man in a suit walked in, a piece in his ear, going straight for a girl about to stuff a cream puff in her mouth. Once he was close enough, he held out his arm for her to take. She looked at it a moment, wiped her mouth with a napkin, glanced back at the desserts once more, and then took his muscular arm. They took a right at the door and disappeared out of the room a second later.

I wonder what number she is and when I'll be up next?

Taking my drink and leaving the room with the buffet, I decided to take a seat on a comfortable chair in the midst of the chaos. Laughter steadily grew louder. Two men in front of me mock-punched each other while one of the women I saw in the food room earlier watched them act like fools. A few more women who had been in the room were socializing with men out here, too.

Were we supposed to flirt if this was some kind of auction? I hated the thought of trying to sell myself. This entire situation was bad enough, but selling the goods before they were bid on? *Impossible.* How was I supposed to compete with all of these beauty queens?

Another one of those men wearing an earpiece came out, his eyes scanning the crowd.

Not me. Not me. Not yet.

I breathed out when his eyes passed me up and landed on the woman laughing at the two men. He strode up to her, gave her his arm, and before he led her away, she said something to the two men. Instead of heading right, this time the man with the earpiece went left. He and the woman were headed toward the stairs.

Huh. He was leading her back outside. Did she even know it?

A few minutes later, the same thing happened to a couple more women who mingled with men in the crowd.

Each time a man in a suit came looking, my stomach dipped. I sat my drink down on a marble coaster, not feeling so hot. No food had been a good idea. I was cold and hot simultaneously, and goosebumps puckered my arms. I broke out in a cold sweat, and I hoped the makeup Sierra had wasn't the cheap kind. I patted instead of wiped, hoping the bruises would stay hidden for a little while longer.

Just as I thought a trip to the bathroom was a good idea, the old man with the suspenders took a seat next to me and said something in Italian.

I shook my head. "I don't speak Italian," I said, my voice close to betraying the nerves making me sick to my stomach.

"Ah," he said, almost like a sigh. "How are you feeling?"

The kind eyes under the glasses took in my face, and I felt no need to lie. "Honestly?" I breathed out. "Not so well. Nerves."

He nodded at this. "I am Tito. And you are?"

"Ma—Sierra. Sierra Andruzzi."

His eyes narrowed under the glasses and he tilted his head to the side. "Sierra Andruzzi," he repeated.

"Sierra Andruzzi."

This Tito knew I wasn't Sierra. He didn't outwardly show his surprise that I gave her name, but I just knew. He opened his mouth to speak, but as he did, another man in a suit, another earpiece, came to stand before me. He looked down at me but said nothing.

It was time. 11:11 P.M.

Make a wish, Mari.

Taking a deep breath, stealing one last glance at Tito with the kind eyes, I took the escort's offered arm. He led me down the hallway, allowing time for my awkward walk, past the room with the food, *right*, and into pitch darkness.

THE SMELL of chocolate seemed more concentrated in the dark. I wondered if my senses were making up for the lost one—sight. I couldn't see a thing, but my escort seemed to know where we were going. We didn't run into anything.

The music in this area seemed more intense, too. It was deep, pulsing, slow. The female singer sang about falling from grace for the man she loved.

It screamed loyalty. She was extremely loyal, even when love made her crazy.

I wasn't sure how long we walked in the darkness—a couple of minutes, at least—but when we came to a stop, I felt my escort push against something. Then we entered into a space that mimicked the darkness.

The room's walls were dark, every place to sit black velvet, and the tables the same color. It was entirely monochromatic except for two decorative additions—the crystal chandelier hanging from the ceiling, burning with more candles, and the ceiling itself. The entire space above was created from mother of pearl.

"Would you like a drink, Ms. Andruzzi?" the escort asked, his voice husky.

I don't know, you tell me, I almost spit out. I had no idea what was in store for me, and I was too chicken to ask. When I had committed to this, I did so with all that I had. I was going to see this through.

Set. For good. My last chance.

Take a deep breath, Mari.

"No," I said, my voice just a whisper, the breath I had taken slipping out. Maybe it was my imagination, but the candles seemed to sway with an invisible breeze in the room, making me feel like I was in a world that existed under this one in the darkness.

My escort nodded once, his eyes glistening with the soft light. "Are you ready, Ms. Andruzzi?"

Maybe the details were best left unsaid. That way I couldn't run.

On the other hand, what if there was some kind of protocol?

If I did something wrong, maybe they'd find out that I was lying.

Maybe not.

If I could just go with it and not stumble trying to make my way out of hell...or was I trading one for another?

Closing my eyes, I nodded.

Whatever will be, will be...

A second or two later, something soft touched my face, and a breath trembled out of my mouth. My eyes were covered by a cool silk wrap, the escort's hands securing the tie, and even if I wanted to open my eyes, I wouldn't be able to see.

I didn't hear him leave, but I got the feeling he had. I was alone.

Or was I? It was hard to tell.

Was it the breath of the candles swaying, breathing, consuming the air? Or was I losing control? My breath came faster and faster. My chest felt hollow, as if there wasn't enough oxygen in the room to sustain me. My skin felt hot. The fires licked my skin but blistered my soul.

What were they going to do to me? Or was there something I should be doing?

When I breathed in, trying to control my breath, all I could smell was chocolate, not even the perfume I'd used earlier. It almost seemed...purposely done, to throw someone off.

Everything here seemed to be done with a specific objective in mind. *Stay hidden.*

A soft, cool breeze seemed to enter the room, making the candles hiss instead of pant. A bead of sweat rolled from my neck between my breasts. I felt its cool race down my skin, trying to cool the burn of the fires around me.

The hands that touched me out of the darkness were warm, pleasant, but my skin contracted at the surprise anyway. Someone had entered the room and stood behind me. I felt his presence, his heat, which was different from the candles. Wilder. Hotter. His breath fanned over my skin, only making me feel...overheated.

He.

He had to be a *he.* Those hands. They were big in comparison to my arms. He was tall. Wide. A force. The strength of him engulfed me.

There was no doubt that this man was a hunter, but what

side would he stand on? Would he kill for me, or make me his prey?

Please don't hurt me. Please.

My knees started to knock together at the thought. At the memories I had suppressed for so long.

If I could've closed my eyes even tighter, I would have. I couldn't. They were starting to cramp from the strain of trying to keep my shit together. The drink I had earlier was a small ember in the background, doing nothing to help ease the uncertainty of the moment. It added to it.

I forced myself to listen to reason, to think this through. *Follow the line of his touch.* It was firm but not hurtful, like his hands were not soft but not rough either. He was feeling me out. Tracing my lines. Memorizing them?

Even though I had no idea who he was, something about the way he touched me, taking his time, made me feel like he was looking for something that went deeper than flesh—a connection? A spark?

Maybe I was losing my mind, imagining that he was not only doing this for sex.

Or maybe it was wishful thinking.

His hands slowly came around my waist, and he pulled me into him, my back to his front. We sort of moved in time to the music, from side to side, until I relaxed enough to almost melt into the embrace. He seemed to know when I did. This time, his hands felt like they were burning through the fabric of the dress.

I inhaled, wanting to catch his scent, but...chocolate. *Bingo*, I thought. I was right. It was the reason why the entire place smelled strongly of the rich scent. He didn't want me to *know* him, to *see* him.

Maybe it was for the best. This would be over soon enough, and maybe I'd be set, and life would be better. I'd never see his face when I thought of the moment that changed everything.

I'd only think *chocolate*. No strings to keep pulling me back into the fire.

Another breath trembled out of my mouth when one of his hands started to venture against my body. In the darkness, his touch reminded me of white lightning streaking across the night sky. The hair on my body stiffened, goosebumps puckered my skin, and something about the way he moved made me feel...pliable, like he could mold me into a shape to fit his.

My mind wanted to shut it out, go along with it, *get it over with*, but my body...it did something it had never before.

Responded.

My body started to shut my mind down, wanting, taking, wanting, taking. I willingly relaxed my hand so that he could hold it in the hand that had been searching my body. He entwined our fingers together, and in a move so smooth that it seemed perfectly timed, he turned me.

We must be facing each other. The candles are brightening my face and he'll truly see me now.

Complete silence.

I waited. I waited. I waited. And waited some more.

What the hell?

Did he leave?

I was ashamed to think it, to feel it, but I craved his touch in the darkness. I wanted his hands on me again. I wanted to feel their soothing warmth. I wanted to feel that security again. The nothing behind the blindfold started to feel imposing. Unnerving.

In the darkness, I didn't feel so wicked reacting to his touch. *To him.*

I lifted my hand, about to remove the blindfold, but hesitated. I knew once I did, the spell would be broken. He had set the scene and the tone. Made it ideal. Romantic even. Made it not so hard to think the words...*I can handle this. Touch me again.*

After another minute or two, I couldn't handle the frantic

beat of my heart, the uncertainty that started to creep in, and went to remove the mask.

He stopped me.

His hands were on me again, in my hair, and his mouth clashed against mine, so roughly that I knew my lip split open again. He had been drinking something spicy, with cinnamon, and it mixed with the iron coming in between our mouths.

At first, he was unstoppable. Not even the blood stopped him. His tongue tangled with mine, and it was starved. Starved like I had been for years. I could feel him, consuming in any way he could. For once, I was the one giving. Maybe that was why it didn't feel entirely wrong.

The head on his shoulders, the body carried by the legs, the arms that reached out and touched, the physical, it didn't seem to matter to me. He could look like an ogre, and for some reason, *beautiful* still came to mind. I had met plenty of beautiful people, and their pretty only ran skin deep. But the people who were kind, the rare ones, they were the definition of true beauty.

Somewhere deep inside of my mind, I wondered if the fear of the last couple of hours, *most of my life*, had somehow caught up to me. My mind was taking a terrible situation and making it ideal so I could handle this.

I called bullshit.

It was more.

It was hard to put it all into words.

Simply put, I wanted to keep kissing him. I wanted him to keep kissing me—touching me.

I wanted *more* of whatever this was. It was feeding me in a way that I'd never known, except for when Keely and her family made me feel like I was a part of theirs. Then again, it was different. The feelings were new, even if I couldn't place them while in the immediate glow.

What had the singer compared the intensity she had for her lover to earlier? A drug.

That was something I never expected. The pull. The push. The high from being lifted up by a cool wave.

The intensity of it almost made me pull away, take a few minutes like he did to compose myself, but on the other hand, my hands refused to let him go. I had taken his shirt in my hands and locked down. Touching him felt like touching life. I had never felt that before.

Life. In my hands. Mine.

Then, in a move so violent that I stumbled back, landing against the wall, palms out behind my back to stop myself from going over completely, he ripped his mouth from mine.

He cursed underneath his breath. The sound of it was as violent as his rejection.

For however long—a minute, a million years—I stood still. I wasn't sure what to say. I trembled from head to toe, just like I'd done after Merv had attacked me. Then something came to mind, and before I could filter it, I spoke into the darkness. "The blood from my lip." I pointed to it. "I'm clean."

He stayed quiet for so long that I thought he left again.

"Don't touch it," he said, his voice full of warning. The tone of it ran over me like rough waves, but the coolness of it slid over blistered skin like a miracle. His voice was low, but with some scratch to it. He didn't seem like he was doing it on purpose. I wanted to hear it again

Get your shit together, Mari! You haven't even seen his face! He could be seriously messed up, a man who just came here to fuck you for money. Or worse. He likes to use blindfolds. Kinky shit.

Liar, liar, liar, my heart seemed to sing, all off tune and shit. *He's beautiful.*

The devil was beautiful, too, my mind shot back.

"Okay," I said, putting my hands down. I was going to

remove the blindfold again when he came at me with "*don't touch it.*"

"You're poor."

There it was again, my favorite sound in the world. His voice. I liked the rasp in it.

Wait.

What?

You're poor.

I laughed a little. I expected him to comment on my *I'm clean* comment. That was why I had brought it up. I thought that maybe once he tasted the blood, he was disgusted and worried. Instead he hits me with "*you're poor.*"

Who leads with that?

"Fabulously so." I sighed. "Anyone poorer than me might as well be down with whale shit. I have no home. No job. No money. I used everything I had to get here tonight. I have no family either." I didn't want to get into Keely and her family. He didn't need to know that. If he was deranged, or whatever was worse than that, better he didn't know they existed.

"Name," he said.

"Oh." I took a breath in and released it. "My name is... Mari. I'm not Sierra. She...she couldn't make it. I took her place. So about the rules..."

"Name," he said again. "Not yours, Ms. Flores. I want the name of the man who did that to your face."

"How do you know it was a man?" I whispered, ignoring the fact the he knew my last name without me even telling him.

"Name," he said once more. I got the feeling he was losing patience with me.

Why would he need the information?

I stood taller, teetering a bit in the heels, putting up a wall against all I felt since he touched me. "That's none of your business. I might not know much about this situation, but I do know this. It pays. I came here to earn money. So do I get the job or not? My time is valuable, Mr...?"

"What would you be willing to do to get the job?"

"I thought *you* were the job I'd be doing."

"Answer me, Mariposa."

I licked at my lip, glad that it had started to clot. I knew it looked bad, though. He had kissed my lipstick off. "I'm here. That means... whatever you want me to. I heard the job pays well."

"Ah," he said, sounding Italian all of a sudden. "It pays very well. Millions. Plus perks."

I didn't suck in a breath, but I wanted to. Millions? Perks? Was he messing with me? No, Sierra had mentioned *for good*. If the girl cared enough to count her cheese slices, she wouldn't have messed around about this. Suddenly, her situation with Scarpone dawned on me. Had she broken up with him for this opportunity? It made sense, if she had.

"Sounds good to me," I said. "Sign me up."

This time, I felt it when he took a step closer. I was highly aware of him. *Lightning searing against my personal darkness.* I tried to take a step back, but he put his arm around my waist, pulling me closer. I stuck my hand to his chest, pushing, but he didn't budge.

"Us," he said. "Tell me about that. What happened in here, between us."

"That's a dirty word. Us. There is no us," I said. "This is business. Whatever I do, and I mean *whatever*, I do as a business transaction. Nothing is free in this life, not even love. I'm past being dirt poor. I have to watch out for me. So, you either give me the *job*, or have one of those men escort me out, like you did to the girls who were flirting with the men in the main room."

"You do me a service—"

"And you pay me," I said.

"Nothing more," he said.

"Not a damn thing."

"For the record, Mariposa." He came in closer, inhaling, his breath fanning over my neck. I closed my eyes again, trying my hardest to keep my heart from frantically beating. I knew he could feel it. "Never fucking cut me off while I'm speaking."

I nodded. "Will do...*boss*." The word sounded like a bitter insult sliding right off my honeyed tongue.

"I never said you got the job, Mariposa."

His nose moved up my neck, touching my ear, then moved back down to my lips. He placed a chaste kiss on the side of my mouth, and then on my lips, right where the cut was. It burned, the area sensitive, but it was the only reminder that this was real. That he had existed.

The burn was still strong as my escort from earlier removed the blindfold—the other man, the *boss*, was gone. The feelings he left behind were as hot as the flames blistering the air around me.

After giving me a second to compose myself, the escort led me outside, no words spoken between us.

7

CAPO

Out of all the clubs in the world, she had to walk into mine.

Mine.

She invaded my space without even knowing she had.

She looked completely different, but somehow, I remembered her.

The eyes. The nose. The lips. The shape of her face. She was my innocence, *la mia farfalla*, but she had matured. Became a woman in the span of years that felt like centuries to me. Seeing her brought back a rush of memories. I was a dead man reliving a life he had left behind.

She was the catalyst for death, for a new life, and now for the season I currently found myself in.

She thought she was clever showing up at The Club with the exclusive invitation, one that belonged to a dead girl, nonetheless. Armino Scarpone had killed her. Like father, like son.

Then *mia farfalla* mentioned Guido when the doorman had caught her, thinking she could slip past my security that easily.

Searching her bag had brought me closer to who she was.

The butterfly clip. The piece of broken pottery with the butterfly painted on it. The book with all of her notes. Coloring books and crayons.

A grown fucking woman carrying around crayons.

She was an odd mixture between a woman and a child.

As the piece of terra cotta in my hand had taken shape, so did the memories stored in my head.

If anyone deserved loyalty, it was me from her.

She just didn't know it yet.

She couldn't have remembered. She was only five.

When I had touched her at The Club, though, she had relaxed, melted into me, and the years disappeared. It brought me back to that place, that time. No matter how much she'd deny it, and she would, she trusted me. She had reason to.

Before I could stop myself, I had let go of the image of the child and kissed the woman standing in front of me. Crossed a line that couldn't be set straight again. She was attractive in a way that was hard to explain. But one word came to mind when I looked at her. Regal. She was a queen. And those lips? They were the softest things I'd felt since my pillow.

Being that close to her made something inside of me restart. My entire world went black, faded out, and when I opened my eyes, the taste of her blood had invaded my mouth.

Red. A reminder.

Someone had touched her. Put their fucking hands on her. The child I had given my life to keep safe.

Whatever happened to her over the years had turned her into a woman who refused to allow anyone to help her. Kindness meant she owed something. It was clear that she refused to owe anyone. Even if it meant being starved. Even if it meant her life.

Most people called me Mac. Others called me their worst fucking nightmare. But no one—*no one*—ever called me *boss*. Not like she did, with a sarcastic twist of the tongue. Despite not knowing the circumstances in which she had found herself in, she was going to set her terms.

She demanded to touch life after merely surviving it for so long.

Her willingness to do whatever it took to get the job, no matter how life changing, showed me just how desperate she was. She had hit a turning point, stumbling right into the crux beyond starved and ready for more. She had run out of options.

No home. No job. No money. She was running on zero, on fumes. The stale bread in her bag was a dead giveaway, not to mention that she was skin and bones and wasn't purposely trying to stay that way.

Desperation doesn't always mean a person is loyal, but after someone has been in the trenches for so long, the hand that helps them up, takes them in, and feeds them will become the hand that inspires trust. For someone like her, who owed me even if she didn't know it, she would become loyal.

Loyalty was rewarded in the world I lived in.

I'd do for her. She'd do for me.

She had the general idea of things already ingrained in her, even though I hated to think how she got that fucking way.

I'd find out about that. I always did.

Blue was once Marietta Palermo's favorite color—the same little girl who loved butterflies and coloring books. I'd know if Mariposa Flores's favorite color was still blue by the time I was done.

Butterflies and coloring books still did it for her. My bet was still on blue.

I'd know if she had nightmares and I starred in them, or if she had forgotten the situation completely. The night at The Club, her body remembered me, even if her mind refused to set the memories free.

I'd learn every scar on her body and hunt down every finger that had ever touched her with evil in mind. I had a multitude of sins to pay for. A few more wouldn't make a difference when it came time for forgiveness.

There wouldn't be a single freckle on her skin that I wouldn't know intimately.

I longed to run my finger down her nose, to memorize how it felt against my skin. I had already memorized the lines of her body. The way she fit against me. How she felt pressed against my chest. The scent of her still seemed to drift underneath my nose when I least expected it.

Back to the fucking point. She owes me.

"*Capo*," Rocco said, reminding me that I was in his office. He was being a wise ass, calling me *boss* in Italian. He was the closest thing to a brother I'd ever known, but we were not brothers. Not by blood, but one thing I learned the hard way, family was not always blood. Family was a title that was earned, not given. Even though we were close, there was still a gap. For him. For me. There always was when it came to the world we lived in.

I turned from the window, the city of New York sprawling around me, and took another drink of whiskey. I set it down on his rich mahogany desk, fixing my tie. "*Sì*," I said. "Get the paperwork ready."

"Her name." His eyes scrutinized me without the weight of judgment.

I checked my watch for the time. I had somewhere else I needed to be. "Let her decide."

"I'll send Guido."

"*Sì*." I grinned. "I'm sure she'll enjoy that, since she knows Guido and the Fausti *famiglia* so well. A familiar face might make this easier."

He returned the grin, nodded once, and then started the paperwork.

8

MARIPOSA

I t had been over a week since The Club and *him*, and so much had happened during that time.

I hadn't heard anything from *him*. After his escort had led me to a waiting car, a car that had tinted windows, a privacy glass, and looked like it cost the amount of a townhouse in New York, a suited driver brought me home. I made him drop me two blocks from Keely's place, though I had a feeling he followed me.

So, that life experience tanked. My body wasn't even worth enough to sell.

I blamed it on my nose and then tried to move on.

It was easier to do when so much good was happening around me. Keely was able to not work as hard when Harrison paid a month's worth of her rent. The situation with Sierra really hit her hard. She was having nightmares after seeing the girl she roomed with for so long dead. The detectives ruled that Sierra had been murdered. Harrison told me she had been brutally stabbed. Armino Scarpone was their number one suspect, but he hadn't been found yet.

It was scary to think he was on the loose, but there were so many like him out there, the fact that *he* was out there didn't really shock us. We prepared and then survived the best we could.

Two days after Harrison was able to help Keely with the rent, she got a call. She got a huge part in a famous Broadway show. We all knew she would someday, but it was a shock when it happened. The best shock any of us could've ever expected. She deserved it and so much more.

Keely had demanded that I stay with her. She didn't want me out on the streets since Armino had seen us leaving that day. He knew Keely and I were home when he'd been banging on the door and screaming. Harrison thought that maybe he'd want to eliminate any witnesses, but it was too late. Keely and I had already spoken to the police since we were both there. We were the last three people (Keely, Armino, and me) who saw Sierra alive, apart from the clerk at the store. She had run out to buy stockings and was ambushed on her way home.

Regardless of my feelings on taking handouts, I decided to stay with Kee. Not because I couldn't face the streets again, but because I worried for her. She was having a really rough time, even when she should've been celebrating. But my rule of no kindness unless repaid still applied, so to make it up to her, I helped her pack. Since she got the better job, she was moving into a nicer place once her lease was up at the place she shared with Sierra.

The teapot went off and she jumped up to do whatever it was she did with it. I wasn't a tea person, but Kee and Co. (her entire family) swore by the stuff. Her mother was what she called "a tea-leaf reader." I didn't want to try and read anything but grind particles floating around in my cup of coffee.

I watched her for a moment and then went back to packing things she wouldn't need for the kitchen.

"Mari?"

"Yeah?"

I looked at her again. She was putting bags in the kettle. Something sweet but spicy filled the air. Vanilla. Cinnamon. *Cinnamon.* It made me think of *his* mouth—I cut the thought off before I could get carried away. I thought I'd only remember chocolate, but apparently, that had been a lie I fed myself.

"I keep thinking...all of these good things started happening after Sierra died. I don't have to work so hard to keep up with the rent for this ratty ass place. Getting the call about the show. It all seems so sudden. Do you think...how do I even say this without sounding like a cold-hearted bitch?" Keely dunked another bag in, studying it. "Sierra had her ways, but for the most part, I felt sorry for her. She reminded me of you."

I swallowed hard. "She did?"

She nodded, pouring the hot liquid into an old teacup. "Not her personality. Her story. How she had to fight to survive. She definitely had a mean streak about her, which you don't, but she was an orphan. And then she went into foster care. I think she had to fight for her food; that's why I never said anything when she'd count her eggs or cheese."

Keely stirred the cup and then took a seat. She tucked a fiery red curl behind her ear. "What I'm getting at is this. I wonder if she was stopping her happiness, therefore mine. I hate—*hate*—that she was murdered, but even before, I was thinking it was time for us to part ways. Now that she's gone, I feel...lighter."

I set the decorative four-leaf clover in the box, resting my hand against her shoulder. It was tense. Sierra had no family, like me, and all that she had left behind went to Keely. It took a lot out of her to make decisions for a woman that no one truly knew. Not even Keely.

"I agree," I said. "There was something about her that made me feel...heavier, too. It's hard to explain."

Keely stared at her tea, a distant look in her eyes. "Maybe

her new start was just about to happen. Maybe her darkness was about to get lighter. The job she was telling me about. She never got to go to the interview. The dress is still on her bed."

"Do you know what that was all about?"

I hadn't told Keely what I'd done or what had happened. I still had no clue what the job was or what it had entailed. After I got home that night, Keely was asleep, and I tiptoed into Sierra's room and put everything just as Sierra had left it. I had my extra set of clothes stashed in my bag, so I changed in the car in case Keely was up waiting for me. I hadn't looked in Sierra's room since.

"No," Keely said. "But I got the feeling she thought the job was *it* for her. She wasn't going to have to struggle anymore. I have no idea what kind of job brings that much security, but she was certain of it."

Certain. I got that feeling, too. Whatever *the boss* had in store for one of those girls, she'd never have to work again. I still couldn't figure it out, though. What would be worth that much to him, or to anyone?

"Hey," Keely said, squeezing my hand. "Let's talk about something else. You never told me what you did the other day. You were gone a while. Did you go looking for another job?"

The first time I left her alone was to take a trip back to Macchiavello's. I sat against the wall again, coloring, waiting to see if the man in the suit would show up. It was stupid, so, so stupid, but something about him inspired trust. With all of the problems building around me, it felt good to see someone who really seemed to have their shit together. He seemed so capable. Like he would know what to do in any situation. He would have the answers to any problem that plagued him.

My waiting wasn't in vain. He showed up about an hour after I did, looking as cool and as fine as ever. Maybe it was my imagination, but as soon as he stepped out of his expensive car, his face turned toward mine like he knew I'd been waiting for him.

We stared at each other until I decided to do what I'd come to do. I unzipped my bag, took out the ice pack, lifted it up, and then set it along the wall. Then I turned and left.

I swore to myself that I wouldn't go back. I had issues, issues that wouldn't be solved by waiting around a restaurant that catered only to the rich. Staring at some unavailable (to me) millionaire in a fine suit was not going to solve anything.

The urge to tell Keely everything that had happened surged up in me. I felt guilty about using Sierra's dress, her perfume, her shoes, her invitation to the mysterious side of The Club, and not telling Keely that I had.

I wanted to tell her about the guy in the suit. I wanted to tell her that no matter if Harrison loved me or not, I had never felt anything toward him except brotherly love. Compared to what I'd felt over the last couple of days—for the guy in the suit and the *boss*— I knew how different my feelings for Harrison were. Platonic. Nothing more.

Keely was all I had in the world, and I hoped she'd understand the reasons behind what I'd done. I hoped that she'd be able to hear the truth behind all of my feelings.

It was time to purge the demons and come clean.

I squeezed her hand and then took a seat next to her. Staring at her cup of tea, I said, "I need to tell you something."

The words seemed to tumble from my mouth. I started with the guy in the suit, then went into what happened the night Sierra died. I told her every detail about The Club. Then I gave her a second before I ended it with my feelings about her brother.

I couldn't read her face, and when the silence became too much, I whispered, "Say something."

"You didn't tell me *something*," she said. "You told me *things*. Lots and lots of things."

"I was holding in a lot," I said.

"You think?" She shook her head. "Why didn't you tell me?"

I shrugged, picking at my broken nail. "I didn't want to disappoint you. I basically stole a dead girl's clothes, shoes, and perfume, and pretended to be her. If I failed, which I did, it seemed like such a low blow. A final blow. You would've told me not to go. That whatever Sierra was going to do was not worth it. But it was. It *was*. For me. And now...I...I'm still not sure what I'm going to do, Kee."

"She was a waitress at The Club," Keely said. "Sierra. That's where she worked. And the guy who owns it is not an ordinary citizen, Mari. He's rich, like multi-millionaire status, or more. He's reclusive. But the shit she would sometimes talk about, the people who frequented the place, like the Faustis, made me understand that it was more than just a club.

"So you're damn right. I would have told you not to go. What were you thinking? What if he would have sold you to the highest bidder? Or...used you for some kind of weird sexual fantasy? You don't belong there, Mari! I don't want you there. You deserve more from life than to be bought. You deserve a man who'd never put a dollar amount on you because no amount of money in the world would be enough! You deserve a man who doesn't think he deserves you!"

"I didn't get the job, Kee!" I stood, not able to sit. "I failed at that, too! I couldn't even sell my body. I'm worthless! I can't keep a job. I can't even stay in school! So I took a chance. It was my *last* chance. And I failed at that, too! My nose or my fucking mouth! I got smart with him at the end."

"Good!" she shouted. "The bastard should be told off! He was probably there to buy a woman for the night!"

"No." I shook my head. "I got the feeling this was different. This was for the long run. *For good.*"

"What does that even mean?"

I shrugged, not sure how to explain it. *Living for the rest of my life instead of merely surviving, for starters.*

A knock came at the door and we both jumped. Keely looked at me and I looked at her, both of our eyebrows rising in suspicious surprise.

"*Grab the cast iron skillet Mam gave me,*" she mouthed to me.

"*I'll stand behind you,*" I mouthed back.

She opened the door a crack, and I stood behind, hiding the skillet behind my back. If it were Armino, he wouldn't see it until I knocked him over the head with it.

It wasn't Armino Scarpone. It was Detective Stone and Detective Marinetti again. It felt like they lived around here these days.

We stood back and let them enter. Detective Stone raised his eyebrows when he noticed the skillet in my hand but didn't comment on it. Figuring they were here to discuss something with Keely, I turned to go back into the kitchen.

"We need to speak to you this time, Ms. Flores," Detective Marinetti said, gesturing toward the sofa.

I brought the skillet with me as I took a seat. Keely took one next to me. The two detectives stood in front of us.

"Are you familiar with a man named Merv Johnson?" Detective Stone asked.

"Merv the Perv?" Keely scrunched up her nose.

Stone grinned at her and his eyes softened.

"I know him," I said, staring at him until he looked at me. "But not well. He was the super at my last apartment, if you can even call it that. A place to sleep that's not outside is more like it."

"Yeah," Detective Marinetti said. He seemed so tired. *Done.* He sighed. "We gathered that."

"What about Merv?" Keely sat up a little taller. "If you've come to tell us that he's dead, good riddance." She fake-spit on the side of the sofa. Something I saw her Mam do all of the time when something disgusted her.

"Merv Johnson *is* dead," Detective Marinetti said bluntly.

I elbowed Keely and she started to cough. It seemed like she was shocked that he actually was. She probably thought they were coming to question me about his character after one of the girls in the building had gone missing.

"What happened to him?" Keely said, stealing the words from my mind.

My mouth was dry, my body full of sweat, and my heart raced. All I could think of was his stunned face after I had hit him in the temple with Vera. Did I kill the bastard? I didn't stick around to find out. And there was no telling how long he had been in the apartment if he was.

The place's personal best was two months. Merv didn't check until the second month the rent was due. He was trading sex for rent with some of the women in the building and went to collect when he needed to get some. I was sure no one, *no one*, went looking for him until the smell became too much. They probably thought it was me, if he was still in my old apartment.

"Murdered," Detective Stone said. "The reason we're here is because we're wondering if you happen to know of anyone that might have wanted him dead, Ms. Flores. Since the incident with Ms. Andruzzi, Detective Marinetti and I felt we've already established a relationship with you. No one at the complex will talk. Mr. Johnson doesn't seem to have many friends."

Keely opened her mouth to speak at the same time that Detective Marinetti sighed. He took a chair from the kitchen and placed it in front of the sofa, taking a seat. He looked bored to death, like he knew where this conversation was headed. Merv had no friends here either.

"When was the pervert killed?" Keely got out. Once you crossed her, there was no going back. Keely hardened herself toward anyone she felt did her or her family wrong. She would forgive, but she'd never forget.

"Yesterday."

That ruled out Vera and me.

"Ms. Flores, can you give us anything at all to help us bring the person responsible for this crime to justice?"

I went to open my mouth, but Keely spoke up. Her neck had turned red and it started to creep up her cheeks. She stared Detective Stone in the eyes. "I can give you something. Merv Johnson assaulted my sister." She grabbed my hand. "Did you notice her face the other day, Detective? He did that to her. He tried to abuse her in that rat-infested place he called an apartment. He traded sex for rent. If you said no, he'd take it out on your face.

"So, no, neither of us know who could've wanted him dead, because the list is too long. But I will say this. I don't wish death on anyone, but I'm glad he's dead. Justice? Whoever has done this has served it for the good of all mankind. Now, if you have no further questions, this has been a long week for us. And after you've gone, we'd like to be thankful for the death of a predator in peace."

———

FOUR HOURS LATER, another knock came at the door.

I looked up from the box that I was packing and blew a wild tendril of hair out of my face. It had slipped out of my makeshift bun. I heard Keely moving toward the door, and swiping the skillet from the sofa, I met her there.

"I'll answer this time," I said.

She took the skillet from me and hid it behind her back. "I have a lot of pent up aggression, so I got this." She nodded toward the door. "Open sesame."

I took a step back, running into Keely after I had opened

the door. "Guido." His name slipped out before I could stop myself. He held a gold wrapped box in his hands.

"Do I have to whack him?" Keely whispered.

I shook my head. "I don't think so."

"Good," she said. "His face is too fine to mess up. If that singer who writes about all of her old flames ever saw this dude, she'd be writing songs about a guy named Guido."

Guido eyed us both in the way that men do when they think the women in their presence are unstable. Then he grinned and said, "There is no need for violence. I have come in peace."

We both gasped a little. It transformed his face.

"I used your name," I blurted without thinking. "The night at The Club. It was wrong, but I thought they were going to bust me. I remembered you from Home Run, when Scarlett came to pick up the framed jersey for her husband."

"Be careful," he said, his tone serious, but there was mischief in those dark eyes. It made him hard to read. "My name is well known, but not all that know me *like* me. They might have turned you away due to my name alone, or put you behind bars for my enemy to take apart. The name Fausti does not always guarantee safety. Sometimes it attracts trouble."

"Shit, Mari!" Keely slapped my arm. "The Faustis!"

I turned a little and gave her a dirty look.

Guido seemed unfazed by her outburst. He held out the package for me to take. "*Il capo.*" He paused, fighting a grin. "He sent me to deliver a message. All that you need to begin is in the box."

"Does she get to work from home?" Keely egged him on, taking this situation more seriously since she knew I'd scored the job, whatever it was.

"Instructions are in the package," was all he said as he turned to leave.

"Guido," I called, my voice barely above a whisper.

He stopped and turned to me. The sun hit his dark chocolate eyes and they glistened. *Fucka me.* What were these men eating in Italy? They were almost too good looking to be true.

"What does *il capo* mean?" I asked.

"It means *the boss* in Italian." He laughed. He laughed all the way to his expensive, fast car.

Gangsters with a sense of humor. Who knew?

After I shut the door, I rested my back against it, because my knees felt like they had turned to putty. The box in my hands could have been a gift or an explosive device.

"Mari," Keely said, forcing my eyes on her. "This just got really serious. The Faustis!" She kept repeating the name like it would make them disappear if she said it enough.

I held my pointer finger up. "Shh. I need a minute."

"I need a drink!" she said, and I knew she was going for Irish whiskey.

I slid to the ground, letting my weight take me while the door braced me. After five minutes, ten hours—who knew?—with trembling fingers, I opened the box.

A pair of really nice tennis shoes was tucked underneath a thin veil of paper. *My size.* A note sat on top of the pristine white shoes.

Ms. Flores,

You should always go into an important meeting with shoes that fit properly. A first impression can be your last.

This is the first pair of many. The cost has already been deducted from your wages. Wear them. No excuses.

I did for you. You'll do for me next. This is not personal. Merely business.

He signed off with "*Capo.*"

"Smart ass," I muttered.

A smaller card was below the handwritten one listing the time and date of the meeting. Two days. *Monday. 11:11 A.M.* The address was listed in Manhattan, some swanky building, no doubt. A driver would be sent to "fetch" me.

Fucka me.

Was I really going to do this?

My eye caught the swirl of amber liquid that suddenly appeared in my line of sight.

Keely dangled a shot glass filled with whiskey in front of me. "I would tell you not to do this, but what good would it do?" She took a seat next to me on the floor, careful not to spill her own glass. She sighed, leaning her head against mine. "Promise me you'll be safe?"

I lifted my glass and she lifted hers. I couldn't promise her something I had no control over. We clinked and then downed, not even bothering with a toast.

9

Monday, 11:00 AM on the dot, I sat in the high-rise building, in some swanky office, in my plastic flip-flops, waiting for Mr. Rocco Fausti to call me back into his office. His secretary gave me a strange look when I asked her what it was that Mr. Rocco Fausti did. There was no writing on the door.

He was a lawyer, she had said, and judging by the riches around me, a very successful one.

At 11:07 on the dot, Rocco Fausti came out of his office and greeted me. His accent was strong Italian, but not hard to understand. He held out his hand and I almost didn't take it because I didn't want to dirty his pretty skin. I felt like a kid about to soil some important marble statue with handprints.

He was tall, much taller than me. His hair was black, his skin gold, and his eyes...sea green. His lashes were thick and black. His lips full. And he smelled...whatever equaled to better than good. His body. There was no hiding the muscular physique underneath the custom-made suit. Whoever this *Capo* was, he surrounded himself with beautiful people. Competent people.

People unlike me.

If I didn't already know how basic I was in the looks department, and accepted it, maybe I'd have grown a complex.

We passed what seemed like Rocco's office—it smelled like him—stopping at a room with a long table in its center. There were twelve chairs situated around it, six on each side, and a circular tray in the middle with glasses and a pitcher of water. He gestured for me to take a seat close to the streak-free glass wall that stretched the backside of the room.

Once I had, he took a seat at the head of the table, right next to me. A minute or two later, his secretary came in and delivered a file full of papers. Before she left, she poured three glasses of water, setting one in front of her boss, one in front of me, and one to the right of him. A third person would be joining us then.

"Mr. Fausti?"

He looked up from his papers, the green in his eyes sparking from the sunlight pouring through the windows. "Rocco will do."

I nodded. "Rocco. Why am I here?"

While he stared at me, I took the glass of water, drinking some of it down.

11:11 AM on the dot, the water went down wrong and I started choking. I shot out of my chair, waving my hands in front of my face, trying to fight the clog. The third person had walked into the room just as the water tried to go down.

I looked up at the ceiling, still trying to breathe, thinking, *Is this sarcasm or just a cruel joke?*

The frigging water burned my throat, and I couldn't stop coughing. Water was killing me. *He* was killing me. What was he doing here?

He couldn't be...

He held out his hand for me to take. "You can call me Capo," he said, "if you wish."

The man in the suit. Mr. Mac. Boss. Capo. Four and the fucking same.

Blue. All I could think was blue. His eyes. They were blue. The kind of blue that you could get lost in, float in, never wanting to return to earth. They were calming, but something about them was guarded. Like if you had to survive hell to earn his heaven.

"Mariposa."

His voice. It washed over me then, like it had done the night in The Club. It was low, gruff, and the sexiest thing I'd ever heard.

Even though my eyes watered, his hand was still outstretched, and I couldn't help but stare at it. I kept thinking about the way he had touched me. Held me. Our moment in the candlelit room.

The hand he held out took a firmer shape, lived in *this* moment, and I noticed a tattoo that covered the entire portion of his opposite hand, his left. It began at his wrist and ended at the beginning of his long fingers. It created the face of a snarling black wolf. The animal's eyes were electric blue, like his.

If this man wanted a woman to have all kinds of sex with him, why would he ever have to pay someone? I was willing to bet my stale loaf of bread that almost any woman would want to be touched by him. He was universally appealing, and he had that something about him that evened out his beauty. It was something wild and rugged. He had something that existed deeper than the physical and couldn't be truly explained.

No. It could in simple terms. He was a brutal force. I could feel him pushing in on me without even touching me.

He cleared his throat, and my eyes automatically went there. It was the first time I'd seen him so close up. Just like I hadn't noticed the tattoo, I hadn't noticed the scar that circled his throat. It was old, almost the same color as his skin, but noticeable.

"Ms. Flores," Rocco said, breaking my trance. "Shall we begin?"

It took me a moment, but after Capo retracted his outstretched hand, I cleared my throat and croaked out, "Yeah, but call me Mari."

Rocco nodded. "Mari." He gestured to the seat.

I took it, my eyes never leaving Capo's. His eyes never left mine. It was intense, but somehow I didn't care. I wanted to stare at him. I wasn't sure if I'd ever get tired of looking at him.

Seeing him from a distance suddenly felt like a sin. All of his features were better seen up close.

Capo took the seat across from me, his cologne filling my nose as his clothes were pressed from the movement. Rocco gave us a minute as he thumbed through the papers situated in front of him.

Capo reached across to take my hand again. "Mariposa," he said. "You can call me Capo or Mac."

I cleared my throat, knowing it was going to sound off when I spoke. I still hadn't taken his hand. I knew how it felt against mine, and I was almost afraid that a spark would go off when we touched. I wondered if a spark had gone off when he had touched me in the dark at The Club? I had felt it. "I'd rather call you Capo," I said, my voice small and full of sand. "And you can call me Mari."

I reached out to make the connection then, not wanting to be a chicken, but when I got close, I slapped at his hand, like I was giving him a sideways five. *Too soon.* It was too soon to touch him again. To be caught up in him. I didn't want my eyes to give away what he possibly didn't see in the darkness. How much he had affected me.

He grinned, but it didn't touch his eyes. "Mariposa," he said, using an Italian accent on the Spanish word. "I'll call you Mariposa. The butterfly."

The butterfly. I moved my head to the side, somehow thinking I could see him better. It didn't make things clearer, but from any angle, he was stunning. The most beautiful thing I'd ever seen apart from my favorite. The butterfly. That was why I hated when people who meant nothing to me called me by my full name. It was the only thing special about me, and when they said it so plainly, like it meant nothing, it reinforced all that I felt—unseen. A caterpillar still stuck in the ugly phase of its life.

Coming from his mouth, those full lips, I didn't mind. I liked the way he had said it, with a roll of his tongue. Mari*posa*. He made it sound...special. Beautiful even.

"Mari, you asked me why you were here," Rocco said, breaking through the fog surrounding me.

I nodded, taking another sip of water.

"Careful." Capo grinned at me. "It seems the water here is thicker than normal."

I narrowed my eyes. *Smart ass.* Then I turned from him, making a deal with myself not to look at him again until Rocco shed some light on the paperwork in front of him.

"Are you familiar with arranged marriages, Mari?"

"Arranged marriages?" I repeated, sounding as dumb as I was sure my face looked. Of course I knew what they were, but why in the hell was he bringing them up during this meeting? I expected words like sex submissive, or discussions about the price of flesh and what I would and wouldn't do for a buck. But marriage?

"An arranged marriage is when—" Rocco started.

I lifted a hand, stopping his explanation. "I know what it is, but what does it have to do with why I'm here?"

"If you had known what you were getting into," Rocco said, giving me a pointed look, "I wouldn't have brought it up.

However, since you were chosen by Capo for this arrangement and you were not previously made aware of the situation, I am here to make things clear. Arranged marriages are not uncommon in our culture, though usually both sides of the family are involved. That aside, Capo wants to take a bride. After spending some time with you, he chose you. That is why we are here, Mari. Capo wants to marry you."

"Marry you?" I repeated, looking between the two men, able to look at Capo again since Rocco had explained why I was there. Neither one of them laughed or looked remotely like they were playing around with me. *However*, I laughed. Cackled like a witch.

Then I became quiet, realizing how serious they were being. "Fucka me," I said, wiping my eyes. Then I turned them on Capo. "You really want to marry me?"

He nodded once, really slow, really sharp. "An arrangement."

"I got that part." I sat there for a moment or two, absorbing all of this. It started to come together.

He'd been vetting all of those women. Maybe playing the field to see which one he had a connection with. He blindfolded them so they wouldn't see him and then recognize him on the street after.

Reclusive was the word Sierra had used to describe him to Keely.

He had the women who'd been flirting with other men escorted out of the party.

Sierra was one of his choices.

Marriage. He wanted me to marry him. He chose me for this *arrangement*.

I stood from my chair, refusing to look at him. I wanted to, just once more, but couldn't. This was hard enough as it was. "I've wasted your time. You picked the wrong girl for this *job*. Marriage is not in the cards for me, not even for an arrangement." I turned to go, but I stopped when his voice struck me like lightning in the back.

"You came *to me* looking for a job, and now that I'm proposing one to you that doesn't include cheapening your morals for money, you're going to walk out. At the very least, tell me what scares you about this arrangement—an arrangement with specifics that you haven't even considered yet. Walking out without hearing the details doesn't make you a champ, Mariposa. It makes you look like a scared child. Now sit down and prove me wrong."

"Okay," I said, turning around. I hung my bag on the chair again, taking a seat. Even though we were discussing marriage, there was no doubt that this was a business meeting. A merger of two lives brought together by paper and pre-thought-out details. If I were going to do this, I had to become as business-minded as possible. Emotions had to be swept from the table, but I had something to air that demanded some feelings first. "Before this meeting officially begins, and all sides have been considered, you have to answer a question."

Capo stared at me for a minute and then nodded once. He picked up the glass of water and took a sip, his eyes never leaving mine.

"Why me, Capo?"

His name felt odd on my tongue. I didn't say it how Rocco did, with an Italian accent, but I did my best to give it its due. He had done the same for mine, so I wanted to give him the same respect. His face changed when I had said his name, though, and for some reason it brought me back to The Club, to the candlelit room. The intensity. The intimacy.

"Do you mind if I return a question with a question?"

I put my arm out, as if to say, *go ahead.*

"Why not you, Mariposa?"

I picked up my glass again, carefully taking a sip. When I set it down, I answered truthfully. No one in this room had time for lies. "I saw the other women at The Club. Your choices. Sierra was my sister's roommate. I saw her first thing in the morning. I saw her when she was tired beyond what sleep could cure. But I never saw her unattractive." I pointed to my face and then slid a finger down the slope of my nose.

His eyes went from relaxed to hard in a matter of seconds. I wondered if the outside world ever considered it a subtle change, something that happened in a blink and then was gone, but I caught it. *Too aware of him already.*

"Will you believe me if I dispute your feelings?"

"Yes," I said. "You don't seem like a man who has time for games."

"You don't look like the rest. You stand out. You could be a queen on a throne. One I'd feel privileged to call wife. You have the most beautiful face I've ever seen." He steepled his fingers, watching me even more...intensely, almost studying me in a way that I wasn't used to: with appreciation. "'The man said, 'This is now bone of my bones and flesh of my flesh; she shall be called *woman*, for she was taken out of man.' I'd be honored to call you bone of my bones; flesh of my flesh. My woman."

It took me a moment to get my head on straight. His words were almost too blunt, but they were filled with so much truth, it made me a little faint.

Finally, I knew I had to say something, or he would see that he'd made me weak with a few words. "No one has ever..." What was I even saying? He made me too honest, admitting things better left in the darkness. *He's too aware of me already.* Those eyes had too much light in them. I knew they were hiding darkness, too, but the contrast between the dark rings around his irises and the blue only made his light even brighter to me.

"Fuck them." He waved a dismissive hand. "They don't matter."

"You do?"

"The only one," he said. "*Il capo.*"

"I'll accept your why," I said, wanting to change the direction of the conversation. "But there's more to this than looks alone. Give me other reasons why."

Rocco and Capo exchanged glances before Capo spoke again.

"What if there are no other reasons? What if the only reason you're sitting here with me is because I want to hear my name coming out of that pillow-soft mouth of yours, and for the rest of my life, I refuse to allow another man to have the same honor?"

I swallowed down a gulp of water, almost choking again. "That's honorable," I said, glad my voice didn't waver. "But not the entire truth."

"It's not," he said. "But don't assume anything with me, Mariposa. That would be a mistake. I'm honorable, but only to a certain degree." His eyes seemed to heat at whatever he thought. The color somehow became darker, a wild storm I could feel in the pit of my stomach.

He was using only a few words to insinuate something much more complicated. *Honorable to a certain degree.* The attraction between us felt like a living thing that couldn't be denied. I wanted to touch it. I wanted him to touch me again. I was the numb sky to his strike of electricity.

"Mari," Rocco said, and I turned to him. "Yes or no. Do you consent to go forward with this meeting? If you do, we will work out the terms, but the arrangement will be live."

Ironic he had used the homophone "live."

Holding Capo's stare, I licked my lips and asked, "Live?"

"You will be my wife," Capo said, his voice dipping even lower.

"Yes," I said, without hesitation. "I say yes. I do consent. Let's go forward with the arrangement."

BEFORE WE COULD REALLY GET STARTED, Rocco went over the most important reason Capo wanted to "take a bride."

"His grandfather's sick," I repeated. At this point, they might as well have called me parrot instead of my name. At every turn, I continued to be shocked.

Rocco nodded and went into more detail. After Capo's grandmother had died, all he had was his grandfather as a parental figure. His grandfather was dying, and one of his last wishes was to see his grandson married.

Before I could even spit out the question, *why don't you just bring a woman home to meet him and pretend like she's your fiancé?*, Rocco answered it. Capo would never bring a woman home to meet his grandfather and lie about marrying her. It was out of the question.

I nodded, meeting Capo's eyes. They rarely moved from my face. Even when I paid attention to Rocco, I could still feel them. "I can understand that," I said. "My—adoptive mother, she died of cancer when I was ten."

"I'm sorry to hear that," Capo said.

"You have no family, Mari, but it will be required of you to travel to Italy to meet Capo's."

"I do." My voice came out strong. "Have family."

Both men's eyes narrowed.

"My best friend, Keely. She's my family. Her brothers, too."

Rocco looked at Capo, waiting for him to respond.

"I'll meet them formally," he said, "at the party her family is hosting. They're celebrating her new job. Around two weeks from today. Sunday."

"How did you know that?"

"I know everything, Mariposa. I know even more when it comes to you." He ticked off her parent's names with his fingers and then named each of her brothers and their ages. He gave me a second before he continued. "We know this is an arrangement, Mariposa, but the people in your circle won't. I will not demand that you lie to your friend, but the truth will be bent. We met today for an interview for a possible position at my club. Once you realized I was the man from Macchiavello's, we had our moment and things changed.

"I felt it was a conflict of interest to employ you. We had lunch, discussed things people in lust do, and you'd like to invite me to their family thing." He waved a hand. "We'll spend time together during the two weeks. I'll pick you up from her place. Dating." He seemed to hate the word, because he kind of spit it out. "Then during their family thing, you'll announce that we're engaged. We'll be married at city hall in New York the weekend after. We'll be married at the end of June in Italy, as well. A proper wedding. Your friends are welcome to attend."

With all that he'd said, I could only concentrate on one thing. "You know everything about me, but what do I really know about *you*?"

He leaned forward, taking his hands together on the table, his eyes not absorbing me in a personal way anymore. "You mentioned other reasons for me doing this. You got the second main one, my grandfather's wish. I hold one heart and more than one vein close to my chest, though. There are other factors at play here, Mariposa. I need you to give me time to bring them to light."

"How many?" I asked.

"*Scusami?*"

I grinned. Even though I had no Italian, I sensed what he had said, something the equivalent of *excuse me*? "How many veins should I expect? The ones connecting to the main heart?"

"You want a number." He leaned back in his chair, studying my face. "Two."

"No," I said. "Pick another number."

"You want me to make something up."

"No," I repeated. "But bad things come in threes. I don't want you to make something up, but I challenge you to find something good about this situation after your two 'veins' are opened up to me. Give me three so we'll come out with four, with the main heart."

He stared at me for an intense five minutes, at least. Then he nodded. "I agree."

Rocco wrote something down.

I liked this. I really, really liked this. Putting everything on the table beforehand. We were hashing our shit out before we committed to each other. Marriage was not supposed to be a business dealing, but in an odd way, I thought that maybe it should be sometimes. *I expect this of you. You expect this of me. You do for me. I do for you.* And neither of us will cross certain lines. It removed a lot of the weight that felt like it had come crashing down on my back when he had first made his *proposal*.

I sat up a little taller and really started paying attention when the mention of the police was brought up, how at all times I was to keep quiet, unless Rocco told me otherwise.

"Are you...involved in dealings you shouldn't be?"

I didn't expect Capo to be so candid, but he was. He nodded once without hesitation. "My hands are not always clean at the end of the day, Mariposa."

"How deep?"

"Does the severity of the sin matter to you?"

"I'm not sure."

"Would it lighten your conscience to know that I only act out of vengeance and not for business gain?"

"I want honesty," I said. "At all costs. If...if I ask. I need you to be honest." In that moment, coming close to his honesty overwhelmed me. If I had too much time to think, I would want honesty at the table, and that might cut whatever we had going. I wasn't sure what type of person that made me, to refuse to consider that he might do terrible things out of vengeance, and I would overlook them to have this.

To have him.

I deleted the thought as soon as it came. There was no room for emotion at this table. I felt none from him. There would be none from me.

He nodded. "I agree."

Rocco wrote something else down.

This was how the conversation continued. Rocco or Capo would bring up a term, we would discuss it, and then we would either agree or not. If we didn't, we went back and forth until we were both satisfied.

Money. I would have access to all of his funds after we were married. The millions and millions he had. He set no limit. However, if I left him or wanted to divorce him, or broke the "central" rules of our agreement, I would get nothing. Not even a penny.

"Final," Capo said, his eyes never more serious. "I don't believe in divorce. You are mine until I die."

"But what...what if one of us becomes unhappy?"

"This arrangement is not about love, Mariposa. You do understand that, don't you?"

"Yeah," I said, too defensively. "I do. You've said it. I've said it. I get it."

His eyes challenged the statement, but he didn't harp on it. "You take love out of this." He motioned between the two of us. "Neither one of us will ever be unhappy. We have our terms, and those should keep us content. We both have a purpose for this marriage. I want loyalty. You want to live. Not all marriages are built on love. Love is a fragile house that crumbles. What we are building at this table will be untouchable."

"Moving forward," I said.

I'd receive a ten-thousand-dollar stipend until we were married. To buy food, clothes, and whatever else I'd need until it was a done deal.

We even touched on specifics such as: how many times we'd travel in the year. We could go over that, if we wanted, but not under it. Two, we decided, was an ideal number. He'd choose one place, I'd choose the other, and there was no three involved unless we went over that number.

The two men had been shocking me the entire time, so I decided to get one in on them. I told them that under no circumstance would I get ass implants. The idea was still fresh in my mind, and I made Rocco write it down. Capo grinned as he said, "I agree. No ass implants, or any cosmetic surgery, unless my wife requests it. However, I'd prefer if you didn't. It would seem like a waste of money. Why paint the butterfly?"

After an hour went by, a knock came at the door. The three of us sat back, the conversation fading, waiting for Rocco's secretary to take our lunch orders. My stomach growled loudly, and my cheeks flamed. Even though I had been staying with Keely, I hadn't eaten much of her food, only when she made me. I was still helping her pack, but it never felt like enough.

Capo ordered for me. He ordered dessert for me, too.

"That was nice of you," I said. I was too embarrassed to order for myself. I knew the food was expensive, and I'd never ordered anything like that before.

He nodded once and then grinned at me.

Rocco's secretary became still. Watching him. She watched him until he turned his eyes toward her. "That's all for my fiancé and I."

She nodded, fixed her hair, and then smiled at him. She tucked the list against her chest when he turned away without a response. I watched her until she closed the door behind her. She was an attractive brunette, runway ready. Giada, Rocco had called her. She was someone I'd expect with Capo. She'd look right on his arm.

Giada & Capo. Their names even seemed right together.

Rocco suggested that we continue the meeting until the food was delivered. I couldn't have agreed more.

I lifted my hand, like I was in school. "I want exclusive rights to you," I said. "Starting now."

"You will have to explain that in more detail, Mari," Rocco said, shifting some papers around.

"She means," Capo said, a slight grin touching his eyes. "She wants us to be exclusive. Right now."

"A little ahead of me," Rocco said, and I could hear the grin in his voice. Capo and I were staring at each other. "We were going to discuss this next."

"However many times Capo wants to take me out on date night is fine by me." I waved a hand. "Let it be a surprise, just not three times a week. But I'm ready to discuss these terms now."

"We have arrived at exclusivity due to the lady's urgings." Rocco flipped a few more papers. He grinned again. I think he found me amusing. "Since you have declared your feelings on the matter of the two of you being exclusive, we know where you stand, but I feel it best to discuss the matter in detail. If you would rather not be intimate with Capo, you cannot expect him to be celibate. He would take lovers, but would be discreet, of course."

"Discreet," I murmured. "Of course." And I'd be made a fool of. And even worse, I didn't like the idea of the brunette secretary slipping in and out of his room while I slept next door, or wherever.

Rocco nodded. "Mari, you would have to be discreet—"

"No," Capo said. "No one touches my wife but me."

The room became exceptionally quiet. When I turned to look at Rocco, he was staring at Capo. Rocco's face rarely showed any emotion, but Capo's response seemed to take him by surprise. He wasn't expecting that.

Was it not a big deal before? I had no reason to think they hadn't discussed a few points of the terms ahead of time. I could tell which ones when Capo became firm on a few things before I even had a chance to think them through.

"It's settled then," I said. "No one touches me. No one touches *you*."

"*Esclusiva. Esclusivo.*" Rocco wrote on his paper.

"Are you a virgin, Mari?" Capo asked.

"Why?" I blurted out. "Will it make my price go up? I don't think it can. I mean, you've already offered me everything, money wise, as long as I don't leave."

I didn't like the way Capo looked at me. He was trying to dig the information out by sheer will alone. Did he expect me to be experienced because I was a poor girl on the streets? *Oh, that's right*, I thought cynically, I basically went to his club looking to sell my body for a dollar. Turned out, I was about to sell my secret in return for my life.

"Does it matter?" I tried one last time.

"It matters to me," Capo said. "Your answer will direct our first time together."

Direct our first time together? What did that even mean? He'd be rough with me if I weren't a virgin?

I stood from my seat, the first time since I'd attempted to walk out on him, and went to the window. The view from this high up was dizzying. New York seemed so beautiful at this height, when your feet couldn't touch the ground.

"I don't know," I said, my voice barely above a whisper.

"You don't know," Capo repeated. I could imagine his face, his dark eyebrows drawing in.

Silence washed over the room. After a little time, he asked me to explain.

"I don't know!" I said a little louder. "When I was sixteen, I was fostered by a rich family. Political. He...would touch me. It didn't go as far as sex, because I left before it could. I refused to let him do *that* to me. Keely helped me get a fake ID, and I worked odd jobs wherever I could. I slept at shelters. Sometimes at Keely's when her Mam would allow it.

"I kept my head down so I wouldn't get sent back to foster care. I avoided the cops, too, until I was old enough to legally be on my own. He did things to me, though, things I'd rather not discuss. I'm sure you're both smart enough to understand why I really...don't know if I'm a virgin or not. But I am clean. A man hasn't touched me before or since. I never had the time to worry about a relationship, but even if I did, I never thought I'd want to be touched again."

"Or to owe anyone," Capo said softly, but there was an undercurrent running through him that I felt from where I stood. It felt cold on my back.

He had figured out the reason why I hated accepting kindness without giving something in return. The foster jerk had told me that he had done me a favor, taking me in, and I owed him for his kindness. At first, I believed him, and would have done anything to make myself at home. *Home.* But when I realized what he expected of me, kindness never felt so dirty.

I was ashamed. Each night I knew he was getting closer and closer to doing something to me that could never be undone. Fingers were one thing, his nasty dick another. So I hid a knife in my bag, and when he tried, I told him that I'd scream and cut him if he did. Living on the streets was better than living in what felt like a cage. He had a wife and children, all sleeping in the rooms surrounding mine.

"Kindness," I said. "I'll never owe anyone for it, if it's in my power."

"Do you want to be intimate with me, Mariposa?"

"There are other factors at play here, Capo." I repeated his words, only replacing his name with mine. "I ask that you give me time to come to your bed."

"*Concordata*," he said softly. And I knew from earlier conversations that meant *agreed* in Italian.

I stood at the window so long that when I turned, I found Capo sitting at the table alone, his eyes on me.

"The meeting over?" I asked, suddenly fearful that my confession might have turned him off. Was I used goods? I had never admitted that aloud, not even to Keely. I had just told her that the political jerk was mean to me, abusive almost, but never went into detail. I think she knew, but she didn't press me, only told me that if I ever wanted to go to the police, she'd be there with me.

"No." The rasp in his voice was strong. "Only taking a break."

I nodded, turning around again.

"Sit down, Mariposa."

Thinking that we were about to eat, or going to start soon again, I did as he said. It was easy to take direction from him. He really did have his shit together.

He rose from his chair, his imposing figure coming to stand before me, before he took a knee in front of me. He placed his hand on my knee. "You didn't wear the new shoes I sent over," he said.

The light hit his eyes, and I thought of the ocean, of depths I wanted to explore. There was no denying that there was something dark beyond the light, but in some odd way, I wanted to explore that, too. I wanted to know that what I'd done, out of fear, out of desperation, wasn't as wicked as I felt it was—not screaming when the political ass touched me the first time. I wanted to know that other people had secrets that were hard to tell, too. I just hoped that I wasn't the only one in history who would trade telling them for a chance to live.

"No." I grinned a little. "You weren't my official *capo* then."

He returned the grin. Then he reached for my bag. When I flinched and grabbed for it, he took his time prying it from my hands. He opened it and took out the new shoes, like he knew I'd packed them. I had. Slowly, he reached down for one of the worn-down plastic flip-flops.

I went to pull back, but he held tight. "They're so dirty," I whispered.

"I've touched worse and worse has touched me."

I let him have my feet, watching as he switched out my old shoes for the new ones. They felt so good on. I hadn't had a pair of shoes that were mine alone since I was ten.

"Your bag," he said. "It belonged to your mother."

It took me a second. "My mother? You mean Jocelyn?"

"No," he said. "Jocelyn Flores was the woman who took you in and loved you as her own. 'Fucka me.' That was something old man Gianelli, her father, used to say when he'd get irritated with the bugs in his garden eating his produce. Sicilians love their gardens."

"You knew my—Jocelyn? Pops?" Pops was Jocelyn's father, my adoptive grandfather. I hadn't met Jocelyn's husband, Julio Flores. He had died before they adopted me, but I got his last name.

He nodded. "I knew them well."

"Pops died first," I said, wanting to tell him. "Jocelyn died a year later."

"Heart attack," Capo said. "Cancer."

"That's right," was all I could say. Their home was the only stable one that I'd ever known.

"You still go back to Staten Island to revisit the house."

"I do."

"I gave them enough money to take care of you."

"You—what?"

"What happened to it, Mariposa?"

I stood, putting some distance between us. "She was so sick.

We used it for her treatment. Then they took the house. There was no money left. No one to take care of me." I bit my lip. "How do you know all of this?"

Capo was still down on one knee, the dirty shoes dangling from his fingers. "I knew your parents, your birth parents, Corrado and Maria. Your name was Marietta Palermo."

"Marietta Palermo." I tasted the name. It felt foreign. Wrong. "I was five when—You had something to do with me going to live with them, didn't you?"

"I did. I brought you to live with them. I changed your name."

"Mariposa," he said, using an Italian accent on the Spanish word. "I'll call you Mariposa. The butterfly."

The bastard had named me.

"Why?" My hands clenched at my sides.

"Marietta means sea of bitterness, or something close to it. I wanted you to have something better to direct you. I wanted you to become the thing you loved the most. The butterfly. You deserved the chance. Both names started with Mari, something your mother called you. I wanted you to keep that part of her with you as well. And I knew it would make the transition easier. For a small child, you could still tell people that your name was Mari. It wasn't such a stretch."

"That's not what I meant. Why did you bring me to live with them? What happened to my mom and dad?" Those two simple words almost ripped me in two, but I held myself together.

"Killed," he said.

"In a car accident?" That was what Pops and Jocelyn had told me.

He set the old shoes down reverently, and then stood, facing me. "The Scarpone family murdered them."

"The..." I couldn't even say the word. *Mafia.*

"They demanded your blood, too."

"I see." I sat, all of my weight plopping down. I couldn't stand, though I reached for the bag to hold it close. It was the only thing Jocelyn said had come with me when I arrived at her door. The bag held two coloring books. One filled with butterfly pictures and the other princesses. A box of colors. The butterfly hair clip.

"Barely," he said.

At the one-word response, my eyes turned up to find his. He was looking at me, always looking at me, with an intensity that kept me rooted but made me feel like I could fly.

"You knew I liked butterflies. Coloring."

Mariposa. Butterfly.

"You told me," he said. "You asked me to color with you. Blue was your favorite color."

"Still is," I said, thinking of the color of his eyes.

I was going to be sick. I closed my eyes, taking deep breaths in and out.

"You..." I had to take another breath. "You've been keeping tabs on me."

"No," he said. "After I left you with Jocelyn and old man Gianelli, I cut all ties. It was safer that way. I had planned on having someone close to me check every so often, to make sure the money was still there and that you were taken care of, but then something happened, and life got in the way. When you showed up at Macchiavello's the first time, I thought you seemed familiar. When you showed up at The Club, I knew. The ice pack you left behind confirmed it. I ran the DNA from your blood on it."

"You saved me. Saved me from those people." *Your people?* The question burned the tip of my tongue. I wanted answers, but we were talking about the Scarpone family—they seemed to be entering my circle a lot lately. Anyone who knew anything about anything knew who the Scarpones were. They were not the Faustis, not by any means, but they were known to be ruthless to the core.

Five families ruled New York, and the Scarpone family was one of them. They were the top dogs. Because of people like them, I had learned early on to keep my head down and my eyes averted. It was one of the reasons I didn't rat on Quillon Zamboni, the man who touched me while I was in foster care. To be curious went against all that I knew, how to keep myself safe, but I was marrying this man. I had to know this, at least.

"You're one of them."

He watched me for a moment, his face expressionless. "I was one of the pack."

"But now?"

"I'm a lone wolf."

"Why? Why'd you save me?"

"You were the most beautiful thing I'd ever seen. So innocent that it broke my heart. You had the butterfly clip in your hair, and all you wanted to do was color. I had never experienced that before, something powerful enough to change the course of my actions. You made me see something different. I saw you, Mariposa. I wanted your innocence to live."

He said these powerful words, but without an ounce of emotion. He could've been talking about what to wear to go outside—if it was cold enough to need a jacket.

"At what cost?" His or mine, I wasn't sure which I asked for.

"A vein," he said. "Another day."

"That's all you're willing to give me?" I said.

"Today."

I knew this was a deal breaker. He wouldn't tell me. And did I really want to know specifics? Would it change the outcome of this arrangement? Once I was in, I was in. No getting out. He had already given me the warning. There was no doubt he was going to act on it. There was something about him that dared you to cross him, but stopped you just before you did. *Think twice.*

I was pretty confident, though, that even though he was one of them, he must've been considered a disposable man, a man who had survived the family's long-reaching arms. Not someone exceptionally close to the family's inner workings, or he wouldn't be here.

Money was at stake, *living*, but for me, it felt like so much more. What, I had no clue, but it felt dangerous. Not something to take lightly. All of my years I craved to live, and here the chance sat before me, beating like a heart, but it came with consequences. *Unhealthy veins.*

"What's it going to be on the paperwork?" Capo said, not giving me more time to think. "Your name."

"Will I be in danger?" It was the first time I thought to ask. I was so busy being dazzled by the chance to live that I forgot about the dim veil of death.

"Yes," he said, no hesitation. "You've always been in danger. I did the best I could with what I was given at the time. You being on the streets, not attracting attention to yourself, kept them off your scent, so to speak. There are other factors as well. The Faustis, for one. No one touches what belongs to them unless they have a death wish. As you can tell, I consider them family. I trust them as much as I can. However, that doesn't change the truth. I can't promise something that isn't mine to give, which is complete protection against life. But I will vow to keep you safe at the cost of my own."

"You already did, didn't you?"

He became silent for a minute. Then he repeated, "What will it be on the paperwork?"

"Mariposa," I said, no hesitation. "Mariposa."

He nodded once, about to go to the door to get Rocco. I could tell he was ready to move forward.

"Capo."

He stopped but didn't turn.

"What...what'll be my last name?"

"Macchiavello." He took a breath. "Mariposa Macchiavello." He sounded satisfied. "It's not the name that pleases me. It's that no matter where it came from, it came from me, and you'll be wearing it like a fucking ring around your finger."

He left me alone then, shutting the door behind with a soft *click.*

I wilted in the seat when I was alone. All of a sudden, I realized that he was the only man I would ever owe. And he knew it. He knew it at all along.

He wanted loyalty. He had secured it at all costs.

But never again would anyone, including the man who intended to be my husband, Capo Macchiavello, kill me with kindness. Because kindness didn't kill you quickly. It ate at you slowly, like acid, until you wished you were dead.

10

MARIPOSA

Two weeks later, Capo drove us to Staten Island in one of his many fast cars. The man had a car fetish. My original assumption about his cars matching his ties was off base, but close to the truth. He seemed to have a car for every occasion.

The one he drove seemed a little overkill for where we were headed: the party Harrison was throwing for Keely's big Broadway break. When I asked Capo what kind of car it was, he said, "Bugatti Veyron." I was clueless when it came to cars, so I just tucked it away as being a matte black beast that could probably be used on a racetrack.

He had been picking me up on "dates" since our meeting. After I explained the situation to Keely, she seemed to accept it, but I could tell she was suspicious. Still, that didn't stop her from making a comment about how fine Capo was when she first met him.

"Shit," she had said. "That singer—what's her name? The one who always writes about her boyfriends?—has no idea what she's missing out on around here lately. Lots and lots and *lots* of creative inspiration. That tattoo on his hand has me wanting to lick it, not to mention *that* perfect face and *that* tight-ass body. Are you sure he's real, Mari? The man doesn't have one fucking flaw."

I hadn't found one yet, except for his coldness. It didn't seem like he meant it, but there was something guarded about him at all times. It seemed like he had to make an effort to remove it when we were together. At The Club, in the darkness, he had been warm, dare I say welcoming, but in the daylight, he was as hard as a frigid wave.

His standoffishness didn't take away from how well he seemed to know me already, though, because already, he was giving me things, *experiences*, I'd only written about in Journey. Our dates seemed tailored to fit me.

After our meeting, he had given me a card with the set amount of money on it. He told me I had to use it or he'd assume I was reneging on my end of the deal. This was, after all, an arrangement with terms.

I needed a new wardrobe. I worked on that.

I needed to start eating better. I *jumped* on that.

I had people to see about our two weddings. I did that.

Rocco's secretary, Giada, made a comment about my hair when I'd gone to meet the wedding planner who took care of things in Italy. Most of my meetings took place at Rocco's office. I still had no idea where Capo lived.

Giada secured me an appointment with one of New York's hottest hair stylists, Sawyer Phillips, the same day. The Faustis had some real pull. Sawyer was kind to me, though, and after we were done, my hair was rich chestnut brown with swirls of caramel in the mix. The change was almost shocking.

My eyes were much more vibrant and my skin glowed from the inside out. It could have been that I was eating well, too, and not as stressed about where I was going to sleep and where my next meal was coming from. But...I had a standing appointment with Sawyer indefinitely after the first one, and two girls who did my nails.

I also had a man named Giovanni who followed me around when *il capo* wasn't with me. I only saw Capo in the evenings for our dates, so I spent more time with Giovanni. He was a nice guy, and I usually didn't mind him tagging along. I couldn't help but notice how...different he was compared to Capo and the men who worked for or were related to the Faustis, though.

Giovanni wasn't as attractive, which made no difference to me, but it seemed like Capo did it on purpose. And Giovanni and I had nothing in common. Zero things to talk about except for the weather and the things he liked and disliked about New York. He was from Italy.

Capo. My appearance. Even Giovanni.

There were so many changes in such a short period of time. I woke up knowing that some part of my life was going to be different. And after the wedding, I felt things were going to change even more. Capo seemed to be biding his time with the "dating" part of the deal. He wanted it to be official. Still, I hadn't expected one thing:

I still felt like...me, just without the extra stressors.

I worried about the price of the clothes I bought. Even about the amount of groceries in my cart. So I bargain hunted, almost afraid the money was going to run out and I'd be left hungry and homeless again, even though I was still staying with Keely until her lease was up and I'd be married.

Some things would never change, I guessed. There'd always be a certain amount of fear in me. A certain amount of *I can afford that, but what about that? Can I have a drink* and *fries?*

All of these changes had to be explained to Keely, though, so she wouldn't get too suspicious. So I told her that even though Capo didn't give me the job, Rocco offered me one. I worked in his office as a gopher girl. To make this true, because

I felt guilty about lying to her, I brought Giada coffee whenever I arrived.

Capo had nodded and said, "*Bene,*" when I had told him about what I had told Keely. We had to keep the story straight.

Capo's hand came over both of mine after I sighed. "Stop fidgeting. It makes you look nervous."

"I am," I said. "Nervous."

I'd been twirling the engagement ring he'd given me around my finger. It was a four-carat antique stunner. The central diamond was oval shaped. There was another surrounding layer of diamonds around the center. And then more diamonds on the sides. It was real artsy, feminine, and I could've sworn the side scrollwork and diamonds created abstract butterflies.

The only reason I knew the carat size was because Capo had told me. He didn't want me to be worried about anything on the ring being a three. As far as I was concerned, he could've given me a simple gold band. The thing was heavy and sometimes I was afraid that someone would cut my finger off for it.

He had made the moment special, though. He'd taken me on a helicopter ride around New York at dusk, and after we landed, he told me to check my bag. I found a new coloring book inside. The title said: *The Mariposa Princess*. I had smiled when I opened it. It was a thick book and the first half of it was filled with character portraits of me in many different poses.

He told me to keep going and only stop when I got halfway through. The second half of the book had been carved out, but the ring sat in the center, and it was made to look like it was on my left finger. The bottom of the page had writing in elegant script: *When you know, you know.* I had slipped the coloring book back in my bag, the thought of it more valuable than the ring.

"That way we have a real story to tell," he'd said. "No lies to keep track of." He had slipped the ring on my finger, and we hadn't spoken about it since.

I told Keely about it earlier that day. I didn't want her to be taken by surprise during her party, and I didn't want to announce it to all of her family. It was *her* day. I told her to tell if she wanted, but I was keeping quiet.

She hadn't kept quiet after I'd told her. *"It's too soon! You hardly know him. He's affiliated with one of the most powerful criminal families in history. And do you know what that means? They're probably the reason he's richer than sin!"*

He was richer than sin.

When we were going over the financial side of things during our arrangement meeting, all that Capo owned was made clear to me. Not only did he own one of the most successful restaurants, but one of the most successful clubs and a string of fancy hotels. I knew his wealth better than I knew him as a man. And if he had criminal dealings? He hadn't disclosed them at the meeting. I hadn't asked either.

Not wanting to listen to her as she continued on the same path, I had taken out the coloring book he had given me, the ring, and showed them both to her. She'd read the inscription at the bottom of the page out loud.

When you know, you know.

"Do you truly want this, Mari?" she had asked, staring me in the eye. "If you say yes, I'll back off."

I grinned at that. "Yeah, Kee," I said. "I really do. But we both know that you're not going to back off."

She barked out a laugh, hugging me tight, kissing my forehead. "You know it. I'm your big sister. I'll always take care of you."

"By two weeks, Kee!"

"Italy. My Sis is getting married in Italy!"

I got the feeling our wedding was going to be considered big news at this party. That put me on edge. I wasn't sure how

Harrison was going to react. After learning about his feelings for me...I hoped my marrying Capo wouldn't make things awkward between us.

Capo had agreed that I could tell Keely early, but I wasn't sure how *he* was going to react to Harrison. I kept thinking about how he'd said, *no one touches my wife but me.* It was intense. Possessive. From the tone of his voice alone, he still ran with wolves. It was as clear as the tattoo on his hand.

"You dropped out of college."

Those five words pulled me out of the nervous fog I was in.

"How—" I went to ask how he knew that, but I stopped myself. When he said he knew everything, he did. "Yeah. It didn't work out."

We were still holding hands, and as lost as I was in my thoughts, I realized that he used his thumb to make a soft pattern on my skin. He was making a 'C.' He held my hand a lot out in public, the only intimacy between us since our night in The Club, but he only made the 'C' pattern while we were in the car. It helped, especially when I realized how close we were to arriving.

"Work got in the way and then you were fired."

"That about sums it up."

"You should rethink going back. You'll have the free time, when you're not busy with me. Rocco suggested law."

"Law?" I laughed, but he gave me a serious look, so I changed gears. "Why law?"

"He was impressed with the way you handled yourself during our meeting. You stood up for yourself. You were willing to bend on the terms you didn't feel were all that important, but the ones you did—" he shrugged "—you took your gloves off and fought barehanded. You're an excellent negotiator, Mariposa."

They were impressed that I stood up to them. It didn't seem like a lot of people did that. Men *or* women. I had nothing to lose when I went into that office, and once I found out that Capo was interested in me, I had something to bargain with. I think he knew that. I think he wanted that from me. Which made me respect him even more. He knew I was going in with nothing but a bag full of old memories, a journal, and stale bread. He gave me a bargaining chip. *Me.*

"I'll consider it." Law had never even crossed my mind. It seemed too unattainable, something only rich people with connections succeeded at. Maybe I'd ask Harrison about his feelings on the matter... The thought of Harrison made my palms sweat, so I changed the subject. "Were you going to pick Sierra?"

"What made you think of her?"

I shrugged, trying not to fiddle. "Rocco. The arrangement. It popped in my head."

We drove on for about five minutes before he answered. "She was one of my top choices."

"Because she was beautiful?"

"No, because she was one of the hungriest."

Ah. It was like that. She was both literally and figuratively starving. He was looking for the hungriest of the bunch, a woman that would fall into the dizzying spell of his magnetic force. He had everything a girl could ever want. Looks. Charm. Money. And he carried a strong sense of *I'll always take care of you if I call you mine.* Throw in a girl like Sierra, *like me,* and loyalty to someone like him would be high. We rarely got chances like him.

"Did...a connection have anything to do with it?"

"Depends on what you mean by 'connection.' If you mean sexually compatible, a strong physical attraction, yes."

My cheeks heated, and not from embarrassment. I was a little jealous that he felt that way about Sierra. Sexually attracted to her. I wondered if they had sex, since she worked at his club, but I didn't want to bring that up either. "Were you going to give her this ring, if you chose her?" I lifted it up and he gave it a sideways glance.

"No."

He smoothly changed lanes and left it at that. I stared at him, hoping he would give me a little more, but it seemed like he had closed down. I sighed, turning to face the window. The world passed by in a blur. We were going too fast for me to catch up.

The quiet in the car was suddenly killing me. I leaned forward, and for the first time, fiddled with some buttons. I could tell Capo watched me from the side, underneath his glasses, but he didn't say anything. Finally, I found the stereo. I grinned when I heard the last music he had been listening to. I kept pressing the forward arrow to see what he had on his playlist.

Bee Gees. 2Pac. Andrea Bocelli. White Snake. Sam The Sham & The Pharaohs. Staind. Seven Mary Three. Frank Sinatra. Nazareth. His fancy car displayed the artist's names and their songs. I had no idea who most of them were, but they were all so different. His music tastes gave me no further insight into who he was. *He is a man of extreme mystery*, I thought sarcastically. And the rest of his list continued in this genre mishmash fashion.

"You're laughing at me," he said. "At my music."

I laughed even louder, and then pinched my fingers, leaving a small gap between. "A little."

"You have a warped sense of humor." He shook his head. "And a wild laugh to go along with it."

"What's a wild laugh?"

"Some people cage it up, train it to be what they want it to be, a quiet animal. Some people fake it, hiding the fact that they have nothing to really laugh about. You do neither."

I continued to laugh, turning on the radio instead of his old man music. He was going to be forty-years old in August, compared to my twenty-two in October. Even though there was an eighteen-year age gap, my time on the streets had aged me. I felt we were close to even on that.

Then a popular pop song came on and the gap widened some. It made me think of Keely and what she had told me about Capo and his family supplying enough creative inspiration for endless songs.

"You can't be serious." He glanced at the radio like it had done something offensive to him. "You'd prefer this chick to Bocelli?"

"Me? Not serious? How could this have happened?" I pretended to pass out against the door, pressing a hand to my forehead. "I've got the vapors! Help me, *handsome sir!*"

"This is what happens when your brain has been on this kind of music for too long. You. You should be the poster child for kids who listen to this." He switched the music to Bocelli, some real romantic Italian ballad.

I switched it back, feeling lighter than I had all day. Actually, I felt lighter than I had in years. "We've listened to your music. Let me listen to mine for a while. And I disagree. I love her music. This is her new stuff. It's beautiful. Especially this song. Listen."

My laugh threatened to burst from the cage I'd pushed it into. He was seriously listening to the song, and when he became serious, his thick eyebrows drew down and his lips became severe.

"You *have* a friend," he said when the song was close to ending.

"I do," I said. "But did you *really* listen? First she mentions a childish kind of love, then a love that takes place while they're growing up, and then they get married. It *is* nice to have a best friend, but when your best friend is also your lover, it completes things. I would think, anyway."

"So philosophical," he said, and I almost laughed again.

"What? You didn't get that?"

"All I *got* is a Tim Burton movie soundtrack stuck in my head now."

"Who's Burton?" I asked.

"Edward Scissorhands?"

I shrugged. "Have no clue."

"It amazes me. You have no idea who Tim Burton or Edward Scissorhands are, but you had a pretty good idea of who the Faustis were when we met."

"It's a sad fact of life on the streets. You try to keep ahead of the things that can kill you." I shrugged. "The rest doesn't really matter when you're hungry enough to rob a small kid for his ice cream cone. I doubt Tim Burton and Edward—" I made a motion with my fingers like I was cutting paper with scissors "—would chase me down and kill me, maybe even torture me, if I saw something I wasn't supposed to."

I had known some about the Faustis, but more about the five families. The Faustis didn't deal in petty shit. They were royalty in Italy and beyond. Their dealings made headlines. So did their marriages when one of them took a bride, using Capo's archaic term. And when I asked Capo just how deep it went, he said, "*Consider the Faustis a lawless land that no president or dictator can touch. They rule their own territories. And whatever they feel belongs to them does. End of story.*"

He glanced at me before he turned back to the road. "You have a lot to learn about the good in life, Mariposa. It'll be my pleasure to teach and show you."

With that, we swapped music until we pulled up to the address Keely had given Capo.

MY STOMACH TOOK a dive when Capo parked in front of the house I'd grown up in until I was ten. "Why are we here?"

He took his sunglasses off and studied my face. "You didn't know?"

"Know what?"

"That this is where we were going, Mariposa."

"No." I shifted in the seat some. "Keely only told me that the party was at a friend's house on Staten Island."

I'd had a dress fitting that morning. Giovanni had taken me, and then Capo picked me up for Keely's party after. She wanted to leave early, so she had given Capo the address while I was getting ready. She wanted to help set everything up. Capo must've assumed I already knew.

Judging by his hard face, he had no idea that she hadn't mentioned it to me. He didn't seem to like surprises. I could tell by the way everyone around him briefed him on everything.

"I thought that's why you were nervous," he said, staring past me toward the house. I wondered if he remembered bringing me there.

"No," I said. "I *was* nervous because you're basically meeting the family. Now *I'm* nervous because I haven't stepped foot in this house in eleven years. This place is the only house I've ever called home."

"That's not going to help." He took my arm, stopping me from fanning my armpits.

It was hot out and my nerves had me on edge. The heavenly perfume worked overtime. The entire car smelled sweet. I loved how the scents seemed to subtly change from time to time. Sometimes I'd smell more caramel, other times, pistachio or sandalwood. It smelled more like almond in that moment.

We became quiet for a while, but my thoughts were running rampant, and if I didn't say something soon, I felt like a blood vessel might burst. My heart felt close to it.

"After Jocelyn died, I was too young to really consider what happened to me. I lost the only parents I remembered. I was thrown out of my safe place, thrown into the system, which felt wild and unsafe. It wasn't until I turned eighteen that I realized just how much I lost when I lost them.

"I never had the time to really think about it, you know? It was survive, survive, survive. And then one night, it hit me. Keely and her family loved me, but I had no parents. I was no one's baby girl. That's what Jocelyn used to call me, her baby girl. They were good to me. So good to me."

"Home is wherever you make it," Capo said, his voice gruff. "Come, Mariposa. Now or ten minutes, waiting is not going to change the way you feel. It'll only make you feel worse."

I couldn't decide what to concentrate on first once Capo opened the door to the car for me. The fact that we were climbing up the steps to the house I had never thought to enter again. Or the fact that Capo wore comfortable clothes—a black t-shirt that fit his chest like a glove, jeans that showed off his thin waist and toned legs, and *that* ass. His boots only upped his level of supreme coolness. Or the fact that when the door opened to the house, Harrison stood on the other side, staring at us with daggers in his eyes.

I wondered if Keely had truly gone to help set up the party, or if she had gone to break the news to her brother before he found out this way.

Before Harrison made a sound, his eyes raked over Capo, and Capo's eyes did the same to him. Harrison's attention stilled on our connected hands before he met my eyes. I felt Capo watching him while he stared at me.

I had no idea what to expect, but the hurt in Harrison's eyes took me by surprise. It hit me square in the chest and stole my breath. He was like my brother. He was my family. Even before Capo, I'd never had romantic feelings for him, or for anyone.

Keely came up behind Harrison and greeted us, making the situation less awkward for me. The two men didn't seem to care. Neither one was willing to make introductions. Keely did it.

"Harrison," she said, a certain level of warning to her tone. "This is Mac, Mari's..." She hesitated for a breath before she said, "fiancé. Capo Macchiavello. Everyone but Mari calls him Mac. Mac, this is my brother, Harrison Ryan."

Harrison nodded once. Capo did the same. The air between them was tense. I hadn't mentioned to Capo what Keely had said about her brother's feelings. I didn't feel it was necessary. Harrison had never admitted that to me, and to broach the subject with Capo felt like a betrayal of Keely. She had told me that in secret.

Capo had picked up on it, though. His grip on my hand grew firmer, and I didn't particularly like the look in his eyes. I'd never seen it before. It was stone cold, not an ounce of warmth to be found. The tension eased a little when we walked outside and there were more people to meet. Keely's parents (they had flown in for the party), a few family members, a couple of friends, and her other three brothers—Lachlan, Declan, and Owen. There was also a man that I'd never seen before. Lachlan called him Cash Kelly, but I heard one of Keely's uncles whisper to another uncle that his name was Cashel. Blond hair. Green eyes. An Irish lilt. His eyes were intense as they watched Keely from time to time.

News circulated around the party about our engagement, and everyone congratulated us. A few of the ladies asked to see my engagement ring and to hear the story of how Capo proposed. I was glad he'd given me a story to tell.

I tried to keep my distance from Harrison, who was quiet, watching me with a force that made me uncomfortable. It was almost like he was willing me to be alone with him. He was drinking and hardly saying a word to anyone, but I knew he wanted to talk to me. Lachlan, Declan, and Owen seemed more comfortable around Capo, even though he was being quiet himself. His eyes absorbed his surroundings, and not in the way he sometimes absorbed me. They were on guard.

The party was mostly contained to the patio. Lights had been strung up, the old garden starting to look like it did when Pops had it going, and the smell of barbecue floated in the air, along with the scent of beer. Keely and her family could drink the best of the best under the table.

Once we were there for a while, I started to relax, able to take in the state of the house. It was in good shape, like eleven years hadn't passed. Even the mural Jocelyn and I had done in the hallway was still there. She had let me pick, and I had picked a blue butterfly to paint.

As evening came, bringing with it a sweet breeze, I noticed Keely going inside. I hadn't had a chance to get her alone to ask her who the house belonged to. And I also wanted to ask her about Detective Stone. She had told me the day before that she had invited him, but he couldn't make it. An emergency had come up. Some politician had gone missing and all manpower had been called in.

I excused myself from Capo's side—he was deep in conversation with Keely's dad and uncle—and went back into the house. I looked for Keely but couldn't find her. Keely's Mam was in the kitchen, and she asked me if I wouldn't mind arranging a dessert tray and making coffee. Her sister was about to leave, and she wanted to say goodbye. I knew my way around the kitchen, and to be honest, it felt good to be back home.

Home.

Footsteps sounded on the floor, but I continued to arrange the little cakes, pies, and muffins. A second or two later, Harrison stood next to me. I looked down, trying to concentrate on what I was doing. My nails were dark, almost black, and in contrast to the white cakes, it made them stand out even more. It was something, anything, to distract me from the heat I felt coming from him. He smelled like a bar.

He stood close to me, his hip leaning against the counter. "You smell good, Strings," he said.

"It's new," I said, trying to keep my voice even. He had never made me nervous before, but I could sense his disappointment, or maybe his anger toward me.

"It smells natural. Like you're not wearing anything, but you are."

I thought the same thing. The perfume worked like magic with my chemistry. But this was petty conversation. He was moving us along, bringing us somewhere. I didn't like where we were headed, so I murmured, "uh huh" before turning to the coffee pot.

"You've changed so much. I hardly recognize you."

"I got a job, Harrison. I'm able to afford things now."

"New hair." He took a strand and analyzed it. "New clothes." He nodded toward my purple silk camisole. I had paired it with a pair of blue jeans and heels that showed a lot of toe. Since I planned on wearing a pair for the wedding, I'd been practicing. "I'd say that job pays really well, Strings."

"It pays enough." I finished filling the filter with coffee and set it in the pot to brew. I didn't want to turn and look at him. The hurt in his eyes was too much. I just wanted to be the way we used to be. "I'd say your job pays really good, too. Seems like you're doing better."

"Keely told you I bought this place?"

I turned on him so fast that I could feel the breath of air that circulated between us. Pistachio drifted off of me. "You bought this house?"

He nodded, picking up his glass from the counter, taking another drink of whiskey. "I didn't take you for the kind of woman to be attracted to golden things, Strings."

"What do you mean? Golden things?"

"Golden things," he repeated, his voice slurred some. "The

man outside. Capo. The ring on your finger. Not this house. It's a paper thing compared to what he can offer you."

"I'd never think of this house as a paper thing," I said, turning from him again. "This house is the only home I've ever known. Even if it was a paper thing, I'd still call it home."

Only a few people could get to me. I never allowed anyone in. But Harrison could get to me because I loved him like a brother, and it was hard to pretend like everything was okay between us when it wasn't.

"There's a war going on," he said, throwing me for a loop.

Maybe he was drunk off his ass. That was usually Owen, but there were a few times I'd seen Harrison drunk, too. He was usually more relaxed.

"I've heard about it."

"I doubt you've heard about this one," he said. "Right here. Home soil. New York."

I turned to him again. "What are you talking about?"

He grinned at me. "Someone's fucking with the five families. Whoever it is started a war. One family is blaming another. Territories are being crossed. Even the Irish are getting in on it. Whoever's fucking with them killed a dangerous name in that world, too. Serious turmoil."

"Are you drunk?"

"Maybe." He grinned. "A little."

"That explains a fucking lot," I said, about to turn around again when he took me by the arm and forced me to look at him. His stare was too...much. "Why would you even care?" I rushed out. "About all of that?"

He shrugged. "I don't. Just bringing up recent news. You work for the Faustis. I thought you should know."

"I doubt they'd get involved. No one touches them."

He shrugged again. "I want you to be careful."

I tried to remove my arm from his hold. "Noted."

Time seemed to stand still while we stared at each other. He wasn't leaving me any room to squirm away from him. I didn't want to cause a scene. I didn't trust Capo. What would he do if he walked in and saw the way we were standing? I didn't want to find out.

"Do you know why I call you Strings?" Harrison said, finally breaking the tension some. "You never asked."

"No," I shook my head. "I thought it was just a cute nickname."

He laughed some, his breath fanning over my face. "Cute," he repeated. "The first time I saw you, you tangled me up, *Strings*. They're still wrapped around my heart. I want you to marry me, Mari. Live here with me. I want to take care of you. Kindness doesn't mean you owe me anything. We can be kind to each other. That's what a husband and wife do. Be kind to each other when they're not tearing each other apart from too much passion. Love. It does wicked things, but it's good. So good, too."

"Harrison," I said, trying to remove myself from his hold. From the situation entirely, but he wanted an answer. I wanted to run. "We're family."

"No," he said. "Keely is family. You're family because I want you to be mine. I've always wanted you to be mine. You know how many nights I couldn't sleep because I was worried that something might happen to you? And you turned down every offer of help I ever offered. I'm not taking no for an answer this time, Mari. Kindness is not your enemy. Love isn't your enemy, either. You deserve love. My love."

"I—" I tried to move away, afraid that if I said the words, *I don't love you like that*, I'd lose my entire family.

"You don't love him, Strings." His hold on my arm grew tighter, but he wasn't hurting me. "You hardly know him. He's just another rich bastard who thinks he can turn a poor girl into something he wants her to be. I love you the way you are. Kiss me, Mari. Kiss me once."

"No," I said, and this time, my answer was harder. He put my hands against his chest, right over his heart, and I pushed against him. "No. I can't do this. I *won't* do this. I'm getting married."

Something made me turn, and I jumped after I did. Capo stood in the doorway, half of his body tilted toward the frame, watching us. How long had he been there? The entire time? I wouldn't doubt it. Was he testing me? Like he'd tested those women at The Club? Would he walk out and then turn his back on me, too?

Harrison held me for a second longer before he let me go. My breath held when he stopped in front of Capo and held his stare. Capo stood like he had no issue, like he had all of the time in the world, but something about his eyes made my heart race. They seemed dangerous. Machiavellian.

"Harrison?" Keely said, coming to stand behind the two men. "Come on. Go outside and get some fresh air."

Lachlan was right behind her, and he took Harrison by the shoulders, leading him outside, whispering things in his ear as they went.

Not wanting to cause any more trouble, I kissed Keely goodbye and we left.

As we met the last step of the house, I could hear the family in the backyard, still enjoying the party. Leaving like we did made me feel guilty, but I'd rather live with guilt than to live with something unforgivable happening between my soon-to-be husband and the only family I had left.

My concentration was on what had happened, so when Capo took me by the arms and brought me to the side of the house, pressing my back against it, I gasped. He wasn't rough, but I knew he wasn't messing around either.

"You love him," he said. His eyes searched mine, digging brutally for the lie on the tip of my tongue, if there was one.

I shook my head, swallowing hard. I couldn't tell if the ball in my throat was my heart or all of the food I'd eaten. I wasn't afraid of him—he could've killed me years ago—but I was wary. Even though we had an arrangement, we still had to learn how to live with each other. The real him ran too deep, and until I could break the surface, we were left trying to figure out how to navigate our terms.

Before I could answer, he hit me with, "You knew that he was in love with you." His tone was accusing and sharp.

"Yeah. I found out about it the night I met you at The Club."

"You didn't tell me."

"Why should I?"

"It's my business," he said.

"No. It's *my* business. It happened before you."

He grinned, but it was fucking frightening. "Anything touches you, it touches me. You get fish instead of the steak you ordered, I know about it, understand?"

"I know the terms, *Capo*," I said, my voice starting to rise. He was starting to piss me off. "Again. This. Happened. Before. *You*."

"There is no before me. There is no after me. You. You're *all* me."

"You can't get pissed about this. You have no right. He feels the way he feels. I feel the way I feel. The end."

"How do you feel, Mariposa? You never replied to your friend when she told you. You never responded to Grumpy Indiana Jones in the kitchen. You never answered me."

I narrowed my eyes. He had read the conversation on my phone when Keely had texted me at The Club. And he'd been listening tonight. No surprise there, but suddenly, I had the insane urge to scream, *you don't own me!* But he did. And I owned him. That was how the deal worked. We both set our terms and vowed to honor them.

"If I loved him *that* way," I said through clenched teeth. "I wouldn't be fucking marrying you! What do you take me for? If love was what I wanted, I wouldn't be standing here with *you*! If love touched me, I'd never, ever sell it out. If love drove my life, I'd be its main chick. Ride or die, Capo. Would I sell my body to live? We both know the answer to that. Would I sell out love for the sake of this arrangement? Never! I'd die first! So, no, I do *not* love him in that way!"

My words seemed to stun him for a moment, though he recovered quickly. He didn't want me to see that some part of my truth had touched him, but too bad. He wanted nothing but honesty from me, so he was going to get it. Even if it meant a dagger to his iron-clad heart. It might not nick him, but it would make a dent that would forever mark him. *Mariposa was here.*

"You belong to me, *Strings*," he said, his voice cold, "and I won't stand for any man to run behind you like you're a dog in fucking heat."

In what seemed like slow motion, my arm came up, and my hand connected with his cheek. The slap rang out in the night air. "You might be my *capo*," I said, "but that doesn't mean I'll allow you to disrespect me."

He didn't even flinch at my slap, but something in his eyes changed. They softened some, but in a way that I wasn't used to.

One, two, three, four breaths, and he took my wrists, raising them above my head, his face coming close to mine. His mouth was a kiss away, his breath warm as it flowed over me, and I breathed him in.

The bulb lights had been turned on in the backyard, and between us, a white spark flared in the darkness. My chest heaved up and down, my breasts pressed against his chest. The friction felt so good. I'd never been more starved for this kind of connection in my life. I had hungered for the unconditional love of parents, for food, for all of the things that money could buy, but never for *this*.

A lover's touch.

He showed me something that I craved the mere idea of. I'd sampled it the night at The Club, and I was already addicted to the flavor.

I inhaled again, breathing him in even deeper. The heat made his scent stronger. Cool. Clean. Healing. His eyes had turned a darker shade of blue, the color of the deepest part of the water. *Sapphire.*

Pressing against me as he was, he never felt more intimidating. He was like a monster wave before it comes crashing down on someone who doesn't know how to swim. He was made up of hard lines, and he radiated power, control, while he swept me away.

His teeth raked over his bottom lip, and in the glow of the lights from the yard, it glistened. I wanted to lick it, to taste his mouth again. "I seem to remember telling you that I'm not an honorable man, Mariposa."

"And I seem to remember telling you that you will not speak to me *that* way," I said, hoping he saw the defiance in my eyes. "If you'd rather a woman that goes for anything, a different kind of *purchase*, you know which way the city is. *Thata* way." I moved my head to the side to give emphasis to my words. "And I'll just see myself back to the party after you go."

"So you can run back to Harry Boy and finish your earlier conversation."

"No." I shook my head. "So I can hang out with family and friends while I wait for you to do whatever it is you feel you have to do. Then, once you come back for me—because I know you will—we'll see Rocco about changing the terms of the agreement. You'll be *discreet* with your lovers, and so will I. If your mouth can't respect me, then your hands have no place on my body."

When I said the words "*you'll* be discreet *with your lovers, and so will I*," his grip on my wrists tightened, enough that I almost wanted to squirm out of his hold. I came close to giving in and resisting, pushing against him so I could turn my back on him and take a much-needed breath. But I didn't. I held my ground.

All of my life, I thought that holding my ground meant fighting for it. In that moment, I realized something. Sometimes holding ground meant going with the flow, saving energy, so when the wave passed, I could go in a better direction.

We had come to terms in Rocco's office, but we both knew there would be times that we'd have to draw lines outside of that room. This was one of those times. And he'd either call my bluff or he wouldn't, but since I was committing my life to this man, *proposition or not*, and he could easily crush me, I had to be as term-oriented as he was. He seemed to like the control it gave him, and for a man who was always in control, I needed to learn to work around him in a way that he was familiar with.

After a tense stretch of time, he lowered his head, his nose skimming my neck. "*Concordato*," he murmured against my overheated skin. *Agreed upon.* "I will choose my words wisely around you, Mariposa. They seem to cost me more than our agreement."

I closed my eyes, giving myself over to the feel of his body so close to mine.

"Never..." he said, pressing his hips against my belly, giving me a taste of what was to come when I was ready. Even though I was nothing but skin and bones, he was still harder than me, and he made me feel...soft, feminine. "...think that I need to pay for a fuck. I never have. I never will. Come tomorrow, you'll be the only one I'll be fucking for good. Plans and dates and times can go to hell." Then he said something in Italian against my pulse. *Il tuo profumo mi fa impazzire.* I think it had something to do with the way I smelled. He kept breathing me in, inhaling my skin like it was air. Sandalwood hung heavy between us.

I bit my lip, not wanting an embarrassing sound to escape from my mouth at how good he felt against me. My lower stomach clenched like a fist, and my entire body was damp, and not only from sweat.

"You taste as good as you smell." He inhaled even harder, and then his tongue trailed from my neck to my heart and back up to my chin, stopping close to my mouth. "Say it, Mariposa."

"*Concordato,*" I repeated. We both had to repeat the word during our meeting in order for Rocco to finalize the term and move on. He was keeping to those rules. I lowered my voice. "We were only talking. Just because Harrison said those words to me doesn't mean I feel the same. I do love him, but like a brother."

The neutral territory we stood on seemed to disappear beneath my feet, and we were back to opposite sides of the battle lines. As soon as the words *I do love him* came from my mouth, I felt the change in him immediately.

"You." His tone was gruff and came against my skin like a hundred stones. "You're my territory. I say who does and doesn't come near it. I'm the only one who touches it."

Territory. Like property. "Your property?" My eyes flashed up to meet his. He was right. He did own me, in a sense. He owned my loyalty, but I wouldn't stand to be treated like some piece of land he could shit on whenever he wanted.

"My fucking property. My territory. You seem to forget that it was you who came to my table willingly. You hashed out the details. Set terms. You signed papers with your blood. We made a deal."

I wanted to slam my fists against his chest, all of my anger contained there. "For all your wisdom," I seethed, "you're not that smart. When you enter a bargain, it not only binds one but two. You might be my *capo*, but I own you, too, don't I? I'm your territory, so you're *my* property."

We were still navigating the real word, the one outside of Rocco's office filled with terms and legal papers, but we seemed to be circling around something personal I couldn't figure out.

After a few minutes, he finally spoke. "I didn't like what I saw. Or what I heard."

There it was. The eddy that kept sucking us under. He didn't like seeing Harrison and me together. Why? It made no sense. Capo had me, all of the parts of me he requested at the table. What difference did it make how Harrison felt or what he said to me? They were just words, unless I made them more. Still, it seemed to take a lot to get Capo to admit that.

"All you have to do is say that. Use all the words, Capo. I'll understand. You don't have to hurt me to get what you want."

He watched me for a few intense seconds, and then he nodded once. "*Concordato.*" But his look didn't cool. It turned into something else, and the maddening desire in me responded automatically when he did something with his hips, pressing even harder into me, so hard that I sucked in a breath and a noise that I'd never heard before slipped from my lips.

Fucka me, I bet he was going to be good in bed. He wouldn't only touch me; he'd consume me. Still. There was hesitation. I wasn't ready to go all the way with him. That severe craving would have to eat at me until every defense had been gnawed away.

Hands on my mouth so I won't scream. Sweat. From him and me. Fingers. Nasty fingers. Disgusting. Wicked. Kindness. Owing.

Capo stopped touching me, and when I opened my eyes, his were on my face. *Seeing right through me.* I didn't flinch from his knowing. I appreciated the fact that he seemed to understand without me having to speak the words again.

Please don't hurt me.

He released my wrists, taking my hand in his—his hand

practically engulfed mine—and started to lead me back toward his car.

The haze slipped a little after he put space between us, and his words from earlier made full entry into my mind. *Come tomorrow, you'll be the only one I'll be fucking for good. Plans and dates and times can go to hell.*

"We're not supposed to get married until next weekend in New York," I said, my voice the opposite of my body. Steady. A few seconds went by and he didn't answer me. "Next weekend, Capo. What happened to next weekend?"

"Too long," he said. "It's happening tomorrow. I'll talk to Rocco in the morning about changing the terms. We'll get married in the evening."

"The dress you spent a lot of money on! It won't be ready."

"Have Giada call the designer. Tell them I'll pay triple to have it finished. If not, wear *paper* jeans."

With that settled, I'd be a married woman the next day. *Monday.* Who gets married on a Monday? That thought flew right out of my head when the next one kicked it out.

I'd be married to Capo Macchiavello in less than twenty-four hours. A force of a man who had me right where he wanted me, locked down in his field for the rest of my life.

11

CAPO

The air in City Hall was cool. It smelled of old papers, my cologne, and something that smelled a lot like love and loyalty, and if I was taking Mariposa's ridiculous song into consideration, friendship. Three different reasons for a man to be standing in the same spot I was, waiting on a woman to commit her life to him.

I looked at Rocco and narrowed my eyes. He had a cat-that-ate-the-canary grin on his face. He was all too curious as to why I was taking my bride today, and not on the original date planned.

Fuck dates.

It was a done deal; there was no reason to wait. The wedding in Italy needed time. Things had to be planned; it had to be meaningful for my grandfather. He deserved to see his grandson married. It was one of his worries. It should be put to rest before he left this world.

However, there was no reason this wedding had to be postponed until later. Another day, another time, were unpredictable. And when I wanted something, I made it happen.

I wanted Mariposa as my wife today.

I lifted my arm, the sleeve of my suit pushing back, and checked my watch. She was running late. *Three minutes.*

"Guido said ten minutes," Rocco said. He and his wife, Rosaria, were standing as witnesses. She sat next to him, rolling her bracelet around her wrist, watching me.

I met his eyes, not one to prolong the inevitable. His smirk was starting to irk me. "*Parla.*" *Speak.*

Rocco rolled his shoulders, getting more comfortable in his suit. "I did not expect this," he said in Italian.

Our entire conversation took place in the language.

"We discussed it before," I said. "This was part of the arrangement."

He shook his head. "We discussed a different date. *Later.* Now here we are. Today." Our eyes held, and then he switched gears. "You did not tell me how the meeting with her family went."

"They're not her family," I said. "Friends."

"She considers them family," he said, not caring if he pissed me off or not. "They take care of her. She trusts them."

"Last I checked, family members are not supposed to cross romantic lines." The blood in my veins burned with the thought of Harry Boy. *Strings.*

He was instigating trouble on more than one account. Bringing up the war to spark Mariposa's curiosity, even though he was a part of it. Harry Boy was the new lawyer for Cashel "Cash" Kelly, the leader of a connected Irish family. Right before Harry Boy took the job, the old leader had been killed, and Cash took his place. He hired Harry Boy not long after. Cash called him Harry Boy, so I did, too. I wanted him to know that I knew everything. Not long after that, he bought the house on Staten Island for the woman I'd be marrying in a moment.

Too late, fucker, I cut those strings. Snip. Snip.

"Ah," Rocco said, the grin growing wider. "One of the Ryan brothers cares for her."

I lifted my arm again. *Seven minutes.* I started to pace the hall. Women took time to do whatever women do, but the clock ticked, and it was loud in my head. It needed to be silenced.

"You should not worry." Rosaria waved a dismissive hand. "I doubt there is a woman alive who would stand you up."

My comment about family not crossing romantic lines was aimed at her, too. Rocco and Rosaria also had an arranged marriage, but their marriage was open, to a certain degree. She had made numerous passes at me over the years. Rocco was like my brother. And Rosaria was not my type.

That aside, Rosaria hadn't met Mariposa yet. She had no idea how different she was, and Harry Boy could offer her something that I couldn't. A no-scars-included history. If Harry Boy fucked this up for me, they'd find him six feet under, or maybe never at all.

Eleven minutes.

"I know I'm late!" Her voice carried to me through the expansive hall, her heels clicking against the marble floor in a rush.

I turned to find her hustling toward me as though she wasn't wearing one of the most beautiful dresses I'd ever seen, and she wasn't the most gorgeous woman in my world.

Her hands clutched the dress, lifting it so the floor couldn't dirty it.

Don't you know, woman, the dirt is what's going to make memories one day, I had the urge to say, but didn't. Whatever she bought, she appreciated, almost reverent about the purchase. It would take her time to understand that, if her life was full of pristine things, she wasn't living enough to wear them down.

Scars on skin meant living. Blood on knuckles meant living. Dirt on white clothes meant living. Living meant taking chances, even if we got soiled up in the process.

The late afternoon light caught the material as she passed by a window, making the silky material glow and the pearls and crystals shine. Her small waist and pronounced collarbone were perfectly displayed. Her tits—the only fat she had on her body—were pushed up, jiggling as she tried to hurry. Her hair was swept back, small tendrils framing her face. The style showed off the regal set of her nose and her softer features, those lips.

"Since this was last minute," she said, barreling right through the fact that I couldn't take my eyes off of her, "I had to rush and get a few things done." She eyed me up and down. "You look..."

"*Sei sbalorditiva*," I said before she could finish.

Her eyes narrowed. She was thinking hard. "You called me stunning. *You are stunning,*" she repeated in English.

"I did." I turned her in a circle. The dress dipped into a deep V in the back. "This dress pleases me." *You please me.*

"You wanted me in a dress, I delivered," she said. "But that's not...I understood what you said to me, without you having to translate."

I nodded once. "You're catching on."

She shrugged, but I didn't give her another second to think about it. I offered her my arm and we stepped into the room with the officiant. After a few minutes, we repeated the simple vows and I slipped the ring I'd given her back on her finger. When it was her turn to do the same to me, I went to speak, to say that we'd be skipping that part.

"Wait!" She turned to Guido. He stepped up and handed her a box. She opened it and took out a chunky white-gold ring with a square black diamond in the center and the letter M done in gold. She handed the box back to him and turned to face me, smiling a little. "Late, remember? Something last minute to do. It wasn't supposed to be ready, but the jeweler took pity on me and rushed the order." She took my hand and slipped the ring on my left finger.

After the officiant pronounced us husband and wife, the

kiss we shared to seal the deal was soft, my mouth finding the corner of hers, hers finding my cheek. Rosaria and Rocco pulled her to the side after, each of them hugging her. As they did, I slid the ring up and down my finger, not prepared for the weight of it, like a leash around a full-grown wolf.

Then something caught my attention on the inside. An inscription.

Il mio *Capo*.

My *Boss*.

"Capo?"

I turned to look at my wife. She sat next to me in the car as Giovanni drove us home. Judging by the look on her face, she had tried speaking to me before.

After we were married, something had been nagging at me until I made sense of what she had done.

She had been miserly in using the stipend, finding bargains, even on food. She was even using coupons. The ring she bought, though, easily cost more than two thousand dollars.

She had spent her money on me.

The only person who would've done this under my nose would've been Rocco. He had invited us to celebrate at the exclusive Italian restaurant he owned with one of his brothers, Brando. When I had pulled him aside to question him about it, he had told me that she came to him and asked him to do her a favor.

A favor.

From a Fausti.

She wanted him to buy the ring so that I couldn't see the purchase. In return, she offered to fill in for Giada while she was on vacation. No pay. Rocco had accepted her offer, but he still had the other women in his office help my wife regularly. He said she had a lot on her plate with the wedding in Italy.

"The *famiglia* jeweler created it." Rocco had waved the issue off, drinking a glass of whiskey. He was the ruthless head of his own branch of the family, and his father was one of the most merciless men Italy had ever seen. Yet Rocco loved weddings and a good celebration. "It has already been taken out of your pocket. Your wife kept her end of the bargain. We are even. A favor for a favor. Let us not discuss this on your wedding day, ah? Business should be kept in the office."

The Faustis had a jeweler on demand. The jeweler's family went way back with theirs, and they worked solely for them. Since I was connected to the name, considered family, he worked for me, too. I had a tab.

Mariposa seemed to understand a favor for a favor better than anyone. It was the only rule she seemed to have. Kindness for kindness—nothing owed. Except for me. She owed me her life. And not long ago—I lifted my watch, checking the time— she had vowed it to me. But for her to approach a man she knew would expect something in return, usually at a high cost, rubbed me the wrong fucking way.

"Have somewhere you need to be?"

The car shimmied and I turned to look at her. Her eyes almost glowed in the darkness. The gold in her eyes, in her hair, and in her skin all seemed to complement each other. Her lips were soft and pink, and when she smiled, almost shyly, betraying the defiant streak in her, I met her eyes again.

"Why do you ask?"

"Oh." She drew the breath out. "You've been distracted ever since dinner. I tried asking you where we were going a minute ago, but you didn't answer. Then you looked at your watch." She leaned over, studying it. Her close proximity made air move between us, and the sweet smell of her made me lick my lips. I knew she was trouble the moment her scent drifted underneath my nose at The Club. Pheromone phenomenon and all its magical bullshit. It leaves little control to the one jonesing to inhale someone's skin like a drug. "For all your millions, you need a new one. That one has rust spots on it."

I shrugged, the white button-down shirt tugging at my shoulders. "Some things are not worth trading in, no matter how old they are." I pointed to the building we were slowing in front of. "We're home, Mariposa."

"Home," she repeated, turning to face the window. "You live next to a fire station! Sweet. That'll come in handy when I cook you dinner." She became quiet as Giovanni hit a button on the dash and the garage door lifted. "You own this entire building?"

"Mmhm."

"It's not what I expected."

"What did you expect?"

"The bat cave?"

"How do you know about the bat cave?"

"Keely's brothers. I was over once when they watched that movie."

I gave a low laugh, burying the thought of Harry Boy further down. "Not a place shiny enough to blind you?"

Why did the fucker still affect my words?

She narrowed her eyes at me. "No, I just thought...something in Manhattan. A penthouse." Then she grinned, my words sinking in. "Still, this is far from a *paper house*."

"Then I'll *huff*, and I'll *puff*, and I'll *blow* your house down."

"The big bad wolf dressed in a fine Italian suit." She touched my hand, her fingers as soft as her lips, where the wolf tattoo seemed to snarl underneath the lights of the garage. "I should've known."

Her eyes drifted to my lips, then back up to my eyes, and when she couldn't hold my stare any longer, she started to fiddle with my tie. *Nervous hands, like flitting wings.* I wanted to feel them against my skin, around my cock, caressing my balls.

She cleared her throat. "Are you going to show me around?"

I knocked on the window once with my knuckle and Giovanni appeared, opening my door. I told Mariposa to stay put in Italian, and just as she had done at City Hall, she seemed to understand without me having to translate. I walked around the car and opened her door. She took my hand and stepped out, still holding the dress up.

"I know why you bought the entire building now." She looked around. "You needed the room for all of your cars."

I squeezed her hand, feeling the tremble in her bones, leading her inside of the building. It didn't seem to be a conscious reaction, but when we entered, she squeezed my hand harder.

"*Fucka me,*" she breathed out, peeking in. "I've never been in a place so...big."

I showed her around, giving her the grand tour, but at the end, I could see that she had something on her mind. She hadn't said much.

"What is it?" I stopped in the closet of the master suite. "Don't get bashful on me now."

She dropped the hem of the gown and shrugged, and then she tucked a long strand of hair behind her ear. "It's beautiful, Capo."

"You can change anything you'd like. Take it apart and put it back together again."

She nodded but said nothing else.

"Let me show you something," I said.

"More?"

I grinned. "Watch carefully."

Her eyes were glued to me as I pressed buttons on my watch. The back wall started to move silently, slipping in front of another wall, and the space behind it opened up. It looked like an elevator. Cold. Sterile. A metal wall stood on the other side. I put my arm out, gesturing for her to step inside. She hesitated, but only for a second. After we stepped into the space, I closed the door in the master closet. A second later, I opened the other side and gestured for her to step out first.

"Okay," she said, her eyes wide. "You *do* have a bat cave. A secret door."

The laugh that broke free from my chest sounded shredded. "Not exactly. This is the fire station."

"Yeah, but it's been redone. Totally redone. It looks abandoned from the outside."

She stepped up to the glass railing, looking out over the lower level of the house. I'd had it redone for her. No one knew it was mine. As far as anyone knew, it was an inactive, abandoned firehouse.

The other side was cold, with sharp lines. This side was for her: warm colors and soft furnishings. Numerous butterfly pictures hung on the walls. It didn't fit the exterior, but rarely did what we see on the outside fit the inside. I had one of my aunts speak to a decorator. She gave them an idea of who Mariposa was, from what I had told her, and the woman ordered everything. I took it from there.

"This is your home, Mariposa. The other side, that's for show. If we have guests over, dinner parties, that sort of thing, we entertain on that side. This side is for personal use only. Seven people, including us, know that this is where we live."

"It's more than I could've ever imagined," she breathed out.

"I'm glad that it pleases you."

"Who are the other five people that know about the secret house?"

The secret house. I almost grinned. "Rocco, my aunt and uncle, Rocco's brother Dario—he's an architect—and Donato. He's head of Rocco's security. You'll meet them soon enough, at the wedding in Italy."

"If no one else knows, how did you do all of this?"

"Dario helped me with certain aspects. He put some hours

into it. The rest—" I lifted my hands "—I've been working on this place for five years. All supplies came in through the other building. I've never lived here until now."

"Reclusive," she whispered.

"You have a watch like mine, but it's newer in style and more feminine. You can change the bands out to match your clothes, if you want. You'll find it on the table next to the bed. But only the seven of us know, Mariposa. No one else."

"Understood," she said. She was playing with her hair. *Agitarsi. Fidgeting.* She was nervous.

"*Vieni,*" I said, guiding her away from the banister. "Let me show you around."

This time as we toured the house, she was more animated, her eyes bright, absorbing instead of trying to figure out where she'd fit in. Her body relaxed, just as it had done the night at The Club when I had moved her in a slow rhythm. That night, her heart beat so frantically that I could feel every one of her pulses racing to keep up.

When I showed her the second master, she nodded and said, "Really nice. Is this where I'll stay?"

"That's up to you. Part of our agreement was that I'd give you time to get used to me." I'd purposely made the second master bland compared to the master suite for my own selfish reasons.

She started playing with the beading on her dress the closer we came to the room. When we got there, she peeked her head inside, almost wary about entering.

"The big bad wolf is out here." I grinned. "You're safe."

"For now," she mumbled, finally stepping in.

She ran a hand along the huge bed, all of the furniture, even the walls. She moved to the bathroom, her eyes shooting straight up to the mother of pearl ceiling, her birthstone, the massive shower and clawfoot tub, and then at the floor made of the finest Italian marble.

She stopped when she came to the entrance of the closet. It was a room inside of a room. It had a hallway, and on each side, glass doors that housed clothes and shoes and places to store jewelry. She had one side. I had the other.

"Not to sound rude," she said, about to rip a pearl off of the dress. Her eyes were glued to a shelf stacked with tennis shoes in all different colors, most of them Italian-made. "But whose clothes are these? I know one side is yours, all of the suits, but what about the other side?"

I almost laughed at how subtle she tried to be. "No other woman has ever been here before." I moved to stand behind her. When I breathed out, my breath fanned against her back and goosebumps appeared on her skin. "Everything is new here. That's why it still smells of fresh paint. All of these things are yours."

"I didn't buy these things."

"You didn't. I did. We'll see how well I know you soon enough, ah?"

It took her a moment, but she nodded. It was overwhelming for her. Even though this was a deal, it was hard for her to go from nothing to everything without feeling like it was too much. I'd pushed her into the deep end without her knowing how to swim.

"I see how you've been spending money, Mariposa, and we need to work on your skills." I didn't keep tabs on her to see how much she was spending. I kept tabs on her because nothing she craved would go unanswered. If I had to order every fucking item on the menu so she could figure out what she liked best, I'd make it happen. And it would take that. She had a lot of catching up to do.

"This is too—"

"We had a deal," I said. "You're holding yours. I'm holding mine. I'm not doing this to be kind and you're not accepting because I did. We have an agreement."

I took a step closer to her, running a finger along her neck, tracing a "C" along the perfect skin there. She trembled, and my dick twitched and hardened. "Soak in your tub, Mariposa." My voice was low, rough, almost shredded. "Wear your clothes. Grab a bite to eat. Watch some TV or listen to some music. Bocelli to get your mind straight. Read a book."

Rosaria had invited her to join her and the other wives— Rocco had three brothers—to enjoy their girl nights. They discussed books, knitted and crocheted, and did whatever else it was that women do. So I bought her a reading device, along with hundreds of paperbacks and hardbacks. When she had walked into that room, she had said, "W*hat, no coloring books or journals?*"

I refused to take away from what she had given herself over the years, so no, she wouldn't be getting those things from me. She had been surprised that I thought of it that way. There were things that were still special to me, even though the world fell at my feet, and unlike a coloring book or journal, no one could replace them.

"Get a good night's sleep. The first of many. Make yourself at home, Mariposa. Because this is your home. *Per sempre.*"

"Wait." She turned to me. "Where are you going?"

"To work."

IT HAD BEEN close to two hours since I left my wife to roam around her house and get comfortable. I sat at the desk in my office, looking over all of the monitors and trying to place the different smells slipping in. A cake baking. Lasagna. Popcorn.

An hour later a knock came at the door, and before I could answer it, she opened it and came in. She had showered. Her hair was damp. The scents of pistachio, almond, caramel, and sandalwood invaded the room. Instead of wearing one of the many items I had bought for her to sleep in, she wore my robe. It was three times too big. Her hands were lost in the sleeves, and it practically hung on her body.

She held a plate in her hand. As she set it before me, her wedding ring peeked out from underneath the fabric. "There must be over a hundred cookbooks in the kitchen. I found a recipe for wedding cake. We have all of the ingredients, and a million other ones, so I tried to bake."

"Tried." I looked at the cake. I picked up the fork and stabbed it. It was as stiff as a board and darker than a white wedding cake should be. Maybe it was supposed to be chocolate. "Seems like you did."

She scrunched up her face. "That's debatable."

I cut a piece of it with the fork and stuck it in my mouth. I paused before I really started to taste it. I looked up at her and she looked down at me, making the weirdest fucking face, like a puffer fish.

"What do you think?" She tucked her lips in. She was trying not to laugh.

I forced myself to swallow. If I knew what a cardboard cake tasted like, I was sure it tasted better than that one. "That the first time you baked a cake?"

She nodded. "Very first."

"Good." My voice was strained.

She pointed at me, full-out laughing. "You are a terrible, terrible liar, Capo!" She laughed even louder.

"You must've forgotten a few things. Like milk, eggs, and butter. What did you do, just add flour? You got any water in the pockets of that robe?" My voice had turned rough from the tightening in my throat and the dry thing she called cake.

She laughed herself out of the room, coming back with a bottle of cold water for me. I chugged it while her wild laughter turned into a satisfied grin.

She walked around the room, studying all of my equipment. "What's all of this?" she finally asked.

"I do private security on the side."

"You creep on people."

"You could say that."

"Do people pay you to creep?"

"Some of them."

"Ooh. I see." She gazed at one of the monitors. "Is that your building?"

"Our building," I said. "Look." I pointed to a spot on the screen and then zoomed in. Giovanni walked around the place, making his rounds. He had no idea we were on this side. He assumed we were in our suite on that side. He would always assume that.

"You're not going to do that to me, right?" Her eyes narrowed on him as he pulled his pants from his ass crack. Giovanni was the ugliest son of a bitch I could find with enough experience to take care of my wife when she wasn't beside me. "Be a peeping creeper?"

"Depends." I sat back in my seat, studying her features in the glow of the monitors. She was refreshing. Something different.

"On?" She opened her eyes wide, something she did when she wanted me to continue or expand.

"How well you behave."

"I'm a good girl." She came to stand in front of me, crossing her arms over her chest, which had disappeared under the massive robe. "But you know what they say about good girls? They never make history."

She closed the gap between us and reached out to touch my tie. I had untied it but didn't take it off. She moved slowly, watching as the black material slithered out from around my collar, and then she set it on the desk. I'd rolled my sleeves up to my elbows earlier, and using her finger, she traced one of my veins, concentrating as she did.

We both became quiet, and when her eyes rose, we stared at each other.

"Do you need something, Mariposa?"

She shook her head. "I was getting lonely. This is a big place. I'm not used to it yet. I was wondering when you were coming to bed."

I lifted my eyebrows and she looked away for a second, at one of the many monitors. "To sleep," she added softly. Then she started to fiddle with the ties of the robe. I could feel her anxiety. She was preparing to either say something or make a move.

"Don't do that with me," I said.

"What? This?" She twirled a tie, making it go around and around, smiling a little as she did.

My hand came out to stop her. "Yes. *Agitarsi. Fidget.* Don't do that with me."

She nodded, and I saw the bob of her throat when she swallowed. "You got it, *Capo.*"

"You mean, *il mio capo.*"

"You noticed that?"

"I notice everything."

"Why do you seem...upset?"

"Going forward, no more making deals with men who are not me."

"You mean Rocco. The ring."

"Yeah. Rocco. The ring. Never again."

"As you wish, Capo."

When she first called me that, I had a hard time not fucking her at The Club. And the more she said it, the more it made me feel like a feral animal in a cage. Not being able to touch her until she was ready was like thinking important words but not being able to speak them.

After a few minutes, she took a deep breath in, untied the robe and opened it, releasing the breath she had been holding after. She was naked underneath.

My eyes feasted on her naked body like they were starved. Somehow our roles had reversed. I was the one who couldn't seem to get enough. She was fucking perfect. The light from the monitors highlighted every one of her bones. Her tits were enough to overflow in my hands. Her waist was small, and her hips had some slope. Her nipples were hard, and a thin sheen of her desire coated the inside of her firm thighs. I could smell her arousal—so fucking sweet I could taste it on my tongue. My tongue darted out, wetting my bottom lip, craving the hit.

"I thought you should see what you committed yourself to exclusively, *il mio capo*. Me. Hopefully I was worth the high price." When I could tear my eyes from her body, I met her eyes, but she looked the other way. "I'm nothing but skin and bone, but—"

When my hands took firm grips of her hips and lifted her onto the desk, she gasped. When I yanked her closer to me, her mouth parted, and a cool stream of her breath came over my burning skin. I pressed her closer to my dick, pushing against her until a breathless noise came from her soft mouth. Her hands reached out, almost clawing through my shirt, trying to get to skin.

My teeth bit at her neck, working my way to her ear. "I got a deal," I said. "You should have demanded more."

"Ah." She sucked in a breath and hissed it out when I bit her neck harder. Her nails sunk into my skin, and the burn made me even hungrier. "Maybe we should go back to the table."

"I'd need unlimited funds, because, *fuck. Un estimabile valore.*" There wasn't a price I wouldn't have paid to have her. No term that I wouldn't have agreed to. She might have come into the deal with nothing monetary, but complete power stood in her corner. There was something about her that possessed me. Made me obsessed.

Then a strike of something else, something foreign, burned me deep.

Jealousy.

The word seemed to come at me like a shock of lightning during a storm—right as I stood in a puddle and next to a tree.

Rocco's face at City Hall, his words, suddenly clicked together.

I was old enough to know better, but I didn't give a fuck. I was jealous when Harry Boy told her that he loved her. When he had called her that pathetic nickname. *Strings.*

The thought made my fingers dig into her hips, pulling her even tighter against my dick. Something wild drove me to claim. To possess. To control. To dominate her scent with my own. My lips drifted down her chest, my tongue savoring the taste of her skin, and when I took her nipple in my mouth, she bucked underneath me.

"Just," she breathed out, "don't cover my mouth."

My pace slowed, not to make her feel that she had caused me to stop with her words. I looked up at her from my position. Her hands fisted my shirt, but her claws had retracted. Her eyes were closed tight. The heart in her chest seemed to beat in my ears but not in pleasure—from fear.

Her wings tried to fly, but she was rooted at the same time.

She wanted me. Wanted this. But that fucker had done something to her that she'd never recovered from. It was the first time I had ever heard vulnerability in her voice. Even at The Club, when she had no clue what she had signed up for, she was martyr-strong.

Vivo o muoi provando. I live or die trying.

At my slowing, she seemed to relax some, and the moment passed. She had agreed to give me time. I had agreed to the same.

"Mariposa," I said, my voice low and gruff.

It took her a moment to open her eyes. When she did, what I saw shocked me. Shame.

I lifted her up, keeping her close. "When you're ready to have sex with me, wear something red. *Consumami.*" Consume me.

"You want a fire in your bed."

She said this like it was questionable. Like fire was a bad word. Like it was something to fear. Maybe to her it was. A butterfly was a fragile creature and could easily be engulfed by flames, but not if they carried it within them. She did. She carried the strength to make the change. "Yeah," I said. "A fire. That way I know you're ready."

"I want to be," she whispered.

"You will be. We'll work on it."

I felt her smile against my chest. She kissed me there and then underneath my neck, around my scar. I froze, but she didn't notice. *Thank fuck.* She yawned and wilted against me.

"Time for bed." I lifted her from the desk, carrying her toward the master.

"We'll sleep in the same bed? I want to. You said during the meeting that it was my decision, once I got here."

That was why I'd made the other room so unappealing. She needed to be next to me.

I set her down in the middle of the monstrous bed and she took the robe off, setting it on the bottom of the mattress. Crawling under the covers, she got closer to the pillow, and then she stuck one leg out. She was looking all right, her one bare leg sticking out like that. Her ass was a soft handful, too. It was the first time I was able to get a good look at it. I wanted to bite it until she cried out. Then I wanted to fuck it.

"You coming?"

I cleared the tightness from my throat. "Later. I have some work to do. If you need me, your watch is on the nightstand.

Press the button on the side and say, 'call Capo.' It'll connect you to me right away. You can call for Giovanni the same way."

"Call him Capo, too?"

"No. That's just for me. You just say *his* name and it'll connect you to him right away."

She made her hand seem like a gun, pointing it at me, and then she winked at the same time she made a *click* noise with her mouth, her "gun" tilting a bit. "Got it." Then she laughed, and I realized she had been fucking with me the entire time. It had been a while—years—since I'd spent this much time with a woman. And none like this one. I was going to have to speed up to keep up.

She sat up, rubbing at her eyes, the covers falling. Her nipples were still hard. "Are you one of those people who can't sleep?"

I shrugged. "Depends on the night." *And if you'll be willing to fuck me all night.*

"So I *really* did come to live at the bat cave."

Far from it, but if it meant that she felt safer here with me, I let it ride.

"Hey," she said, stopping me before I left. "Do you have time to watch a movie before you go to work? Maybe we can make root beer floats? I've always wanted one. We have all of the stuff."

This place was big. It was new. She was having trouble adjusting. Then I thought of the house on Staten Island, how comfortable it was, and that forbidden word flashed through my mind again. *Jealously.* Harry Boy had thought that out ahead of time. The place was comfortable for her.

Back to the point. She'd just have to get used to it.

I removed my shirt, holding it out to her. She moved up on the bed, taking it from me. Our hands brushed and that electrical storm that had been brewing inside of me all night seemed to send a shockwave up my arm. She took my offering, but her eyes raked over my bare chest as she did.

"Put that on," I said, my voice low.

She nodded and slipped it on. It hung like an oversized dress. "So that's a yes?"

"What'll it be?"

"How about Freddie Scissorhands? And I'll make the floats!"

12

CAPO

The lights of my car lit the garage at one of my buildings. A second later, it opened and I pulled in, putting the car in park. One of Mariposa's ridiculous songs came on the radio. I felt my brain shrink each time the chick hit a note. Mariposa loved it, though. And sometimes, when a particular line would play, she'd point at me and lip-sync the lyrics.

It was one of the weirdest fucking things I'd ever seen anyone do. But then I'd have to remind myself that she was young. That innocence I wanted desperately to save had somehow been preserved, and when she felt free enough to reconnect with it, it came out at times like those.

My boots were silent against the pavement as I made my way inside. Donato had sent two guys over to keep watch, so my eyes narrowed on a third figure before they relaxed.

I held out my hand and Donato took it. He pulled me in and we slapped each other on the back.

"I hear congratulations are in order," he said in Italian. He lifted a glass from the table and we clanked before we both said, *salute*, and then downed the excellent whiskey.

"He still singing like a canary?" I slipped my gloves on. I'd be hard to see at first, dressed head to toe in black.

"We are past this. He is angry now. Demands to speak to the man who has ordered his taking. He assures us that he will pay any ransom."

We both grinned. I patted Donato on the shoulder, and he took his men and left.

I slipped a ski mask over my face before I stepped into the room. The light was faint and only lit the table and two chairs. Other than that, there was only a cot. A bathroom stood off to the side, bare to the bones, only a flushing toilet. There were no windows in either room, only brick walls.

The man I came to see stood from the bed, trying to be quiet but failing. He was breathing heavily. "I got you now, you fucker." His voice had a little thrill about it. "You leave a gun behind and you don't expect me to use it on *you*?"

He cocked the hammer and then—

Click.

Click. Click. Click. Click.

I laughed as he hurled the gun against the wall.

"Son of a bitch! You played me!"

He charged me and I stopped him in his tracks, using my fist to impale his stomach. His mouth opened and closed as he gasped like a fish out of water. I took him by the collar and threw him toward the table. He landed on the floor, and instead of getting up, fighting back, he stared up at me.

"Take a seat," I said.

His eyes narrowed. "Do I know you?"

"Nah," I said.

He licked his lips and held his dirtied hands up. "I told the other guys, the ones without the masks, I'll give you anything you want. I'm connected. I'll do whatever it takes. Whatever you want is yours. All you have to do is say the word."

"Ah." I breathed out. "Your people aren't going to kill us anymore?"

He had been mouthing off about how connected he was and how we were all dead men when I first picked him up. Dead *men*. He had no idea there was only one *man* who had taken him. Me. The rest were just guard dogs until I came back to finish this.

His eyes narrowed even further, almost closing, trying to see past the darkness that cloaked me. "No, they'll go easy on you if you let me go now. I'll make sure of it."

"Why didn't you use the gun, Quillo?"

"I tried to! It had no bullets."

"I meant before. On yourself. You didn't even check for bullets."

He tried to make it subtle when he scooted away from me, but I noticed everything. "What good is a gun without bullets?"

"You know the game," I said. "I was giving you an easy way out."

One of Donato's men had left the gun on the table. He had given him an option: Take the easy way out, put one bullet in his brain, or it would be me who ended it. Except Donato's man didn't mention me by name. He called me Fate and told him what a cruel motherfucker I was. But the problem with men like Quillon "Quillo" Zamboni is, they think they own the world. Therefore, he thought he'd make it out of this alive.

He was *connected*. His father had been before him. But he knew how the game was played, and if someone powerful enough wanted you dead, you'd be dead. And if you were a coward, putting the gun to your own brain and blowing it out would be easier than whatever fate had planned for you.

He never once tried using the gun on himself. Never even contemplated it. One of Donato's men stood guard at the door, and not one click had gone off. If it had, he would've been given a bullet to try again.

A sick fucking joke. If he made his mind up to end it all before the torture really began, he had to go again because the gun didn't have one bullet. It was my way of fucking with him a little more.

It took a moment, but when he realized what I'd called him, he stood up, swaying like he was on a boat during a storm. "You called me Quillo." His head tilted to the side.

"What? You too good for Quillo, *Quillon?* You were always a prick, but you never showed off how much of a pompous prick you were until you ran for office. Quillon sounded more proper than Quillo, I'm sure. You political fucks who start in the trenches are all the same. Trying to prove you're something you'll never be." I picked the gun up from the floor before I took a seat at the table, across from him. I sat the weapon down and relaxed in my seat. "Honest. *Sincero.*"

He swallowed hard, taking a step closer to the table. "Show your face," he said. "I *know* you."

"Ah." I took the top of the ski mask in my hand. "You thought you did. No more." Then I removed the mask completely.

He gasped, his feet automatically bringing him back, right into the cot. It slammed against his knees and he went down, then popped back up.

"No!" He shook his head, his hands waving frantically in front of him. "No. You're a ghost! I'm dead. They must have killed me. I'm in hell. With you. I need forgiveness. Dear God, deliver me." He fell to his knees and started praying the Holy Rosary. His fear scented the air with bitterness. It had the same tang as fresh blood.

"Stop being dramatic." I used my leg to shove the other chair closer to him. "Sit. Let's have a chat. It's time we catch up."

"Vittorio." He shook his head, like he was trying to wake up. "You're a ghost. What do you want with me?"

I called him a fool in Italian. "You're afraid of a ghost. You should be more afraid of me. I still bleed. I can be killed. Again. So you know what that means? I'm dangerous. I'm the living ghost you should fear."

He stood, still swaying some, and pushed the chair closer to the table. Even though he wasn't at ease, he had relaxed some, thinking he could talk me out of this. Thinking he could try and play on our history to squash whatever this issue was. He assumed it had to do with business.

"May I?" He put a hand close to mine.

I nodded, and he used his pointer finger to touch the pulse in my wrist. He pulled back when he felt it.

"You're not dead."

"Apparently."

Then he smiled, and it lit up his face. A wave of relief washed over him. "Son of a bitch! You're alive." He stood for a second and then, too excited to stand any longer, took the seat. "And when was that ever an issue? You *not* being dangerous? Tell me something I *don't* know, like why I'm here."

"In time," I said, watching him ease into being this close to me again. Being next to him felt like old times, but this time, I was going to rip his throat out and watch as he bled out at my feet. Or maybe I'd get more creative. "You need to tell me things. First."

"Wait." He held a hand up. "You're the one starting the wars between all of the families. Did your father order you to? My Pops is in real hot water. I thought maybe this had something to do with him, but then I thought on it some more. He's been in hot water since Angelina—" He stopped there, not going further.

Yeah, his old man had split town after what happened. Quillo didn't have time to react, so Arturo started using him for whatever he needed. Quillo was the equivalent of an indentured servant. He had to pay for the sins of his father and the sins of a sister who screwed two brothers. The fact that she screwed us both didn't matter. It was that she'd been passing secrets—secrets no one asked for—and then set one of us up. Her loyalty had been tested and proved to be as thin as water. *You want to stay in this game, you need blood.*

"I have no father," I said. "I have nothing but enemies."

"Shit." He ran his hands through his hair, making the blonde strands stand up in thin spikes. "So you're orchestrating a massive war. You killed the heads of those families. Their sons. You're fucking insane! What you're doing. It's insane. A suicide mission. After your death, well, not death but—"

"My death," I said.

"Arturo has gotten even stronger with Achille at his side. He doesn't care who he kills. He's a savage. He takes the lives of innocents without even blinking. He's a fucking rabid wolf. The only family the Scarpones ever backed down from is the Faustis, but no one takes them on."

I opened and closed my arms. "It seems my life has always had a short expiration date on it. Achille made sure of it. Arturo went through with it."

"He had to. You can't give orders and have your men disobey you."

"Disobey." I tested the word. "Is that what you'd call saving a little girl from a fate she didn't deserve?"

He seemed to sense something from me then, but he had no idea what, unless he knew who she was, and I doubted he did. If he did, he would've handed her over to the Scarpones when he had the chance.

His gaze landed on my scar, and then he met my eyes again. "Why did you save her? Palermo's kid? He'd never done you any favors. He tried to kill Arturo right in front of you. The only man to ever wound *Lupo*." *Wolf.* "Palermo worked for your old —Arturo for years. Arturo trusted him, like a son. And he double-crossed him in the worst way. So why?"

"I had my reasons," I said.

"Reasons. And where the fuck did those get you? Living like a ghost in your own town? Silenced?" We watched each other for a few minutes; the only sound was the toilet running in the bathroom. Then he spoke up again. "I get it now. You've come back to take them all out. You're starting a war so they have no idea who to trust anymore. One family trying to destroy another. Even the Irish have gotten involved. What did they ever do to you?"

I smiled. "It's mayhem, isn't it?"

"Yeah." He nodded once. "You can say that."

"I said that. Now you tell me something I don't know."

"You seem to know everything. The only thing you never knew was that Achille would seize on the opportunity to run back to Arturo and rat you out for not killing Palermo's kid in front of him. That wife of his, too."

"Ah." I smiled again. "I knew."

"Then I *really* don't understand why you did it. Some say they'd rather face hell than face Arturo Scarpone."

"I faced hell and I survived." I sat forward a little, getting closer. "Tell me about the girl you fostered five years ago."

He bit the inside of his lip and looked up at the wall. It was his fucking political thinking face. He looked like he was taking a shit.

I stood so abruptly that the chair fell over behind me and he didn't have a chance to react. I grabbed him by his throat and squeezed until his eyes started to water. When I let him go, he fell back into his seat, gasping for breath. I picked my chair up and set it down, sitting again. "You know me, Quillo. I'll snap your neck for fucking less than playing stupid."

"Five years ago," he choked out. "Five years ago..."

I wondered how many innocent children he and his family had fostered over the years, and how many of those children he had touched while his bitch of a social-climber wife ignored it.

She came into Macchiavello's regularly with her fake friends. He had fucked half of them.

"Mari—" He went to say her entire name, but I shook my head, daring him. "Do you want her last name?" He had caught his breath, but his voice was like sandpaper.

"Yeah, give it to me," I said.

"Flores."

"What do you remember about her?" I rolled my teeth over my bottom lip. "Specifics."

He caught the gesture and nodded. "Just give me a second." He took a few deep breaths and then sighed. "Young. Around thirteen, maybe younger."

No, you fucker, she looked younger because she was in foster and never had a steady stream of proper meals. Which made his offense even worse. He thought she was younger, and he still put his hands on her.

"Her face had the potential to become something special. Her nose was weird, but her body was tight. She had nice tits. And that ass? She was skinny, but it was already *boom*." He laughed. "We touched each other—" When he caught the look on my face, the roll of my teeth over my lip again, he was quicker and smarter this time. He changed his story. "I touched her. All right! *I* touched *her*. She was irresistible."

"She fought."

"Not at first. She didn't expect it. The last time she pulled a knife on me. Then she was gone. Took off. They had her down as a runaway for a while, but she was a system kid. No one really looks."

"You made her believe that kindness comes with strings."

"It does. I took the homeless bitch in." His face was pinched, but all of a sudden, it relaxed. "That's her! Palermo's kid! You're looking for her." He was stupid in some ways, but too perceptive in others. He knew if I was asking, there was a reason.

"The Scarpones have a hit on her."

He made a disbelieving noise. "*Yeah*. There's money on her head. Has been since that night. It only grows with time. More interest gained with the years. The first one to bring Arturo her severed head gets the entire sweet pot. *Man*." He shook his head and whistled.

I knew he wished that he would've pieced it together sooner, recognized her, so the entire sweet pot could've been his, along with full access to her pussy before handing her over. The pot wasn't about the money; it was about being in better graces with Arturo and his attack dog, Achille. If Quillo had to answer to Arturo, he dealt with Achille on a regular basis.

"I still can't get over you calling the Scarpones the Scarpones. Man, have times changed." He sighed and then his eyes widened. "I do remember something else about her. Her lips. Those lips." His eyes softened at the thought. "You looking for her now? I can help you out. I can't remember hair or eye color, but it's really no issue. I know people, and I'd recognize her anywhere. And if you're worried about me running back to tell your family, you know I won't say anything. You and my sister—"

He stopped himself, and lucky for him he did. I was about to sever *his* head and deliver it to the Scarpone family free of charge.

"Just offering." He held his hands up.

I leaned to the side, took out another small gun from behind my back, and set it on the table. Quillo glanced at it before he trained his eyes back on me. I leaned forward and steepled my hands, my fingers covering my mouth. "I don't need to look for her, Quillo. I know where she is right this fucking second."

"You do?"

"Yeah, I do. She's at home, in our bed, sleeping. My wife. You fucked with my wife, Quillo. You touched her when she was a child in your care. What should have been a safe place, you made into a scum prison. You wanna know why I did what I did? Why I saved Marietta Bettina Palermo?" I rolled my teeth over my lip.

"I saved her because she was innocent. I traded my life so her innocence could live. And then you know what I learn, Quillo? I learn that a sick fuck made her believe that kindness was a nasty thing. That it came with *strings*. You took all that I sacrificed for her and twisted it up. You took that innocence and made her feel ashamed. You made something that was supposed to be clean, the only time in life it can be, seem filthy by putting your hands on her. How do you think I feel about that, Quillo? What do you think I'll do to make sure you never do it again? Not to mine. Not to anyone."

He didn't say anything for a while. He didn't even try to deny it or defend it. He couldn't. There are some men who will sit and listen to excuses. Not this one. There was no excuse that could save his life. Business matters could be negotiated, but a personal offense? Unforgivable.

He was sweating again, his lips pursed. "You fell in love with her. You fell in love with Palermo's kid."

I smiled and Quillo moved his head back in response, but he was about to use anger to cover his fear. Old habits die hard, but I never forgot.

He pounded the table with his fist. The gun trembled. "You fucking love her! The spawn of that fucker Palermo! He was as evil as your father! My sister. She was a good girl. She didn't deserve what happened to her! And you sat there and watched it. And now you sit in front of me and condemn me when your conscience is as filthy as they fucking come. You watched them tear my sister in two, and you felt nothing! She wanted you to love her! She *loved* you. And you couldn't even say it. You didn't even fight for her! And now you marry Palermo's daughter. A whore! A bi—"

I leaned across the table and grabbed him by his throat again, and this time, he tried to fight me. He clawed at the glove but was otherwise subdued. "You're out of shape, Quillo. All those rich, fatty meals have gone straight to your heart. All that wheezing." I shook my head. "It's not good. Careful with that mouth, or I'll have to take that tongue out. Open your airway up a bit."

Once he relaxed and stopped fighting me, I released him, and he fell into the chair again. He wheezed this time, banging on the table for air. I picked up the gun, examined it, and then set it down when he calmed.

"This is not about love. This is about loyalty. Respect. Something your family never knew anything about. So." I pushed the gun toward him. "What'll it be? The gun or me?" I smiled at him, showing some teeth.

He snatched the gun from the table, put it to his temple, and closed his eyes. He shot me the bird, said, "F*uck you, Pretty Boy Prince. I'll see you in hell one day,*" and then pulled the trigger.

Click.

It took a second, but his eyes sprang open when he realized the gun was empty. *Click. Click. Click.* His finger was frantic as it continually pulled the trigger.

I threw my head back and laughed. "They might've killed me, but some things always stay the same, Quillo. Apparently, the same goes for you. You never learn." I sighed. "You should know better. I'd never go that easy on you." Then I rose from my seat and hit him so hard in the chest that I felt his bone crack against my glove. Then I set my hand over his mouth and nose, draining the life out of him.

13

MARIPOSA

"What do you think, Vera II? Should we add more rosemary? More basil? Or how about thyme?" I lifted it to my nose and sniffed too hard. Then I sneezed and coughed. "A little of that will go a long way. But rosemary? I love the smell of it." This time, I didn't put the bottle up so close.

Vera II looked exactly like Vera I, except her pot was different. After Capo had shown me around, and I started to get comfortable, I noticed Vera II sitting on the table next to my side of the bed, right next to the watch. The original Vera's leaves were skimpy, and the same was true for Vera II. I could've sworn they were the same plant, but I knew better.

How could he have given me the same plant?

It just seemed odd, how alike they were. And I would've thought that he would've bought a plant with more aloe to it.

This time around, I swore to bulk Vera II up. She already had a dose of plant food for succulents. Every once in a while I moved her around so she'd have equal amounts of light and rest.

During one of my doctor's appointments—that was a term

during our meeting, I had to see a few of them since I hadn't in years—I read while in the waiting room. The magazine stated that talking to your plants makes them grow faster. It also said that plants seemed to react to female voices better than they did male ones. So whenever I was home alone, Vera II and I had conversations.

Since I was making dinner and home alone, she got an earful. I could've called Keely, but I decided not to.

I'd been married for two weeks, and even though I talked to Kee, it wasn't often, and our conversations seemed...short. I knew she still loved me, but she was struggling with Harrison's romantic feelings and my platonic ones after he confessed to me how he felt. We were on unsteady ground. We usually talked about everything—mostly how we were going to survive—but since everything had been turned upside down, we traded what we once called "poor people's problems" for "rich people's problems."

It was an entirely new world to me, and I was still playing catch up. So many things that I'd written in my journal were happening all at once. And somewhere deep down, a dark fear ate at me. I kept waiting for the shoes that fit to disappear, and the ones that were too tight (and used to make me bleed) to reappear.

I looked down at my feet. They were bare. I loved the way the floors in the fire station felt beneath them. Cool. Clean. And in some rooms, so soft I wanted to cry.

This place. It smelled like home to me. It *felt* like home. I never wanted to leave, and since I'd arrived, I'd only gone out to meet with the wedding planners at Rocco's office, have the fittings for my second wedding gown, and buy groceries. I had a sleek black card that my husband insisted that I use. It had my name on it, *Mariposa Macchiavello,* and no limit.

The black card was nothing compared to my new I.D. and passport, though. My eyes welled at that one.

"How about this, Vera II? Does this consistency look right to you?" I lifted the bowl, showing my plant the mixture I'd made to go between the layers of the pasta boiling on the stove. I was trying to make *lasagne al forno.* When Capo brought me here after the wedding, a full tray of it had been in the fridge. It was the best thing I'd ever tasted, so I looked in one of my many cookbooks and found a recipe for it.

As of yet, I hadn't made a meal that truly tasted good, but since I had nothing but time on my hands, I was determined to get it right at some point. Setting the bowl down, I decided to get the ingredients I'd need for an Italian cream cake. It was sort of like trying to touch the tops of two mountains in one day, but go big or go home. Either way, win or lose, I was square.

"*Fucka me,*" I breathed out. The monstrous size of the pantry always shocked me. It was bigger than the apartment I'd rented from Merv the dead perv (Kee's new nickname for him). And rat free.

While rummaging around looking for things, a popping sound rang out from kitchen, and at first, I thought someone was shooting at me. I clutched the sugar to my chest, wondering what was going on. Then the smell of smoke assaulted my nose and a loud alarm rang out. "Shit! The pasta!"

Still holding the bag of sugar to my chest, I ran so fast that when I entered the kitchen, I slid on the shiny, sleek hardwood floor. Capo had beaten me to it, though, taking the pan off the stove and running it under cold water. The pan sizzled and popped, truly pissed off, and more smoke thickened the air.

He nodded toward the stove. "Turn the fan on."

I set the sugar down on the counter and did what he said. It took a few minutes, but the air started to clear, only swirls of white highlighted by the sun lingering. And the smell. It was a mixture between burning plastic and something I didn't even have a name for, except for *gross.*

After he set the ruined pan in the sink, he turned to face me. "Maybe I should have kept this place as is. A fire house."

I couldn't answer. He was shirtless, only a towel wrapped around his slim waist. His skin was smooth and tight, slick from a hot shower. His hair was combed back—true black when it was wet—and droplets ran down his shoulders and chest.

His eyes were even more electric. They were such a stunning blue, I wondered if the color was stolen from a hidden ocean. Even though the rancid smell still lingered, the shower had made his scent stronger. It was like he had just walked off a beach, but ten times better.

This was the first time I'd seen him like this, with hardly anything on. His shoulders were broad. His muscular chest and stomach seemed carved out of stone. He probably had seven packs instead of six. The towel rode low, showing two deep indentions on either side of his hips, making a V. A thick patch of black hair peeked out. His arms looked like they belonged in one of those fitness magazines. His legs were long and lean. They seemed strong, but not too bulky.

The thing about my husband—something I'd learned during our short time together—was, even when a situation became awkward, he didn't care. He seemed to eat it up. My eyes were glued to him, no shame, and his were glued to me. He wouldn't try to distract me or pretend like he didn't know what had come over me. He wouldn't wave the ruined pan and say *dinner, remember?* He'd say, *you're not wearing red, and you're not in my bed, so I know what that means. You're not ready to fuck me yet.*

Then we'd either explore each other some more, or we'd do something else. We'd watch movies or listen to music or talk about places we could travel to or things we could do to the house later. He wanted me to add my own touch to it once I figured out what I wanted. Thing was, it was perfect as is. Even the clothes, shoes, and jewelry he had chosen for me in the closet. It was all such a dream come true.

Maybe he was, too—on the surface. He hadn't pulled me into the deep end yet.

Finally, I made sense of the words dying to shoot out of my mouth. "When did you get home?"

"About the time you were reading the recipe for *lasagne al forno* to—" he looked at the plant on the counter and then at me again "—Vera II. She's not much of a talker."

"No," I said, leaning against the counter. My eyes kept flickering to his towel every other second. He wasn't hard, but there was a gigantic bulge. I couldn't pretend that I wasn't curious to know what it looked like. What *he* looked like. Naked. I took a breath in and released it slowly. "She's a good listener, but not much of a gossiper."

"Got something to get off your chest?"

"Why? Are you gonna listen?"

"Isn't that what husbands do?"

A huge bubble of laughter exploded from my mouth. "I might not know anything about being domesticated, but I know, *know*, that men are not good listeners. Selective hearing."

"Selective hearing," he repeated, a suspicious tone to his voice. "Where'd you hear that?"

I smiled. "Girl's night."

Rocco's wife, Rosaria, had invited me to join her and the women of the Fausti *famiglia* for their girls' nights. Some were just friends, but they were all mostly related by marriage. Rocco had three brothers. Brando, Dario, and Romeo. Brando was the oldest and the most intense. He barely nodded when I'd asked him if he liked the framed jersey his wife, Scarlett, had given him.

I had invited Keely to come with me one night, but she'd seemed jealous of how well Scarlett and I had gotten along.

After that, I didn't invite Keely again because I didn't want things to get awkward.

When Scarlett first saw me, she said, "*Told you I'd see you again!*" And then she wrapped me in her petite arms and hugged me. She was a famous ballerina, and compared to her husband, so tiny. I couldn't say what it was about her, but she made me feel lighter. She made me feel like I belonged with them. She and the other wives made me feel like family.

Girl's night was always held at one of their houses (next weekend at ours, in the building next to the fire station), and that made Capo cool with it. After our wedding at City Hall, he had upped our security. I had three new Giovannis, which made four, and Capo seemed...a little on edge when we were out in public.

The nights out were fun for me, though. We talked about books we read, some of the girls crocheted or knitted, and at some point, we'd always end up talking about our men.

Our men.

My man.

Capo was mine.

The truth of those words stole my breath.

I was someone's wife.

His.

I touched the ring on my left finger, a reminder. *This isn't a dream.*

He stalked closer, pinning me against the counter, one arm on each side of me. His wedding ring clanked against the marble when he rested his hands against it. I reached up and tugged at the ends of his damp hair. Droplets ran down his chest.

"What were we talking about?" he asked.

I smiled. "See? Selective hearing. Girl's night—oh." I started laughing. "You're messing with me!"

"You *gotta* speed up to keep up, Butterfly." He kissed me on the forehead.

Butterfly. He had never called me that before. Only Mariposa.

"Yeah," I said, my voice soft. "If I want to run with the lone wolf, I need to up my game."

His mouth drifted from my forehead to my nose, his lips soft but firm. He kissed the bridge of my nose, once on each side and one on the center, before his lips met mine. As usual, I responded to him, starved for his touch. My hands reached out to touch him, to bring him closer, and I skimmed my nails along his side, over his ribs.

At the light touch, his eyes opened, staring into mine. When my nails moved toward his back, my touch harder, he made a wild noise in his throat and his eyes closed. His tongue moved faster, harder, twirling with mine, and everything around me seemed to fade.

Lifting my arms, he removed my t-shirt, a shirt I had worn because the color reminded me of his eyes. The kiss broke, but only for a second, not long enough to bring me back to reality. His hands palmed my breasts, his thumbs stroking my nipples. A soft, whimpering sound escaped from my lips. My nails sunk into his skin, wanting more.

He broke the kiss again, almost violently, his head moving down, the water from his hair cool against my overheated skin. I hissed out a breath when his mouth replaced one of his thumbs. He sucked me hard, making my lower stomach clench. The pulse between my legs burned, begging for relief. My underwear was soaked.

"Please," I said, not even aware I had even said the word until after I did. I didn't care. "More."

"Say my name, Mariposa. The name you gave me."

"*Il mio capo.*"

His hands made quick work of the button on my jean shorts. They slipped down my legs and I stepped out of them. I kicked them across the room. I did the same with my underwear.

Capo lifted me like a rag doll onto the counter, my ass against the cold marble. "Steady yourself." He nodded to my arms.

Hardly breathing, I set my arms behind me, palms down on the counter. His mouth came at mine again, and it was a beautiful war between our tongues. A throaty moan came from my throat, and he seemed to swallow it down. Then his mouth moved down—making me lick my lips to taste him again while my head tilted back—and my eyes closed. He licked me from my neck to my belly button, then back up, and down again.

My entire body felt like it was about to explode. Shatter into a million pieces. The ache between my legs had no name. Not even *starved* seemed to be enough. My thighs trembled from expectation. The stubble on his face scratched my skin, his tongue the exact opposite, and the dampness from his hair still made a cool trail. He pushed my thighs further apart, and when his mouth closed over me down *there*, I had to press harder against the counter to keep steady.

Fucka me.

Fucka me.

Fucka me.

Nothing had ever felt so good.

The feeling was contained to one area, the area where his mouth and tongue worked its magic, but it sent shockwaves throughout my entire body.

I bucked against his mouth, not an ounce of shame, his name on my tongue. "Capo. That feels so..." I hissed out a breath when his hand came up and started twisting my nipple. "That feels sooo, sooo good, *il mio Capo.*"

He constantly made a liar out of me. I was traumatized by what Zamboni had done to me, but whenever Capo touched me, I responded to his touch without fear.

My breaths were coming fast, too fast. I was panting and making noises I'd never heard myself make before. If he stopped, violence would come from my hand and land on his body.

He did something to me, something with that magical mouth that sent me over the edge, spiraling out of control. He bit me, *hard*, down *there*. My arms gave out, but before I could go flying backwards, Capo caught me.

I kept my eyes shut tight. "I'm so dizzy," I said. "Is that normal?"

He laughed softly, kissing the top of my head. "Yeah. When it's good."

"So good," I whispered. "So, so good."

We stayed that way for a while, neither of us moving. That was the furthest we'd ever gone. And even though I hadn't made it to red yet, I was getting closer and closer to the fire. I wanted him more than anything, but there was something in me that stopped just short of going all the way.

Zamboni was the main reason, but there was another reason, too. I didn't realize it until after I had moved in, and I found myself flirting with desire, so close to giving myself over to it. I wanted the connection to grow between us before I gave him my body. Love was not an option, he made that clear, but that didn't mean everything else we agreed to couldn't deepen.

A deeper relationship. A deeper sense of intimacy. A deeper loyalty.

Maybe even a deeper friendship.

Maybe I was a fool, but I needed to feel more from him, a little more warmth, so that after it was over and done, my soul didn't feel so lonely. It would sound like total bullshit if I'd said it out loud, but deep down, I knew it was true. His cold nature could be so hard sometimes. Nothing could break it down, not even fire.

Before Jocelyn died, she tried to cram years into months.

One night, when her mind seemed to be sharper than usual, she told me, "*There is nothing lonelier than waking up to someone you've given your all to, only to realize they only gave half in the night. It'll happen, and it'll hurt, but you'll survive.*"

Could I survive this arrangement if that were to happen between us?

I could live without love, the kind that people sacrifice their lives and souls for in romance novels and movies, and I guessed in real life sometimes, too, but could I live with not feeling... something mutual from him?

The answer didn't matter, only my response to it. My loyalty to him ran high, as high as heaven. He had secured that long ago, when I was five.

I'd *live* with this arrangement, but I'd merely *survive* the sex.

He looked me in the eye, and then he leaned in and kissed my lips. "Get dressed."

He took a step back and the towel made a teepee in front of him. His size didn't seem... normal. The towel and how hard he was left little to the imagination. And I imagined a snake. A humongous python. It was one thing to suspect, but another to see the outline of it so close. It was in striking distance.

How was *that* going to fit in my oonie?

"It'll fit," he said, reading my thoughts. "Your body was made for mine."

I nodded, looking up at his eyes. My nails tapped against the counter. What he called *agitarsi* in Italian. *Fidgeting.* I stopped because he didn't like it when I did it. He said there was no reason for me to be nervous. Ever. But if he'd seen what I just did for the first time? He'd be nervous, too.

"Where are we going?" My voice sounded raw, as if I'd been screaming. Every part of me felt drained, but in the best damn way. In some primal way, I liked that he had left a mark on me, something deeper than skin. He had touched muscle and bone.

"To Macchiavello's for dinner." He looked me over, naked

except for my lace bra, sitting on the marble counter. "Nothing I put in my mouth tonight will compare to what I just had, though." He raked his teeth over his bottom lip. "*Vieni.*" He held out his hand. "Time to get dressed."

WHEN WE WALKED into the master suite, Capo sighed and said, "Tell me what you're so nervous about."

Besides the fact that I just saw a mighty python? I was going to say, but I didn't. The ice that followed him around sometimes was thick. I chose to be honest about something else.

"The, uh, guy that…well, I don't know what he does. He runs out to meet you when you arrive at the restaurant. He was, kinda, mean to me." This would be our first time eating at his restaurant. The big-mouthed guy, Bruno, who told me that he'd squish me like a bug, was hard to forget. He reminded me of Zamboni. And the same feelings of shame went straight to my soul like acid.

Capo stopped short, and I almost ran into his back. He let my hand go and turned to me. I almost took a step back but didn't. His intensity could be threatening sometimes, but one good thing about girl's night—I learned it wasn't just Capo. All of the men in that circle seemed to be similar in that way.

Stand your ground, Scarlett had told me. *You're just as powerful as he is.*

Her advice ran through my head, but I kept seeing a deer running from a wolf. I glanced down at his tattoo and then my eyes met his again, thankful that he called me Butterfly, not something that was prey.

"What do you mean?" His voice was stern. "*Kind of mean.* It's either, *yes,* he was mean to me, Capo, or, *no,* he wasn't mean to me, Capo. There is no in between, Mariposa. Use all of your words with me."

Great. He was throwing my words back at me from the night at Harrison's.

I held my hands in front of me, holding them out, popping my knuckles. "It's not that simple. Maybe I was doing something I wasn't supposed to. I'm not sure what you hired him for. If it was to run strays away from your window so they don't scare customers, then, no, he wasn't mean. He was just doing his job, showing sharp teeth and big claws. If he's *not* supposed to make poor people feel ashamed for not being able to afford a steak at your high-priced restaurant, then, yeah, he was most definitely mean to me. Past mean. An asshole."

He studied my face for a moment. "Why did you come to Macchiavello's? Our restaurant. Did you remember something?"

He made sure to say "our" in a powerful way so that I'd accept his business as mine. It was hard when, half of the time, this all still felt like a dream.

I shook my head. "No. I used to pass by sometimes when I was going to Home Run. You can see people eating from outside. It smelled really good. I was hungry." I shrugged. " No one ever came out with leftovers, so I figured the steak must be worth a kidney."

He chin-flicked, copying what I'd done outside of his restaurant when Bruno had given me a hard time. "It makes sense now. Why you said what you did."

"After I was done being ashamed, I got angry. Your guy pissed me off."

"You kept coming back."

"I'm not sure why. You made me...curious." I bit my lip but stopped when he narrowed his eyes. "Did you remember me then?"

"You looked familiar, but no, not fully. You've grown up."

"Some days." I smiled, but it was weak. "It was hell getting to the days when I am."

"Mariposa." He touched my chin and then kissed my lips softly. Then he took my hand again and led me to the humongous closet.

It took only a few minutes for him to find what he was looking for on his side. Even though everything was organized for me, dress clothes from casual, winter, spring, summer, and fall, it took time for me to find things.

I was still rummaging around, trying to find the right outfit, when he told me to meet him in his office when I was done. He wore a black suit with a white shirt underneath and a black tie. He reminded me of a gangster from the '20s. All of his suits were dark, either black or navy blue. For some reason, the view of him reminded me of the tattoo on his arm—all darkness except for those electric blue eyes.

Some men had it so easy. Ten minutes and...done.

I sighed, pushing around the many hangers until I came to an embellished black chiffon dress. The fringe on it reminded me of cascading water at night, the edges tipped with silver, like moonlight was touching them. It had an ombre effect. Holding the dress up to my body, I saw that it landed right above my knees. It was classy and sexy at the same time.

It took me a while to do my makeup and hair. Sawyer's team had taught me how to do both. I kept my eyes simple but used blood red on my lips. I curled my hair, but I didn't do full curls. Wavy. After, I slathered myself in the cream Capo loved so much and sprayed the perfume. Then I got dressed.

Three white-gold bangle bracelets, encrusted with diamonds and sapphires, and a pair of matching earrings came close to completing the outfit.

"*Fucka me*," I breathed. I hoped the jewels in the bracelet weren't real. I had enough to worry about with the ring on my left finger. Maybe they'd just chop my wrist off and be done with it. They might even go after my ears if they noticed the earrings.

Shaking off the shock, this was *my* life, I found a pair of heels that were high and black and made pretty patterns against my feet.

All done.

"Mariposa—" Capo stopped when we met in the "hallway" of the closet. It was the first time I'd truly dressed up since we were married. I liked how he looked at me, like he had when I opened my robe and showed him my goods the night of our City Hall wedding.

"What do you think?" I turned a little for him. "Good enough?"

I wanted to make him proud while I was on his arm. I wanted to look good, *no*, stunning for him. I'd never thought I'd use *I* and *stunning* in the same sentence, but things had changed. This man was so good looking that it made it hard to catch my breath sometimes. And he chose me. The girl with the strange-shaped schnozzola.

"*Sbalorditiva*." He raked his teeth over his bottom lip. "You make me proud, Mariposa."

Sbalorditiva. I knew what the word meant without Capo having to translate. *Stunning*. There were times when I had no clue what he was saying, but others, I did. It was strange understanding words I'd never heard before in a different language, but somehow knowing their meaning.

Then the last part of his compliment made it to my mind. *You make me proud.*

Before I could say something stupid, he lifted my hand to his mouth, placing a soft kiss on my fingers. "I don't deserve your time or company, but regardless, it's mine. For the rest of my life." And with that, he took my hand and we left.

CAPO'S CAR pulled smoothly into his reserved spot in front of Macchiavello's. He had driven his Mercedes AMG Vision Gran Turismo. It was all silver and sleek and looked just like the bat car. Which was what I felt he was aiming for, since we lived in what seemed like a bat cave.

At our arrival, a few people stopped to stare. Anytime he pulled up in one of his cars, it seemed to cause a stir. Or maybe it was Capo. He caused the stir. But his impressive collection of vehicles seemed to be the only thing he did that was loud enough to draw attention. It didn't exactly fit with his reclusive lifestyle, but I was finding I couldn't assume anything with him.

Capo coolly stepped out, ignoring the men pointing at his car, striding to my side to open the door. He fixed the button on his suit before he did.

I hesitated, waiting for Bruno to come barreling out. I didn't expect him to be mean to me like he had the last time—after all, I was his *capo's* wife—but I hoped he didn't spit on my steak while it was coming out of the kitchen.

"Out," Capo said, holding out his hand.

I set mine in his, and the lights from Macchiavello's caught all of my jewelry, making the diamonds and sapphires glisten against my skin. My heels tapped against the pavement in a pretty melody. This time, instead of the dumpster assaulting my nose, his cologne and my perfume seemed to float in the air, caressing it. The smell of steak came on stronger the closer we got to the door. My stomach growled, ready to maul something.

"Are you sure I don't have to sell a kidney for this?" I joked.

He lifted my arm and placed a firm kiss on my wrist. "I believe you've sold enough. You're off the market, Mariposa. You belong to me. No one will be touching you, least of all something as valuable as a kidney."

At the door, a man waited, decked out in the finest suit, holding it open. "Mr. Mac." He nodded. "It is a pleasure to see you tonight."

"Sylvester." Capo nodded, then pulled me forward, trading my hand for my lower back. His touch was warm, soothing, and as firm as his kiss. "My wife," he said. "Mariposa Macchiavello."

The man took my hand and shook it lightly. He congratulated me, called me Mrs. Macchiavello, and then led us away from the door.

"Sylvester is the night manager," Capo said.

As we walked, Capo and Sylvester spoke in Italian, and I was able to pick up on a few things. Their conversation was about the restaurant. Business matters. But I couldn't help but notice how all of the staff were looking at me—with nervous glances. The patrons were different. They looked at me with open curiosity.

Who was this normal chick walking next to the force of a man?

Instead of concentrating on the shit going on around me, I decide to savor the experience. I remembered how much I wanted this, *the steak*, and decided to make my first visit the best.

The restaurant was as classy as I figured it would be, but it was also romantic. Some walls exposed what I guessed was the original brick, while others were painted a deep red. The chairs and tables were black, and the bronze chandeliers held real flickering candles. Each table held a single white rose in a crystal vase.

The bar was on the other side, an entirely different section of the building. From what I could see, the shelves were packed with hundreds of uniquely shaped, shiny bottles. The area reminded me of the old speakeasies Pops used to tell me stories about. That entire side had brick walls, mirroring the ones in the restaurant. The floor was black and white striped marble. A few tables were set up around a small dance floor.

Men and women in expensive clothing sat along the bar in vintage leather chairs. Some of them were turned to each other, conversation flowing, laughter rising over soft music. A man dressed in black tie sat at a grand piano in the corner, playing the instrument and crooning.

The smells...my mouth watered. It wasn't just steak either. Rich sauces and wines lingered in the air. Below the surface, something sweet circulated. I sniffed harder. Chocolate, and it reminded me of the scent at The Club.

Sylvester stopped at a door that didn't really look like a door at all. It was brick, matching the wall, and only a golden ring stuck out. He pulled it open, revealing a humongous room. A table that probably could seat forty sat in the middle of it.

The room smelled really sweet, like chocolate again, but even stronger, and the candles made the room feel warmer. Richer. Sexier. The diamonds on my hands and wrists softened when we walked in. So did the dress. The chiffon seemed to shimmer, the light catching the silver and sparking.

This room reflected the restaurant, but on a smaller scale. It was intimate. The music tinkled in here, carried through a speaker somewhere in the room. What caught my eye next made me walk further in to look out. It wasn't a window, but more like a square piece of glass. I could see the entire restaurant.

"We can see out, but they can't see in," Capo said, walking up behind me, looking out at his world.

"The mirror?" I guessed. I had noticed it when we first walked in, but I really didn't think anything of it. It was fancy, bronze detailing around it, but it was just a mirror. Apparently not. It was a way for him to watch without anyone knowing.

"You're perceptive," he said.

"Not really. If I hadn't seen this room, I would've probably made sure my lipstick still looked fresh when I passed it."

He laughed, real soft, and his breath fanned over my skin, making goosebumps rise on my arms. His chest pressed against my back, and I had the urge to lean back and rest my head against him.

"What do you use this room for?"

"Private parties, but it's exclusive."

"Exclusive," I repeated. "Like for the Faustis?"

"Yes." He turned me toward the table, and then pulled out a chair for me. It was next to the chair at the head of the table. His spot. He sat, looking at me after he did. "So what do you think, Mariposa? Does it live up to the hype?"

"It's beautiful," I said. "But I need that steak first to say for sure."

He smiled at me, his eyes a deeper blue in this light. Sapphire, the same color as the ones on my wrist.

"It must be nice to be you." I sighed dramatically. "You own one of the nicest restaurants in New York."

"So do you," he said. "And even though I enjoy the food here, my favorite place is Mamma's Pizzeria. But don't tell my aunts when we get to Sicily. They'd have my head on a platter. Some of the recipes we use here are theirs, the ones that never change. Anyone who cooks in the kitchen has to be sworn to secrecy. As serious as the *omertà*."

"Mamma's. Really? Compared to this?" I had been to Mamma's. You could get a humongous slice for three bucks, or an entire meal—salad, drink, and a slice—for five. It was a poor man's heaven.

"You've been?"

"Yeah. I went with Keely and Harri—" At the look on his face, I stopped. His eyes narrowed and his lips became severe. "I've been."

"We'll go one day. Take the bike. You'll eat here tonight and then we'll compare after we go to Mamma's."

The bike. He had a few of them, but there was one that he told me he was going to take me out on one day. It looked sleek and fast. I told him *sure* and then set my hand on a car. Any car. He had only grinned. I think he took it as a challenge.

A girl dressed in a stylish black pantsuit entered the room

holding a glass filled with gold liquid. She set down a napkin and then the glass in front of me. "Enjoy, Mrs. Macchiavello."

She didn't even look at me, and before I could say anything, like, "What's this?" she was gone.

"What's this?" I asked Capo instead. I had seen a woman at the bar with one.

Capo explained that it was a cocktail called "the golden prince." He thought I'd enjoy it, so he took the liberty to order it for me ahead of time.

I took a sip and fell in love.

Placing it down carefully, I said playfully, "What? No cocktail named after me?" I sipped on it some more. "This is delicious."

He grinned, and when the same girl came back in, he told her to bring him the most popular drink on their bar menu. She came back a few minutes later with a dark blue drink in a glass that had a light blue butterfly sitting on the edge. The butterfly was made of sugar.

"For real?" I laughed. "You do!"

"It seems a man can't have secrets around you." He winked. Then he turned to the girl. "Tell my wife what the name of this drink is, Liza."

"Of course, Mr. Mac." The woman named Liza with the stylish bob haircut turned to me. "That is our Mariposa, the most popular drink on the menu."

The Mariposa was sweet. I honestly couldn't decide which one I liked the best. And then numerous servers started entering the room, one after another, delivering tray after tray of food. By the time they were done, the entire table was filled with steaming dishes. It seemed like every item on the menu had been ordered.

"How are we supposed to eat all of this?" I looked over our private buffet. "Are we expecting more people?"

"You can try a bite of everything." He waved his hand casually, like it was no big deal. "I had them do it family style. That way we can take what we want and not touch the leftovers."

"I get that." My body felt warm from the drinks. "But this is a lot of food. I don't want it to go to—"

He took my hand and squeezed. "We'll give it to people in need after. I'll have our people box it up. To go."

"Okay." I nodded. "Let's eat."

Conversation was light as we ate. It was a feast fit for a queen. That was how Capo made me feel. He encouraged me try a little from all of the plates. *The steak*—so worth the kidney —but honestly, what I thought I'd sacrifice my precious organ for came in second. I fell in love with a pasta dish filled with cream sauce and lemony crabmeat. It was worth a kidney *and* some blood.

Capo even fed me a bite or two after I'd made him take a bite from my plate. I was so caught up in food ecstasy that I didn't even think about him eating here before or owning the place. It was just the two of us, the rest of the world silent, even though they passed by the peeper glass constantly. There were so many people trying to eye themselves when they walked past without *really* wanting others to see.

Capo gave a throaty laugh when I called it that—a peeper glass.

After the main courses, he suggested that we dance, since he requested that dessert come a while after dinner. The dancing in this place was different than the way people danced at The Club. A jazz band had started up, accompanied by a woman who sang with a voice like a bird. Capo taught me a few steps, since I had no clue what I was doing. He was smooth and a surprisingly a good teacher.

I knew I'd always remember how much I laughed that night.

"Where'd you learn to dance like that?" I asked, close to breathless as he pulled my seat out again in the exclusive room.

I was surprised that the table was still full of dinner foods. I figured after he had mentioned dessert, we'd be getting that soon.

He took his seat again. "My mother."

"You don't talk about her much." He rarely talked about any of his family. I knew his grandfather was in Italy, and he had an uncle (since he mentioned him knowing about the secret firehouse) and aunts (since he had mentioned them that night), but other than that, he didn't bring up his family.

"She died when I was younger."

"It seems we have something in common then," I said.

"Seems like we do."

Our eyes held. Slowly, oh so slowly, he leaned closer and placed a kiss on my lips. When I opened my eyes, he was watching me with an expression I couldn't explain. As a few servers entered again, I sat back, feeling light-headed.

"Mr. Mac? Are you ready for me to clear this—"

Fucka me. It was Bruno. I hadn't even noticed him come in the room. I had assumed Capo had given him the night off, or maybe he only worked days. Capo said that Sylvester was his night manager. I had only seen Big Mouth during the day. I had never come here at night. Instead of a fine suit, like usual, he was wearing cleaning garb. Something red was smeared across his forehead.

At the sight of me, he stopped dead. Even in nice clothes, with expensive jewelry on my finger, wrist, and ears, he recognized me. The shock in his eyes came and went in a flash, and then it was replaced by coldness.

He hid it well when Capo called his name and then introduced me as his wife.

Bruno wiped his hands on his dirty apron, and then went to hold his hand out, but Capo shook his head, bringing his drink to his lips, not even looking at the man.

"Your hands are dirty. Too dirty to touch my wife."

My cheeks burned and I looked away. I knew what Capo was doing. I hated it. It only brought attention to something I didn't want to acknowledge.

"Of course, Mr. Mac," Bruno said. His voice was small. "I wasn't thinking." Then his voice lowered. "I'd like to talk to you about my position. I don't know—"

"I'm out with my wife," Capo said, cutting him off. He took another sip of his whiskey. "We'll talk business later. Right now, you have a job to do. And that's to clean this table. I want it spotless. After, you'll help Emilio box the leftovers. Then you'll search the streets for the hungriest people you can find. You'll feed them."

"Yes, sir." Bruno started clearing away everything we'd eaten, and I tried to avoid his eyes and the nearness of him when he came close to grab a dish or silverware.

It was so fucking awkward that I wanted to kick Capo in the shin with my sharp heels for doing what he did. Who did he think he was? The king of New York? He couldn't react this way whenever someone was mean to me. Beyond that, this made me feel even worse. It shone a big light on what had been done, and it proved to Bruno that he had gotten to me. He had made me feel small. Insignificant.

Whenever a server would enter, Capo would dismiss him. He wanted Bruno to handle it all by himself while I sat and watched, like that would make me feel better.

After all of the plates had been cleared and Bruno had wiped madly, polishing the fancy table, he came close enough to me that I could smell the dumpsters on him. A missed crumb fell in my lap, and he apologized, but when I met his eye, he gave me the coldest look. When I looked at Capo, he was staring straight ahead again, raking his teeth over his bottom lip.

A second later, Capo was out of the chair, the heavy wood turned over onto the floor, and he had Bruno pinned against the wall. A few servers came in carrying desserts, Sylvester right behind them, and when he noticed what was going on, he shooed the servers in and shut the door. The servers and Sylvester stood clustered in a darkened corner, watching.

I stood, squeezing my fingers, not sure what to do.

Capo's voice was low, but understandable. He was telling Bruno that he knew what he had done to me, when I was out on the street, and when he was cleaning the table, and if he ever saw him so much as look at me again, he'd fuck him up beyond repair.

I glanced at the servers. None of them would even look at me. No wonder. They were too afraid.

Without making a sound, I slipped out of the room, passed the dining area and bar, and went out the front door. Giovanni appeared out of nowhere, calling for me to wait for Capo, but I refused. I didn't stop until Capo grabbed me by the arm, forcing me to.

His eyes almost glowed in the darkness, looking murderous. "Where the fuck do you think you're going?"

"I don't know! But I need some space."

"Space, ah?"

He took my arm, leading me out of the way of pedestrian traffic. There was a sports bar on the corner, where televisions playing a variety of games lined the walls. One television played the news.

I flung my arm out of his hold when we were to the side. "Space, Capo. Do you need the definition of the word?" Damn Caspar. His definition clause had gotten to me.

Capo took a step back, glaring at me. "Space." He spelled the word. "Position (two or more items) at a distance from one another. I know very well what the word means, Mariposa. What I don't fucking know is why you want it."

"Ass," I said. "Do you know the definition of that one?"

"You're testing my patience."

Oooh, I wanted to say, but didn't. "You embarrassed me!" I shouted. "No one, not even *Bruno*, has ever made me feel that small." I started to pace in a circle, making circles with my wedding ring around my finger. "I'm no better than those people who serve you, and they're afraid to look at me now! They're behaving like I'm *someone*. When I'm not. I'm not—" I flung my arm out. "I'm not you. And that asshole Bruno? You basically told him what he did hurt me!"

"It did."

"So? He didn't know that! Not until tonight!"

"As your *capo*," he snapped at me, "I protect you. If anyone touches one of the girls at The Club, there are consequences."

I'm not one of your employees; I'm your wife! I wanted to shout. But a second later I realized how wrong that was to think, much less share. It was a lie. He was my *capo*. I even had it engraved on the ring around his finger to prove it.

He continued, not missing a beat. "Most people know better, but the ones who don't catch on quick enough. You're *my* wife. Your flesh, blood, and bone belong to me, and so do your feelings. Someone hurts you. They hurt me. *Capisci*? I hunt for you only. And always remember this, Mariposa. 'It is better to be feared than loved, if you cannot be both.' People *will* fear you. Why? They see me standing behind you. I don't cower. I don't fucking bend. I kneel for no mere man on this earth."

I looked away from him for a second. My eyes caught the tattoo on his hand. All that he had just said suddenly made sense—why he had gotten the permanent mark on his body. *I don't cower. I don't fucking bend. I kneel for no mere man on this earth.* That was my husband. All of him. He had never done anything to make me believe otherwise.

"They all know who you're married to now," I whispered. *A girl from the streets. A girl who has nothing to offer, only take.* No one knew about this arrangement, so from the outside, it looked one-sided.

"Mariposa," he said. "That's who I married. The girl who had a drink on the menu before she showed up at the door."

"You named the drink after me before we were married?"

"It was the first item on the menu. I didn't name any of the others."

"Why?"

"A reminder."

Again, I couldn't read the look on his face. He was still pissed off, but some of the ice had melted. When I couldn't hold his stare any longer, I turned from him, staring into the window of the sport's bar. My eyes narrowed on a strip of news playing at the bottom of a screen.

Breaking News.

A picture flashed on the screen.

Quillon Zamboni found dead.

Strangled.

In the end, he *couldn't breathe.*

Neither could I.

Capo's hand touched my shoulder, and I looked up at him. He removed my hand from my face. It was covering my mouth.

People will *fear you. Why? They see me standing behind you.*

My husband was the big bad wolf, snarling at anyone who came too close. *I hunt for you only.*

I swallowed hard, feeling like my throat was closing up, but the air around me moved, entering my lungs. "Capo." His name came out solid, though I felt anything but. "Do you know a guy named Merv?"

"Knew. Briefly." This time he looked away, at the screen, no expression on his face. "I should have told you. Vera II is actually Vera I. She was a welcome-home gift. Those plants. They seem to have roots made of steel."

I took a deep, deep breath, sighed it out, and then, with a trembling hand, slipped mine into his steady one.

14

New York had become a battleground I'd survived for too long. Every sound was a war cry. Every season gave reason to run and hide, some unknown element coming at me. Every smell was bloodied. Every sight was someone fighting to live.

Italy, *Italia*, was the promised land after the long and grueling fight.

Every sound was musical. One friend calling out to another, something in Italian that sounded heated but was actually friendly banter. Summer felt like a warm breeze in the evening against my skin. Every smell held the promise of some new food to try. Every sight was peaceful. People chatted and laughed in the piazza, eating gelato and enjoying life.

I had never felt so tired but so alive at the same time.

The flight from New York was long, and I'd barely slept during it, so I swayed on my feet, refusing to move. But I didn't refuse to move because of the tiredness.

I pulled at the straps of my backpack. "You didn't tell me I needed to dress for this."

Capo gave me an impatient look. "What you have on is fine."

I looked down at myself. A pretty blue sundress and a pair of leather sandals with crisscross straps. Seeing that I was having trouble knowing what to pack, Capo had helped me decide what to bring to Italy for our long stay. I loved everything in my suitcase, it seemed to fit the vibe here, but he didn't tell me we'd be taking some kind of motorcycle to his grandfather's place from the piazza.

"Why didn't you ask the car to wait? That guy has my luggage. How am I going to ride on *that* if I'm wearing *this*? I can't change now."

A car that looked like it could survive a bombing had brought us here from the private airport, and the driver took all of my things with him after he dropped us off.

Capo lifted his glasses and then sat them on his head. The bright light hit his eyes, and the blue seemed to explode like stained glass when the sun hits it. He was wearing a tight shirt that showed off all of his impressive muscles, a dark pair of jeans, and leather boots. The tattoo on his wrist looked even fiercer when he wasn't wearing a suit and his entire arm was on display. His old watch looked exactly like...an old watch. Even if it was an expensive one.

"Use all of the words, Mariposa. Are you afraid?"

"No, not exactly." I hesitated but only for a second. "I don't want to hurt my oonie."

"Your bag? It'll be fine."

"Not my bag, Capo. Who names a bag? My *oonie*."

His eyes narrowed. "You name shit all of the time. Vera. Journey. I figured your bag had a name, too. So if it's not your bag, what are you talking about? And why would it get hurt?"

I pointed down. "That's my oonie."

He followed my finger. "I'm not following."

"My vagina," I whispered.

His features relaxed, then went blank, before he exploded with laugher. "Oonie? Where did you hear that? Or is that something you named it?"

"No!" I was on the defensive. "Jocelyn. That's what she called it! She told me to be careful on bicycles, since they could hurt my oonie. After what happened with...Zamboni, I don't want to...maybe...mess up what still might be intact."

Zamboni had used his fingers on me, so I wasn't sure if he'd done anything to mess me up—my monthly came that night. If he hadn't, it was important to share that part of me with someone I trusted. It would mean a lot to me to know that he hadn't altered me physically. Because emotionally, he had caused some damage.

At the mention of Zamboni, all of the amusement faded from Capo's face. I didn't want to bring it up, but he had pushed, and I needed to be truthful about why I was hesitant to ride the bike.

Not wanting Zamboni to have the power to ruin our time —*my first trip to Italy!*; *to anywhere*—I decided to try and lighten the mood. I grinned. "Jocelyn used to watch me from the picture window when I was playing outside with the Ryans. Whenever I'd wear a dress, and she felt I was getting too 'loose' with it, she'd bang on the window and scream, 'Mari! Keep your dress down, or the entire neighborhood is going to see your oonie!' Then she'd bang some more. The entire neighborhood thought she was nuts."

"She was, but she was a good person."

"Jocelyn and Pops treated me like their own."

"I knew they would. Jocelyn had always wanted children, and Mr. Gianelli loved them. I knew you'd be safe there."

"Yeah." I blew out a breath, fanning a few small tendrils of hair that had come loose from my waterfall braids. I mumbled something about how much I missed them in Italian.

Capo watched me for a moment. "I think the reason you

remember so much Italian, recognizing the words, is because that's all your parents spoke to you. When I brought you to Jocelyn, she only spoke to you in English. They didn't want anyone to know that you spoke Italian."

I didn't know what to say to that, but thinking about the parents I'd never known made my heart feel heavy.

Capo seemed to pick up on it. "We're in Italy. Everything that belongs to New York stays in New York." He wrapped his arm around my waist, pulling me closer. "What do you say, *mia moglie*, are you ready to ride with me? I vow not to hurt your oonie." His grin was wide. "It's safe in my care. And neither will the entire neighborhood or village see it. Sit close to me so your dress doesn't fan out. We both know how I feel about sharing what's mine. I don't."

I laughed at how ridiculous *oonie* sounded coming from his mouth. But he was right. Italy was too perfect to waste on things that couldn't be changed. "You? Share?" I scoffed playfully. "Not in a million years."

"You didn't answer me, Butterfly."

"*Sì! Facciamolo!*" Yup! Let's do this!

Capo released me, swinging his leg over the seat. I sat behind him, sticking to him like glue, and he handed me a helmet once I was settled. He started the bike and I could feel it vibrating beneath my legs. I wrapped my arms around him, holding on tight.

He took me on a scenic ride around town for a while before we started to make our way to the outskirts. Every once in a while we'd stop at a light, but the further out we got, the less lights we stopped for. He picked up speed and I almost yelled for him to go faster.

I was totally free. Not a care in the world.

We rode for a while, following twisting and turning roads, huge mountains in the distance growing closer and closer, but finally we came to a driveway that seemed like it was three miles long. Hundreds of trees lined the pathway on both sides. Workers were out, picking fruit. Crates overflowed with lemons and blood oranges. Capo had told me that his family owned citrus groves.

Down the road a little was a gate, and beyond it, the land opened up, and a humongous villa sat in the center. It was tan with green shutters and a matching tile roof. Two other villas sat on either side of the main villa, but I wasn't sure if they were places where people lived or something else. Little pathways lined with greenery led from one place to another. The smell of chocolate was strong in the air.

Before we stopped, people started to spill out of the main villa. *A hell of a lot of people.*

"Oh shit," I muttered.

I thought I heard Capo chuckle but wasn't sure. My heart started beating fast, and my stomach plummeted. It had never crossed my mind that his family could be big. Judging by the number of people flowing out of the door, they needed all three places for them to sleep in.

The wedding planner never mentioned how many guests were going to attend. She just said that whatever I wanted, Mr. Macchiavello said to give it to me, and she would accommodate. It hadn't occurred to me that I'd have to impress *all* of these people with what I'd planned.

As soon as Capo turned the bike off, they rushed us. I wasn't sure who I hugged, who kissed me on each cheek, and who held me at arm's length, speaking in such rapid Italian that I couldn't keep up.

Finally, Capo took pity on me and pulled me to his side, taking control of the situation. I was too busy trying to take mental notes, but I think they'd done the same thing to him. When he was able to fight his way out, he latched on to me and started introducing me to everyone.

I'd need another journal to keep track. His mother's sisters

—Stella, Eloisa, Candelora, and Veronica—stood out, since he had brought them up at the restaurant. Capo's mother's name was Noemi. I heard Stella tell him that she'd be proud. Then she looked at me.

All of his uncles, cousins...I'd do my best not to mix names up or get them wrong. I noticed that everyone called Capo *Amadeo*. I wondered why? And then I wondered why he hadn't given me the choice to call him that. It was either Mac or *boss* or Capo, but no Amadeo.

The sea of people parted all of a sudden. A hush fell over the crowd. Then an older man came up the line, Candelora helping him. He wore a wide-brimmed hat and an old-time suit with suspenders. Even though he struggled, he kept his head up. The undertone of his skin was olive, but the surface was pale, which made him seem sickly. His brown eyes were alive, though, even if the shadows underneath were dark. When he smiled, his silver handlebar mustache twitched.

Capo met his grandfather before he made it to us. The old man slapped at his cheeks and said something too low for me to hear. Capo turned to me and said something back. When the old man finally made it to me, he knocked on the helmet still on my head and I exploded with laughter. I had forgotten to take the damn thing off.

"Let me see you." He smiled. "Let me see the woman who has chosen to take my grandson as her husband. Let me see if *she* has a hard enough head to deal with him."

I took the helmet off, setting it back on the bike, and then turned to face him again.

"Ah! *Bellisima*." He took both of my hands, squeezing, while he leaned in and kissed both of my cheeks. "I am Pasquale Ranieri. You can call me *Nonno*, if you would like."

"This is Mariposa," Capo said, trying to keep up with *Nonno*. His grandfather hadn't given him the chance to introduce me. "My wife."

"Not yet!" Pasquale chuckled. "Did Amadeo tell you that I made him wait until June before he could get married?"

I looked at Capo and then at Pasquale. I shook my head. "No."

Nonno made a dismissive motion with his hand at Capo. "You will be married on the date that I was married. I refused to attend my grandson's wedding unless he agreed to this. I also refuse to die before then, but this is between me and—" He lifted his face toward the sky.

"I'm sure it'll be very special," I whispered, squeezing his hand. It was cold, even in the heat, and nothing but skin and bone, but I liked the way it felt in mine. I liked him. Immediately. He put me at ease.

"Mariposa," he repeated my name slowly. He watched me for a minute before he smiled again. "Such a beautiful little butterfly."

15

CAPO

She fit in.

It had been a week since we arrived in Modica, Sicily, and the changes in my wife were subtle to others but so pronounced to me.

Instead of questioning her decisions like she had before we left, there was a quiet confidence about her that made her take charge—no more was it "yours." It was "ours."

Her laughter was even louder, even freer, than it had been with me. My grandfather ate it up. She made him laugh more than anyone ever did. Except for my mother.

My *zie* (aunts) had fallen in love with her. They taught her how to cook. They even gave her the secret recipe to the Modica chocolate they were famous for. *Cioccolato di Modica.* It was a recipe from the 1500s brought to Sicily by the Spaniards, a direct descendent to the Aztec tradition.

My wife would come to me with a huge smile on her face, brown smears all over her skin and clothes. She was as happy as a child who got to play in mud all day. She'd smell of it, too, the chocolate I loved so much. It reminded me of my mother.

And it brought me joy to think that she would've spoiled Mariposa the same way the *zie* were.

They were spoiling her with their time and attention. They were treating her as family. *Zia* Veronica even went after her with a wooden spoon when she tried adding rosemary to her pot of whatever.

One day while I watched Mariposa make a mess with the chocolate, smiling at nothing and everything, I overheard *Zia* Candelora tell her, "*Your parents should have named you after me. You glow like you have eaten an internal flame and your skin is made of wax!*"

Zia Candelora was known for her hyperbole, but she wasn't off her mark. Mariposa was glowing. Her smile was so bright that the gold flecks in her eyes seemed unreal. She was moving in the right direction. While she was, she also had a chance to rest, to truly find peace.

Mariposa slept like the devil was no longer on her heels because she had an angel at her back. I knew how that felt. I once had an angel, too.

At the hottest time of the day, she'd take one of her books, or the reading device, and find her favorite place to be—the hammock between two chestnut trees—and read. She always wore a big floppy hat, and before getting comfortable, she'd kick her sandals to the side. After an hour had gone by, she'd fall asleep with the book against her chest. In New York, she slept, but it was broken, like she couldn't afford to sleep for more than an hour at a time.

In the evenings, she'd rush back to the villa and come out with my grandfather, the man she called *Nonno*, on her arm. They'd usually go to his private garden since he couldn't walk that far. She'd keep the floppy hat on while she got to work. He directed her. He told her to move this plant to another spot, or pick the fruits of that one, or whatever he felt needed to be done. I could hear them laughing together. Every day she'd tell him a new joke.

"Wanna hear a peppery joke?" I heard her say, when she didn't think anyone else was around. She gave him a few seconds before she said, "Sometimes I'll order a pizza without toppings. When I'm feeling *saucy*."

His laughter rivaled hers.

After the garden was tended to, she'd take a seat next to him, wrap her arm around his, and then rest her head on his shoulder. He'd tell her stories, or read to her, or recite poetry. Some days he'd do all three. My grandfather was a world-renowned poet and novelist. He'd won the Nobel Prize in Literature in the 1970s. His poetry was known for being lyrical and full of passion.

Mariposa's wild laughter enchanted him, and he had somehow made her fall madly in love with him.

I rarely spent time with my wife since we'd arrived. Everyone wanted a piece of her. Once in a while I'd take her for rides on the motorcycle, or for a walk in the groves, but I gave her the time to get comfortable, to make my family her family. But even when she didn't think I was around, I was, and I took the time to see her. To see the person that she had always had the potential to become—the child I'd given my life for, and the woman who was now my wife.

Two shadows stretched along the walk. A few seconds later, my uncle and aunt appeared. Tito and Lola. Tito was my grandfather's first cousin, even though everyone called him uncle. Lola was Marzio Fausti's sister. Marzio was one of the most powerful and ruthless leaders the Faustis had ever seen. Tito was a doctor, one of the best, and he saw to them personally. He saw to me personally, too. He'd been the angel at my back. And besides my grandfather, he was the only honorable male figure in my world.

Tito had met Mariposa the night she snuck into The Club

as Sierra. When she'd given him Sierra's name, he knew she was lying. After Mariposa had left, he advised me not to choose her as a bride, especially with what I had planned. She was different and didn't belong in this life.

I disagreed. Her loyalty had the potential to become ruthless if someone meant me harm. She was exactly the type of queen a powerful king needed at his side.

As Mariposa rose to meet them, I could tell she recognized Tito. Her cheeks flushed a little when my grandfather introduced her as Mariposa, not Sierra. Tito made a joke and she relaxed, laughing. Lola pulled her close, and I winced in sympathy. Her happiness came out in either a crush or a pinch. At least I knew she liked Mariposa. Lola only crushed or pinched the people she was fond of.

"Amadeo!" a soft voice called. "Amadeo!" When our eyes met, Gigi ran toward me, crashing against my chest when she was close enough.

After she was finished hugging me, she messed up my hair. "It is not fair how handsome you are, Amadeo. A beautiful devil." She grinned. "I know ten of the most famous faces in Hollywood that would kill to be *you*."

"I'm glad you could make it," I said. Georgina, or Gigi as everyone called her, was a famous actress in Italy, and since I lived in America, I didn't get to see her that often. "I heard you were somewhere in the French Riviera living it up with some rich prince on his yacht."

"Yesterday." She waved a hand. "Today, I am here for you. I had to see this monumental occasion for myself. Amadeo married. What do the Americans say? Hell might freeze under." She punched me lightly on the arm, and we both smiled. "So, where is she? This woman who has tamed your wild heart."

"In the garden with grandfather," I said in Italian. "They sit and talk every evening."

We both turned to look in that direction.

Mariposa stood, a hand shielding her eyes, trying to see us better. I suppressed my grin. She had no idea that I'd been watching her, but when Gigi was loud enough to attract attention, she must've noticed the two of us. She didn't seem to like it.

"Amadeo," Gigi said, and it seemed like she had called my name before.

"Ah?"

She smiled, but it didn't touch her eyes. "She is pretty, but not what I expected."

"No?" I spoke in Italian. "Who did you expect?"

"Someone like me."

Gigi was considered one of the most beautiful women in the world. I was never one to be swayed, though, by the popular vote. In my eyes, the woman standing across from me, full of dirt from the garden, was the most beautiful woman in the world. She had something that I'd never seen in anyone else. *Or felt from anyone else.* Maybe attraction had the same rules as pheromone phenomena. Whatever attracted me to Mariposa was mine alone—therefore, what a fucking rare treasure.

Zia Stella and *Zia* Eloisa stepped into the garden. They wanted Mariposa to shower and get ready for a dinner they'd planned with all of the women. All of the men were going to play baseball. Mariposa wouldn't move. She refused to stop staring at us.

Gigi groaned. "I will catch up with you later." She quickly kissed my cheek and then hustled in the opposite direction. Lola had started to make her way toward us.

This time my grin came slow and satisfied. After Gigi had gone, Mariposa allowed my aunts to cart her off.

"There you are!" Lola said when she reached me, pinching my cheeks. "How are you, *bell'uomo*?"

"I'm fine, *Zia*, and you?"

She smiled. "I love her, Amadeo! She will make a wonderful

wife. She seems like a wonderful girl." She hesitated for a second, then opened her mouth but quickly closed it. "Your grandfather and uncle would like a word with you," she said in Italian, nodding toward the garden. "I'm going to find Gigi. I need celebrity gossip!"

Before I could reach them, one of the guards stopped me. He spoke in Italian. "A man has come to the gate. He claims he is looking for the place where the women make the chocolate. He was told that he could find some here."

My aunts had shops all over Italy, and the one in Modica was extremely busy, especially during tourist season. Once they sold out, they sold out. You'd have to come back the next day, but no one would direct them here. The chocolate operation was a family business, and our secrets were our own, including where we lived.

Over the years, a couple of men had done the same thing, except their excuses for stopping had varied. This was the first time any of them had claimed the workers at the shop had given them this address. They were getting low on lies.

It wouldn't have surprised me if the king wolf himself had showed up. He felt the devil on his heels lately. And with Armino missing, Achille was adding to the flames.

"Bring him to one of the villas deep into the property," I said in Italian, nodding behind the main villa. "Wait with him and do not let him leave. Do not tell him he has come to the wrong place, either. Do not tell him anything but that he must wait."

"*Sì.*" He readjusted the gun hanging from his shoulder and dug in his pocket for a pack of cigarettes. He lit one up and said, "I will inform the others."

The scent of smoke lingered even after he'd gone.

TITO WAS TALKING to *Nonno* about new treatments for cancer when I walked up. He was listening but shaking his head. I could've told Tito to save his breath, but he never did. I had tried to talk my grandfather into more treatments, but *Nonno* refused to even entertain the idea. He said he was old enough, had lived enough, and when his time came, he wanted to be at home, in the comfort of his own bed. It was time for him to see my grandmother and my mother again. A life full of living had given him the grace to accept death.

Their conversation slowed when I pulled up a seat in front of the bench, but Tito didn't stop talking until he felt he was done. After, silence filled the space between us until my grandfather knocked his cane against the ground. His eyes were heavy. He was tired.

"You wanted to see me," I said.

Tito looked at me from underneath his explorer hat and crossed his skinny legs. "Mariposa looks different, Amadeo."

"She does," I said. "She's flourishing."

My grandfather leaned against his cane and then cleared his throat. "You did not tell me," he said in Italian, "that Mariposa was the child you traded your life for."

My eyes locked with his. "She told you."

"I told her a story, a story of a man who traded his life for a woman he hardly knew, the greatest sacrifice known to man. She told me she knew a man who was as honorable as that. When I asked her who was this great man, she told me *you*. I am dying, but I have not lost my mind yet."

The old man was sly. He had taken her comment and connected it. He probably asked her how old she was and did the math. Then he had tricked me into admitting it. The only way he knew that I would.

He slammed the cane down again, looking away from me. "Tell me, grandson, will you give her the life she deserves?" He met my eyes again. "You saved her life by sacrificing your soul.

What will your sacrifice mean if she ends up hiding in a closet while the only man she loves is killed because he is a reckless fool?"

"*Amore*?" I laughed, but both men narrowed their eyes at me. I continued in Italian. "Loyalty. That's what we share. That's our foundation."

"What of love? Now or in the future."

"Love makes us foolish."

"Says the man who has never opened himself up to it," Tito muttered.

I narrowed my eyes at him. He narrowed back.

"Perhaps love does," my grandfather said. "But what would you know about it, Amadeo? How can you speak on such things when you have no idea what you're speaking about? Or do you? Prove me wrong." He eyed me hard for a minute, and when no answer came, he grunted. "Perhaps to men who have loved, *you* are the fool." He tapped his cane once, twice, three times against the ground. "Remember, Amadeo. Fools will go where even angels dare not to tread."

"Once more," I said to my grandfather. "Tap once more."

He did without asking me why. Then he cleared his throat. "Mariposa reminds me of my Noemi in so many ways."

I looked away this time, knowing where he was going with this. If he were anyone else, I would've walked away, but I owed him more respect than that. These were his last days, and if speaking of things I'd rather not gave him peace, I'd listen. I'd sacrifice for him as he had sacrificed for me.

"In a way, Mariposa is childlike, and in another, a woman. It is a delicate balance to be enough of both without taking away from the other. Being too much of one eliminates the other completely. Mariposa has mastered the balance. Your mother was the same. I knew when she married your father that he would not nurture the child; he would kill it. He wanted a cold-hearted woman. The life he chose to live demanded it. I grieved for the child in my child even before she was murdered. Arturo murdered that vital part of her before her soul left this world. When a woman has both sides, if one dies, the other follows. Because the two together make a whole, you understand."

Left this world. Left me. By her own hand. By her own choice. My mamma committed suicide. My love wasn't enough to keep her here.

"I will not waste the time I have left speaking in riddles," he barreled on. "I am going to tell you what I think."

He always did.

He went to continue, but numerous cars pulled up the drive, and the guests for the dinner in Mariposa's honor spilled out. The men were ready to play baseball, including Rocco and his brothers. My grandfather wouldn't speak of personal things in front of them. It wasn't that he didn't care for the Faustis—he considered them *famiglia*—but he never condoned their lifestyle.

My grandfather and Marzio had been friends before a bullet had accidentally killed Marzio. Ettore, one of Marzio's sons, had held the gun, and the bullet had been meant for Luca's oldest son, and Marzio's grandson, Brando. The bullet had hit Marzio instead. But Marzio had enjoyed spending time with my grandfather. They would argue over just about everything, but they respected each other enough to be friends at the end of it. Marzio was a poet at heart, and that was the only thing they were square on.

Poetry was a love language.

Violence being the key to reaching peace was not something Pasquale Ranieri believed in, though. My grandfather was a firm believer that, if you live by the sword, you will die by it. Marzio believed that everyone was going to die anyway, and no matter how you went, death was death. Peaceful or not.

My grandfather didn't support my lifestyle. I made no secret of my plans. Or who I was. He loved me despite it, but he never kept his feelings quiet on the matter. He felt it was his duty as my grandfather to try and steer me in a direction he felt was the right one. He had lost his daughter to a violent end, one he believed was her husband's fault. My grandfather had tried to stop my mother from marrying Arturo, but she was hardheaded, thinking her love could save him from himself.

In the end, she couldn't save herself from his violent nature. He didn't want a wife to lead the pack with him. He wanted a pretty toy he could use until he didn't need her anymore. A beautiful Italian-speaking girl from the old country had impressed his *capo* at the time. Then, after he had used my mother to put the *capo* at ease, Arturo slit his throat and took over the family. He'd been standing on that bloody ground ever since.

My grandfather looked away when Rocco, his brothers, and a few of the higher-ranking men entered the garden. They were all ready to play ball. I looked at my grandfather, but I knew he'd wait for them to leave before he spoke again.

Tito sat up, narrowing his eyes at us. He fixed his glasses. "Baseball is a game. It is supposed to be competitive but fun. If I see a man getting too rough—" he lifted his pointer finger "—off with your HEAD!" He made a slicing motion with the raised finger. "The doctor is off today!" He had a habit of elongating his r's when he was mad.

Every man around him grinned, except for my grandfather.

Rocco pulled up a chair next to mine. "We must speak before the game."

"The man at the gate," I said. "Arturo sent him."

"*Sì.* New York is a war zone. I have had five families come to me about the problems they are facing."

"Five." I grinned. "The great Arturo *Lupo* Scarpone has finally come to you for help."

"Help," he said, "or information. He thinks he is smarter

than me. He asks questions with the intent to hide their true meaning. He asked permission to speak to Lothario."

Lothario was one of Rocco's uncles. Marzio had five sons, and Luca was the oldest. Some people called him a nightmare. He was even more ruthless than his father, but something had happened, and he ended up in jail in Louisiana. Some say it had to do with a woman, Brando's mother, but the Faustis kept a tight lid on things they wanted to stay sealed.

Ettore was the son who was set to rule after Marzio had passed, but since he accidentally shot his father trying to kill Brando, Lothario took over the family. He wasn't his father, and he was nowhere near the formidable shadow Luca casted, but so far, he was honorable enough to keep the deals his father had made before his death with me. All of the Faustis lived and died by a code. Their word was as good as their blood. *La mia parola è buona quanto il mio sangue.*

In order to speak to Lothario, you had to go through channels. Arturo went through Rocco to try and reach him.

Would Arturo demand they tell him if his son was still alive? Marzio had given me permission to use whatever means necessary to have my vengeance. I was still, technically, under his protection.

So I wasn't surprised when Rocco said, "Lothario denied his request, but I do not want him involved. As you know, the Faustis are at war from within." He set his glove on his lap. "Calling Lothario closer will do no good for anyone. He has his own agenda, and in time, he'll be dealt with, but for now, we must keep this between us."

I nodded. I'd rather keep him out of it, too. Rumor had it that he wasn't as honorable as the rest of his family.

Rocco flipped his baseball glove over. "Arturo is speaking to all of the families in New York. Even though they are at war, he is trying to convince them that he isn't the cause of the war. He is convincing them that an outsider is at work. Be prepared.

Now that the smoke has cleared some, their eyes are open, and some may be directed at you."

I smiled. "All eyes on me." Let the games fucking begin. It was getting boring playing a five-person game with only one player. When they didn't know a game was being played, they couldn't cheat, but that was about to change.

Rocco and I stood. He held out his hand and pulled me in, slapping me on the back. "No more talk of business," he said. "It is time to play ball!"

"Eeeuuuu!" His brother, Romeo, yelled, and then all of the men started for the field.

Rocco waited for me.

"I'll meet you," I said.

He looked at my grandfather and then nodded. Tito walked with Rocco toward the field.

I took a seat next to my grandfather. He gazed into the distance. "What are you looking at?"

"I am not looking, Amadeo, I am thinking."

"That's right," I said, hiding my grin. "You were going to tell me what you thought."

He turned to me and raised his hand, like he was going to slap me. I moved away, bracing myself for it. No matter how old I was, he was my grandfather, and he'd bust my ass if he thought I was making a joke out of something he considered serious.

After a second, with his hand still raised, he smiled at me. Then his hand came down on my head and he moved it back and forth, growling at me. "You make me furious!" Then he pulled me in roughly and kissed my head. "I will miss you the most, Amadeo, after I am gone."

His sickness was a snake around my heart, and it made it hard to breathe when I thought about him leaving me. He had always challenged me to see things differently. He was the only one who had the balls to.

I looked down at the ground. "*Non voglio parlare di questo.*" *I don't want to talk about this.*

"We must talk about things we find difficult," he said in Italian. "Or we will never conquer them."

We became quiet for a while. I couldn't look at him, so I continued to stare at the ground, my head empty of thoughts. My grandfather looked at nothing again, but I could tell his head was full of them.

"When Tito told me what happened to you," he continued in Italian, "that day was the first day I had spoken to God since your mother died. I hated God. I did not understand why a faithful woman, such as your grandmother, had to suffer such a loss when all she did was pray. Pray for the protection of her children.

"Why hadn't He protected my child? Why hadn't He sent her home to us when she needed us the most? The anger consumed me. We are what we love, Amadeo. I loved to hate. It was easier than feeling that I had somehow been forgotten by a God that *I* hadn't forgotten."

A few of my cousins walked along the path, talking, and he became quiet. Seeing this, they waved but didn't stop. A minute or two after the group was far enough that they couldn't overhear, my grandfather twisted his cane against the ground, continuing his train of thought.

"The first time I saw you, I saw so much of your mother in you, and I felt you were my own. Arturo called you the prince, but you were always my boy. My Amadeo. *My own*, and Tito could not tell me if you would live or die. Again, I found myself in a position to lose it all. When we love, we are at the mercy of life and death. Love sets us in a position to lose it all. A chance —*there is a chance he will make it*—can make or break our soul.

"The miraculous thing is, even if we lose it all, we somehow build it up again. That tiny part of us, the ember of whatever is left in us, becomes our all until we add to it. I stood to lose the little I had when Tito called and told me of your condition. It would have destroyed me. I couldn't survive it." He sighed. "I drove to the church and stepped in front of the cross, willing to bargain. I said, *'If You will save him, I will give You myself in his place. There are worse things than death that can take a man. I don't want the worse again. I want my grandson to live. I want him to touch love and experience the good in life. Let him experience the indescribable feeling of falling in love, of loving enough to die for the woman worth his sacrifice. Let him experience the indescribable joy of becoming a father. Let him fall in love with his life! Let him live with love in his heart and not vengeance in the deepest part of his soul.'"*

I looked at him from the side of my eye. He had battled cancer on and off for years, after I had come to live with him.

"*Sì.* I found out soon enough that He took me at my word. You were saved, but I would face death. Even so, I hadn't lost it all again. I still had part of my Noemi to keep here. She lives through you." He leaned on his cane some, twisting it a bit. "After you came to us, I was told that you had saved a child. You had given your life so that she could live. My sacrifice was rewarded. It was not done in vain. And neither was yours.

"I hoped the fact that she lived would be enough to keep you content. But I saw. I saw how hate ate at your insides like acid. I went to Marzio and asked him to help you, even though I did not agree with his idea of a means to an end. It is not in my blood to be such a man, or to understand him. Sometimes I do not understand you, my own blood, but I can understand hate. I hated once myself, to the point that it ate *me* like acid. The difference between us is that I take to my pen while you take to your sword.

"Marzio denied me. He said that you were a grown man, and if you needed his ear, he would listen. We know that he did, and after, even though death stood with you, I could see life in you again. It gave me hope." He set his hand on the back of my head, shaking me some.

"So I will tell you what I think now, Amadeo. I think that you fell for that little girl's innocence because she reminded you of your mother, in better times. That is why you saved Mariposa's life, sacrificing your own. You know what true sacrifice is, and what is worth your soul now. Do not sacrifice the second chance you've been given for something that will mean nothing tomorrow. Do not shield yourself from love when the man sitting next to you loves you enough to give his life for yours. Allow love to consume you, Amadeo, because we become what we consume. What will you become if you continue to consume vengeance? What will it do to the butterfly you gave your life for? Your sacrifice will be in vain. Yours and mine. It will be worth nothing if you cannot feel anything but hate. That is what I *know*."

16

CAPO

We had planned a dinner with our immediate family the night before the wedding. Torches made the night air smoky, light music played, and people sat at a table built for a hundred, eating and laughing.

The evening was so busy that I hadn't had much alone time with Mariposa, but she was never far from my view. She was speaking to Keely and her family. Right after Mariposa said something to Keely's father, Keely's mother said something to Mariposa. Mariposa's face fell, she nodded, said something else, and then walked away with her head down.

It rubbed me the wrong fucking way. I'd make sure to find out what it was about and deal with it.

A minute later, Mariposa took a seat next to me. She kept fidgeting with the napkin on the table.

"Tell me what's wrong," I said.

"Nothing."

Standing, I gave her my hand and told her we were going to take a walk in the groves alone. Keely flew past us, her neck red, and I turned to look at her family before I turned back to Mariposa and urged her to move.

The groves were lit up, lighting our way as we walked. The men who worked the fields had helped me string up countless solar lights in the trees for the special occasions.

Mariposa was quiet until she wasn't. "A walk in the groves, huh?"

"I haven't had a chance to talk to you in private."

She nudged me with her arm. "Getting cold feet?"

"My mind rules my feet, and my mind is set." I glanced at her dress. She looked like a Roman goddess. The color was light blue, the material almost sheer, and it draped over her arms. When the wind blew, the dress fluttered like wings. The hem swept the ground as we walked, and I noticed she didn't hold it up. "Your favorite color. Blue. It looks beautiful on you."

She looked at me, right in the eye, and I had to catch her before she fell over a crate left on the ground. She exploded with laughter. "Too much wine."

She hadn't had a drop to drink.

"Is that what the kids are calling fun these days?"

"Are you accusing me of lying, Capo?"

"Depends. If that's what the kids are calling it." I shrugged. "You're telling the truth. If not, your pretty nose is going to grow like Pinocchio's."

"Ooh!" She laughed even harder. "Who's lying now? *Pretty nose.*"

"You're beautiful," I said. "The most beautiful woman to me."

She wiped something from my face. "Are you sure about that?" She showed me her hand. It had a smudge of red lipstick on it.

Gigi. She had kissed me on the cheek earlier. Mariposa noticed it. I even caught her mocking Gigi. She'd pretend to laugh like her and then shake her tits. Gigi hadn't noticed, but I did. Mariposa hadn't even met her yet. They never seemed to be in the same place at the same time. And when Gigi would appear, she'd talk to me when Mariposa wasn't beside me.

"I don't say things for the fun of it, Mariposa."

I almost laughed at the sour face she made in response, but I didn't. I didn't want to fight the night before our formal wedding. There was nothing to fight about.

We became quiet after that. She had her thoughts and I had mine.

Then she inhaled, bringing me from mine. "I love the smell here. It reminds me of the new perfume." She lifted her arm and I inhaled the scent on her skin. It was from the same designer who made her other one, but this one was different. It had notes of orange flower and the sea. Both perfumes seemed made for her, but the new one even more perfect.

I kissed her pulse and then held her hand. "This way." I led her deeper into the groves, wanting to go as deep as possible, as far away from people as we could get.

"Capo," she whispered, not looking at me. "That was a nice thing you did for me tonight. Switching my dinner."

Before she had the steak at Macchiavello's, she had told the planner to serve it for dinner that night. After she ate there, she had fallen in love with the pasta and crab dish. I had the planner switch her order at the last minute, after I'd found out that she'd ordered the steak before she knew what the pasta tasted like. She wanted to thank me for it, but we had a deal and it wasn't necessary. We both did for each other.

I nodded. "You've been great with my grandfather. He really enjoys spending time with you."

She stiffened. "My arrangement is with you," she said, keeping her face straight. "Not with anyone else. I enjoy spending time with him. Because *I* want to."

I hadn't meant to offend her, but I did.

"Tell me, Mariposa, if you were to ever fall in love, would love cancel out your kindness law?"

"Law?" She almost scoffed, but she took a moment to answer. "I'm not sure. I'd need time to think about it."

Or feel it.

I sighed, pointing to two overturned crates. "Here we are." I motioned for her to take a seat and I took the one next to her.

The silence was welcome after being surrounded by family since we arrived. When I had come to live here, sometimes I'd walk the groves to be alone. I'd sit on a crate and clear my mind from all thoughts. After, I did my best scheming.

"Is something wrong, Capo?"

I realized she'd been talking. She was looking at me, waiting for me to reply.

"No. It's peaceful here. I'm content."

"Okay," she whispered. She looked down at her hands, and I set mine over hers, making her look at me again.

"I didn't want to do this in front of everyone. I wanted to give you this in private." I dug in my pocket and pulled out a rosary made from real pearls. The spacers were made with sapphires. The cross was gold. I opened her palm and set it in the center, closing her hand around it. "That was your mother's. I thought you'd like to have it. You can carry it tomorrow, if you want. Something old."

"My mother's." Her voice was soft as she opened her palm, as though I had given her an invaluable treasure. "Where did you get it?" Her fingers gently caressed the beads, maybe trying to find a connection, trying to remember something. When she came across a blood spot, she tried to wipe it clean but it was stained for good.

"You," I said. "Your mom prayed with you every night before bed. You'd recite the rosary with her in Italian. The night I took you with me, it was near your coloring books, and you handed it to me."

"You kept it."

"Close," I said.

After a few minutes, she placed the rosary down on her legs, putting a hand behind her back. She lifted a small box toward me. "When you told me we were taking a walk, I decided to give you what I had, too. If not, I would've had to send it with someone tomorrow. Tonight feels right."

I grinned at the fact that she had tucked the box in the soft wraps of her dress without me noticing. This small girl could've brought a knife and stabbed me in the back with it and I wouldn't have had a clue until it stuck in my flesh. I realized in that moment how much I trusted her. It might have been foolish, but since I was running a race on uncharacteristic decisions when it came to Mariposa, why not add one more to the list?

The grin slipped from my face when I opened her gift.

"Your family jeweler probably hates me because I didn't think of it until we got here, and he had to rush the order again. I thought...I thought you'd like to carry a piece of your mom on...our wedding day. This felt like a clever way to do it. You have so many of them at home."

She had given me cufflinks, cufflinks that had a picture of my mother on each one.

"Mariposa—" I started but couldn't finish.

"Remember our deal," she whispered. "I do for you. You do for me. You do for me. I do for you. We're even."

Far from it, but I didn't respond.

"She's so beautiful," she said, looking over at the cufflinks. "You look a lot like her, just a manly version."

I grinned. "My grandfather," I said. "She looked like him, just more feminine. She had his features, but the blue eyes are from my grandmother's side. So technically I look like him when he was younger."

"Either way," she said. "I've never seen a more beautiful woman."

I thought so too, until I looked at you, I went to say, but then stopped myself. I cleared my throat, closed the box, and then stood. I gave her my hand. "Time to go, Butterfly. We have a long day tomorrow."

"Stop fidgeting." I repeated the words like a mantra. Over and over and over. The words were almost a chant underneath my breath. I peeked inside of the church for the tenth time. It was filled to capacity. All of the voices were at low volume, but it almost sounded like the hum of bees, and it made goosebumps rise on my arms.

I took a step back. "*Agitarsi. Stop* fidgeting, Mari." I couldn't shake my nerves today. They clung to me. The New York wedding seemed simple, over and done, final in minutes, but this one? This one had meaning.

Nonno sat at the front of the church, talking to friends and family, and the day was doing him good. He looked...healthy. He kept smiling, laughing, and he waved everyone off when they went to help him. He wasn't just surviving; he was living. It gave me hope for the future. If he could keep having days like this one, maybe they could do something to help him.

Happiness was the best medicine, right?

Therefore, the day needed to be perfect for him. I wanted to walk down the aisle with my head held high, my strides perfect, and a wide smile on my face. But I kept having visions of exploding laughter shooting out of my mouth, or tripping over my own two feet, or my veil. All *seven* feet of it.

I looked down at my gown. My hands were splayed against my waist to try to stop the fidgeting, and they were trembling.

The dress. I sighed. I was in love with it. It was form-fitting with long sleeves, a low-cut back, and a train that flared out, but not too much. But what I loved most about it was what the designer called "geometric patterns" that ran through the soft fabric.

I had told her that I wanted something inspired by the butterfly, but nothing too frou-frou. Like my engagement ring, I wanted something artsy, a subtle nod to the name he had given me. *Mariposa.* But the dress shouldn't make the connection too obvious. It was something between us that we could share, like a private joke that no one else would get.

When I stepped into the evening light, candles burning all around me, the details of the dress came alive. The sheer detailing on the train and the deep geometric patterns gave the impression of a white butterfly when it stretches its wings during sunset. All of the lines across its wings, the ones that made it look like it was made of silk, were on display.

Mariposa. The way he said my name, his voice deep and throaty, made me shiver just thinking about it. I had connected the rasp in his voice to the scar around his throat. Sometimes he drank water to try and ease the strain.

Thinking about the sound of his voice made me even more nervous. "You're *so* going to trip, Mari." I had almost bit it the night before when he had looked at me and the lights in the trees made the color of his eyes do this...hypnotic, shimmering thing. Like when the moon touches the dark ocean and paints the surface silver.

"You're going to be fine, *bella*," a soft voice said, and I almost collapsed in relief.

Scarlett. She and the other women from girl's night had become family to me. They were with me all day, normalizing the moments but also making them special. They treated me like family, as one of their own. Right before we left for the church, I'd showed her my mother's rosary, not sure where to put it but wanting to carry it with me.

She took it from me, along with my bouquet, and told me she'd give it back to me before the ceremony.

"I hope you like it." She held out the hundreds of orange blossoms for me to see. She had wrapped the rosary around the bottom, around the white silk that held the flowers together, and the cross dangled in the front.

"It's..." I couldn't even find the words.

She smiled at me. "You don't have to say anything. We're family, and that's what we do. We're here for each other through thick and thin."

I looked up at her and we both smiled.

Scarlett reached out and grabbed my hand. She held it tight. "I wanted to tell you this the day I met you at Home Run, but I didn't really know you then. Now that I do..." She sighed. "It's hard to imagine a night that we wish would never end, especially when all we know are nightmares, but trust me, some nights are worth wishing they could go on forever. Amadeo—"

"Mari."

At the sound of the voice, Scarlett and I turned to look.

Keely slipped through the doors separating us from the church. She looked between us. "I'll wait—"

"No." Scarlett squeezed my hand again. "I was just going back." She hugged me and whispered in my ear, "This. *This* was meant to be." Then she left us.

Keely watched Scarlett shut the door before she said, "I can't help but think about gangs when I see them—the Faustis and their wives. The dynamics. They take people in who have no one and treat them like family. Make them feel accepted because there was no one there to accept them before."

I squeezed the bouquet, my nerves getting even worse. "Is that what you came to talk to me about right before my wedding? Scarlett's different. She's a good person. And so is Capo's family. It's okay that I have more people to add to my family now. You're still my family, Kee."

She waved a hand. "I know. Maybe I'm a little jealous."

"You don't have to be. I'll always be your sister. Scarlett and the other girls, they're cousins."

Keely turned to me and looked me over from head to toe. She smiled, her eyes getting watery. "Mari, I know I told you this already, but you look...so beautiful. Really. And you smell so good, too."

I smiled. "It's all of the orange blossoms."

"You're just like a butterfly, always attracted to the sweet." Then she looked away from me. "I know I should wait to tell you this, but I want to tell you now. I'm sorry, Mari. I'm so sorry for the way Mam treated you."

I blew out a trembling breath, trying to keep it together. Keely meant well, but I didn't want to talk about what her Mam did. Since I had no father to walk me down the aisle, I stupidly asked Keely's dad if he would at our rehearsal dinner. His face lit up, and he was about to answer when Catriona had spoken up.

"Nay," she had said. "It's nice of you to ask, but he can't accept. He only has but the one daughter, and he needs to walk her first. It would take away from Keely."

I wasn't sure why it had hurt me as much as it did. Maybe because I'd always considered them my family, and I thought it would be nice to have someone familiar walk me down the aisle. Someone who had known me as a child.

All I could do was nod, more like bob my head uncontrollably, before I left and buried my hurt feelings. I refused to let Capo see it. After what he had basically admitted to doing to Merv, I was afraid to let him see how emotional Catriona had made me in fear of what he'd to do to her or her family.

Asking Harrison was out of the question, too, considering how he felt about me. It would've been a raunchy thing to do.

It didn't matter. I didn't even want to think of it again.

"Keely," I said. "Don't apologize for something you didn't do. And I understand why she feels that way."

"Not entirely, but still. It's not right. You have to know that *I* would never feel that way."

"I do." I stood taller and kissed her cheek. "Now go take your seat. I think we're about to start."

Stop fidgeting. Stop fidgeting. Stop fidgeting. Stop fidgeting.

After Keely had gone, it was all I could do. I kept fidgeting with the cross in front of the bouquet.

Uncle Tito came out of the doors, and when he saw me, he stopped. He placed a hand over his heart and mimicked the beating. Fast. I had fallen in love with him just as much as I had fallen in love with *Nonno*.

After Capo and I had returned from our walk in the groves, he said he had business to attend to and that I should get a good night's sleep. I couldn't. So I sat around with the family and enjoyed another hour or so with them.

Before I got up to leave, Uncle Tito had taken a seat next to me. He took my hand, held it close to his heart, and asked if I would give him the honor of allowing him to walk me down the aisle.

My mouth had fallen open.

How had he known?

I caught Capo's shape in the distance. It almost seemed blue from all of the torches surrounding us. He had been watching us.

"It would be my honor, *farfalla*," Uncle Tito had said, calling me *butterfly* in Italian. "Because my wife and I were not gifted with the ability to have children, I will never have the chance to walk a daughter down the aisle. This would mean a great deal to *me*."

My answer came in the form of the bone-crushing hug I'd given him. He was an angel disguised as a doctor.

"*Farfalla*," he breathed, bringing me back to the moment. "I am thankful to God for one blessing on this day. That I have eyes that see you in this moment." He took my hand and kissed my knuckles softly. "It is a great honor to be at your side."

No one had ever touched me deep enough to make me cry out of happiness. I couldn't help but wonder if it was because this one, small man had touched me that deep, or if I was starting to soften because my feelings were not buried as deep as they once were. I wasn't as afraid of them getting bruised and battered, used and tattered, twisted into something nasty and horrible. Something owed.

My time in Italy had changed me.

My time with *him* had changed me.

A soft voice in the church began to sing.

It was time.

I took a deep breath in and sighed it out.

Uncle Tito lowered my veil before he offered me his arm. I looped mine with his, using his strength to keep me upright.

Hundreds of people.

Hundreds.

All watching.

Waiting.

To see me.

The doors to the church opened, and hundreds of people stood. When we took a step forward, a collective, soft gasp seemed to fill the air.

All eyes were on me.

But there was only one set that I looked for.

His.

Candles lit the way, the evening sun giving way to darkness, and the soft light went straight through the material of my gown, like candlelight goes through a mosaic in church. It highlighted all of the lines on the fabric. All of the struggles the butterfly goes through to reach a state of living.

Capo met us before we made it to the altar. He shook Uncle Tito's hand, but before Uncle Tito let go, he told him, *"I have taken responsibility for this beautiful girl; you will take responsibility for this beautiful woman for the rest of your life."* Capo grinned at him and patted him on the back. Uncle Tito lifted my veil and placed a soft kiss on my cheek before he sat with his wife, Aunt Lola.

Capo offered me his hand and I took it, never gladder to be physically connected to him. His confidence fed mine, keeping my steps steady. I kept my head up, but I wanted more than anything to wipe the tear away from my cheek. I had no idea when it happened, but it had. I didn't want anyone to see.

Glancing up at Capo, I thought, *let him see.*

Let him see the good and the bad, the dirty and the clean, the ugly and the beautiful, the happy and the sad.

Let him *see* me. *All of me.*

Dare to live.

This was me daring to live, to show someone who I really was. To allow them past the surface and into the secret depths that used to be mine alone.

"Bocelli," Capo whispered as we made our way to the waiting priest.

"And Pausini." I grinned, squeezing his hand. "I wanted to keep my head on straight. Get my mind right."

When we stopped in front of the priest, I turned to Capo and he turned to me. He took both of my hands in his.

All the words were spoken. All the promises were made.

He slipped a new ring on my finger, a diamond and sapphire band. I slipped his wedding ring back on, the one I had given him in New York. Il mio *capo*.

Before the priest announced us as husband and wife, Capo leaned in and used his lips to collect another tear that had fallen from my eye, and as the priest said the final words, he reached my mouth and kissed my lips, sealing the everlasting deal.

Tutto suo. Tutto mio. Per sempre.
All his. All mine. Forever.

THOUSANDS OF BUTTERFLIES fluttered around us, small bursts of color exploding in the night air. All of the flower arrangements, thousands of orange blossoms, were misted with butterfly nectar. Maybe they'd all have a drink before they flexed their wings and took off for wherever they were headed. A blue butterfly landed on my shoulder before it flew to another spot.

It was a surprise from Capo. So was what we were doing in that moment.

"I didn't realize we were doing this," I said.

My husband moved me on the dance floor that had been set up behind the property of his grandfather's villa. Hundreds of people watched as we enjoyed our first dance as *marito e moglie*.

His eyes were steady on mine even though we swayed. "You do for me. I do for you."

"Ah." I smiled. "Bocelli for this chick." Capo never referred to the singer by her name, only *this chick*.

He had requested the song we'd listened to in the car on our way to Harrison's as our "first song." When it first started playing, I'd exploded with laughter, thinking he was playing a joke on me. With his hand held out, he gave me a narrow look, so I took it, and there we were. Moving to the tune he'd once said should be on a Tim Burton soundtrack.

"You know what this means, right?" He twirled me out, and then I came back into his body with a soft *whooo*. He was a smooth operator when he danced. My left hand pressed against his chest, and the new band there sparkled like his eyes. It was simple, delicate, matching the engagement ring, but not as heavy. "Your head's not going to be on straight for the rest of the night. All of your screws are going to be loose. Like mine."

His grin came slow. "That's the way it's supposed to be. Your head is supposed to be on straight for the ceremony, but for the reception—" He shrugged, his broad shoulders stretching the fine, custom-made suit. "You're supposed to get a little wild. It's a celebration."

It was.

I'd never been to such a fun party before. Hundreds of people ate, laughed, and danced. I was starting to understand what Scarlett had meant by wishing a night would never end.

I wished for a magical glass jar.

I wished I could lasso the full moon over the groves.

I wished to take the night and the moon and all of the laughter and the warm weather and bottle it up for as long as I lived. And then after I died, escape to it as my heaven.

It was mine. It was his. *Ours.*

The only disturbance was Harrison's arrival and that Gigi character's presence. I was told that Harrison wasn't coming, and given the circumstances, I thought it was best. He hadn't showed up at the church, but he decided to crash the reception, in a way.

Harrison asked me to dance, and I did, but reluctantly. I didn't want an issue. I had never had a perfect night before, much less day, and this was coming damn close to it.

"You look beautiful, Strings," he said, moving me, but in a way that was different from Capo. With Harrison our moves felt familiar, brotherly. With Capo, I couldn't still my heart or the butterflies. "Are you happy?"

I looked up at him. "I am, Harrison. I really am."

"For now," he said.

I went to remove myself from his hold, but he refused to let me go. "Don't do this," I pleaded, keeping my voice low.

He watched me for a moment and then leaned down to kiss my cheek. I closed my eyes, not wanting to see the hurt in his.

"If you say you're happy, I'm happy. But when he hurts you beyond repair, I'll be waiting to take you home. Remember that, Mari."

I shook my head. "You don't understand, Harrison. It's not that simple. I'm in—" Whatever words were about to pour out of my mouth stopped right before they did. It was none of his business anyway. "I'm where I belong."

Capo cut in then, taking me from Harrison's arms. I could tell Capo was irritated. When he said he didn't share, he meant it. I knew he was trying to give me what I wanted, the people I considered my family at my side, but there was no patching what had happened at Harrison's house. And I didn't miss the intense looks Capo gave Keely's Mam.

When she had made a comment about how close he was to his family, he gave her the definition of family, and then tacked on at the end, "*People who are there for you through thick and thin, not only blood. If they're neither one of those, they mean nothing.*" I got the feeling he was telling her that she meant nothing. Whatever his issue was with her, I hoped it wouldn't come between Keely and me. There was already an issue with Harrison.

After Uncle Tito cut in on Capo, I watched as Gigi took the opportunity to dance with him. She fit with him. Silky black hair. Razor sharp features. Feline-shaped eyes. She wasn't tall, but she was built, curves in all of the right places. Her lips were usually siren red. When Capo caught me staring, I turned away and back to my dance with Uncle Tito.

I decided not to give her room in my head. Capo had married me. We had an agreement, and no matter how much history existed between them, because I could tell there was, we had agreed to be exclusive.

Why does it burn me up that she's that close to him, though? That he might think she's prettier than me?

Scarlett saved me from the maddening thoughts. A fast song replaced the one we'd been dancing to, and she pulled me further onto the dance floor. Surrounded by all of the women from girl's night, we kept time to the beat.

My skin was slick with sweat, my cheeks burning from the strain of smiling so much, and for the first time in my entire life, I was thankful for hurt feet. I had danced so much that my arches were killing me.

Capo took me to the side, set me down on a bench under a grape arbor, and sat next to me. He took my heels off, placed them on the ground, and then started to massage my feet. I closed my eyes, making noises that were indecent, but it felt so good, I didn't even care. At his touch, the ache seemed to melt.

"It's nice to have a friend," I said with a smile, "who has good hands."

"Good hands, ah?" I couldn't see him, but I could tell he was grinning. "It's nice to have a friend," he said and pressed even harder, making me moan softly, "who reacts the way you do when I touch you."

"Friends are not supposed to make friends make embarrassing noises." Then I exploded with laughter at my lame attempt at a joke.

A second later it faded when Capo leaned forward, took me

by the back of the head, and pressed his lips to mine. My hands ran up his chest slowly, to his shoulders, and I tried to pull him even closer.

I was starved for something that ruled me.

His tongue twirled with mine, slow and soft at first, but when I opened up to him, he became rough, demanding, our mouths at war. My attraction to him was out to destroy me. When he kissed me, I lost all sense of myself and somehow faded into him. Nothing, not a damn thing, mattered.

Scarlett had once told us at girl's night that people in ancient times believed that when you kissed, you lost your soul. There was more to it than that, but that was the gist of it.

The more Capo kissed me, the more I lost a vital part of myself to him.

I was once willing to trade a kidney for a piece of steak. I was willing to trade something that helped my body run properly for something that would feed my need for life.

Wasn't it normal, then, to lose a vital part of myself to the man I called husband?

I fisted his dress shirt in my hands, not willing to bend or break this. I wanted his hands on my body, his mouth on mine, like he was giving me air to breathe.

I give him something I can't live without. He gives me something he can't live without.

I wanted. I wanted. I wanted. I wanted more of...*him*... of...*this.*

Wasn't it normal, then, to trade something that helped my body run properly, like my heart, for something that would feed my need for intimacy?

He broke the kiss, and it took me a minute to realize we'd separated, that I was entering reality again.

There he was. There I was. Separate.

I kept my eyes closed, my hands on my lips, demanding to keep the feelings close.

Loss.

One simple word sent my heart in a different kind of spiral, and fear clung to me. I couldn't open my eyes to look the feeling in the face, to open my mouth and tell it to fuck off, because I was at war with not wanting to lose what I'd just experienced. I wanted to savor it.

An explosion went off in the distance and I almost jumped out of my skin—I visibly flinched.

"Open your eyes, Mariposa," Capo said.

I did. Fireworks exploded over our heads, lighting up the sky in the prettiest colors. Hundreds of people crowded together, eyes to heaven, enjoying the nighttime show.

Capo took my chin in his hand and made me look at him. "Your dress. All of your hard-earned lines are on display, *Mariposa*. Your veins made of silk."

"You noticed," I said.

He had told me that I was stunning in Italian on our way to the reception, but he hadn't commented on the lines, or what they meant to us.

"I'm careful with my words now, even though I use all the words." He grinned. "Time and place."

I smiled. "You brought me here to tell me."

"In private," he said.

I smiled even wider. "You got the private joke."

"I'd never call this dress a joke." His finger traced a line up my arm. The material was sheer there, but the lines were as deep as they were on the train. "But it's something only the two of us know about. Ours." His path continued over my shoulder, down my chest, ending at my heart.

My hand came over his, trying to hold the feeling again. I met his eyes for—I wasn't sure for how long—but then turned to look up at the sky, not able to match the intensity.

"Don't do that with me," he said.

"Do what?" I continued to watch the fireworks.

He turned my face and I met his eyes. "Look away." He searched my eyes, but I wasn't sure what he was searching for. But I felt it when he found it. The lock turned, and the sound of something inside of me opening echoed through every part of me.

"Amadeo."

Capo stared at me for a second longer before he turned to face one of the guards. I refused to look at the guard. I refused to give him a second of our time. Guards only meant unrest, and whatever war existed outside of the gates, it wouldn't touch our night—not then, not a hundred years from then.

My eyes scanned the party while Capo and the guard spoke in Sicilian. People were still dancing while the fireworks continued on. Harrison danced with Gigi. Every so often, his eyes would search the crowd. It seemed like he was looking for someone.

"He's trying to make you jealous."

I blinked, realizing it was Capo's voice, and only then did I look away from the night and at him. "He—what?"

"Harry Boy. He's dancing with Gigi to make you jealous."

What about you? Are you jealous that she's dancing with him? I was going to say, but again, she wasn't getting any space in my property. It didn't matter if Capo was jealous or not. We'd made a deal. He was going home with me.

"He's wasting his time." I hesitated but had to ask. "Everything okay?"

He sighed and stood, picking up my shoes, holding the straps in his fingers. Then he held out his free hand for me to take. After I gave it to him, we started walking back to the reception. Even if Capo denied it, I knew something had changed.

More guards were headed toward the front of the property. The ones who stuck closer seemed to be on higher alert. A few of them had taken positions around *Nonno*, who was so drunk that he laughed at nothing and everything.

Capo made a dismissive motion with his hand. My shoes hung from his fingers and they clanked. "A guest that wasn't invited."

"Anyone I know?"

"No." He stopped for a moment in the midst of the crowd. "How has your night been, Mariposa?"

"This has been the best night of my life," I answered honestly. "If I had the power to stop time, I would've stopped it at the grape arbor."

"The end?"

I nodded once, but I was trying to figure out what that meant, exactly.

"I need to use all of the words." He spun me around to the tempo of some fast song that played. "Are you ready to call it a night?"

"Ooh." I laughed. "Yeah, if you are." It was his party, too.

He looked at his grandfather, smiling from ear to ear, enjoying a cigar with Uncle Tito and a bunch of the Faustis, and then at the men going for the gate.

"One more song," he said, and it seemed like he was determined to do what he wanted. It almost seemed like he was daring the uninvited guest to cross the gates and try to stop him.

After four more dances, my feet still bare, my dress smudged with stains on the hem, we held hands while a line of sparklers sent us off to a private villa somewhere on the property.

THE VILLA HIDDEN DEEP on the property was old school and small, but whoever had come in and prepared it made it as romantic as possible. The air felt warm against my skin, like the night air had clung to my dress and filled the glowing space. Hundreds of candles clustered in an arched brick fireplace brightened the darkness. I had only seen pictures of setups like that in magazines. The smell of orange blossom almost overwhelmed.

I knew then that Capo's aunts had come in and made the place extra special. They had four signature candles that they sold in their stores. Orange Blossom. Lemon. Pistachio. Chocolate. I had connected the dots to the chocolate smell at The Club. Capo must've bought the candles in bulk.

A huge wooden bed with a carved headboard sat in the center of the bedroom. The gold sheets were crisp, but the cover was thick and soft and had been turned down. Between two equally large pillows, a single, perfect red rose had been placed. Above the bed was a simple wooden cross.

"You or me?"

"You or me...?" I turned around to find Capo staring at me. His tie had been draped over a chair in the corner, and his dress shirt was unbuttoned. His sleeves had been rolled up to his elbows since earlier.

In front of the fire, I had to admit, he made me nervous. No matter how I looked at him, he was intimidating, and not only in physical appearance.

All of the fear from the grape arbor hit me hard and knocked the wind from my lungs.

"Shower." He nodded behind him, toward an open door.

I looked down at my feet. They were still bare and dirty, but luckily, I hadn't stuck anything in them on our walk to the villa. This was because Capo had insisted on carrying me. He went to step right over the threshold with me, but I'd stopped him.

"Aren't we supposed to kiss or something for good luck?" I'd said.

His laughter had been low and raspy, but he had kissed me.

It was over much too soon, but then, being inside the villa gave me insane butterflies.

"You first," I said. "I'd like to stay in my dress for as long as possible. I only get to wear it once. It seems like such a waste to—"

He stepped forward and kissed me. His hands fisted into my hair and he kept me solid against him. When he pulled away, my eyes were still closed. "Your mouth is fidgeting," he said.

I smiled, but my bottom lip trembled. "And you refuse to allow that, *Capo*."

Before I could open my eyes, he was leading me away from the bedroom and toward the bathroom. "What are you doing?"

"It's safer if you stay close to me. The bathroom doesn't have any windows."

"Why? Is something wrong?"

"People keep showing up without an invite."

People? More than one? "Do you know who they are?"

He released my hand and went to the simple shower, turning it on. Once the flow started to trickle, he threw his shirt over the chair in front of the mirror. He undid his pants, throwing them over the shirt. His socks came off next. And then his boxer briefs.

I felt like one of those cartoon characters when their eyes bug out. He was lean and had muscles in all of the right places. And I was right about him being a python. His size only added to my anxiety. I was so out of my league. He was beyond fine.

I didn't realize I'd been gawking until I met his eyes. "I didn't mean to stare—"

He grinned. "You didn't mean to? Or you wanted to and did, and now feel guilty for getting caught?"

I shrugged. "I've heard that it's impolite to stare."

He threw back his head and laughed. "It's only impolite if it doesn't belong to you." Then he sighed, but in a good way—like he had enjoyed the release. "I like when you stare at me, Mariposa."

"I like when you stare at me, too," I whispered as he stepped into the shower and shut the door. He was almost too big for the small space. He was tall and his shoulders were wide. At least the tub next to it was big enough for two.

His back was full of muscles, and when he moved to wash, they rippled. The water and candlelight made his skin shimmer. I took a seat on the chair, not willing to look away from him, but not able to stand any longer. Just watching him wash made the pulse between my legs throb. My lower stomach was as clenched as a tight fist. My breasts felt like they were straining against the dress all of a sudden, so tender that they ached.

I licked my lips.

I swallowed hard.

I craved friction.

His back still faced me, and when he turned, his erection touched the glass. He started to wash himself while he watched me watching him. His penis bobbed each time he stroked it. He raked his teeth over his bottom lip, and when I made a noise deep in my throat, his eyes became more serious, more hooded.

I felt faint. The little bit of steam in the room was getting to me. *He was getting to me.* Then I opened my mouth. "Are we in danger?" *Am I in danger? Not from them but from* you.

He blinked at me, like he had to remember who he was with—the girl in the white dress. Not the one in red. Then he started to rinse the soap off, our moment over. "We're all in danger, Mariposa. Some people more than others."

"We're the 'some people,' I'm guessing."

He nodded and then shut the water off. I turned and grabbed a towel from the counter and handed it to him. He took it and then turned to dig in his bag. After he gave me a great view of his fine ass, he secured the towel around his waist.

I stood and turned toward the mirror. I watched him walk closer from behind. He stopped when he was at my back. I could feel the heat from his body through the dress.

He moved my hair to the side, and then he helped me lower the top of the gown. My fancy white adhesive bra glowed against my skin. He kissed the nape of my neck, watching me as he did, and then his fingers barely caressed my arms.

"Butterflies have least favorite colors when it comes to flowers. Do you know what they are?" His voice was low, almost hoarse.

"No," I whispered. A shiver waved over me from his constant touch, his gravelly voice, and it made me tremble.

"*Ti piace la mia bocca sulla tua pelle. Tremi per me.*" He said the words almost to himself, something about me liking his mouth on my skin, me trembling for him. Then, smoothly, he brought us back to his comment about the butterfly. "Blue to green."

My eyes lifted to meet his. Blue to hazel.

"Good thing I'm not a real butterfly then, or maybe I would've taken the warning the first time I saw your eyes and flew away to something lighter."

"Good thing." He ran his tongue from my nape to the center of my back, and then trailed firm kisses on his way back up. His hands moved to my hips, and he moved us slowly. "If you only knew the thoughts I've had of you since the night at The Club, the fantasies, you would've run away."

"No," I said, sucking in a trembling breath, releasing it slowly. "Now that I've found you, I can't fly away. I'm attracted to blue—all shades. It's my favorite color. It seems to heal me, not hurt me."

His hands caressed above my breasts, circling the cups, until he removed them. With a touch so soft that it made me want to moan, he caressed my nipples.

I melted into his back and he seemed to absorb me. "I—" I barely got out. "I need to shower."

He nodded once and then kissed me on the side of my neck, his lips against my pulse. He stepped away and slipped on his sleep pants.

"Wait," I breathed when he went to leave. I felt lightheaded. "Where are you going?"

"There are no windows in here, Mariposa. You're safe."

With that, he left me alone.

18

MARIPOSA

He was asleep when I walked into the bedroom, propped against the massive headboard, his laptop on his lap. I tiptoed toward him, still rubbing the sweet-smelling cream on my arms. I tried to be even quieter the closer I got to him. He was a light sleeper. In fact, I couldn't remember a time when he fell asleep first. I was usually the first one out, and each time I woke up during the night, he'd still be up.

In Italy, though, I slept all night. I still didn't think he did.

His hair was still damp from the shower, he smelled like the ocean, and I had to stop myself from reaching out and touching his face. It wasn't softer in sleep, but more relaxed. Except for the frown. It was only noticeable when he rested, as if he had to fight to keep it off of his face when he had control. I had once told him that he was going to get premature wrinkles if he kept it up, and he only shook his head and said, "S*cars don't bother me. They only mean I've earned my place in this world.*"

I took another step closer and reached out for the computer, a hand on each side to slide it toward me and away from him. "Some watch wolf," I whispered.

When I went to move the computer, he grabbed my hands. "I'm not sleeping. I'm resting my eyes."

If anyone else would've said it, I would have laughed and said, *yeah, right*, but I believed him. He was always on guard.

His eyes slowly opened to mine. Then they took in the red silk on my body.

"I'm ready," I whispered. Even though my voice was firm, every part of me trembled as if I was cold, which made me feel almost...achy. My insides were hot.

The shower had done me no favors. After he had walked out, he left me on fire, and not even the cool water could put it out. Every defense of mine had been consumed, leaving me empty. The emptiness demanded that his touch take the place of the fear that had stopped me from doing this with him before. It didn't matter if we were married or not, whether it happened a week ago, on our wedding night, or the next day. I knew when the time was right.

Now.

He looked me in the eye for a moment or two and then flung the computer onto a bag beside the bed. Then he was off the bed, his body colliding with mine. I thought he'd be gentle with me, but he was the exact opposite. Rough. His mouth started another war with mine while his hands fisted in my hair, keeping me as close as skin. Maybe my lip had busted. Or his.

My hands groped for skin to touch, to claw, returning what he gave. When I raked my nails down his bare back, he hissed, and his touch became even rougher.

My back slammed against the wall and the kiss broke, but his mouth kept working. The scruff on his face burned my skin as it scraped against me. His teeth nipped. His tongue licked. He pushed my breasts up, making them pop out of the silk, and when he took my nipple between his teeth and bit down, my knees almost gave out. The shock of it went directly between my legs.

"You came to me in *rosso*," he said, his mouth greedy on my skin, his hands cupping my ass. His fingers dug into my flesh, keeping me pinned against him. His erection was hard against my soft. I wondered how *it* was going to feel between my legs. How *he* was going to feel, over me, in me, all around me. Consuming me. If I thought on it too long, it made me nervous, but caught in the moment, I craved nothing but him.

"You wanted a fire," I barely got out. He moved my neck to the side, and I hissed when he bit and sucked at the skin there. "*Sono tuo, Capo.*" *I'm yours, Boss.*

"Put your arms around my neck and wrap your legs around me."

I did, and he lifted me up, his arms under my behind. We kissed as he moved us toward the bed. Once there, he sat me down, his eyes as greedy as his mouth and fingers.

"You're so fucking beautiful." He raked his teeth over his bottom lip. "*Mia Mariposa.*"

I set one foot on each side of him, right above his hips, and once I had a good grip, I shoved his pants down. The length of him sprang free, and I'd never seen anything so erotic—this man standing in front of me naked.

When he started to creep up the bed, I pushed back some, making room for him. His lips came for mine again, while his two strong arms were like bars on either side of my head. He nipped and licked and teased. Then his mouth moved down, his tongue making routes along my skin. He pushed the red silk down, and my body, my breasts, was his for the taking. I pushed against his mouth, wanting more.

The ache between my legs begged to be eased. And I didn't realize that I was whimpering, moving my hips up, until his hand reached down and touched me *there*. He whispered something about me being ready, *wet and hot*, in Italian. A noise that

I had no control over trembled from my lips. I didn't care. I had no shame.

There would be no shame here. He killed it.

The more I responded to him, the more he seemed to want me. When I made noises, his touch would become harder, or his mouth would bite or suck. And when he ripped the gown from my body and flung it across the room, it fluttered like a butterfly that had been set on fire in the darkness.

He leaned back, taking in my naked body with eyes as dark as sapphires.

"Don't stop," I breathed out. "Please."

His hand slid up my body, his fingers caressing my nipples. A soft *ahh* left my lips and I lifted my hips, begging for him to move further south. His eyes moved down to my oonie, and then he gently parted me, opening me up to him. As he started to touch me, he watched. He watched what he was doing to me, and then he'd watch my face. And when his mouth came against me like it had before, I screamed out in pleasure. I was so close. So close to being shattered by his tongue. But I wanted more. I hungered for all of him, like I'd never hungered for anything before.

"Make me yours, Capo," I said, breathless.

He knelt over me, his dick in his hand, stroking it. "This what you want?"

"*Dominami.*" I took a deep breath and it left my mouth in a slow push of air. *Dominate me.*

"*Ti domino.*" His voice was low and rough. And I never wanted to forget the look on his face. He was losing control, though somehow, he had every ounce of it on lockdown in this bedroom. "One word, Mariposa."

"You," I barely got out. "Inside of me."

"That's four."

"Yes." Yes. Yes. Yes. YES!

He lowered down, and I opened my legs to accommodate

him as he came in between. I could feel the tip of him close to my entrance, and I almost lifted my behind, refusing to wait another second. I wanted to feel him pressed against the fucking ache that wouldn't quit.

His face was close to mine, and he licked me up to my ear. "This is going to hurt," he whispered.

All good things are worth bleeding for, I wanted to say, but didn't. Using no words, I pulled him closer, my nails digging into his back, drawing blood.

Blood for blood.

The violence behind it urged him to move. He entered me slowly, his size stretching, stretching, stretching my walls, and I wasn't sure if it would ever be comfortable, but I wanted it. I wanted him to fill me up, to move harder, faster. I wanted him to send me over the edge.

He moved in even deeper, and I hissed out a breath. Pain. So much pain. A burning, like a match lit from inside. I was close to crying out, making him take it out, but then he moved in even deeper and the pain subsided, warring with pleasure. He had breached me, went beyond the pale, and moved into a space no one had ever touched before. A strange noise, between a cry and a soft whimper, escaped my lips. That spot he kept hitting, it was like...nothing I'd ever felt before.

"That's it, *mia Mariposa*." His voice was strangled as he slipped in even deeper, every inch of him pushing in on me. "Relax. *Fuck*. You're so tight."

His eyes were lowered, like he was drunk. His forehead was creased. His mouth was parted, and he made a wild noise that came from his throat. I wanted him to make it again. It made me feel powerful, as drunk as he felt. He had made it because of me.

He started to move a little faster, pumping in and out of me, and while he did, his hand came down, between my legs. He dragged the same hand across his chest, over his heart, and it left a smear of bright red blood, the color of the silk that had been ripped from my body.

So many feelings hit me at once.

This. What we were doing.

That. That part of me was still mine to give to whoever I wanted to, and I had given it to this man. *My husband.*

He put my hand over his heart, where the blood smear was. "We have made vows," he said in Italian. "But none like this one. This is a blood vow between the two of us. Between our flesh." He pulled out of me, and then came back, making me lose my breath. "You belong to me in all the ways now, Mariposa."

It was useless to fight the feeling of being overwhelmed by him. There was no room to move, to hide, to escape him and the intensity, and if I didn't give over to the pressure, it would split me in two. I couldn't hold back. A wave of intense pleasure surged inside of me, and I let go, giving over to the sensation. To him. My nails dug into his flesh even harder, my back arched, and I cried out. He seemed to swallow my pleasure without his lips even touching mine.

My entire body trembled, draining me of everything but him. The pain was there, still burning, but the pleasure shot through every other part of me, the shock of it so great that it seemed to stop my heart.

He moved even faster, making noises that I drank down like a bitter wine or a sweet poison. Only time would tell if he was my saving grace or my greatest enemy. There would be no in between with him.

He went even deeper and I cried out again, so sensitive after what he'd just done to *me.*

We had already hashed out the details of protection. It was up to me. I wanted children—*Fine by him.* If I didn't—*Fine by him.* It was my choice to make. I decided to wait on birth control when the doctor asked. I wasn't sure why, but I wanted no barriers between us the first time.

Whatever will be, will be.

"Mariposa," he growled out my name, and a second later, his head tilted back, his mouth parted, and his eyes shut tight. All of his muscles seized and then he spilled himself inside of me. I felt the combination of my want, my blood, and his seed mixing together.

He didn't pull out of me. Not right away. He looked down at me. I looked up at him. He kissed me between the eyes, making me close mine.

The ache between my legs became real, not from want but from what we'd just done, and every part of me seemed to hurt. I was instantly sore. When he pulled out, I winced, as if he'd pulled a knife out of sensitive flesh, suddenly feeling alone and cold.

Bleeding out.

Instead of two, I felt like we were one.

The connection made me feel... What had the priest said? *And the two shall become one flesh. So they are no longer two, but one.* There was no way to ask for it again, either. I wasn't sure if I could move. Or how I would handle it again later, or tonight if he wanted to. It had been so...penetrating, and not just physically.

"Mariposa." He studied me. "It's normal to hurt the first time. To bleed."

"I know." The sheets beneath me were soaked with blood. When I asked my doctor what to expect the first time, she told me that blood was normal. No blood was normal. Everyone was different. She had given me the lowdown on every circumstance so I wouldn't be surprised.

He kissed my lips. "Use all of the words."

I didn't expect to feel closer to you I wanted to say. *I didn't expect for this... connection to grow even deeper inside of me so fast.*

All of the fear I felt at the grape arbor was not because I was afraid of sex, but of the emotional strings it came with. Strings scared the shit out of me because I was married to a man who had a severe aversion to love. Even if I wanted that, which I didn't, it could never happen that way.

"Was it...good for you?" I bit my lip, not really wanting to share my deeper fears. I chose a surface one instead.

Maybe it was stupid, but I wanted him to enjoy me, too. Even though we never discussed his history in detail, a man like him probably had a lot of women. Women like Gigi, and Rocco's pretty secretary, Giada.

"So innocent," I thought he said in Italian, and then he answered me in English. "I said fire. You brought it. The kind that consumes water."

"Not yet." I smiled, kind of shyly, and I wasn't sure why. "I wasn't sure what to expect...tonight. Now that I do..."

"You'll kill me."

"Me?" I rose up on my elbows, getting closer to his face. "Kill *you*?"

"You have no idea," he whispered. "What you do to me." His eyes lowered and he caressed my thigh, coated in dry blood. "*Vieni*." Come. "I'll wash you clean in the shower, *la mia farfalla*. Then we'll take a bath. It'll help ease your muscles."

Without asking, he scooped me up from the bed, both of us still naked, and brought me into the bathroom. After showering together, I fell asleep with my head against his chest, his fingers caressing my back in that delicious 'C' pattern, in the warmth of the bathtub.

I heard nothing but the sound of his heart beating against my ear. I smelled nothing but his skin. I felt nothing but *him*.

I NEVER LEARNED how to swim (and I couldn't remember how to ride a bike), but I knew what it sounded like to be submerged underwater in a tub. Sounds came in echoes, so close yet so far away. The closer to the surface, though, the clearer the sounds became.

Cars zooming. Background music. *Mouth of truth. Legend is, if you're givin' to lying, you put your hand in there, it'll get bitten off.* More music. Laughter. *Let's see you do it.* Higher voice. Feminine. *Sure.* Deeper voice. Male. More music. *Dun. Dun. Dun.* Screaming. *Hello. You BEAST!*

My eyes slowly came open. Where was I?

Same sights. Same smells.

Still at the hidden villa.

I yawned and stretched, consciousness snapping awake, and the sounds in the background took form in my mind. A movie. *Roman Holiday* with Audrey Hepburn and Gregory Peck. We had started watching it and I must've fallen asleep.

It had been two days since our wedding and I was blissfully sore and tired all of the time. I took naps whenever I could. Then I'd wake up, he'd kiss me, or touch me, and we'd be at it again.

"You make bubbles with your mouth when you sleep."

Even though my brain was on, my eyes were slow to open. I blinked at him. He was leaning on his hand, his perfect bicep bunched like a hard knot, watching me.

"Were you watching me sleep?" My voice was rough, almost shredded. We had been having some wild times.

He grinned and I pushed at his bare chest. He kept my hand there, sucking on my pointer finger.

"That's so creepy, Capo. It's like you're stalking me in my sleep."

"Your dreams." He chuckled, the sound coming out raspy and low.

"And what do you mean?" I narrowed my eyes at him. "I make bubbles?"

"Like this." He pushed his lips out using air, making a soft popping noise when his lips parted, and then he relaxed them, and then did it again. It was like he had no control of his lips, and a light push of air kept making 'bubbles.'

My laugher rose to the ceiling. "I must be drowning in my sleep. Or maybe I'm part fish."

"You sleep hard lately."

"*When* I sleep." I smiled.

He leaned in and kissed me softly. I made an mmm noise and he cupped my boob, like he was weighing it in his hand. I couldn't remember the last time I wore clothes.

"Tell me something about yourself, Capo." My voice came out soft, as soft as the kiss had been.

I had come to learn that other than the occasional kiss, there was nothing soft about Capo Macchiavello. The first time we did it was as gentle as he got. And I liked it. I liked when he almost tore me in two. I liked when the orgasms he gave me were so intense that dizziness followed. I was lightheaded day and night.

"You know everything worth knowing."

"Not the heart."

"In time."

I nodded and gently touched the scar on this throat. I never left my hand there long, but sometimes I ached to find out the story behind it. How it had happened. I never asked, but even if I had, he didn't seem ready to share. Sometimes when I touched or kissed him there, his muscles contracted.

"You put a lot on the table, but I want something that's not part of the deal, Capo."

"Something given without terms."

"Yeah."

"Boundaries are there for a reason, Mariposa."

"You didn't say that we couldn't share *anything*. You only said that in time you'd give me the heart and all its veins. Just like I said in time I'd give you my body. I did."

He sighed. "Twenty fucking questions."

"Ooh! I'll go first."

"I didn't agree, Mariposa."

"You didn't say no, either. And you *kinda* said yes. You said—"

He put his hand over my mouth and I tried to bite him, but he didn't have enough fat on his palm. "I know what I said."

"Ten questions." My voice was muffled.

He released my mouth. "Two."

"Two? That's one each. That's measly. That's nothing. That's being *tight*. You're so free with money, why not with all your words?"

"Words are worth more than money."

"Words are free, Capo. This is costing me nothing. See? There is no little man running around with a collection jar, screaming, 'Tab! You have a tab!' There is no tab for words."

"Both questions are for me and I'm sure it'll cost me *something*."

"You don't have one for me?" That was about right. He knew everything about me. And what he didn't? It didn't matter. I was boring. All I did was survive. I hadn't even had sex until him.

He studied my face for a moment. "Actually. I do have a question."

"Just one?"

"*Uno*."

All right, I mentally rubbed my hands together like a villain in a romantic novel. I had a bargaining chip. "For your one question, about me, I can ask you more than two, as long as they don't cross any invisible lines. And I go last."

"Twenty fucking questions." He sighed. Then he dipped down and took my nipple in his mouth, and as his tongue did really magical things to me, I pushed against him. My lower stomach contracted, and immediately, the ache between my legs started to make me feel sensitive all over. He bit me, hard, and I pulled his hair. He released me suddenly. "Ask."

"What?" I panted. "Now?"

He chuckled and told me to stop pouting. "You wanted to do this. Play this ridiculous game of info hunting."

"I do." I lifted up, resting on my elbow, facing him. My nipples tingled, craving the friction against his chest, but I soldiered on. "Have you ever been in love?"

"No. Next."

"Wait. Wait." I held a hand up. "That's it? No?"

He narrowed his eyes at me. "That question deserves no more than a 'yes' or 'no' answer."

I waved a hand, dismissing his clipped tone. "What's your favorite color?"

"Gold."

My questions continued in this vein for a while. I kept the questions basic, because after the first one, I knew he'd say that I tripped some invisible line and use it to get to my question. I was saving the burning questions for last.

After I ran out of the basic ones, I asked, "Is your dad a bad man?"

I had seen pictures of his mother, was told stories of her, but no one had ever mentioned his father. It was like he was a hot subject that no one wanted to touch. I tried to bring him up with the sisters, but they refused to gossip about him, claiming that he was rotten, and that was all I needed to know.

He became quiet. "He's not a bad man. He's a bad soul."

The intensity in his eyes made me turn mine away. I looked at the sheet, picking at nothing. "Is that why you're so close to the Faustis? They treat you like family?"

What Keely had said to me before the wedding, about how lonely people find criminal crowds to get close to, came back to me. Was that what had happened to him? Was his father missing from his life? Abusive? So he ran to the Scarpone family? Then to the Faustis when that didn't work out—when he refused to let them kill me?

From what I had learned about the Faustis, their word was as good as their blood, and if they took you into their fold, you were there for life, as long as you didn't double cross them. They seemed exceptionally close to Capo.

Of course, Uncle Tito shared blood with Capo, and Uncle Tito was married to Lola Fausti, so there was a connection. But it seemed stronger than that. They were loyal to him. Just as loyal as he was to them.

It seemed...a little overkill to me, though. Why go looking for that kind of family, swearing fealty to them, when you had an amazing one, a real one, right at your fingertips?

"Use all of your words, Mariposa, since they cost so little."

I breathed in and then out. "Do you...do illegal things for the Faustis?"

"Yes." The word was clear-cut, but far from simple. "I have and I do. The Faustis were there for me during a really hard time in my life. They didn't have to help me, but they did. I call the people on this land my family because I share blood with them, and they've never been anything but good to me and mine. Including you. The Faustis are my family because when I was in the trenches bleeding out, they sat beside the angel and promised me that vengeance would one day be mine."

"You'd kill for them."

"I have."

I swallowed hard. "Do they...protect you?"

"They keep an eye out, but for the most part, I make my own way. I asked one thing of them, Mariposa. That they give me time—that means a few different things. They keep an eye out. They tell me when someone that's not supposed to come close does from time to time. I needed to secure time to set things in motion, and that's what they've done for me. But when the time comes to collect dues, it'll be my enemies and me. No one else."

"I really don't understand." His words made me nervous. I knew he was into bad dealings from the moment I saw him outside of the restaurant. Each time I was near him, something around him alerted me to the fact that he was powerful, in control, and there were people who wanted to test those hard lines.

He had never hidden anything from me, but I knew there was more. The heart, as he had called it during the meeting, and all of the veins that led to it. When was he going to share them? My life was on the line. So was his. And that made me nervous. More than it should have. The thought of never seeing him again did wicked things to my thoughts and feelings.

Keely and her brothers, the Faustis, all of Capo's family, they all felt like veins in my body. Capo. He felt like my heart.

Shit. Shit. Shit. Where did that come from?

"You will," he said. "In time."

I couldn't understand the look on his face. Either he had gone deep enough to see the thoughts I'd just had, or he was close to discovering them. Even though it wasn't love, it had to do with matters of the heart. He couldn't find out, or he might terminate the deal on grounds that love, or anything close to it, was never supposed to be a part of our deal.

"Time to pay up." He squeezed my thigh, bringing my attention back to him.

My eyes found his. I'd been staring at the tattoo on his hand. "If words have a price, take my money," I barely got out.

"Have you ever liked a boy?"

"You mean like a crush?"

"Whatever you kids call it these days."

Despite my sudden fear, I smiled to hide my earlier thoughts and the feelings they left behind. "No." *Lie.*

"Have you ever been in love, Mariposa?"

I squeezed the sheets, and then pulled the covers up to hide my breasts, or maybe my heart. "That's two questions."

He shrugged. "Since your words cost *niente*, I might as well go for broke, since they cost me so much. Tell me if you've ever been in love."

"Love wasn't created for girls like me." *Avoiding a lie.*

He was right. Words were not free, and mine had cost me *il tutto. Everything.* I had never been so broke in my entire life.

The breath *whooshed* out of me when Capo suddenly flipped me on my back, his body hovering over mine. When I'd thought of him as a wave sweeping me out to his ocean? Yeah, I'd hit the mark. Half of the time, he could steal my breath without even touching me. Luckily, he hadn't slammed into a metaphorical rock yet.

"Game over, Mariposa." His eyes were intense on mine. After a few heartbeats, he said, "You trust me."

That took me for a wild turn. "What? Are you in my head now, Capo?" His chest barely touched my breasts, and a soft, whimpering sound came from my mouth.

"More than words, Mariposa," he said. "Learn what it means to speak to me without words."

I wasn't sure what he meant, exactly, but my head was getting too clouded by him to figure it out. I looked at my wrist pinned in his grip. "I do. Trust you."

"You do. I had my hand over your mouth earlier and you didn't even notice."

Shit. I hadn't.

"You trust me," he said again.

Something told me his statement had nothing to do with my feelings, but something more...sexual. I was thankful for the turn. Maybe he wouldn't see how broke my words had made me while he was busy with other...things.

"I do," I said again, pushing my hips up to meet his erection.

He grinned and the look went straight between my legs. His hands slid between my thighs and I sucked in a breath, slowly pushing it out. His fingers slid, slid, slid, until he started to massage my behind. "See, you do," he whispered. "You understand me without the use of words."

Whatever he had in mind was *the* best distraction, and inevitably, I would understand without the use of words. I'd be consumed by nothing but feelings.

19

MARIPOSA

Before I knew it, we'd been married (again) for two weeks. When we had first arrived, I couldn't keep my eyes on Capo long enough to keep track of him. After we were married (again), his eyes were always on me, mine on him, and we were inseparable.

It seemed like he was purposely trying to make an effort to spend time with me. Maybe it was because our honeymoon, to some unknown destination that Capo had picked, had been postponed. It didn't seem like he had it in him to feel sorry for anything, but it seemed like he was trying to make up for it. After all, it had been a part of our deal.

We had forever to honeymoon. There was no telling how long his grandfather had left, and I wanted us to stay and hang out with him.

Since we had some time on our hands, and Capo found out that I didn't know how to ride a bike, or how to swim, he took the time to teach me how to do both.

The beaches in Sicily were something out of an aquatic fairy tale. The colors of the water were vivid, from sea-glass green to sapphire-lagoon blue. The sun was hot and the sand white. And the smells—lemon, fresh water, coconut, even seafood—made me drunk on summer.

It took me about a week to really feel secure in the water, but I didn't worry too much because Capo stood close to me at all times, even after I felt secure in what he had taught me. Evening swims were my favorite, when the sun sunk down into the water and the prettiest colors lit up the sky, right before the stars fell from heaven.

Heaven. I decided it had to be real after being consumed by something so perfect as the ocean.

Capo taught me how to ride a bike in front of our hidden villa on the days we didn't go to the beach. I did a lot of shimmying from side to side at first. I fell three times and then once on purpose. After that, I caught on, and some evenings we took rides through the groves not long before sunset.

The air was perfumed with fresh lemon zest and overly ripe blood oranges. The scents came out in the evening, like they had been holding on to the heat, and after the blazing sun went down, they released their perfumes. Sometimes we continued to ride even after the sun had set so I could get lost in the fallen stars.

Paradiso. I decided it had to be real after being consumed by something so perfect as a simple bike ride through hundreds of fruit trees.

How kind and good the world seemed when the devil stumbled and fell over your heels instead of being on them.

Some days, Capo came with me to the hammock I liked to sleep in at the hottest time of the day. The oversized hat I wore shielded my eyes from the sun while my body soaked up the heat. He'd read to me his grandfather's poems. The old man never would. He'd said that if I wanted to read them, I was welcome to it, but he'd rather make up stories, or read to me from someone else's book.

When it was bearable for his grandfather to enjoy his

garden, Capo walked him out and then took a seat next to him on a wooden bench. While the two men sat close, I listened as *Nonno* directed me—*move this there, it needs more sun. Move that one there, it needs less. Prune that a bit. Let that one go for a while. It needs time to grow wilder.*

During one of our visits, he had told me that plants were a lot like people. They were all so different, but at the same time —*they all need the basics to grow, and without roots, none of them can survive.* Right after he had said the words, he had searched for Capo and found him watching us from afar.

"He enjoys your beauty," he had said to me. "He does not feel that he deserves such a gift."

I had fixed the floppy hat on my head and continued to water. Enjoying my beauty was stretching it, I thought, but Capo had been watching us. Even though we had spent time apart before the wedding, I never felt like he was too far away. Part of it, I knew, was the fact that his grandfather was dying.

I saw the way he looked at *Nonno* when he thought *Nonno* wasn't looking. It was like Capo was trying to absorb the memory of him, but he didn't want to face the last moments he'd ever have. Whenever someone made a comment about how tired *Nonno* was becoming, or how his coloring had turned paler, or he wasn't eating as much, Capo turned away and refused to listen.

Maybe the family saw something I didn't. Comparing the man I first met to the man sitting on the bench, his face turned up to the soft sun, I thought he looked better. He looked... content. When I'd first met him, I felt no peace, but I didn't know it then.

After we'd arrived, and especially after our wedding, something in *Nonno* had changed, something that made me feel the life in him again, even though all of his doctors said that he was fading.

Turning from the plant I'd been pruning, I narrowed my eyes at the sight in front of me.

Both men said nothing as they sat beside each other, watching me tend to the garden. They were being quiet with each other. Whatever Capo held back bothered *Nonno.* I think *Nonno* knew that Capo wanted to tell him things, things he'd never be able to tell him again, but his refusal of the situation stopped him.

I wanted to tell Capo that even though I was a girl from the streets and didn't have much experience with living life, I knew that he didn't have to use his words to speak to his grandfather, just like he'd told me to look past words and understand something deeper in him.

Since *Nonno* had worked with words all of his life, he seemed to understand what words could only hint at. There were deeper meanings to be found, if we only opened our hearts, not our eyes or ears, to them.

Nonno wanted Capo to be happy.

Capo wanted to tell his grandfather all that his mouth (or was it his heart?) refused to say, but he couldn't; that would mean *final.* So Capo found joy in nothing. Even when we were intimate, he buried the pain of this. Sometimes, of what felt like so much more.

I knew Capo Macchiavello was not a good man, but he was mine. As long as I lived, I'd be the woman standing next to him. I'd do whatever it took to take care of him like he took care of me.

An idea hit me then.

Grinning, I lifted the hose, testing out the water pressure. The world had turned pink from the setting sun, and as a soft shower sprayed out, it reminded me of glitter being tossed in the air. A second later, it settled on the ground like dew, and I did it again.

The action got *Nonno's* attention, but Capo was watching

some of the men who worked the groves as they came and went.

Pressing the handle, I sprayed again, and this time the spray was more like a bullet shooting out of a gun. "Precision," I whispered to myself. "Is a girl's best friend."

Then I lifted the hose, squeezed the trigger, and hit Capo directly on the forehead. It took a moment for him to realize what I'd done. He blinked as water ran down the slope of his nose, and then his eyes connected with mine. Before he could move, I shot him again, some of the spray hitting *Nonno*.

The old man was already in hysterics. His laughter caused some of the family to gather around, and it seemed like they kept multiplying from there. His daughters all touched him while he laughed. They were laughing, too, shouting out taunts.

Capo had shot up from his seat the second time I'd hit him and, moving like a wolf on the prowl, was trying to get the hose from me. I wouldn't go down without a fight, and until he had the weapon, I refused to let up on the trigger.

I stuck my tongue out at him. "You can't catch me!"

"You are so childish," he said. His hair was saturated, and when he slicked it back, those eyes were the color of sapphires, reacting to the draining light.

I grinned. "Maybe so, but who has the hose?" I hit him right on his crotch.

He was getting closer to me, and the closer he got, the more I lost it. I couldn't control my laughter. It grew in volume when I hit Gigi next. She let out a blood-curdling scream, which made everyone else laugh even harder, too. Here, they treated her like everyone else, but in *her* world, she was treated like glass. Her eyes narrowed into an 'I will get you, child' look.

"Oops!" I yelled toward her. "I can't keep my arms steady!"

My revenge had caused me to turn a blind eye on the wolf, and he'd grabbed me around the waist while we wrestled for the hose and it sprayed wildly. All of a sudden, everyone was throwing buckets of water at everyone else. Kids giggled. Adults shrieked like Gigi when that first blast of cold water hits warm skin.

Then it was on. The garden and surrounding areas were in mayhem.

I was still trying to hold on to my weapon, but Capo had somehow turned my weapon on me. My simple summer dress was soaked and clinging. My laughter did me in in the end— slippery fingers were a disadvantage, too—and he got the hose and refused to let up on me. I ran around, trying to dodge, laughing like a loon (one of *Nonno's* favorite words) while Capo took his revenge.

Having had enough of his vengeance, I ran right out of the chaos. I had no idea where I ran to, laughing like I was, but my feet seemed to have an agenda. Capo handed his grandfather the hose, and it thrilled me to the core when he took off after me. As we ran, my laugher echoed behind me, and right before we reached an area of the property with a dilapidated villa, I realized he'd been herding me this way on purpose.

The villa had fallen apart, probably years ago. It had no roof, but the foundation stood strong, and so did some of the brick walls, even if vines clung to them. The light was still fading, but the air felt heavy with leftover sunlight, and it snuck in through all of the crevices, causing the area to glow.

Slowing, breathing heavy, I turned and walked backwards, my hands held up in surrender. "Don't do it," I whispered. "Think this through. Remember. You're more man than animal. You have more than basic needs."

That Machiavellian smile came to his face. "You should know better, Mariposa. You should always think before you *act*. When it comes to fucking you, I'm all animal."

Thoughts of the night before barreled into me—him pounding into me, and then him letting me climb on top of him. I rode him hard, the friction between us a fire between our bodies, and we cracked the headboard from our insane momentum. Being with him was like talking about good food while you ate good food.

"Hungry wolf," I whispered.

"What about the hungry wolf?"

"That's how you're looking at me."

"You're wrong."

"If I am, it's not by much."

He howled softly and then grinned. "I'll never get the taste of you off of my tongue, and I'm fucking starving, not hungry. I crave you, being inside of you, like I've never craved anything in my life."

My back slammed against the brick. He pushed me even further into the rough wall when he crashed into me, his erection hard against my stomach. My leg came up, wrapping around his hip, and his hand slid against my slick inner thigh, going toward my ass. My fingers tugged at the ends of his hair, feeling the droplets of water that continued to saturate his shirt.

Our eyes connected. It lasted for only a few seconds in time, but to me, the moment seemed to span a lifetime. Something moved between us, and I wasn't sure what it was, only that it felt stronger than it ever had before. It consumed me like the most beautiful ocean, and then wrote his initials on my soul.

The fear from the grape arbor hit me with what felt like a blow to end it all. The serrated walls around me might as well have stabbed me in the heart. My palms tingled, my stomach filled with poison-winged butterflies, and my heart pushed into my throat, making it hard to breathe. The roar of my blood filled my ears. A hard-earned breath escaped my mouth in a deep *whoosh*.

Waves the color of his eyes had me too far from shore. I couldn't catch my breath. I was going to drown in my feelings for him.

The fear sucker punched me at the most unexpected times. I'd buried it down so far below the surface that it was usually hidden from the light, but when Capo created havoc on my heart, the way he looked at me, with hooded eyes and an expression that was somehow confused but determined, it freed the panic from its cage.

I couldn't swim fast enough to hide it again. So I did what I could. I punched fear right in the fucking face. I wanted this, him, more than I was afraid. My words, or what I didn't say, had already cost me everything.

Being with Capo, I realized, felt a lot like living—and living meant taking chances.

The fear shattered and blew out when his mouth slammed against mine, his hands cupping my ass, pulling me forward. I reached down and undid his jeans, pushing them down as far as they would go, and then his boxer briefs. They were soaked and sticking to his skin. I was too lost in his mouth sucking the beads of water from my skin to even notice that he'd ripped the lacy underwear from my hips.

He stuck them in his back pocket before he lifted me up some, my leg still wrapped around his hip, and then he entered me so hard and so deep that my head knocked against the wall. He pumped into me so fast that my world spun from the sudden overflow of sensations.

For every ounce I gave, he took two. For every ounce I took, he gave four.

I didn't need him to touch me with his fingers to make me shatter into a million pieces. He knew where to reach me, and he kept touching the spot, sometimes battering it, over and over. So it was hard to keep up, to not give in, but I held on, drawing out the moment, stretching the connection.

"That's it," he rasped against my neck. "Give yourself to me, Mariposa. Always."

Not conquer. Not own. Give. Maybe he'd realized that no

matter how much money a man had to *buy* things, there was nothing like a woman *giving* herself to him.

The noises we made were animalistic, and they echoed around us. The smell of water, the earthly smell of a vacant building, and our sex filled the warm air. He seemed to know that I was holding on, not letting go until he did. Even though I was wet, I could taste salt on my lips from how hard he worked my body.

He slowed, his strokes easier, but no less filling. I bit my lip, making it bleed, and he came forward, licking the spot. "Come to me, Mariposa," he said in Italian. "Come now."

He thrust so hard, once, that I felt shockwaves throughout my entire body. I hissed out a breath because I was pretty sure he had rammed my uterus. He slowed, only to hit me again, until his pace picked up and I couldn't deny the tension any longer.

It consumed me. It consumed him. I cried out at the same time he spilled into me, and his mouth slammed against mine again, swallowing it down.

We stood that way for a while, both of us breathing heavy, my head pressed against his chest. When he pulled out of me, I winced, always craving the feeling of being one with him.

"*Vertiginoso.*" His voice was raw. *Dizzy.*

I looked up and met his eyes. This time, I wasn't sure who he was talking about. I held up four fingers. "How many?"

"Eight," he said, and put my fingers to his mouth, biting them. He used my underwear to clean me up some. After he was done, he stuck them back in his pocket.

A little boy chasing another ran past our secret spot. They were laughing, still trying to fling water on each other. By unspoken agreement, we left the abandoned villa hand in hand. When we got back to the garden, the kids were still at it, the adults still laughing. *Nonno* was still after them with the hose.

Capo stood with me for a minute, watching, and then letting my hand go, he took a seat next to his grandfather. He pointed out kids to spray, egging the fun on. *Nonno* started laughing even harder when a little boy slipped and went down in the mud. Capo grinned as he directed his grandfather's hand to spray the poor kid while he was down.

Our absence hadn't lessened the joy, but since we were back, it felt even more complete. My heart raced when Capo took his grandfather by the head, pulled him in, and kissed him there. Then he said something in his ear. *Nonno's* smile was immediate. Then they both looked at me, before Capo pulled him in once more, shaking him a bit. Maybe the joy of living had lessened the hurt of saying goodbye, in the only way Capo could.

A BUTTERFLY GARDEN.

Where the plants to create one came from, I had no idea, but when I stepped out of the villa, a cup of espresso in my hand, they were at my feet. Capo was unloading them from a cart with four wheels. It had a handle like a wagon. He wore a tight white tank top, khaki pants, and work boots. His top was already smeared with mud.

"What are you up to?" I asked.

He was usually somewhere in the villa when I woke up, but that morning, he was gone. Since our second wedding, he hadn't left me alone. The first thing I thought was that something had happened to *Nonno*, and I started to panic. But I knew Capo would've woken me up, so I calmed down and fixed some coffee before I found him in front of the villa. Unloading.

The muscles in his arms and back flexed when he took a humongous rock, which looked older than the mountains surrounding us, from the bed of the four-wheeled cart. Then he thought better of it and set it back.

"Where do you want this?" He looked between the rock and me.

"Did *Nonno* send all of this over?"

"No." He wiped a line of sweat from his brow. It was early, but the sun was already baking the earth. "Where do you want it?"

We had stayed up the night before, *all night*, so Capo had only gotten, maybe, two hours of sleep. I felt tired to my bones. So I had no idea where I wanted anything.

"Capo." I took a sip of coffee. "I'm confused. Where did all of this come from? And why would I want to put it anywhere? I don't live here."

"You do," he said. "When we come to visit. This is my villa. We can have it redone. The look of it never mattered to me. It was just a place to sleep."

"The plants?"

"A garden. For you. You need to plant all of this."

Ah. He had done it, but he didn't want to come out and admit it. *Hardheaded capo.*

Judging by the amount of plants already unloaded, he had already made a trip or two. I didn't recognize all of the flowers, but I figured they had to be what *Nonno* called nectar plants. They'd attract butterflies. Capo had enough of them to create a border around the villa. Maybe even more.

Walking further out in my slippers, I surveyed the land. He walked with me, both of us quiet. When we returned to the front of the villa, I nodded.

"I want to go around the villa with all of the different flowers. I want an arbor in the backyard for grapes. We'll do a bigger butterfly garden back there, too. We'll place the rocks in different spots so the butterflies can bask in the sun. We'll need a birdbath, or something similar, to put the sand in. We're not supposed to fill it, only soak the sand in water. *Nonno* said butterflies like the moisture."

I tapped at the coffee cup, thinking. "I'll ask *Nonno* where he thinks we should put the plants. I mean, which spots would be better for each one. How about you go and get him for breakfast? You can bring him back on the four-wheeled contraption —" I nodded toward it "—and we'll get to work after we eat."

Capo didn't move. He looked at me like I was a new person.

"What?" I had the strongest urge to fidget. I felt like I had grown an extra head and had no idea she was sticking her tongue out at him.

He shook his head. "You're bossy."

"Who knew?" I grinned.

"Me." He hesitated. "I knew it was coming." Even though his lips pinched, something about his tone seemed satisfied.

After he unloaded the rest of the cart, he pulled it back toward his grandfather's villa. Before he left, he gave the men that stuck around orders to keep an eye on me. He never left me unattended. He had more men around ever since the uninvited guests had showed up.

I hurried inside and quickly dressed for the day. I had no time to worry about how I looked, not when I wanted to freshen up the villa and make a delicious breakfast. It took me five minutes to clean and twenty to make the meal. I made more coffee (café latte), croissants (*cornettos*), and a simple omelet. I set out numerous different spreads on the lazy Susan on top of the table. I even went outside and picked fresh wildflowers to put around the house. There were no vases, so I used old jam jars.

The sisters had taught me so much.

I heard *Nonno* chuckling over the crackling wheels of the cart as it rolled over the rough terrain. I untied my apron and ran outside. He sat in the back, surrounded by more plants, still laughing. The sight of him made my smile grow wider.

"It was a bumpy ride, *Farfalla*, but I have made it!" He wiped his face with the handkerchief he kept in his pocket.

Zia Stella strode up right behind the men, a smile on her face. "You should have seen him!" She came toward me as Capo practically picked his grandfather up and set him on his feet. Capo held on to him while they made their way toward us. "He demanded that Amadeo take him all over the property. And if there was a hill, he wanted to go faster! He carried on like he was on one of those scary rides and he was seven again. He lifted his arms in the air and went, *weeeeee!*"

Close enough to grab me, she kissed my cheeks and then entered the villa. I kissed *Nonno* on each of his cheeks and gave him an arm to help him inside.

"A woman's touch," he said softly, looking around, "makes all the difference in a home."

We had an enjoyable breakfast. *Zia* Stella and *Nonno* made over how much they loved everything. Capo said nothing, but when he got up to wash his dish, he kissed me on the cheek and said, "*This time, I tasted all of the ingredients.*" He'd even gone back for seconds.

We spent the rest of the day planting. *Nonno* helped me decide where to place all of the different flowers so they'd prosper in their new homes. When Capo wasn't looking, he nudged me with his elbow and said one word, "*Radici.*" Roots.

Capo worked on the arbor mostly all day. Every so often, when the sun was too hot for *Nonno*, he'd go sit close to Capo under the tree in the back and tell him what to do.

I couldn't believe how good *Nonno* looked. He almost glowed. It seemed like he'd gotten a second wind and was riding the wave. We even enjoyed a light lunch outside, and by the time evening met us, we were done.

The villa and the yard suddenly had promises to hold onto. And in some odd way, I felt as rooted as the new plants getting used to their new homes. I made a wish—I wished that any butterflies that found their way to our home would find shelter.

Zia Eloisa brought us dinner. We gathered around the table and dined family style. Platters moved from hand to hand, lots of wine was poured, and the laughter that was shared was more filling than the food and the wine put together. The stars were out by the time we were finished.

The sisters and a few cousins left first. Capo had planned on bringing *Nonno* back to his villa in the cart, but he wanted to sit in the yard and enjoy all of the new additions before he left.

Capo and I both helped him outside, and he took a seat on the bench, while we took a seat on each side of him. He turned his eyes up the sky and became very quiet.

None of us said anything for a while. We all seemed to be lost in our own thoughts. After thirty minutes or so had gone by, Capo asked his grandfather something about the arbor. He didn't answer.

At first, it seemed like he had gone to sleep. Capo sat up faster than I thought possible and shook him. "Papà!"

I sat up too, wondering why he wasn't answering.

After a second, he answered, but his words made no sense. They were slurred, and his eyes looked drunk.

"Mariposa." Capo jumped up from his spot, going toward the front of the villa. "Keeping talking to him!"

I took one knee in front of *Nonno*, holding his hand to my heart. "*Nonno*," I said, trying to make my voice sound as calm as possible. If he was dying, I didn't want him to feel chaos, to feel my fear, because I shook, my heart breaking. "*Nonno*, please don't go. You have so much life left to live. You need to stay with us. Please. Don't leave." I kissed his hand, over and over.

He lifted his free hand and rested it on my head. His words were slurred, but I could make them out. "I have lived a long life. I have lived a full life." He took a breath, and I could tell it was shallow. "I did not receive all that I asked for, but I received all that I ever needed. My last days have been filled with joy. I have retouched firsts. The first time I tasted air. The first time I felt the sun and the moon upon my face. The first time I fell in love. I have received all that I needed. My work here is done. My sacrifice was not in vain."

I hadn't realized that Capo had pulled me from his grandfather until I saw him from a distance, Uncle Tito sitting beside him, checking his pulse. Under the stars, *Nonno* looked peaceful, content, like all of his wishes had come true. All of his needs had been met.

Nonno's found peace was the opposite of the cries that met my ears when his daughters and the family crowded around, grieving for the man who had meant so much to so many.

I HAD EXPERIENCED death in my life.

My parents.

Losing Capo the first time.

Jocelyn and Pops.

In some ways, I never truly grieved for my parents, or for Jocelyn and Pops. I didn't have time to. After I was relocated from one home at five, and then the only home I could remember at ten, my entire life from that point forward was consumed by survival. I'd often think of them, but not for long. It hurt too much. And in order to keep breathing, I had to keep my head on straight.

So death was not unfamiliar to me, but still, I hadn't experienced loss on this level—this close and old enough to know what the loss meant in the moment.

Everyone wore black to the funeral, and I'd never heard someone cry as loud as one of *Nonno's* daughters when they closed his coffin. It made my knees go weak. Capo had to hold me up to keep me from falling over. It was the type of cry that everyone fears—the sob of a soul grieving for the one person who took half of her with him.

After the funeral, we returned to his grandfather's villa. I tried to keep quiet, keep out of the way, and help as much as possible. My heart felt like it was bleeding, so I couldn't even comprehend what the people closest to him felt. He was one of those souls that the world would never forget. His words had been burnt into paper. He'd be forever immortalized between the pages and in the hearts of all who loved him the most.

Unlike me, who, at one point, thought that I might be found in a New York dumpster. The only people to remember me would be Keely and her brothers. I hadn't even made a mark on this world. Not even a paper cut. Another Sierra.

I sighed, my eyes scanning the crowd, looking for Capo. He had been slipping in and out of my vision all day. He'd check on me and then disappear.

"Rocco," I said, touching his arm. He was finally alone, getting a drink. "Have you seen Capo?"

"In his grandfather's office."

I nodded and went looking for him. The door was slightly open, but no Capo. I stepped in, noticing that a few of his grandfather's books had been taken out. Before he died, he had written a letter to each of his children, grandchildren, and great-grandchildren. He had written them poems and stories. When I got close enough to his desk, I noticed a book there, opened.

Mariposa,

The smallest creature can make the biggest impact. You have been seen and you are valued. Share this with the great-grandchildren I will not meet. This is for them as much as it is for you.

You have put down roots in my heart and taken shelter there for always.

Nonno

I took a seat and opened to the first page. It was an illustrated children's book.

A black wolf with shocking blue eyes sat in a dark forest, a full moon hanging over his head. He was a lone wolf, no pack to lead, because he demanded to be the alpha. Then a dull brown caterpillar came to the wolf on page three. The caterpillar told the wolf that the reason he's so lonely is because he lost something that had once belonged to him. Or maybe it had been stolen.

"Who would dare steal from me?" the wolf snarled at her. *"Tell me what I have lost so I can find it again and call it mine."*

She crawled onto his nose and said, *"Follow me and I will show you."*

The wolf thought that what he lost was something tangible, something he could bite with his sharp teeth, but the caterpillar never told him any different. She let him believe.

Some have to be shown, not told, she thought.

What happened next was a journey. They met other creatures in the forest. They got turned around and lost. And finally, when the wolf was about to eat *her* for taking him on a foolish expedition, she led him to a magical garden.

There, he found a rabbit to eat. There, he found shelter from the blistering sun. There, she hid him in the darkness so he could rest, and she alerted him when someone was near. She became his companion through it all. Even when she was tired and bruised from her own struggles, she never left him alone.

During their journey, the wolf started to realize that the caterpillar had nothing for him to touch, but she had offered him so many things to feel. The feelings were even more tangible than the rabbit he had devoured. Through the caterpillar's actions, she had loved him all along, a creature so different from her; a creature that could end her world with one snap of his mouth, or a swipe from his massive paw.

What I hadn't expected next was the caterpillar's death. The wolf mourned for her, both of them realizing at the very last second how much they meant to each other, and what lessons there were to be learned about living and dying. It took death to make them understand what life had been trying to teach them.

What the wolf had lost was his ability to love. For so long he'd been running with the pack, biting and snarling, always fighting for his position until he was banished. When he found himself alone, he was left with...himself. The wolf had forgotten that he was capable of love. He had to be shown how to give and receive it again.

What the caterpillar needed to understand was that her struggles were not in vain. In the end, she would be remembered for all she had done. Even if it was this one snarling, violent animal that remembered her. He would never forget her. She had taught him how to love without forcing him to be something he wasn't. Weak. Her love only made him stronger.

The last page showed a blue butterfly nestled in the wolf's thick fur, the moon high above them, sitting in the magical garden.

"*Nonno.*" I shut the book and rested my head against the hard cover. He had written a children's book for his great grandchildren. He had written a children's book in honor of the girl he'd said was both woman and child. He knew I'd love and cherish it. Even the artwork was something out of a whimsical fairy tale.

"I believe that book was his last."

I jumped at the sound of Rocco's soft voice. He stood behind me, looking at the book. I ran my hand over the cover, wanting to lock it away and keep it safe.

"Have you read it? It's...I don't even have words."

"Some. Your husband was reading it when I found him here."

"Where is he?"

"I do not know, Mariposa. He is...struggling."

"I know," I said, thinking over the words in the book, trying to find a deeper meaning. "Can you drive me to church, Rocco?"

He took a seat on the edge of the desk, one leg dangling, watching me. "Why church?"

His grandfather had told me that he had made a deal with God, and it was the first time he had returned to church after Capo's mother, his daughter, had taken her own life. Maybe I was wrong, but I felt it in my gut.

"Where would a man go to fade yet be seen?" I said.

He chucked me under the chin. "Clever girl."

Rocco drove me to the church where Capo and I were married in a steel-gray Lamborghini. If I'd hoped to make it there in record time, my wish was granted. As we made our way toward the steps, two men in suits were just about to enter.

Rocco slipped his hand around my waist and pulled me closer. I was about to step out of his embrace, because he had never touched me like that before, but at the subtle shake of his head, I stood where he'd placed me.

"Arturo," Rocco called, stopping them right before the other guy, the younger one, opened the door.

Arturo, the older of the two men, narrowed his eyes at us before he and the younger guy started toward us. "Rocco." He held out his hand for Rocco to shake when we were close enough, but Rocco didn't take it.

There was nothing remotely friendly about Rocco in that moment. I'd never seen him that way, and honestly, it sent a spike of fear up my chest. The Fausti was coming out in him. Some people called them lions. He had a tattoo of one on his forearm, a rosary around its mane and a sacred heart in its middle. It wasn't noticeable under his dress shirt, but I had seen it before, when he rolled his sleeves up.

Arturo was American, and he looked familiar to me, even though I'd never seen him before. Bold features. Thinning black hair with stripes of silver. Broad shoulders but a bit paunchy around the middle. Brown eyes. The man next to him was solid all around, but with blonde hair and brown eyes. He shared some of the same features with the older man.

After Arturo took his hand back, he slapped the younger man on his back. "You remember Achille."

Achille took a step forward and nodded.

"What brings you here, Arturo," Rocco said, totally dismissing the man with the strange name. *Achille.*

I saw fire in Achille's dark eyes then. He didn't like being dismissed. I watched the two strange men carefully after that. Something about Arturo made me want to take a giant step back, but Achille made me feel like he breathed down my neck even though he stood across from me.

My breath caught in my throat when I noticed Achille's hand. He had a tattoo. Both of them did. Arturo had one on his wrist, and Achille had one in the same spot as Capo, on the front of his hand. Black wolves. The eyes were different. All darkness, no blue like Capo's wolf.

I forced myself to look away, not to draw attention.

Arturo looked at me and then back at Rocco. "Is this your wife?" A second later, he held up his hands. "I don't want to seem rude."

Rocco grinned, but it was far from friendly. "You know of my wife," he said. "This is Amadeo's wife."

"Amadeo," Arturo repeated. He seemed to be thinking the name over. "Stella's son?"

"You don't belong here today," Rocco said, no longer subduing the irritation in his voice. "The family grieves. Your presence will be taken for what it is, an insult."

"I heard about the old man," Arturo said, shaking his head

sadly. "I was sorry to hear it. I was hoping to deliver my condolences in person."

Sorry my ass, I almost said. I had no idea who he was, but he was such a fake. And Achille refused to look away from me. He watched me with hard eyes, eyes that made me want to shrink into my skin and disappear.

"I'm Achille," he said slowly, reaching out a hand to take mine. I kept mine close, refusing to touch him. He grinned at my discomfort. He was the type who knew and enjoyed it. Achille was *Merv the Perv, the Remake,* but more dangerous. He wouldn't run out of breath. "They don't make girls like *you*—" he pointed at me "—in America. If you were not married, maybe I'd be interested in making an *arrangement* with your family. I wonder how much you'd cost."

It dawned on me then...he thought I spoke only Italian. That was why he was speaking to me like I was slow. *Stupid ass.*

Rocco pushed me behind him and got in Achille's face. He stared at Achille in a way that made me cower. I took his shirt in my hand, holding on.

"You do not belong here," Rocco spoke to Arturo, but he stared at Achille. "Take your boy and leave. If you want to deliver your condolences in person, you will call first. The family has not warmed toward you, and I doubt they will after today. Send flowers. That is appropriate if you feel you must express your grief."

Arturo stood still for a minute. His eyes moved between the situation—*us*—and the church, and finally he sighed. Arturo put a hand on his *boy's* shoulder and pulled him back, thanking Rocco in Italian for his time. Achille snapped his teeth at me before he followed Arturo's command to leave.

As Rocco watched them go, he made a phone call. He spoke in rapid Sicilian. He was sending men to watch the Americans. After they left, he put his hand on my lower back, urging me toward the doors to the church. He opened one for me, but he made no move to enter.

"Are you coming?" I said.

"In a minute. I have another call to make."

I hesitated.

"Do not be afraid, Mariposa. I will not allow them to hurt you."

"Are they...bad men?"

"*Sì*. They are two of the worst. If you ever see them on the street, turn the other way. Are we clear?"

"Crystal." I knew they were bad news, but I was hoping he'd give me a little more information.

Leaving Rocco to make his call, I entered the church. It was quiet, and in the stillness, memories from our second wedding assaulted me. The day had brought so much joy.

Nonno.

I'd never forget how alive he was. Hours ago, he was a silent figure in a coffin.

Churches were like hospitals in that way. The invisible line between life and death were constantly being tripped over.

My heels barely made a sound as I walked, but when I entered into the actual church, I stopped and hid in the shadows. Capo sat on one of the pews, and Gigi sat right next to him, her hand on his shoulder. When she started to cry, he reached out and squeezed her neck.

"Amadeo," she sniffed. Then she rested her head against his shoulder.

I never thought of myself as a vengeful person. I never had a good enough reason to get someone back. Most of the time, if a person made me run, I kept running to keep out of trouble. But on a day when so much had been sealed, never to be opened again, it was still hard to tame down the sudden urge to hurt her. Hurt her as much as she was hurting me.

Capo was *my* husband. Not hers.

My lack of experience, especially in comforting a man when he was down, was never so apparent in that moment. She was offering just enough strength for him to feel it, but at the same time, just enough vulnerability so that he wouldn't feel weak. And she had used his special name. *Amadeo.* She always did. The name he'd never given me the option to use.

After a few minutes, Rocco entered the church. When he saw me standing there, he looked between the two sitting in front of the altar and me. Then he continued ahead and called on Capo. Gigi turned to look but Capo didn't. Before she stood, she placed a soft kiss on his cheek, probably leaving a red smear behind.

Rocco took a seat next to Capo, and his words were heated and low.

Gigi grew closer to me. Her perfect face looked even more stunning with tears. She took a tissue out of her purse and dabbed at her cheeks. "He is all yours," she said. "Take care of him."

I said nothing, looking away, trying not to breathe when her expensive perfume lingered in the air after she'd gone. Rocco and Capo's voices were still hushed, but Rocco had stood. Whatever Capo had told him, or not, made him angry.

"Would you like me to bring you home?" Rocco said as he prepared to leave.

"No," I said. "I'll stay with him."

He nodded and then left.

I took slow steps to where my husband sat, a lone figure in a massive church. I replaced Rocco, sitting right next to him. He hadn't even looked at me when I sat down. His eyes were raised, and nothing showed on his face. It was cold and hard. I wondered if it was truly a waste of time to keep trying to avoid his massive waves. Would he ever truly let me, or anyone, in?

We were silent for a little while. Then his hand reached out and stilled my leg. I hadn't realized it was moving up and down nervously.

"Speak your piece, Mariposa."

"Capo." I took a deep breath in and then released it in a whispered push. "Life is short. It's too short not to live, and not to keep love after you've found it. You should be with Gigi. You obviously love her. I—I don't want to stand in the way of that. Whatever it is between you two, you should go for it."

I stood, about to leave, when he said, "You would leave me that easily." He never looked at me. He kept staring up, but the tone of his voice stopped me.

Easily? That *easily*? He had no idea how much I suffered, too. How much his grandfather and his entire family meant to me. How much *he* meant to me. But getting to know his family, his grandfather, had given me the courage to say the words. *You should go for it.*

Like a recipe, sometimes it took more fear than anything else to make courage, to make selflessness. Even though it hurt me in a place in my heart that I never knew existed until him, and it made me furious to think about them together, if Capo had found love, and Gigi was what he wanted—I refused to stand in the way. Whatever reason sent him looking for me was not good enough. A deal was not good enough. Nothing was good enough if true love found you.

"It's not that easy," I said. "It's not that simple. You know my feelings on love. Loyalty is the foundation, but love, love is the entire house. It trumps all. One reason. *Amore.* The only reason to send me walking away from you."

Love was both the reason to stay and the reason to go.

"You're taking the path of the real mother," he said.

He was grieving, and apparently, not using all of his words. "Real mother?" I asked, confused.

"An old story. It goes something like this. Two women were fighting over one baby, both claiming to be the baby's mother.

The king finds out about the feud and summons both women to his chamber. He listens to both sides but has no idea who the real mother is. So he does what a king does best and makes his ruling based on what he knows.

"He tells the two mothers that since he can't truly make a decision, the baby belongs to both of them. He's going to take his sword and cut the baby in half. Each mother gets half. One mother agrees to this. The other mother refuses. She tells the king the other woman can have the child. She doesn't want to see him hurt. The king gives the selfless woman the baby."

"She loved the baby enough to sacrifice her own heart for him," I said.

"Even cared for him would do. It didn't have to be love."

"I guess you can call me the real mother then. Though, when Gigi left, she told me to take care of you. So what happens if we both give you to the king?"

"Neither of you will be giving me to the king," he said.

It was odd, but I could've sworn his next words would've been, *because I am the king.*

"Capo—"

"I don't have the patience for this right now, Mariposa."

"I understand. It was stupid for me to even bring it up." It was. I let my emotions get the best of me, but truly, I wanted him to be happy. His grandfather's death just proved that we only have the here and now—one life to live. "Take care of yourself, *Capo*," I whispered before I started to walk away. Money aside, I never asked for much, but in that moment, I demanded clarity on this, on love, like I demanded his respect.

"You don't need permission to call me Amadeo," he said, and I stopped, my back to him. "*Nonno* gave me the name. He wanted that to be my name since birth. That's why my family calls me Amadeo. It's your right to call me whatever you want. I'd never allow another person to call me *Capo* or husband, though. Those are yours alone. You named me, Mariposa, just like I named you. The rest." He sighed. "Doesn't matter. Names are just names. Labels that are only surface deep."

He must have felt my hesitation, because he cleared his throat. "Gigi is Stella's daughter. My first cousin, so what you're implying is incest. It never seemed to come up in conversation who she was to me, and honestly, I enjoyed you being jealous when you thought she was *someone* to me."

Instead of saying something that resembled an apology, I said, "You enjoyed that?"

"Your reaction was cute."

Cute. I hated that word. Puppies are cute. Babies are cute. Even tiny vegetables are cute. But a grown woman shouldn't be cute. She should be—

"Your mind is fidgeting." Then he hung his head, leaning his forehead against his steepled hands.

I tiptoed back to the pew and slid in next to him again. I lifted my hand slowly and put it on his back. His muscles were tense, almost stiff, but at my touch, he seemed to relax some.

Me? I tried not to fidget. The thought of going this deep with him made me anxious. Beliefs and faith were personal. They were two of the few things in this life that were truly ours to keep, and apart from love and our sins, what else was there to take when we died?

Capo came to church for a reason. *I need to fade yet be seen.*

Suddenly the weight in my pocket called to me. *Fiddle with me,* it seemed to whisper, but right in my ear. I pulled out my mother's rosary, rubbing the cool beads between my fingers.

For the first time, he looked over at me, at what I was doing. A beam of light went straight through the stained glass and hit his eyes. He became the mosaic—the glass holding back the tide. I glanced down at his throat. Someone had tried to destroy all of his defenses. Whoever it was had shattered him, and then he'd put himself back together. The hard, metallic lines that keep the glass whole were so apparent on his face, if someone had enough courage to see.

I need to disappear yet be seen.

Ti vedo.

I see you.

I see right through the beautiful blue shattered glass. I see the hard lines that keep you together. I have the courage to see past the hunter and into the man's eyes that connect to a beating heart.

I see you, *my* husband. I see you, *my* capo. I see you, *my* heart. I see you, *my* everything.

I held the rosary in one hand and reached out to touch his cheek with the other. "It's nice to have a friend who...doesn't mind the stillness, no matter how loud the silence." My voice was as soft as my touch.

"It's nice to have you, Mariposa." His voice was rough. "*La mia piccola farfalla.*" *My little butterfly.*

Then we said no more, meeting in the depths of his silent grief that somehow seemed so loud inside of my heart.

20

MARIPOSA

After we left church, Capo sped back to his grandfather's place. He instructed me to pack. He told me we were going on our honeymoon. I felt guilty. We were leaving the family at a time when family should stick together, but Capo said they gave us their blessing. His grandfather would've wanted us to go. Something was off, though, and I knew it had something to do with the two men who were outside of the church.

The tattoos on their hands matched Capo's. It was understood that he'd run with them at one time. But I wondered... maybe the scar on his throat had something to do with them? I wasn't sure, and when I asked a few questions, Capo told me to keep packing. I took his refusal to answer as a *yes*. Maybe he wanted to lead Achille and Arturo away from his family?

It took us two hours to say goodbye to everyone. They made me promise to bring Amadeo back soon. They felt he was away from "home" for too long. I had no idea how to respond when they kept telling me they loved me and were going to miss me.

What surprised me the most was that a few tears slipped

down my cheeks after we left. I hid my eyes behind dark sunglasses to try to hide them, but Capo noticed.

He wiped a tear from my skin and rubbed it against his lips. "Leaving doesn't mean you'll be gone forever. You'll be back."

I still had no idea where we were going, but after we boarded the biggest boat I'd ever seen, I knew we were going on a nautical journey. Capo met the captain as soon as we boarded. He was related to the Faustis in some way—of course.

Capo corrected me when I called it a boat. It was a *yacht*. Boat. Yacht. Floating mansion. It was all the same to me. It had numerous plush cabins, numerous efficient workers, and anything we *desired* was only a request away.

I fell asleep somewhere in Sicily and woke up in Cala Gonone, a city in Sardinia. We spent the day there. The water was sapphire, topaz, and a green I couldn't even describe in words. I could see straight to the bottom. It was like a watery dolphin hole bringing swimmers to another world. The sea was cool, my skin hot, his lips salty when they touched mine, and I couldn't imagine a more perfect spot if I tried.

That night, I fell asleep in Sardinia and woke up at a port somewhere in Greece.

Greece!

I knew Capo had probably gone through my things when I'd handed them over at The Club. Being in Greece took that probably and turned it into a solid *for sure*. I'd written in Journey about Greece and how badly I wanted to go. One of the customers at Home Run was from Greece, and he'd tell the most wonderful stories about the sunrises and sunsets, the bright houses, the blinding sea, the windmills, the mountains, the food, and the people.

The first thing Capo did after the tender dropped us on land was find a shop that sold cameras. He told me it was unacceptable that I was squaring my fingers, putting them in front of my face, and then making a *clicking* noise when the sight I never wanted to forget was in frame. If I wanted a camera, I'd get a camera.

He bought me a fancy one, and it took me two hours to figure out how to work it, but once I did, there was no stopping me. Rarely was it not around my neck. And I must've gone through five digital cards, filling them all to capacity.

Sunrises and sunsets, white-washed houses, blinding seas, windmills, mountains, food, and people. Capo and me. Just... Capo. The camera loved his face and body.

During our time, I got to meet a different side of him. He was more at ease, and when he felt like I was chickening out on life, he urged me to do things I'd never imagined before. Swimming naked at night under the stars with him, hiking to places that were only occupied by wildflowers and goats, crashing a wedding and dancing until my face felt like it was permanently stuck smiling, rafting on Mount Olympus, kayaking over water so clear that the surface resembled glass and the depths blue and green treasure, having sex in secluded coves, and eating things that took some guts, like sea urchin salad (straight from the sea) and lamb. I drew the line at fried ink sack from an octopus and snails that popped when you put them in a pan. I fell in love with pomegranates, though, and the chef kept the kitchen stocked with them.

We'd been in Greece for a month when Capo received a call from Rocco. Capo had to plug his ear to hear what Rocco was saying. My husband had surprised me with a night out in Athens. The Greek National Opera was performing *Carmen* at the Odeon of Herodes Atticus.

The Odeon of Herodes Atticus was an outside stone theater that had been there since 161 AD. It was steep-sloped, almost like a bowl with high sides. Beyond, the city of Athens glowed, while the mountains in the distance created rugged shadows. I'd never been to a place with so much history. Not only could I touch it, I could smell it in the air.

Capo ended the call and raked his teeth over his bottom lip. With him, passion and anger were closely related. He only rolled his teeth over his bottom lip when he wanted me or when he was pissed off.

"Something wrong?"

He didn't look at me, just stared at the actors playing their roles on the stage. "Boo, bam, *boo*."

I stared at him until he met my eye.

"We leave tonight, Mariposa."

I'd been dreading this day, but I knew it would come sooner or later. "Why?"

"One of my buildings in New York was blown up."

That line concluded our time in Greece.

We'd be back in New York, back to reality, by the next day.

21

CAPO

Every step I took was planned. Nothing I did was by accident. In my world, unforeseen circumstances could get you killed. After my death, I had learned to time my breaths to each second that passed. I remembered all too well how sixty seconds equaled a lifetime—the next possibly my last.

I had caused the wars. I went in unsuspected and killed brothers, sons, uncles, and good friends. All evidence pointed toward the Scarpone family. I even fucked with the Irish. And as I'd planned, all hell broke loose. No one trusted anyone, not even a cent. It was a cent that usually kept them square with each other.

I knew whom to kill in each family. I knew how to set it up, how to make it look. At one time, that was who I was: the king's prince, the one he sometimes called the pretty-boy killer. When Arturo wanted someone dead, someone who had done something personal to him, he called on Achille or me to handle it.

We were the wolves after sheep to slaughter. Arturo never thought of anyone but the Faustis as competition. He called them lions, a different breed of animal. We didn't have to worry about them or take them down because they had territory of their own. But when it came to taking other wolves down, the ones who challenged him, wanting to be the alpha, we were sent in to destroy.

I'd let the daughter of another wolf go, and in Arturo's eyes, the sin was unforgivable. So he sent a pack of wolves after me. They came close to tearing my throat out.

Then I became a ghost. I saw it on every face of every man I killed after my death. They thought I had come to lead them to hell. It was especially sweet to see the recognition on the faces of the animals that had a hand in my death. The cowards who held my arms while the knife cut me deep. The ones who held a woman against her will and assaulted her in front of me until they tore her apart.

One thing about death—you have nothing but time. So that was what I did. I bided my time. I got lost in Italy for a while. I started going by the name Amadeo, to begin with. Then a visit with Marzio Fausti brought me back to life. He loaned me enough money to invest in tanking businesses. In return, I'd kill for his family, until I paid him back every cent with interest. He'd offered to kill Arturo, but I asked that he be spared. I wanted to do it my way.

I wanted to seek revenge in a way that fed the soul that had been ripped from its body and starved for too long.

After my investments paid off—the hotels, the restaurant, The Club, plus numerous investment properties, along with investments Rocco made for me—my plan really started to take shape. It looked like a vengeful wolf with teeth sharper than the rest. I left little clues here and there, enough for them to catch a hint of a new but also familiar scent.

Vittorio?

No, it can't be.

Ah, but it is motherfuckers, it is.

Small clues led to medium clues until medium wasn't

cutting it anymore. My schemes became bigger. Not enough to give me away, but enough that the scent got stronger. Every so often one of the Scarpones made a trip to Italy on the guise of "visiting with family."

I laughed, a cold breath forming out of my mouth. "Family." I said the word like a taunt, a joke.

After the father and son's last trip, when Arturo and Achille almost discovered me in church, they started creeping around buildings in New York. Buildings owned by one Amadeo Macchiavello. *If* I was still alive, they were trying to draw me out in the only way they knew how—striking. They couldn't seem to find proof of my existence any other way.

Achille had even tried to find me at The Club after his son had been killed. I watched him from the private floor above. He was mad with loss of power. He kept grabbing black-haired men and turning them around, looking for me in their faces.

For the record, they never found Achille's son's body. My empty grave was the last place they'd look.

There was a meaty story. After the man Arturo had sent to kill me thought he did, he was supposed to take my body and dump it in the Hudson River with the rest of the fleshy scraps that were disposed of. However, they hadn't counted on an angel to arrive.

Tito Sala.

He showed up not long before I took my last breath, and he saved me. Rocco and Dario were with him. The man who slit my throat was killed in a car accident two days later. His brakes had gone out. Apparently, he never told Arturo that he hadn't dumped me because he didn't want Arturo to kill *him*. After all of the men had fled, and only the man who had "killed" me was left, he had seen the shadows coming for him in the alley next to Dolce. He had taken off, going straight to the King Wolf to deliver the lie—*yeah, he's gone.*

His lie hadn't saved him. Nothing would've. Arturo never

left witnesses. It was too risky. So he had the man killed. It worked out for me, though, because Arturo killed him before finding out the truth.

Angelina was already dead, our blood mingling in the alley. It was a fitting final goodbye.

The Faustis left my blood in the alley, but they also left traces leading to the Hudson. I didn't want to be found, and I knew this was where the man was bringing me next—while he sliced my throat, he had whispered in my ear, "*You're not even good enough to leave on the street next to the dumpster. Your old man wants you down with the fish in the Hudson, a watery grave.*" He talked too much when he'd been attempting to slit my throat.

The detectives labeled our cases, Angelina's and mine, as murders, but after no clues pointed to the murderers, the case went cold, and the evidence box was sealed shut.

Yeah, they hadn't looked too hard. Even if they had, they would've never found me. I was a ghost, as some called me.

The Scarpones were feeling the pressure of that ghost. When medium clues got too boring for me, I started dropping the big ones, the ones that would lead them a little closer. I wanted to fuck with their heads before I chopped them off.

In an attempt to convince the other families that it wasn't the Scarpones starting the wars, killing their men and taking their stolen shipments, they pinned it down to one man.

Me.

A man they didn't know. A man who, from out of the blue, started stomping on all of their turfs. Of course, Arturo never mentioned Vittorio Lupo Scarpone to the other families. If he did, it would paint Arturo unstable, and the last thing he wanted was to be labeled mad, unless it came to violence.

Seeing ghosts? Believing the son you had killed had come back from the dead? Yeah, not good for business.

So the heat was on me. I was getting hit from all different sides, but after a couple of months, the other families moved on, convinced that the Scarpones were to blame, since no man looking to start a war had been found.

However, the Scarpones hadn't let up. They were determined to smoke me out, make me show my face, or throw my fucking ashes to the wind. For every property they set on fire or blew up, I did the same to two of theirs. And their shipments of stolen goods? Gone. Gone. Gone. Never arrived. Then, a few days later, some of their items would float up from the Hudson.

I'd never seen Achille cry, not even over his son, until millions of dollars worth of drugs went missing. I saw him on the docks, talking to a paid-off foreman, pulling his hair, twisting around, cursing the sky.

Waaa. Waaa. Waaa. Waa.

His perfect life was imploding from within, and there was nothing he could do to stop it.

That's what happens when you try to catch a man you made into a ghost.

Months had gone by since our honeymoon, and I'd lost a substantial amount of property and money, but it was nothing compared to the payoff I received that had nothing to do with *la moneta*. I had fucked up a family that no one was able to touch before.

The Scarpones, led by the King of New York and his mad son, The Joker.

Word on the street was that the families who had originally decided to help them smoke me out, a man none of them could find, had actually pulled out because they wanted the Scarpone family destroyed. Their willingness to help had been a war tactic. They had agreed at first, but then they pulled out in hopes that I would take the Scarpones out. Completely.

A little more time, and the entire city of New York would owe me.

Movement made my eyes turn up. A shadow crept closer to the upstairs window, peeking out. Arturo had two wolf-hybrids as pets, and they didn't even bother to look away from their treats. They lay at my feet licking the blood from the steaks I'd brought them. I ruled his house, even his dogs.

Yeah, come on down, we can end this here and now if you want, old man. Arturo was old, and any ruling he did, he did from his office. Achille had complete control of the body, except for the brain and the heart. He hadn't been born with either.

As I stood underneath Arturo's window, dressed in black, he couldn't see me, but I could see him. I could even hear his wife, the blonde-haired bimbo with fake tits, talking to him. She came into the restaurant, too. And she was a fucking hoot. She was dumber than a sack of bricks. No wonder she gave birth to a joker when she was only seventeen.

No one would ever be able to replace my mamma. She gave Arturo a prince, and he destroyed her. He had killed her innocence. Slaughtered it. Then she killed herself because of it. He took something that was supposed to be unique, innocent, and turned it into something dirty.

My phone lit up. A picture of Mariposa and I from our wedding in Italy appeared on the screen. Not even a second later the song Mariposa and I danced to came through the speaker, the one that sounded like a song that should be on a Tim Burton soundtrack. My wife constantly changed her profile picture on my phone and the ringtone. So I started doing the same to her.

This time, though, she had caught me at a bad time. It was my own fault. I should've put the phone on silent.

Arturo was going to get curious, so I sent her to voicemail and silenced the phone. I quickly sent her a text.

Me: At work. You okay?

A second later her response came through.

Your wife (she programmed this into my phone): Fine, just lonely in this big house without you.

I grinned.

Another text.

Your wife: It's nice to have a friend who stays home and watches old movies with me. I'll make some popcorn and root beer floats.

The lights in the yard came on, and the dogs jumped up, going toward the back door. A second later, Arturo appeared, holding a gun.

"Who's out there?" He narrowed his eyes. Then he called for his men to check the yard. He was getting too careless in his old age. He should've known. Send the men out first. One bullet and his life was mine.

Too fucking easy, though.

I was gone before his watchdogs even made it behind the tree.

My phone lit up again as I opened the door to my car. Snow covered the windshield, and the leather felt like ice. My breath fogged when I took another deep breath.

Your wife: On second thought. Can you stop and get marshmallows? We ran out. Since it's cold out, hot chocolate will be better.

Me: You're going to owe me.

Your wife: That was my plan.

Then she sent me a smiley face winking.

I sat in the cold for a while, staring at my phone. I clicked on the picture she had uploaded. We'd been sitting under the grape arbor, and I'd been rubbing her feet. The photographer had caught us in a candid moment. Mariposa loved it so much that she had it blown up and hung it over our fireplace. I used my finger to scroll through the other ones. Some of them I had taken in Greece.

In that moment, I was a liar. In my life, I had once done something that was not in my plans.

Her.

My wife.

She changed the entire course of my life.

She had been a surprise the first time, and again when she came back into my life. It would take a fool to think that fate doesn't exist, that some things in this life *don't* belong to us, no matter how much we fight them.

Mariposa Macchiavello was mine in every way. She had been since the moment I found her on a night like this one. Dark. Cold. Snowing. The air had been almost blue with cold. No stars in the sky. She'd been only five at the time. Only five. Her innocence had been a blow to my heart.

Her mother's big bag had been pressed against her little chest as we drove away from the place Palermo had been hiding them.

"Where we going?" she had asked me in Italian.

"You're going home, Mariposa," I had answered in the same language. It was mostly all she'd spoken. Her father spoke mostly Italian at home, but on the streets, English. Her mother left Sicily and went straight to America. Her English was limited.

Her eyebrows drew in. "To your house."

I didn't answer and she continued to stare at me, her legs so short that they hardly reached the end of the seat.

"Do you know what Mariposa means?" I asked her.

She shook her head. "Non."

Non ho capito. She didn't understand.

"It means butterfly," I said. "Farfalla ma in spagnolo."

She thought it over for a minute before she nodded.

If the Scarpones found Mariposa, the game would be different. No longer would I have nothing for them to steal or to blow up. No longer would I be a ghost, but a man with everything to lose.

She was the one thing in this world that was worth something to me.

Everything.

She had been worth everything to me ever since that cold

night in December when she'd asked me to color with her, when she had given me the rosary because she said that *I* was fidgeting. She had unnerved me the first time I saw her. Looking at her was like looking at my future, and unless she lived, the rest of my life didn't seem to matter. It was like trading my evil so one ounce of good would be left in the world.

"*Fucka me*," I breathed out. Where was I before I had gone too fucking soft? *Mariposa fidgeting.*

Her mamma, Maria, knew that about her, and instead of her giving her something childish, like a soft blanket or a stuffed toy, she had given Mariposa the rosary to caress when she was anxious. When I saw her doing it in church, after my grandfather's funeral, it brought me back to when she was five, and I couldn't help but question how much more Maria had instilled in her, even at that young age.

Get the fuck outta here, Capo. Thinking of your wife while on Scarpone territory is only going to get you killed.

Not yet.

I flipped the headlights on, snow swirling in their beams. I set the gears and pulled off. I'd go to a separate building before going home. I'd use the connecting buildings to walk to another one, and then take another car, leaving from a different exit. I'd know if they were following me. I tracked them all on my computers.

Even computers didn't inspire enough trust, though. That was why my wife was in the firehouse. Even if they blew up the other building, she was safe on the other side. Besides, the entire block was "owned" by Luca Fausti, Rocco's father. No one touched him. If they did, they'd regret it.

The Scarpones wouldn't even drive down that block, much less put a finger on one of his properties. Luca Fausti disliked Arturo. Always had. And after Marzio had filled him in on what had happened to me, he was all too eager to put his name on the block as a front.

Still. I took one extra step to make sure Mariposa was safe. The abandoned firehouse wouldn't get a second glance.

Though, I didn't fucking like the Scarpones seeing her, getting that close to her, like they'd done in Italy. They knew that if anything would draw me out, it would be my grandfather's funeral. I'd been seconds away from being discovered when Rocco—actually, my wife, since she came looking for me —stopped them.

At the time, I didn't care. It was easier to die than to feel the pain of losing the man who taught me everything about living. Then *mia farfalla* brought me back. The life in her made me hungry again.

I hit the brake when a man jogging down the street decided to cross. He ran right in front of my car, slowing when he made it past the hood. He stopped for a second, putting his hands on his hips, breathing heavy. The wolf tattoo on his hand stood out, the glow of my lights highlighting the ink. He narrowed his eyes on the car, trying to see through the tinted windows. He couldn't.

"Joker." My voice was low, rough. "You're trying to see someone who doesn't exist anymore."

I lifted my hand in greeting. He narrowed his eyes again but didn't move. I took off slowly, watching him through the rearview mirror. He moved from the curb and stood in the middle of the street, trying to read the license plate. *Be my guest.* He'd get some random name and number.

He was always a stupid motherfucker. Couldn't see beyond what was right in front of his face.

Yeah, my wife was protected from them, from this life of vengeance I chose. The jury was still out on my fate. I didn't know who was more dangerous to me—the Scarpones or her.

22

He was late. I was too, but that was beside the point.

He had been "working" more late nights ever since we got back from Greece. He didn't bring up what had happened to his building, or whatever else was going on, but call it wife's intuition—I knew he fought a battle that was kept under wraps.

I thought his building, or *a* building, getting blown to smithereens would've made the news, but it hadn't. I watched the news every night and... nothing. The supposed "wars" between the connected families had died down, the news reported, and soon after that was settled, it was all about politics again.

Usually, I didn't mind when he was late, but tonight was important for two reasons. *One.* Keely had her debut on Broadway. She was playing the lead. Some kick-ass Scottish warrior who was an excellent archer. *Two.* I didn't want to think about reason two. It made me nervous to keep dwelling on it, so when it happened, it happened.

"Mariposa," Capo called out, coming into the bedroom. He

found me sitting in the bathroom naked, touching up my makeup.

He stopped, his suit jacket over his arm, looking me over. "Just the way I want you," he said, his voice low. "Stand."

As I did, he threw his jacket on the counter and loosened his tie, his eyes never losing contact with mine. The frenzy that existed between us, something carnal, seemed to feed his desire as much as it fed mine.

A long moment seemed to stretch before something seemed to explode inside of me, before his body created the physical equivalent between his chest and mine. Our bodies crashed into one another, my fingers hungry against his skin, his mouth devouring mine. My back slammed against the shower, and without him having to instruct me, my legs wrapped his waist, urging, pleading, *demanding* that he settle the ache.

I'd come to know that whatever *thing* stood between us, was primal but basic, animalistic. And that's how we were tearing at each other, like animals that didn't know right from wrong, that had no other thought or feeling but *this* and *now*. It had only been hours, but the ache screeched...*right now!*

The noises we made echoed around the huge bathroom, and the noises his mouth made from pleasure reverberated inside of me, reaching every hollow, pinging from bone to bone, sliding right through my bloodstream.

He drove me higher and higher, my back sliding against the doors to the shower, his thrusts hard and crazed. He read my body language, maybe the way I started to quiver, and how loud my moans were becoming—maybe the pleading was getting worse. Then, in another explosion, we came together, his guttural growl swallowing my softer one as he spilled into me with so much pleasure that it made me feel like the most powerful woman in the world.

We stood connected for a moment, our breaths settling together, and when I finally had the energy to open my eyes, I smiled at him. He'd been watching me.

"Welcome home, Capo," I said, my voice shredded.

He grinned and set me down on my feet. "My favorite time of the day," he said.

"Mine too," I whispered, dazed, as he carted me into the shower and wet all of the makeup I'd applied and my hair.

We were going to be *so* late.

I hurriedly redid what he had wrecked, my face, and tried to the do the best with my hair without having to fuss too much. Tonight was a reason to dress up, so I wore a sapphire silk jumpsuit, and diamond, sapphire, and gold bangles on my wrists to match.

"Blue." He grinned as he stepped out of the closet, handing me a pair of shoes I had asked him to find. It had taken him ten minutes to get dressed.

"My signature color," I said.

He nodded. "*Sempre bella in blu.*" *Always beautiful in blue.*

We stared at each other for a moment or two. The intensity in his eyes was hard to meet, especially when images of the night before, when he had brought the marshmallows home, did things to me that made my skin shiver in remembrance. Out in public, the man was as reserved as could be, but behind closed doors...he was an insatiable *animale*. And when he had time...delayed gratification was his specialty.

"It really should be a crime for any man to look as fine as you," I said, not able to help myself.

"That's why I married the most beautiful woman." He slipped my dress coat over my arms, helping me into it. "No one will be looking at me, but at you."

I sometimes forgot how much of a recluse he was. Even though women stared at him wherever we went, he didn't seem to notice, or care. The sooner he was behind closed doors, the sooner he opened up to me.

Ever since the day of his grandfather's funeral, after what had happened in church, something had changed between us. *Nonno* had told me that all life changes begin with a crux. He explained to me what it was—*the decisive or most important point at issue, the heart*—and when it changed, it changed the entire course of things.

"Compare it to taking a different road," he had said. "Sometimes we do this by accident; sometimes we do this by will, but it changes everything beyond that point. It changes history that has yet to happen."

Greece only helped. Capo was more relaxed, more at ease, even though I knew he was grieving. Somehow, though, I knew Capo was teaching me how to live (almost through death), and it seemed like it was in honor of something. Though I didn't know exactly what. Maybe the fact that he had saved my life? And the cost to him, because I knew there had to be one, would be in vain if I didn't make the most of my time here.

Nonno was a philosophical man. His grandson was, too. I tried to keep up.

Giovanni drove us to Broadway. The show was packed; sold out completely. I waved to Keely's family as I took my seat. I was so nervous for her that my foot kept tapping against the floor.

Capo squeezed my thigh, stopping me. "*Dov'è il tuo rosario?*" *Where is your rosary?* he asked in Italian.

I dug in my clutch and pulled it out. The soft lights made the pearls shimmer against the darkness of my nails as I rubbed a bead between my fingers. He rarely had to remind me to use my rosary to ease my anxiety, but tonight, my mind was running in too many different directions, tearing me apart.

The lights went off completely, the curtain lifted, and the show began. Capo took my hand and we watched.

To say that I was proud would've been an understatement. If Keely didn't make the news with her performance, the entire Broadway community could stuff it, as far as I was concerned. After the show, we were invited backstage. I handed her the flowers I brought and hugged her longer than necessary. She invited Capo and me to dinner with her and her family, but I declined. It was awkward, and the less time spent together, the better.

I noticed that the guy who was at the party at Harrison's house, the one who went after Keely, was there. Cash. It didn't seem like Keely wanted to be around him. He'd talk to her and she'd ignore him. When she had to answer him, her answers were clipped.

The entire time, Capo kept his hand on my neck, the one with the tattoo, my hair covering it. It seemed like he did it on purpose, but I wasn't sure.

I didn't take an easy breath until we were out of the theatre. The night was hard with cold, and snow fell in flurries. It actually felt good, and I didn't feel like going straight home. This was the first winter that I didn't fear my teeth chattering all night.

To buy some time, I suggested we get something to eat. Capo agreed. We walked the streets, his hand still on my neck. The city was decorated with holiday decorations. Thousands of lights were strung up, Santas waved bells from street corners, and windows were decked out with pretty things begging to be bought.

Capo had been quiet most of the night. I wondered what he was thinking about.

I glanced up at him. "You've been quiet."

"Can't get much talking in during a Broadway show." The breath rushed out of his mouth in a cloud.

I smiled a little and he pulled me closer. After he did, I felt his grip tighten on my neck, as if he'd seen someone he'd known in a previous life, someone he wanted to avoid. But when I looked up at him again, he was looking at me.

Slowing our strides, I stopped at a window display. It was a bunch of porcelain baby animals. In the center of the scene, an entire Ferris wheel went around and around, all filled with happy little animals in their seats. More little figurines were in motion, rotating in a circle on the ground, like they were at a carnival.

An elephant held a blue balloon. Two giraffes were in a hot air balloon. A tiger flew an airplane with a scarf around his neck. A hippo wore a tutu, holding pink cotton candy. The kicker: a black wolf with its head upturned, a blue butterfly resting on its nose.

The little figures looked like antiques. Maybe French. I could've sworn I heard tinkling music coming from behind the glass.

I turned away from the display and toward the man next to me. Snow fell in his hair, on his lashes, and his eyes seemed even bluer. "I'm not just saying this because you're my husband. You really are the most attractive man I've ever seen." He went beyond attractive, but I didn't want to sound too girly by calling him beautiful.

His eyes flew to mine. "You've complimented me enough tonight." His voice was rough, like the cold clung to his scar and made it hard for him to talk.

I looked down, the buttons on his coat suddenly catching my attention. I fiddled with one, rubbing it between my fingers. "I'm pregnant, Capo."

It was hard to meet his eyes. Would he be angry? He told me the choice was mine. I wanted a baby with him. *Fine.* I didn't want a baby with him. *Fine.*

He was quiet for so long that I took a deep, deep breath and then finally looked up. I wasn't sure what to expect, but what I didn't expect was how pale he looked all of a sudden. His hands trembled when he touched my face. His eyes looked so...uncertain. I'd never seen that before.

It scared me, but I didn't want him to see, so I kept talking. "The baby is due in August. The doctor said everything looks good. I was waiting for the perfect time to tell you, but my mind keeps fidgeting, so..."

He lifted my chin, forcing me to look at him. Without a word, he came in slow and kissed my lips.

That was it. A kiss.

Maybe he was overwhelmed? Even after we started walking again, he didn't say anything. *This pleases me. This fucking sucks.* Nothing.

When we got to an expensive Italian restaurant, Dolce, I stopped. Whatever they were cooking inside smelled really, really good. I hadn't had morning sickness or anything, so when the doctor confirmed that I was pregnant, it was hard to believe. I was worried that my lack of sickness meant that something was wrong. She assured me that pregnancies were as unique as the women who experienced them.

I did have some symptoms, though. Tender breasts. A more sensitive oonie. I needed sex more often to satisfy the craving, which was saying something, because it seemed like that was all we did. Extreme exhaustion, which I had thought was from all the sex, was another symptom. Oh, and some foods smelled so delicious that it was impossible to pass them up.

"What about this place?" I stuck my thumb toward it. "They're known for—"

"Veal *parmigiana.*"

I studied his face harder. Was he sweating? In the snow? His voice was lower, even rougher.

"Capo," I whispered. I took a step closer to him and he took a step back, his eyes turning toward the alley that ran along the side of the restaurant. He narrowed his eyes, like he could see through the darkness. Maybe he could.

Something was wrong, but I had no idea what. "We can go somewhere else," I said. "We don't have to eat here."

A bunch of voices drifted from the alley. Men. Maybe drunk. They were being loud. Obnoxious. Before I could react, Capo had me pressed against the wall of the restaurant, shielding my body with his. He was hurting me, almost crushing me against the wall, but I didn't make a sound. Instead, I lifted my arms, wrapping them around his neck, trying to hide him.

"Ooh!" One of the men squealed like a woman. "I can't believe you would do this to *me*!"

"After she tried to play you and him?" The other man scoffed. "She deserved everything she got."

"Bobby, you got a cigarette on you?"

When the men grew closer, Capo pressed even harder, and then came down and kissed me, the hand with the tattoo in my hair. As they passed, I could smell whiskey like a fire in the air.

Capo's entire body trembled beneath my hands. He *was* sweating. And after the men had gone, I truly noticed his eyes. His pupils were dilated, all of the blue chased out by black, and he looked...mad. Not angry, but almost insane.

Four more men came from the alley a second later, and it felt like my heart was stuck in my throat. The brick dug into my back from the pressure.

These guys were younger, and they didn't even bother to look at us. One of them looked familiar to me, though. He reminded me of Armino Scarpone. I tried to see if any of them had the wolf tattoo, but they moved too fast, leaving behind strong scents from the restaurant.

It still wasn't made clear to me how my husband knew the Scarpones, or what he'd done for them, and why he had saved me from them, apart from the fact that he felt I was innocent in whatever war my father had gotten himself into. Capo had told me that much. My father's actions had set the Scarpones on my mother and me. We were to pay for his sins.

Even after the men had gone, Capo still held me against the wall, not moving. It was getting hard for me to breathe. "Capo," I whispered, sliding my hands underneath his arms. "It's all right. Come on. Let's find somewhere else to eat."

He didn't answer me. It was freaking me out. He had never acted this way before.

"Capo," I tried again. "I'm cold. We can eat at home." I squeezed his coat, resting my head against his chest. I kissed him there, hoping he felt it. "We have leftover *lasagne al forno*. Let's just go home. Call Giovanni and have him pick us up. I'll press the button on my watch."

Finally, his hands covered mine. He pulled me to the side of him, almost making me stumble, and before I could say another word, he forced me to walk. Keep up with him was more like it. As we passed the alleyway, he moved me faster. Not fast enough that my eyes missed it, though. The area seemed colder, and steam rose in white, ghostly shapes from the kitchen. I shivered, and goosebumps rose on my arms.

I had no idea why the sight of it scared me, but that night, I had a nightmare.

Capo's blood collected on the cement right outside of the kitchen in large, dark pools. The smell of iron was thick in the air. His eyes were too blue for his pale face. His lips were almost white. The rosary I'd given him was clutched in his blood-stained hands. His warm breath in the cold night made fog.

Once. Twice. Then he took his final breath.

His third breath. The devil comes in threes.

My limbs were too heavy to move. Frozen solid. I couldn't save him, and I screamed out in agony—the same noise that I'd heard from one of the *zia's* when they closed *Nonno's* coffin. Someone had taken my Capo away from me and torn my soul in two.

Forcing my eyes open, I reached out for Capo with one hand, and with my other, the rosary on the bedside table. As I set the light beside the bed on the softest setting, my eyes were drawn to a spot on the rosary that was stained with what looked like rust. His old watch had stains of the same color.

A sob almost tore out of my throat when I realized it wasn't rust, but blood.

23

February was brutal with cold. No matter how many layers I wore, I still felt the chill. But I often wondered if it had to do with the weather, or the freeze that had settled over us after what happened in December, after Keely's Broadway debut.

Capo had never felt so far from me. He worked more than he ever had, and not once had he brought up the baby. I knew that it was my decision. He was my responsibility in the real sense, but I was hoping Capo would at least show some kind of emotion toward having a son. I hoped that someday he would look at him with more on his mind than what Rocco had called him in the meeting—Capo's financial responsibility.

A son. *He.* The ultrasound technician had said that, even though there was a possibility she could be wrong—we still had what she called the "big ultrasound" to confirm—the tech was almost positive the baby was a boy. His tiny parts were already visible to her. Capo had come with me to that appointment, and it was the first time since Dolce that I'd seen some kind of emotion flicker across his face. It died as soon as we were out of the doctor's office.

I tried to talk to him about it, about everything, but he'd always change the subject. I wasn't any closer to the "heart" and the "veins" he had promised me during our arrangement meeting.

When? I often wondered. *When will he trust me enough to share his secrets?*

Whatever happened that night in front of Dolce had hardened him, and I found myself on the outside again. He had drawn a hard line without giving me an explanation, setting us back. His demands on me became harder, too. The places I could go were limited. The Faustis sent in more reinforcements to watch over our place. And Giovanni was on higher alert at all times, to the point where I felt smothered.

I couldn't take it anymore, so I decided to call Keely and ask her if she wanted to grab a bite to eat. We agreed to eat at Macchiavello's. Giovanni deemed it safe since it was listed on his "allowed places to go" sheet.

"I'm driving," I said to Giovanni. Capo had surprised me with a candy-apple red Ferrari Portofino for Christmas. It was automatic, so I wouldn't have a problem with gears. He had taught me how to drive in Italy. He'd even made some joke about keeping me off the main roads until I was a safe enough driver to not run some poor three-wheeled car off the mountainside. I hadn't driven the Ferrari yet, and I wanted to. It seemed like the perfect time.

I needed some kind of control in my life. I needed to... just *do* without having to get permission from a man who reminded me of an Italian version of Shrek. Keely had put the thought in my head after she had seen Giovanni. She wanted to know why I got the ogre when everyone else had Italian gods to guard them.

Giovanni really didn't look like Shrek. I tilted my head. Much.

"Not today, Mrs. Macchiavello." Giovanni swiped the keys

from my hand too fast for me to even jerk them back. "Mac's orders."

Forget looks. He *acted* more like Shrek at the beginning of the first movie. Instead of *get out of my swamp!* it was *gimme those keys!*

I called *Mac.* "Why can't I drive?"

He sighed. Impatient. "It's not safe. I'll see you tonight."

I looked down at my phone. He had hung up. *"Uomo scortese."* I stuck my tongue at his picture on my screen. I had taken it of him in Greece, his eyes challenging the water for who wore the color blue best.

Giovanni's mouth twitched. He didn't want to outright laugh. I had called his boss a *rude man.*

We beat most of the traffic and made it to the restaurant at the same time Keely did. Bruno looked up from where he was cleaning a table. His eyes flew back to the dirty dish he was placing on a tray when he realized it was the bug, *me.*

We were brought to the private room. The man who usually waited on Capo, Sylvester, came in, taking our orders. Keely and I had the steak. It was cold out, and besides, the crab dish was seasonal. When Sylvester came back in with Keely's drink, she stopped him before he left.

"Wait. What do you want to drink, Mari?"

I lifted my water. "This."

Her eyes narrowed. "You're not getting a cocktail? They're so —" Her eyes widened.

Sylvester left without a sound. So quiet compared to Keely's screech.

She slapped the table. "You're pregnant!"

I smiled and gave her all of the details.

"I'm going to be an aunt!" She lifted her glass, toasting to me, to every chair along the table, pretending like there were people sitting in each one. "That baby is going to be so pretty." She took a sip of her drink. "Why didn't you tell me before?"

I shrugged, tucking a strand of hair behind my ear. "The thing with Harrison—I didn't want things to get more awkward. I've been...staying away. I don't want to lose you. And I don't want to make him feel bad."

She watched me for a minute before she held my hand. "Things have been different, right? I've been giving him time. You, too. But no matter what, you're my sister till the end."

I squeezed her hand and we both smiled.

After our dinner came, conversation flowed, as easy as it ever was. This time, though, both of our lives seemed to be moving in the right direction, and it was fun to talk about all of the positive things instead of survival tips. We laughed more than we ever did.

I asked her questions about Broadway. She asked me questions about Capo and the baby.

"Is he excited?"

I shrugged. "Hard to tell. He's been working a lot."

She still didn't know about our arrangement, so it was hard to open up. I couldn't tell her a version of the truth without giving her the complete truth.

"Hmm." She took another drink. "You're not being totally honest. I've kept quiet long enough. I know he loves you, Mari, but you've been keeping something from me."

My fork hit the plate with a loud *clang!* when it fell from my fingers. "He loves me."

She threw back her head and laughed. "Duh. You goof. He's your husband. Of course he loves you. At least, I'd hope so. Or why would he marry you? Just for your smoking bod? You have one, but in New York, and with a man as fine as him, bodies are a dime a dozen. There has to be more. Animal attraction. True love. I see and feel both."

I didn't want to seem overly excited, so I kept my tone even. "You can?"

"Actions, Mari. Not words. I can tell by his actions. I saw the look on Capo's face when Harrison confessed his undying love for you in the kitchen. Jealousy is a mean bitch, and she was slapping Capo all around. Then in Italy. The way he'd look at you when you weren't looking. When you walked down the aisle? I doubt anyone else existed in that moment. I could tell the wait was killing him. One of his gorgeous friends— Rocco? — had to put a hand on his shoulder to keep him in place." She sighed. "Your first dance. The way he was rubbing your feet under the arbor."

"You saw that?"

"Yeah. I sent the photographer over to take a picture. I didn't want you guys to see. It was so...touching."

"That's one of my favorite pictures," I said.

She smiled at me. "I've never seen you so happy, Mari. And honestly." She looked around. "I know it has nothing to do with...all of this. Money seems like the answer to everything when you have none, but when you've been hungry for more, for things like passion and love, even security, you find out what you were truly starved for when you get what you never knew you wanted or needed."

She was right. I couldn't measure my hunger for love and passion when it had been overshadowed by basic survival. Fear sucked the life out of everything.

Fear of being too cold or too hot.

Fear of being attacked on the streets and having no one to protect you.

Fear of becoming so hungry that'd you resort to digging in the trash.

Fear of dying before truly living.

I took a sip of my water and looked out of the peeper window. My breath caught in my throat. Achille Scarpone sat right next to the mirror, laughing with one of the young guys from the alley. The young guy had a wolf tattoo on his hand, too.

Keely turned to see what I was looking at. "That's kind of creepy." She scrunched up her nose. "It's not as bad as having one in the bathroom, or in a dressing room, but still, I'd hate it if I was eating and someone I didn't know was watching me without me knowing."

"You wouldn't hate it," I said. "You wouldn't know."

"You know what I mean." She squinted. "Capo has a tattoo like that. Do they know each other? What does it mean?"

"I don't know," I whispered, like Achille could hear me. "He's not a friendly, though."

A minute later, the young guy put his elbow on the table and Achille did, too. The younger guy got up after they shook and moved out of the window's frame. Maybe he had left? Achille stuck around, ordering another drink from the waitress.

I hit the side button on my watch, the screen turning into a touchscreen keyboard, and sent Capo a text. *One of the men from Italy is here. Sitting right outside of the peeper window. Achille.* I hoped that I'd spelled his name right. It was odd. *A-kill-ee.*

My watch lit up a second later. *Stay in our private room. I'm on my way.*

A knock came at the door and I looked up. Sylvester. "Mrs. Macchiavello, I hate to disturb you, but Detective Stone requests a word with you."

I stared at Sylvester for a moment. What fucking timing. Detective Stone wasn't allowed in this room. It was used exclusively for Capo and his guests. Stone was not on the guest list. And if I met him out front, Achille might see me and recognize me, and then maybe he'd hang around more. The thought of being close to him made the steak feel like jerky stuck in my throat.

"Can he come back? I'm having dinner." It was almost gone, but he didn't know that. "Or have him call and make an appointment."

"No." Sylvester shook his head. "He says he needs to speak

to you now. If you are eating, he will wait until you finish
dinner."

"Have him meet me in the kitchen," I said.

"I'm going to get going." Keely stood abruptly, throwing her
purse over her shoulder. She gave me a hard kiss on the head.
"Call me tomorrow. We'll go shopping soon for our baby boy."

"Keely." I stopped her. "What's going on with you and
Stone? Is that why he's here?"

"Nothing. Between us, I mean. I'm not sure why he's here. If
it's about me, tell him you have no idea what's going on."

"I don't."

"You're better off." She threw me a kiss and then left.

Giovanni escorted me to the kitchen, his hold tighter than
normal.

"Do you think I'm going to run to him?" I yanked my arm
out of his grip.

"I apologize," he said. "Detective Stone wants to speak to
you. Alone."

"What for?"

Giovanni shrugged. "Mac is not going to like this."

"Let's hope I can answer his questions before Mac gets
here." I entered into the kitchen alone. It bustled, and all of the
hustling bodies and stoves made it feel like a degree before hell.

Detective Stone stood in the corner, trying to stand out of
the way, and when he noticed me, he called me with a finger.

Before I could get to him, I overheard Bruno talking to one
of the other busboys. He was talking about how he couldn't
wait for someone to take "Mac" out. He hoped Stone would
do it.

I tapped him on the shoulder. He froze. A second or two
later, he turned around slowly, facing me.

"You're fired," I said. "Gossiping about my husband's business is not tolerated. You signed the agreement when you
started working here. Get your shit and go."

"Fired?" he repeated.

I opened my eyes wide, trying to press the point. "Do you need a dictionary?"

His face turned a mean shade of red. He opened his mouth to say something, but then he closed it as soon as Stone came close to us. Bruno turned and left, and after, a few of the kitchen staff applauded softly.

Stone took me by the arm after the kitchen drama and led me outside. I protested, but it was no use. He said that he refused to speak inside of the restaurant. *Why?* Then I worried about Achille rounding the corner, seeing me. He couldn't kill me in front of a detective, could he? *I guess that depends on if Stone is in his pocket,* I thought cynically.

"You could've let me grab my coat!" I crossed my arms over my chest, trying to ward off the cold. It was like going from one side of hell to another in the span of a second. "What's this about?"

"Where's Keely?"

"I don't know." I shrugged. "If it's Keely you want, go find *her*. It's freezing out here!"

"What do you know about Cashel Kelly?"

"Besides his name? Nothing." I held up a hand. "Honest."

He watched my face for any signs of dishonesty for a minute. Maybe looking for a tell? I stuck my hands in my pockets, not wanting to fidget.

"It seems like you girls keep a lot of secrets from each other. I thought ya'll were friends."

"You're right. We're not. We're sisters."

"Well, that makes more sense. Sisters don't always get along as well as friends."

"Is this visit about Keely?" Smoke purled out of my mouth.

"Yes and no." He watched me again, this time with his hands on his hips. He had a coat on. Gloves. A hat. Maybe he thought if he made me stand out in the cold I'd break sooner.

"Do you girls always go for the bad boys you'll never be able to change?"

"That sounds like a lot of nonsense to me, Detective Stone."

"I'm a little late on the congratulations, Mrs. Macchiavello. I heard you married Mac Macchiavello, one of the richest men in New York. He's a man whose face is rarely seen. He glides just under the lines."

"No need to wish me well in my marriage. You hardly know me. And again, *nonsense*. I'm out here freezing my ass off for nonsense."

"What do you know about the Scarpone family, Mrs. Macchiavello?"

"At this moment? One of them is sitting inside of the restaurant. Having dinner."

"His name is Achille Scarpone. He's Arturo Scarpone's youngest son."

"I assume the other guy that was in there with Achille a few minutes ago is Arturo's—"

"Grandson," Stone answered for me. "Achille Scarpone has four sons. Well. Had. You remember Armino Scarpone?"

"Yeah."

"He's presumed dead." He let that hang in the air between us.

"So...?"

"So. It seems like ever since you hooked up with Mac Macchiavello, everyone who has threatened you in some way has disappeared."

"Like who?" I lied.

He lifted his pointer finger. "Quillon Zamboni. Strangled." He lifted his middle finger, which was suitable for the next name. "Merv Johnson. Beat beyond recognition." He lifted his ring finger. "Armino Scarpone. Still missing."

"Let me refresh your memory, Detective Stone. I met Armino maybe three times. He knew I was home the day he killed Sierra. He's a Scarpone. He might not be dead, if he's just missing—after all, he killed a girl and all signs point to him. So what does he have to do with me?"

"Forget Armino. What about the other two?"

"I don't associate with Quillon Zamboni."

"Wrong. He fostered you."

"And that means what, exactly? I haven't seen him in years."

"Where did you go after you ran from his house, Mari? What made you run?"

"Do I need my lawyer, Detective?"

He smiled. "This is a private visit."

"Then let's get on with it." I really started to tremble. And it wasn't only from the cold.

"Arturo Scarpone has one son now, but he had two."

"We've already went over—"

"You seem to know who Achille is, but do you know his oldest son?"

I shook my head, holding my arms closer to my chest. "I haven't had the pleasure."

"No." His voice was low. "You wouldn't. He's presumed dead. Vittorio Lupo Scarpone. The case was never truly solved. Rumor has it that he was dumped into the Hudson, on a night like this one, cement blocks around his legs. But he was already dead. Someone cut his throat.

"It's been rumored that the King of New York—that's Arturo—had his own son killed. And Achille, the next in line to the infamous Scarpone throne, was only too eager to see his older brother—they called him the Pretty Boy Prince—dead. They call Achille the Joker. You ever hear of a joker passing up the opportunity to be king?" He paused for a second. "Nah, I didn't think so.

"Arturo, they say, killed his son because he didn't kill the child of a mortal enemy. Last name Palermo. First name Corrado. Apparently, the Prince found some scruples. He was against killing kids, even the kid of his father's enemy. Little Marietta hasn't been found either. That's Palermo's kid."

"W-w-what does t-t-his h-h-have to do with m-m-me?" My teeth started to clack and my bones trembled. Suddenly, so many pieces clicked into place, and I was terrified that Stone would see the truth on my face. I was thankful that the temperature had dropped, the wind sharper, and the dress was thin.

He shrugged. "Thought you should know the kind of people your husband entertains in his place of business."

"He a-a-also entertains t-t-the F-F-Faustis."

"Even worse. Luca Fausti killed my aunt and her unborn child. Drunk driving. They, unlike the Prince, have no scruples."

"How about a-a-actors and a-a-actresses? M-m-musicians? World f-f-famous artists? Are those b-b-better?"

"Not by much."

"T-t-there is n-n-no p-p-p-pleasing you." I took a step closer to him. With the same clacking, I asked, "Who is Cashel Kelly, and why do you care if he's with Keely or not?"

At first I thought he hadn't understood my question. My teeth chattered so hard my speech was almost unintelligible. But after a second, I felt it, too. Another presence. Wearing all black, he seemed like a detached part of the night taking shape, appearing behind us. My husband's blue eyes seemed to emerge from the darkness, making the resemblance to the wolf on his hand identical.

Capo slipped my coat over my shoulders and then pulled me closer, tight into his side. "Detective." His voice came out gruff. The cold played havoc with his voice. It gave me chills. "The next time you request to speak to my wife, you will call our lawyer first and make an appointment. I believe you've met him before. Rocco Fausti."

At Stone's nod, he continued. "My wife was accommodating enough to agree to speak to you in the kitchen, where it was warm, but you led her out into the cold. Do you make it a habit, Detective, to make pregnant women step outside in negative temperatures without a jacket?"

"I didn't realize she was pregnant." Stone's voice couldn't hide his shock—not at the pregnancy comment, but at seeing the man standing in front of him. Stone's eyes traveled to Capo's throat before they went to his hands. His coat's collar came above his throat, and the hand with the tattoo was stuck in his pocket.

Had he evaded the police all of this time?

"Even if she wasn't," Capo said, his tone sharp, "I don't appreciate my wife being out in the cold and you harassing her for no reason."

"Harassing?" Stone's face screwed up. "We were just talking. This visit was personal."

"In that case." Capo raked his teeth over his bottom lip. "No fucking more. You have a problem with my wife's friend, you take it up with her. You have a problem with my wife's friend being connected to Cash Kelly, you take it up with her. Or him. None of this nonsense comes close to my wife again. Are we clear?"

A low whistle sounded in the air. At first, I thought it was the wind. Then I realized it was a person. I turned to look, but Capo kept me firmly in place.

"Deeee-tect-ive Stone! Is that you? We should have a chat outside of the precinct for once. Hell, I'll even buy you a drink. You gotta be human under that cheap suit, right?" His throaty laughter echoed.

The familiar voice made the cold feel even colder. Achille. Capo squeezed me tighter to him. He glanced at me once, and then he met Stone's eyes. Stone didn't seem like he knew where to look the longest. At Capo or at Achille, who moved closer to us.

"It seems our business is done here." Stone nodded at me once and then headed in the direction of Achille.

Capo directed me back toward the kitchen, almost shoving me through the door to get me back inside, before his brother saw us both.

———

CAPO HADN'T SAID a word to me on the ride back to the fire-house. I thought that was for the best. We both had too many thoughts to offer normal conversation. If he were to ask me if I were hungry, I'd probably blurt, "You're a Scarpone? Are you fucking kidding me?"

I knew he had run with them, was maybe one of their men at one time, but he was *one* of them. The King of New York's son!

Then there were other issues. The first being—you killed my parents. The second—if his father was the King of New York, his brother the Joker, and my husband the Prince, what did that mean for our future? For this baby? The third, and probably not the last—in the eyes of the world, my husband was dead, a fucking ghost wearing expensive men's clothing.

No wonder Capo had refused to give me the heart of the matter and the veins, as he had called them, at the meeting. The heart he was going to offer me had no beats, no blood flow, because, again, it was dead.

The man walking beside me into our house was not supposed to be using his legs. He was supposed to be submerged underneath the Hudson River, cement weights attached to his ankles, drowned long ago. When I was five years old. After he had saved my life. His fucking bloodthirsty family had slit his throat because he hadn't killed me.

Who told on him?

Was it his brother?

That bastard looked like the Joker. He looked nothing like my husband, the man Stone called Vittorio, the Pretty Boy Prince.

And Arturo? What a fucking king he was. To kill your own son? And that savagely? Someone needed to take *his* head off.

Hold up, Mari. I stopped the thoughts before they got carried away. Why was I getting so upset about what they'd done to him when I should've been upset about what he'd done to me? The least he could've done was told me who he was from the start. He had told me who I was, what he had done, but he had left out a vital part of the conversation.

He killed my parents before he saved me.

He hadn't swooped in while someone else from that vicious family took care of my parents— he had done it, and then changed my name, my address, and gave me new people to take care of me. He basically wiped me clean.

Why didn't he tell me?

If it had something to do with me accepting his offer... why did it matter if he married me or not? Sierra or me, another one of those faces at The Club or me, he just wanted a starved woman, a woman who wouldn't bite the hand that fed her. For a Gucci purse, Sierra would've spit in Stone's face.

Why didn't he just let me go after he realized it was me?

Why is he playing these games with me?

"I'm going to take a shower," I said, leaving him in our room. "I'm still cold."

He stood at the entrance of the bathroom, leaning against the frame. "You disobeyed me, Mariposa."

I stopped, my back turned to him, but I could see him through the mirrors. "How?"

"You left the private room at the restaurant when I told you to stay there."

"I didn't tell Stone anything!"

"You didn't." He raked his teeth over his bottom lip. "Still. Not the fucking point."

If he wanted a fight, he was barking up the wrong tree. He wanted a wolf—he was about to get a she one. "What *is* the point?" I said through clenched teeth.

"I need to keep you safe. You're my wife. The mother of my son."

That shocked me. His tone. It was softer, but still raspy. My anger simmered some, which would give me time to find out what I needed before I confronted him. I wanted all of the facts before I went to war. I knew after talking to Stone, I wasn't dealing with an average man. This man had lived half of his life as a ghost. In honor of what? Vengeance?

"I'll be in the office."

When I turned around, he was gone.

I must've taken the quickest shower in my history at the secret fire station. I tried to act nonchalant as I dried my hair and then prepared for bed. I put on the thickest pajamas in my closet, still feeling the cold from earlier, and even thicker socks. I slid into bed, propped my pillows against the headboard, and then took out my laptop from the side table.

The last page I'd been on was a site for saving ideas. I was thinking about the baby's room. Nothing compared to those little French figurines I'd seen in the window that night, though. I wanted to go back and get them, but I was hesitant. Dolce seemed like a main hangout for the Scarpones. Maybe I'd ask Keely to swing by and get the store's name. I could call them, buy the figurines over the phone, and have them delivered.

Lowering the page, I opened an entirely new search. I typed in four words: *Scarpones of New York*.

Thousands of results appeared on the page.

"Too many." I sighed. I read the first couple of articles, though. *Ruthless. Pack of Wolves. Cunning. Social climbers.* Those were the most prominent adjectives used. I found a few pictures of Arturo and Achille. *Ritzy functions. Political dinners. Shaking hands. All smiles.* There was a picture with Arturo and his current wife, Bambi, who was Achille's mother. Achille was the perfect mixture of them both. My husband looked more like his mother's side of the family.

It clicked then. That was why they called him the Pretty Boy Prince.

In a house full of savages, he stood out.

I scrolled some more, but only "suspected" criminal dealings came up. Things the Scarpones had been questioned for but never indicted on. This time, I narrowed my search down.

Vittorio Lupo Scarpone

"Can't be," I muttered, narrowing my eyes against the glare of the screen. There were only three articles that mentioned him. The first had a picture of a beautiful woman smiling as she walked down the street. I could tell it was someplace in New York. I could tell she was going somewhere, trying to get away from the cameras, but still smiling, showing her best side. If the other side was as perfect as the one she shared; she had no flaws.

Two Kingdoms Come Together to Form One Powerful Family

The "Prince" of New York set to marry into one of New York's finest political dynasties.

Vittorio Lupo Scarpone, son of Arturo Scarpone and the late Noemi Scarpone, and Angelina Zamboni, daughter of Angelo and Carmella Zamboni, will be wed at the Cathedral of St. Patrick, followed by a winter-wonderland themed reception at the bride's parents' estate in Upstate New York.

"Son of a bitch," I whispered. Was Quillon related to Angelina? They had the same last name, and when I looked at her a bit harder, there was something there. Not immediate, but something about the way they smiled. Nothing else, though, connected them. She had a slim face. Tan skin. Long, dark blonde hair. Dark eyes. Tall. She seemed very tall. And her nose was...perfection, along with her lips. She was the Italian Princess to the wildly gorgeous Italian Prince.

I pulled up a separate page, typing in her name. Very few results showed for her, too. Quillon *was* her brother. The rest of the articles focused on her murder.

Her *murder*.

Men, more than one, had attacked her in the alley beside Dolce, the restaurant that gave me the creeps. It was speculated that Vittorio went down fighting for Angelina before the men raped her and then put a bullet in her brain. She had suffered a gruesome death, the article stated. She was also pregnant at the time of her demise.

I had to close the computer for a second, take a deep, deep breath. Then I opened it again when I felt I could breathe normally.

Vittorio's blood had been all over the scene, enough of it that they had suspected he was brutally stabbed and then his body dumped in the water somewhere. They hadn't found him.

"Of course not," I said to the screen. "He's sitting in the next room. *I* found him."

I couldn't stand to read more details about Angelina's murder, or continue to see pictures of her, so I went back to my other search about Vittorio.

The second article went on about the wedding, the A-list guests that were expected to attend, how much the wedding of the year was going to cost. I clicked that off, too. I couldn't read an article about their wedding after I'd just imagined their horrendous deaths.

The third and final article gave details about Vittorio's death. It was all speculation, though. No one really knew what had happened to him, but I could tell the article hinted at his father and brother, but the writer was too afraid to come out and directly say it.

Vittorio Lupo Scarpone had become an urban legend, in a sense. Some people, the article claimed, didn't think he was dead. They thought that after his attempted murder, he took hidden money and lived on a private island somewhere, to escape the evil clutches of his family.

Like 2Pac. Or better yet, Niccolò Machiavelli. The root of the 2Pac theory. Even Elvis. All of those *"is he or isn't he dead?"* magazine headlines.

"Fucka me," I said.

I sat there for a minute, biting my lip, until I took my rosary out. I settled some after rubbing the pearls, but not entirely. My anxiety rose even higher after I searched for Noemi Ranieri Scarpone. She was even more beautiful than Angelina. Black hair. Blue Eyes. Tan skin. Thin. Big smile. The very first article spoke about her killing herself. It was rumored that she had a long history with a mental disorder.

I scrolled down a bit, familiar with the story, but what I hadn't known was that she had left a note behind for Vittorio.

The article claimed that no one had ever seen the note, but it was rumored to have said: *Marry for loyalty, not for love. Love kills the soul quicker than a sharp dagger to the heart.*

Even though it didn't make me feel any better, if Noemi had left that behind, it explained so much about my husband's aversion to love.

"Looking for something?"

I made an *ahh!* noise, jumped, and the computer flew through the air, my knees liftoff point. We both scrambled to get to the computer at the same time, but he was quicker. It didn't matter anyway; we had to have this conversation sooner or later.

I thought he was going to look at what I'd been looking at, but instead, he handed me the computer. Then he took a seat on the bed, his back to me. Instead of the computer, I grabbed the rosary, worrying it between my fingers.

Time. So much time went by—ten minutes? Which felt like a lifetime to me. Finally, I couldn't stand the tension any longer. "Why didn't you tell me who you are, Vittorio?"

"I gave you permission to call me any name you'd like. You even named me. Capo. But that name...that one is off limits. It belongs to someone else."

"A ghost," I said.

"A ghost."

"You killed my parents," I whispered.

"There was no other choice." He sighed. "I didn't mind killing your father, but I didn't want to take your mother away from you. She was a good woman, but she married the wrong kind of man. She knew I had to. She begged me to. If I didn't kill her, give her an easy death, Achille would've been sent in my place.

"He's stupid in some ways, but when it comes to locating someone, he's relentless. He would've sniffed her out eventually. Too many people knew her face. Even in Italy they would've found her. They have connections there, too. At that point, your parents had little money. They'd been hiding from Arturo for a while. What I did to her was a mercy compared to what Achille would've done. The only thing better for Achille would've been making your father watch as he did it."

"He never found me." I squeezed the rosary, hoping it wouldn't pop from the strain.

"There's one person who's better at tracking than him. Better at hiding, too."

"You."

"I was certain they wouldn't find you. They didn't. I even went as far as renaming you in the blood database."

"How did—how did they know you let me go?"

"A man playing two sides of the game was hiding in your parents' place that night. He was getting information from your father and then delivering it to Arturo. If Arturo seemed like he was worried about something, or growing weaker, the rat would tell your father. He didn't know who to place his bets on. You were an unforeseen circumstance that I didn't bargain for. I should've checked the place twice but didn't. I wanted to get you out. The rat came to me the next day, telling me what he'd done—he told Arturo that I didn't kill you, that I hid you. I killed him after, but it was too late. He'd already ratted to Arturo and Achille."

"Your father had you killed because you let an innocent child go?"

"Yes and no." He sat forward some, pressing his palms together. "Yes. In that world, you leave no member of a rival family alive. For example, if you would've found out later on what I'd done to your parents, you might've wanted revenge. If you no longer existed, that takes care of that. The yes also includes disobeying his orders. I was instructed to make your father watch as I killed you and your mother in front of him. Arturo wanted him to suffer for challenging him, for trying to slit his throat. Your father had that same ruthless streak about him. He was hungry to lead and thirsty for blood. He wanted Arturo's place in that world. If I wouldn't have killed Palermo, even knowing you and your mother were in danger, he would've gone after Arturo again."

"Why else?" I said when he stopped talking. "You said yes and no. You gave me the yes."

"It was only a matter of time before I did something to get myself executed. Achille wanted the throne for himself. Time and time again, I proved myself as ruthless as him, even smarter, and he couldn't stand it. No matter what I did, he'd run back and tell Arturo how I somehow fucked it up. I was *'too pretty to rule.' No one would take me seriously.* Arturo gave me an out, and I refused to take it. I even told him I'd challenge Achille to a fight, if that's what it took. He told me there was no need to fight Achille. I'd rule beside the king, and after he was too old to rule, the kingdom was mine.

"Then one night we were at a party. All of these powerful political figures were there. Arturo had been out to get this one guy in his pocket but never could. Arturo saw the two of us talking and came over. Political told Arturo that he wanted someone like me to work for him. I was smart. Had a plan. 'As charming as they come.'

"After that—" He paused, stretching his shoulders, like the custom-made suit had grown too tight all of a sudden. "—I noticed a difference in him. He talked down to me more and gave Achille more to do. And when Achille complained about me, the pretty-boy prince who got everything he wanted, Arturo ate it up. He was starved for it. He was worried that once I married Angelina Zamboni, an arrangement he made, I'd take over his kingdom without him handing it to me. Angelina could charm a vagabond out of his last penny, if she wanted to. She had high expectations for her life, for her husband."

For her husband. The man sitting beside me. *My* husband. "Why did they kill her?" I asked softly.

"Punishment. They did to her what I was sent to do to your mother and you. Kill you in front of your father. But Angelina's fate was worse. They didn't just kill her. They violated her from every side until they tore her in two. I couldn't stop it. There were too many of them and only one of me. The man they sent to slit my throat had already started cutting—sometimes the moments are a blur. Other times, I can still smell the blood."

"That's..." I didn't even have words.

"They probably would've raped her and let her go, if it was only me they meant to punish. But she was fucking Achille and me at the same time. She told me she was pregnant the night it happened. He admitted, right before he left us to be slaughtered, that she'd been telling him things about me. Loyalty is valued in that world, Mariposa. Valued above anything else, even money and gold. Achille had the woman who was pregnant with his child killed because she had double-crossed *me*. The man he was about to send to his grave because he threatened to take all that he wanted."

"The baby wasn't yours," I breathed out.

"No. His."

Click. Click. Click. The pieces started to fall into place.

"It happened right outside of Dolce." I bit my lip, hard. "And she told you she was pregnant on the way."

"Right after a Broadway show," he said.

"She set you up."

"The Zambonis have gone down in history as traitors. None of them were ever truly loyal. They were all out to rise above the rest, no matter the cost. Shiny things. They loved shiny things to collect. If you would've searched a little more, you would've found that most people have dubbed them the family of Judas."

"You were controlling the results of my searches."

"I control everything," he said.

That's why there are no pictures of him. He took them all down.

We both became quiet, but a burning inside of me refused to allow me to keep quiet.

"Did you love her?"

It took him a moment. "Who?"

"Angelina," I said. "Your fiancé."

He smiled and it gave me chills. "No. It was an arranged marriage. Love kills the soul quicker than a sharp dagger to the heart."

I swiped at my eyes, hating that tears were on the edges, blurring my world. I didn't know how to feel about all of this. I softly got out of the bed, afraid that if I made any sudden movements, it would disturb something. *Him.* And all of the fight had drained out of me. I needed time to think, to process all of this.

I stood by the door, and he tilted his head to the side, watching me.

"Why weren't you honest with me before? Why didn't you tell me from the start that you killed my parents? You gave me no choice! I had no idea...I thought you maybe ran with the Scarpone family. I had no idea you were *one* of them. The king's son. His prince."

He was on me in a minute. I tried to back away, but I couldn't. The wall pressed against my back and I was forced to look up into his cold, cold eyes.

"I let it slide when you called me Vittorio. I'll let that last comment slide this time, too, since you have no fucking clue what you're talking about. I'm not his son. I'm not his prince. When you call me the king's son. When you call me his prince. When you call me Vittorio. When you call me anything that has to do with *that* life, you're speaking the ugliest words of all to me."

Suddenly, an ember seemed to burst into flames out of nowhere. The last fight I had in me. "The ugliest words? No, I don't think so. You want to hear three ugly words, *my husband*? Words that are nastier, and more twisted, than all of those words you strung together? I love you, and there isn't a damn thing you can do about it. And what's even better, I don't want to! I don't want to love you, but I do! I love you. I love you. I love you! You've damaged me with this...love! That dagger? You stuck it right in my heart. You made me fall in love with you before you were honest with me—before you used the dagger on me."

Without taking any of my stuff, I started for the spare room, the room I planned on decorating for the baby. My husband followed me, no expression I could make sense of on his face. But I didn't want to see his face. I wanted nothing to do with him.

He killed my parents.

He saved me and then he hid me.

And the Scarpones had killed him for it. Made him watch terrible things. They were going to throw him in the Hudson after he bled out on the cement right in front of a bunch of dumpsters. The Prince with Scarpone blood running through his veins. *Blood that belonged to them.*

Then I found him years later.

Then he saved me, again, from a fate he'd put me on a path to. His father and mine both at fault, too.

Then, in the midst of all that fucking madness, somehow, I fell in love. So deeply in love that I couldn't tell the difference between passion and anger anymore. I wanted to slap him and kiss him all at the same time.

Slap him for not telling me.

Kiss him for saving me. For suffering for me. For all that he had been through in my honor.

Marry for loyalty, not for love. Love kills the soul quicker than a sharp dagger to the heart.

He had taken a dagger to his throat. For me.

I took one to the heart. For him.

I touched my stomach. I'd forever be connected to him, the proof of his blood vow taking up space in my womb.

We both had to bleed for this.

I wondered if tomorrow our arrangement would be null and void due to...love. A weapon he had no defense against.

It didn't matter. Nothing mattered. After he'd slammed me into that metaphorical rock, I was set adrift.

I slammed the door in his face right before I slid into bed and hid myself in the darkness.

A WEEK HAD GONE BY. We hadn't spoken. We hadn't touched. We hadn't even looked at each other.

In the morning, I used to cook him breakfast before he left for work. We were in contact during the day. We'd make dinner plans. Sometimes he would even send me a dirty joke. There wasn't a night since our wedding, or day for that matter, that we didn't have sex. I hadn't gone even a day without seeing him. When he worked too much, I felt it, the absence of the most important person to me.

I struggled with missing him and wanting nothing to do with him. When I smelled coffee in the kitchen after just waking up, or his cologne in our bathroom, or saw one of his shirts in the hamper, it made me want to burn it all down, but at the same time, savor each scent, each touch.

Love doesn't make you sick, like people claim. It silently goes in, nick by nick, causing cuts that might never heal. Noemi was right about one thing: Love isn't a disease. Love is a dagger.

On the seventh day of silence, I got an unexpected visitor.

Uncle Tito.

He hugged me tightly before patting my stomach. "How is our boy?"

I patted the same spot. "The Dr. said all looks good. He's still looking like a little boy."

Uncle Tito laughed at this. He handed me a loaf of what looked like bread. "Scarlett wanted me to bring this over. Would you mind putting on some coffee so we can enjoy it? The baby will like the blueberries, I am sure."

After pouring him a cup of coffee, I cut us each a slice of the cake, and we ate in silence. Every once in a while, he took a sip of coffee. On one sip, my eyes rose to meet his, and the kindness in them almost knocked me off the chair. It happened at the most unexpected times.

"I know," I said. "You were the man who saved...my husband." It was hard for me to call him anything but husband. The other names seemed wrong, and when I thought of the name he was given at birth, *Vittorio*, it made me think of talking about a dead man.

He patted my hand. "A different time. A different place. I am only thankful that I was there for him."

Silence came between us again. I didn't know what to say. I still hadn't settled on one feeling. Loyalty kept me rooted. Love was killing me because it gave him the power to stick the dagger in further. His secrets were the poisonous tips.

When I looked up, Uncle Tito was watching me again. "He sent me here."

"Who?"

"Your husband. He is unsure."

"That's a new one for him, right?"

"Right." He nodded. "In my humble opinion, it can do a heart good to feel things it has never before. He is feeling everything now, not just existing for vengeance."

"I disagree about the heart. Sometimes when the heart feels things it never has before, it hurts. Really bad."

"Good thing the heart has the amazing capacity to heal itself after time when it comes to such things, ah?" Uncle Tito took a sip of coffee and then placed the cup down. "All that Amadeo did, *farfalla*, he did for you. You understand that, don't you? You showed him something he had not seen in a long time. Such innocence...an innocence he hadn't seen since his mother."

"Why..." My knee bobbed under the table. "Why didn't he tell me? Who he was? What he'd done?"

He smiled, but it made the kindness in his eyes turn to sadness. "He was unsure then, as well."

"Unsure of what?"

He picked our plates up and set them in the sink. "Perhaps in time you will understand. It is not my place to say. The words should be shared between husband and wife. If you would like to know, speak to your husband. Open the lines of communication." He took a deep breath. "You speak of the heart. The heart cannot beat without an open flow. If it has clots." He shrugged. "It will die. Think of a marriage in these same terms."

The good doctor stayed with me about an hour longer, and after we shared normal, family gossip, from Noemi's side of the family, he kissed my head firmly and left.

After he'd gone, the house seemed too quiet. All I did was stew on the same issues over and over, my brain starting to short circuit, my heart bleeding out or maybe backing up. Uncle Tito had given me more to consider, which made my need to get out stronger.

Giovanni would have to okay it with my husband before any plans were made. I knew my husband would make me take Giovanni if I left the house.

I needed to be away from *everything* related to him.

Maybe without his influence, I could think clearly, and if things were not as bad as they seemed, maybe my heart could start to heal. Or maybe get rid of the clot, as Uncle Tito had said.

I called Keely and told her to meet me at our place in thirty minutes. We could have some of the cake Scarlett had sent with Uncle Tito.

You see, I'd figured out a few things after I moved in.

My husband really knew everything, but the watch was a way for him to keep track of my movements. Giovanni, too, once I crossed over into the other side of the house. I always came down from the bedroom, so he had no idea about the secret firehouse.

Right before the thirty minutes, I asked Giovanni to look for a pair of boots in my closet. I told him my legs were hurting. *Lie.* He gave me a suspicious look but did as I asked. I'd never asked him to do anything for me before. I quickly called the control room and told them to check the cameras in the back of the house. It seemed like two men were fighting out in the street.

Leaving my watch on the kitchen counter, I took off out of the front door, using my hands to signal to Keely to *not* get out of the car. She understood right away and restarted the car before I was even in it. She took off once I was in, and I had to slam the door shut while we burnt rubber.

"Okay." She eyed her rearview mirror, making sure we were not being followed. "Why are we running from *your* house?"

"I...need a break. I don't feel like being surrounded by men today."

"Ooh. The honeymoon is over. Let the games begin!"

"It's not a game, Keely. It's marriage." I waved a hand. "We just had a fight."

"Over what type of diapers to use?"

Only if our issues were that domesticated. I couldn't give her the entire truth, so basic would have to do. "Something like that."

"Answer one question. Do we hate him or not?"

"Not." My answer came quick. How could I hate him after he sacrificed his life for mine? But how could I not be angry with him for not telling me the complete truth right away? Having enough of my issues, I turned to face her. "Who's Cashel Kelly?"

The car swerved and I glanced at the mirror, wondering if one of the guys had caught up to us. It seemed all clear, but they were sneaky. I expected them to act like cops and pull us over at any minute.

"Cash," she said underneath her breath. "Almost everyone calls him Cash. And Stone told you about him."

"Not exactly. He was fishing for information the night we had dinner."

She nodded. "What did you tell him?"

"What could I tell him, Kee? I have no idea what's going on!"

"Cash Kelly is Harrison's new boss."

I waited a few minutes. "And...?"

"He's not all he seems to be."

"That seems to be a trend lately. Go on."

She turned to me and narrowed her eyes. "Wait. Where are we going?"

I told her about the little figurines, but asked if she could just pass by, so I could get the name of the shop. She agreed and took a detour, heading in the right direction.

"Are you in love with Cash, Kee?"

She threw back her head and exploded with laughter. "If New York was a wild cement forest, I'd be the archer and he'd be my target."

"I don't like the picture you painted in my mind. I keep seeing him running away from you, a bullseye on his back."

She grinned. "We shouldn't talk about this anymore. The baby. Let's talk about the baby. Tell me more about these figurines and the theme you're going for."

Even though I wanted to call her out on her odd comment, I told her about the figurines and how cute they were. When she found a parking spot not far from the store, right in front of Dolce, I shook my head. "I only need the name, Kee! Let's go. We'll go shopping somewhere else."

"Why is your face pale? You have bubble sweat over your lip, and it's colder than a polar bear's oonie outside. Did something happen to you here?"

I bit my lip, fiddling with my purse. "Yeah. I had some bad veal *parmigiana*. Just awful."

"Liar." She squeezed my hand. "You stay put. Keep the doors locked. I'll just run in and see if they're still there. They obviously mean a lot to you."

Before I could stop her, she was out of the car, hustling to get to the little shop.

"Shit, shit, shit," I chanted. I was in the heart of Scarpone territory. *Dolce.* The name almost made me want to puke. There was nothing sweet about that restaurant or what had happened right outside of its doors. I wondered how many people had been murdered in that alleyway. If the Scarpone family owned it, there was no telling. My legs bobbed up and down. I pulled out my rosary, worrying the beads again. This time I kept thinking *please let her hurry up.*

As I looked up, I saw four men coming out of the restaurant. Achille. Arturo. One of his grandsons, I thought; the one who looked like Armino. And, maybe, the guy Achille called Bobby.

They all looked like big dogs with their expensive coats and suits, three out of four smoking cigarettes, and all of them wore identical "I own this fucking place" looks. The wolf tattoos only upped their scary factors.

Keely came down the street at the same time they walked toward her.

Achille stopped, watching her walk past. It was hard not to notice her. She was a bright flame in complete darkness. Her hair was curly, wild, and flaming red, and she'd pulled it up on the sides, making her seem much taller than what she was. Drawn to her, maybe because he was so fucking cold, he watched her walk all the way to her car, where he noticed me sitting next to her. His eyes narrowed and he took a step closer. He whistled and his son and Bobby came to stand next to him. He nudged Bobby in the ribs.

"Keely." My voice came out so low that I made myself talk louder. "Get us the fuck out of here!"

"You know them?" She narrowed her eyes in their direction, while she started the car.

"Fucking go!" I shouted.

"All right! All right!" She swerved into traffic, barely missing a taxicab. He shot us the bird as he whizzed past. Then he got in front of us and kept tapping on his brakes. "Was that the Scarpones?"

"How do you know that?"

"Fucker!" She laid on her horn. She whipped around the taxi driver, giving him the bird as she passed *him* up. Then she did the same thing to him. Cut him off and then started tapping on her brakes. "I've heard things. I was curious so I looked them up online. I didn't find anything too juicy, but those tattoos mean something, don't they?"

"It doesn't matter." I waved off the tattoos, trying to downplay the fact that my husband had one, too. "They kept staring. It scared me."

"It should. They're insane."

"Yeah, I got that."

"Bad news." She blew out a breath. "No more figurines."

My heart pounded overtime, but at that, it sank. "What happened to them?"

"Someone wiped them out." She checked her outside mirror and then went a different way. "Maybe you can find another store that has them. They're French, like you thought. Antiques. The seller said they're rare. Expensive. He told me to try a place in Paris. He wrote down the name. I have it in my pocket. Maybe you can ask Scarlett if she knows anything about it. I remember her saying that she lived there for a while."

I shouldn't have risked the trip for the figurines. I should've asked her to look when she was alone. When I wasn't in the car. It bothered me that someone had bought them, but what bothered me even more was what I'd done.

Maybe I'd put my husband in more danger. If Achille connected me to Italy, to Amadeo, maybe he'd make sense of something. Or become curious enough to find out what I was doing on his territory, after he'd seen me on the church steps in another country, the day of *Nonno's* funeral.

To make matters worse, the figurines were gone. The risk wasn't even worth it.

It took me a few minutes to realize we were headed in a familiar direction. "Where are we going, Kee?"

"Harrison's. I told him I'd swing by later, but then you called. I've been meaning to give him his baseball glove from when he was little. When we moved out of Mam's place, somehow it got mixed with my stuff and I kept telling him I forgot it at home whenever he asked me for it. I took it to Home Run without telling him and had Caspar frame it with his old jersey. I was hoping to surprise him. I never bought him a house-warming gift. And he got a new puppy. I've been dying to see it."

"I don't think that's such a good idea, Kee. I should go home."

"Come on, Mari. You can still be friends with him. We don't have to stay long."

I thought about it for a minute. If the Scarpones were tracking us, maybe it was better not to go home right away. I didn't think they were. I'd been staring out of the outside mirror since we left, but chancing it wasn't worth it. Maybe I'd have Giovanni pick me up from Harrison's. Or better yet, wherever we went shopping after leaving his place. Yeah, that was a better idea. I wouldn't even mention Harrison or the house on Staten Island.

I didn't want to have to deal with my husband's fury when he found out that I'd slipped out without telling him right away, or any of the men at the house. I'd played them all and knew I was going to have hell to pay.

24

CAPO

Did she really think I wouldn't find her? Just because she didn't take her watch didn't mean I couldn't track her a different way.

It didn't take me long to find them. It didn't take me long to realize where she'd gone first and *who* stared at my wife. The Scarpones. She must've realized it, too, because not long after her friend got back to the car, they took off like the devil was on their heels.

He was, but the wrong one.

I followed them to Staten Island. My gut told me they'd be headed that way. After her friend parked the car and they stepped out, Harry Boy met them at the door, the biggest fucking smile on his face when he noticed his sister wasn't alone.

The smile was for my wife.

She smiled back, but not as wide. When he got closer, she held up her hand, and he looked at it a minute before he caught on. Instead of hugging him, she offered him a high five. His smile dropped a little, but I knew it wouldn't deter him for long.

Then a puppy came bounding out of the door, a white German shepherd. My wife sat on the porch, letting the dog attack her with his tongue, while she laughed that laugh that twisted my heart in a weird fucking way. Harry Boy ate it up with an invisible spoon.

So this was where she went when she ran from me.

She told me she loved me.

She fucking loves me.

Then she runs to her old stomping ground and into Harry Boy's safe house.

It took a lot to stump me, and Harry Boy was far from it. Even though he bought the house without me in mind, he knew someday, when we'd fight, she'd run to him—to a place she felt comfortable.

Fuck. That.

Fuck Harry Boy, too.

Fuck love.

Where is the loyalty she vowed to me?

My wife stood, trying to keep the dog down, and then said something to Harry Boy. He made a gesture like, *you don't have to ask*, and a second later, she disappeared behind the front door. His sister stood outside with him, putting her hand on his arm. Then she went to the car, dug around for a second, and after, brought him a framed picture of a baseball glove and a jersey.

He hugged her, but the woman inside was more important.

He said something to his sister. She said something back. And then he turned around in a circle, running his hands through his hair.

I wondered if Harry Boy's sister told him about my wife's pregnancy.

He didn't seem happy. In fact, he was livid.

I smiled.

His sister nodded and then touched her stomach before she

touched him on the arm, and when he waved her off, she left him outside by himself. She must've been confirming the news. Mariposa was pregnant with my child.

The time was right. Tempers had ignited from both sides.

With each step that I took, the clocks reversed, and I was seventeen again, going after my adversary. The one who kept trying me, but this time, it was over a woman, and that woman was *my* wife.

There was a moment of clear clarity between my boots on his lawn and the first hit, but that shocking word flashed across my mind in that thin space. *Jealousy.* It felt like a poker right out of hell that wouldn't stop stabbing me in a raw spot. I was jealous that this motherfucker had my wife's attention.

She refused to talk to me. She refused to look at me. She refused to feed me. She refused to sleep with me. She refused to fuck me. But here she was, strolling down memory lane with this loser, petting his hairy dog.

He had seen me coming, so it was no surprise when my fist slammed into his face. I wasn't here to kill him, but to fight him. Death was easier. *This.* This was fighting for her honor. I wanted him to know and to remember. I wanted him to remember my fist hitting his jaw when he thought about her.

This fight felt like it was a long time coming.

He was giving just as much as I was. Before long, neighbors started bringing their lawn chairs out, watching us go at it like two snarling dogs on his front lawn, fighting over a piece of territory.

"You stole her from me!" he grunted out.

I landed a blow to his ribs, and the neighbors made a collective *ooh* sound. "She's always been mine, Harry Boy. You couldn't steal her even if you tried. She's in my fucking front pocket."

He landed a blow to my mouth and one of the neighbors hooted. "I told her." He swung at me again but missed. "When you fucked up, she'd be here with me. And where is she? In *my* house."

I rammed him like a bull with my head, right in the gut, and we went down to the ground, grunting, landing punches wherever we could.

The first watery hit didn't register, not until the cold clung to it. Adrenaline pumped in my veins and my blood ran hot. The sprays kept coming. Harry Boy jumped up first, lifting his hands in surrender, spitting blood from his mouth. I stood right after and received another sharp spray to my chest.

His sister had the hose. "That's enough!" she yelled. "The both of you!"

"I—" Harry Boy went to defend his actions, no doubt, and his sister hit him with the spray again, this time in his mouth.

"Harrison." Her voice was mean. "Knock it off. You know I won't let up until you stop with the excuses. Now get your ass inside before you catch cold!"

"Sissy boy," I muttered.

She hit me with the hose again. "You! I'll get you some dry clothes, but only if you shut it!"

I narrowed my eyes at her, and she narrowed back. No wonder Cash Kelly wanted her. She wasn't fucking playing around. She was an archer, too, and from what Mariposa had told me, she had unchallenged aim.

Instead of staring at her, I looked toward the porch, where my wife stood, holding on to the railing. The dog sat next to her, looking up, tongue hanging out. She had his loyalty already.

"What are you doing here, *mio marito?*"

Not Capo. *My husband.* Not that I minded, but she refused to use my name, my real name. The one she'd given me. It was the only name I called mine.

Her friend took the hose and started rolling it up, going to the side of the house. Giving us privacy but not.

"I've come to collect my wife. She ran out on me."

"No." She bit her lip and shook her head. "I needed some space."

"There's enough of that between us."

"You're not mad that I left on my own?"

"No. I'm not mad." I rolled my teeth over my bottom lip. "I'm livid."

She watched me for a moment. The sun fell on her just right, and something in my heart twisted again. Her sweater showed the bulge of her growing stomach. I swallowed hard, ignoring the fact that my throat strained.

"You're owed that," she said.

"But nothing else."

"No, that's the problem. You're owed *everything*."

I took a step toward her. She didn't move. She stood her ground while my entire world rocked.

"You owe me nothing," I said.

"Not even loyalty?"

"You give it if you want to." I took another step toward her. This time she went right, toward the steps, and after I took a step up, she looked down at me. "I refuse to accept anything that's not given anymore."

"From me?"

"Only from you. I'll take what I want from the rest of the world and not give a fuck. But you, if it's good, I want you to give it, and once you do, never take it back."

She nodded. "I didn't come here to see—"

"It doesn't matter." In that moment, it didn't. Being close to her again felt like living to me. Her absence in my life felt like death. True death. I knew the difference.

"It doesn't?"

I stopped when I was right below her and fell to my knees on the steps. "I don't bend. I don't fucking break. I kneel for no mere man on this earth." I didn't look at her, so I used my fingers to guide me. I took her hips in my hands and rested my forehead against her stomach. "Except for you, Mariposa. You can bend me. You can break me. You are the only woman who has the power to bring me to my knees. I need your mercy."

"You wounded me deep," she whispered, a tear slipping down her cheek, landing on my arm. It wounded me deeper than the scar around my neck. It broke the heart I'd had no idea I had until her. "You should've told me. Why didn't you?"

"This." My voice was shredded. I held on to her tighter. "Us."

She ran her hands through my hair, kissing the top of my head. "I love you, Capo. I'm so in love with you that it's hard to breathe sometimes. You...crash into me and I want to be swept away. I don't care if I drown in you. *Per sempre.* And I don't love you because of loyalty either. I love you because I...just...love you."

I looked up at her, and her eyes were so damn sincere. It wasn't easy for her to say those words, but she did with a honeyed tongue. Maybe she thought she was hurting me again. Or maybe she was trying to heal something no one else ever could.

"I didn't come here to run away from you, Capo. Keely wanted to give Harrison a gift that has been in her trunk for too long. I went inside because I had to use the bathroom. The baby." She touched her stomach. "That's it."

"Have you seen that car before?" Her friend appeared from the side of the house, looking toward the street.

Mariposa and I both looked at the same time. It was a typical car, meaning nothing stood out about it, except for the tinted windows. I stood, keeping Mariposa behind me.

"No." Mariposa peeked around me. "I haven't."

"I have," Keely said. "It's passed a few times."

The window started to roll down.

"Down!" I roared. I pushed my wife to the ground, but her

friend froze, watching as the gun pointed toward the house, about to spray bullets all over the front porch.

I jumped on her, bringing her down just as the first spray of bullets crashed into the house. From my place on the ground, I pulled out the gun from behind my back, aiming for the tires.

Target hit, two of them blew out. As soon as the car came to a stop, I jumped to my feet, watching the doors. Two men jumped out, and before I could take them out, the driver put a bullet in the passenger's brain. He must've had orders, and those orders were to make sure that no one talked. Including the guy in the passenger seat.

This was retribution from either the Irish or the Scarpones. The Irish were at war. Cash was battling for the streets of Hell's Kitchen after his old man had been murdered. Or Achille had somehow tracked my wife to this house. His whiz kid son probably found something that tied her friend's car to this place. I'd been too busy fighting an internal war when I should've been present in the physical one.

I was about to find out who the man belonged to, but before I could, more racket came from the house, and when I turned to look, it was Harry Boy, gun in his hand, aimed at the driver's chest. The driver was about to take off on foot, but for some reason had turned toward the house again.

Harry Boy must've come outside sometime during the attack, his body over my wife's. Not going to lie. He had decent aim, but the motherfucker made a grave mistake. He killed the asshole before I had a chance to grill him.

The dog whined from inside, wanting to be let out. After Harry Boy sat up, my wife tilted from left to right for a second, blinking.

"Mariposa." I got down on one knee next to her and touched her face. When she focused on me, I ran my hands all over her body. "You're fine."

She nodded but pointed to my arm. "You've been shot!"

"I'm all right. Get in the house."

Harry Boy helped his sister from the ground, and after she made it up the steps, she told me she'd take Mariposa into the house.

Harry Boy followed me as I approached the car. If this was a gift from the Scarpones, there might be a camera in the mirror. The Scarpones sometimes required proof that the hit they ordered was carried out. They started this after my death. They didn't want more than one ghost lurking around. I doubted this particular car had a camera, though. It wasn't one of their cars —they were fond of cars with deep trunks—but then again, maybe they were trying to do something different.

Achille's youngest son, a whiz kid, was the one who monitored the cameras. He had a twin brother who was ten minutes older than him. The whiz kid knew how to make evidence disappear after they got what they wanted.

Either way, they wouldn't get a good look at my face. Not today.

I took out my phone and texted Harry Boy so he could get in touch. "Let me know how this plays out."

"How'd you get my number?"

I waved him off. "Call Kelly and fill him in. He needs to know about this. There's no telling who he fucked with and pissed off. This might be retribution in the form of a life he considers important to him."

"How did you know about—"

"Get to work, Harry Boy. It's not safe to chat in the street."

Sirens grew closer. I needed to get my wife and get out.

"Mac?" Harry Boy called.

I didn't even turn around.

"You saved my sister."

"Make sure you tell Kelly he has a tab."

25

"Capo," I said, squeezing his hand. "Talk to me."

He'd rushed me out of Harrison's house, given me the keys to a truck that seemed faster than a sports car, and had told me to drive.

He gave me directions, but it was to a place I'd never been before. He called Uncle Tito and told him to meet us at the "rendezvous" spot.

After he hung up, I kept talking to him because the amount of blood he was losing scared me. He told me it was a good thing Keely had hosed him down with cold water and it was freezing outside. The cold worked like a tourniquet to slow his bleeding. I wanted to put the heater on in the car, but he refused to let me.

"You're afraid I'm dying," he said.

"*What!* Are you?" My entire body convulsed from fear. I knew I loved the ass, but I had no idea how much until I watched as he took a bullet for my friend. The woman I considered my sister. If I lost him, I lost everything.

"For the hundredth time. No. This is nothing." He grinned. "You're cute when you worry."

I slapped him on the arm and he hissed. "Don't play with me, Capo. I'm not in the mood. And don't call me *cute*! I'm not a baby cabbage."

"Baby cabbage," he repeated slowly. "Like a Brussels sprout."

He told me where to turn a couple of times, and then he became quiet. He stared out of the window with a far-off look in his eyes. Every once in a while, a violent shiver tore through him. When the silence went on for too long, I cleared my throat.

"I remembered something, Capo. When we were at the house on Staten Island. I remembered you. The memories were in reverse, though. I remembered running out of the door, crying for you to come back after you left me with Jocelyn and Pops. I didn't want you to leave me.

"You fell to your knees on the step so I could look you in the eye. Just like you did before those guys shot at us. I was standing at the very top. You were kneeling on the step below. You told me that I was safe. That you made sure of it. You would always look out for me. Then I gave you the rosary. I put it around your neck."

I could feel his eyes on me. I had his full attention. "Your mother gave it to you to stop you from fiddling," he said. "You slept with it at night. You were a nervous child. I was touched that you gave me the one thing that made you feel safe."

I nodded, clutching the steering wheel. "Then I remembered being in a house. Hiding in a closet. You made me hide in there?"

"Yeah."

"You gave me my crayons and my coloring book. I told you my favorite color was blue. You told me to color the page with the butterfly. So I did. Then I heard some noises that scared me. A few minutes later, you came back for me."

"Then I brought you to Jocelyn."

"Then you left me," I breathed out. "Don't leave me again, Capo. Life is not worth living without you."

It wasn't anything money could buy all along. It was my husband. The love I felt from him.

I felt it, even if I didn't know what it was then. No man sacrifices himself the way he did for innocence alone. They say it takes guts to do something like that, but I disagreed. It took love. Maybe what he felt at first was an innocent kind of love—I was only five—but as I grew into a woman, the same love grew and developed into something else.

He turned toward me, his hand sliding against my stomach. I could feel the warmth from his touch even though he was cold. For the first time, the baby fluttered. It wasn't a hard kick. More like wings tickling me from the inside. It was the strangest thing I'd ever felt, but the most wonderful.

I smiled. "He moved. Just now."

Capo pushed his hand against my stomach, trying to feel it, too. I told him it would take a while for him to feel it, the movement was as soft as wings. Then I glanced at him and what I saw in his eyes made me lose all focus. He seemed...excited.

"Shit!" I yanked the steering wheel in the opposite direction, a near miss with traffic from the other side. Goosebumps scattered on my arms, and not from the near miss. A box on the back seat had started to play music. "What's that?"

"Keep your eyes on the road." His voice was firm, back to being *capo*. He turned around and dug in the back for a second. Then he lifted his hand so I could see. It was the black wolf with the butterfly on its nose. "For his room."

"You bought them?"

"They're in the backseat, Mariposa." He pointed out the obvious. "The owner of the shop was missing a few from the collection, so I called a shop in Paris and bought those, too. You have a choice. We can either pick them up or they'll ship them."

An explosive laugh mixed with an equally explosive sob burst from my mouth. Tears blurred my vision. Then I sobered up some after I realized. "You went there. To Dolce. After all that happened. If they would've seen you—"

"They didn't. I know them, Mariposa. I know their habits better than they do. I could've slit their throats a hundred times since they killed me."

"Why haven't you?"

"I'm a ghost that won't leave them alone. Once I kill them, it's over." He became quiet for a second. "I was in the shop when Keely parked across the street from Dolce. Achille saw you."

"Is that why he shot the house up?"

"It's a possibility. Or it could be someone else."

"Someone else?"

"Cash Kelly's made it clear that your friend belongs to him. He has a lot of enemies right now. He's fighting for territory. Word gets around that something is important to him." He shrugged. "They'll destroy it to make a point."

"And if Cash thinks the Scarpones tried to kill his—whatever Keely is to him—he'll retaliate."

"He's not that strong yet, but he's rising. He'll just cause more trouble for them."

"He'll be a pain in their asses."

"You speak so eloquently." He grinned.

I grinned, too. "It's the truth, right?"

"Yeah, the truth. They don't want more trouble right now. I caused a lot of strife between all of the families. I made it look like the other was to blame. I'm a ghost, Mariposa. They believe I'm dead. Arturo and his son couldn't tell the other families that they suspected it was Vittorio fucking with all of them. Even if it *were* true, why would I target my own family? They'd all know then, for sure, that Arturo had me killed. They're all just starting to play nice again, since Arturo convinced them that an outsider started the wars. The Scarpones can't afford longer battles. I've been stealing their shit."

"You've crippled them."

"Close to it."

Yeah, he was Machiavellian all right.

"Right here—" He pointed toward a building. He hit a button on his watch and the garage opened. "There's no time to look around. Stay close to me. We're in and out."

"What do you mean...out? Uncle Tito's supposed to meet us here."

We were already hustling to get inside of the building. Capo had grabbed the box with the baby's figurines and was practically making me sprint. The building was plain but huge. It had a ton of mismatched shit in it. All of the stuff he'd stolen from the Scarpones, probably.

"Another place."

"Your arm!"

"It'll be fine."

He wasn't fine. He was bleeding. His shirt was pasted to him.

Three buildings down, at least, he led us to another garage. He hit the button on a massive off-road type of vehicle and told me to drive again. This time I really hauled ass to get where we were going.

Another warehouse.

Uncle Tito, Rocco, and Rocco's brother, Dario, were there when we arrived. Before Uncle Tito started to get to work, Capo secured my watch around my wrist.

"You take this off again—" he narrowed his eyes "—you'll be punished."

"I—"

He shook his head, *no excuses*, and went to sit on the table. There were two in the room, one on each side. The entire room had been set up to look like a doctor's office, or a small emergency room. Uncle Tito made Capo remove his shirt, and when he did, rivulets of blood ran down his chest from a hole. The bloody smell was strong, mixing in with all of the antiseptics. Uncle Tito assessed the wound and then instructed Dario to slip a blood pressure cuff on Capo's arm.

"Mariposa," Capo said.

I had to blink a few times to focus on him.

"*Sto bene.*"

I'm fine, he had said.

I nodded, but I didn't feel so well. When Uncle Tito took out a scalpel from his bag, the entire room faded to black. When I woke up again, I was on the opposite table, and Capo was grinning at me.

"Nice nap?"

I tried to sit up, but Uncle Tito stopped me. "Rest, *nipote*." Then he slid across the room, to the other bed, on a chair with wheels. He checked the bandage on Capo's arm.

"What happened?" I rubbed my eyes. "Are you okay?"

"You passed out," Capo said. "As soon as you saw the scalpel. And I'm all good." He patted Uncle Tito on the head. "The angel of life stopped death once again."

"Ah!" Uncle Tito slapped at him. "Nonsense! Do not allow your husband to play on your sympathies. This wound is nothing! The bullet was close to the surface."

I looked at a silver bowl sitting on a silver table. A bloody bullet was in it. I didn't realize I'd passed out again until I woke up in the firehouse. Rocco carried me. I looked to my right. Capo stared at us, the coldness back in his eyes. It wasn't aimed at me, though, but at Rocco.

"I can walk," I croaked out.

"Nonsense," Uncle Tito said.

Capo gave him a dirty look.

"Your husband is upset that I refuse to let him carry you. His wound is not bad, but he should not be carrying a weight, no matter how light!" He pointed at Capo. "You listen to *me*, or I will tape your hands together!"

I laughed softly but hid it when Capo turned the dirty look on me. Then I laughed some more when I thought of Giovanni watching all of us disappear into the master suite and not come out for a while.

Capo told me to get settled in bed once we were on the secret side. He was going to walk Uncle Tito and Rocco out. Before they left, I kissed them both and thanked them. Uncle Tito waved it off and gave me instructions on the medicine Capo had to take and what he could and couldn't do.

My husband came back in the bedroom a few minutes later. I couldn't seem to move. All that had happened seemed to catch up to me.

"Shower," Capo said, pointing toward the bathroom.

I shook my head. "Shower for me. You can't get your arm wet. Doctor's orders."

"You have two options. Shower with me. Or shower with me after I've thrown you over my shoulder."

He grinned at me when I wrapped his arm in plastic wrap from the kitchen before we got in. I used the shower handle and aimed it away from him. But when I washed all of the bloody spots off, his shoulders relaxed, and I could tell he was at ease. And no matter how much I protested he refused to let me wash myself.

After the shower, while we dried off, he stared at me.

"What?" I whispered.

"Your stomach." He nodded to it. "You're starting to show."

I turned to the side and smiled. "I am. I wonder if he's going to be big like you? I hope he has your eyes."

A moment passed and neither of us said anything. He took my hand after and led me toward the bedroom. I climbed in and patted the spot next to me. My eyes narrowed when he started to creep toward me.

"Capo," I said. "I'm not giving in on this one. The doctor said—"

"I don't give a *fuck* what the doctor says. This is what I need. You. Underneath me. Crying out my name. That's my only medicine. My only cure in this diseased world."

I bit my lip, not sure what to do. When he came close enough, he used his mouth to pull my lip from my teeth, and he gently sucked on it.

"*Ah*," I released a soft breath. Then my hands fluttered over his shoulders, down his arms, over his sides.

He hissed out a breath and pulled me down with one arm, setting me beneath him. He kissed me, softly, slowly, until I felt like he had taken my soul and I was lost to anyone but him, and then his tongue went deeper and harder. But his touches were...light.

"What are you doing to me?" I whispered when his tongue trailed down my throat, all the way to my breasts.

"Something I should've done before. Something different."

He said nothing after that, but when he entered me, it wasn't hard or rough. He took his time, moving in a slow, sensual rhythm. He demanded that I keep my eyes open, and his were on mine, his teeth sunk into his bottom lip.

"Mariposa." His eyes closed then, and he made a strangled noise in his throat.

The sound of my name on his lips made me dissolve into him, and my orgasm tore through me, even though what he'd done to me was far from hard. He pounded into me after, relentless to chase his release, and I came again with him.

He didn't move after, though he trembled. I was scared to look at the bandage to see if he had done something to his arm and blood was gushing. The thought of it made me queasy. Blood usually didn't bother me but his did. The dream kept coming back to me, so fresh in my mind.

I wrapped my arms around him, burying my face against

his chest. I kissed him in the spot four times. He tried to rise, but I refused to let him go.

I had so many things to say:

Love is not the dagger you think it is. It's only used as a weapon when the one you love turns it on you. Love is a shield against the rest of the world. Only the two of us can allow strangers beyond our gates. Love stems from so many different things. Companionship. Friendship. Loyalty, and loyalty can breed love. Or love can breed loyalty.

I kept quiet, though, because I didn't want him to think that I was trying to convince him or convert him. I didn't want to point out the obvious. *You love me, too.*

He seemed to sense my thoughts. "In my world, love will only get you killed, Mariposa." The sound of his voice, low and shredded, made me pull closer to him. "That's why my mamma left those words behind. She knew what I'd be facing. She used to tell me that I was too pretty. That they were going to eat me alive. But she didn't see it in me. She didn't see that a pretty face doesn't cancel out ruthlessness in the blood. I'm as savage as they are. I held my own. I proved my worth."

"You're still holding your own." I kissed his neck softly. He smelled like the beach, like our time in Sicily and Greece. "You have nothing left to prove. Not a damn thing, Capo."

He leaned down and kissed me on the head. Then he slid out of me, leaving me empty and reaching out for him. He rested on his good arm, facing me, and he took my hands in his, cradling them. "You're owed a heart, Mariposa. The veins you already have."

"A heart—*oh.* The veins are the three bad things. Now for the good?"

He brought my hands to his mouth. "Orange blossoms." He inhaled around my pulse and then released the breath in a slow stream of warm air. "You want to know why I didn't tell you who I was? *Semplicemente.*" *Simply.* "I didn't want you to figure it out. If you did, it made me...anxious to think that you'd walk away from me, that you'd tell me to go to hell, to marry someone else. I didn't tell you because, *semplicemente*, I want your companionship. Your time."

I need to disappear yet be seen. He was lonely, so fucking lonely, because of those ruthless bastards.

"I need you for the rest of my life, Mariposa. I need all of you to belong to me only. *Ossa delle mie ossa; carne della mia carne; la mia bella donna; mia moglie.*" *Bone of my bone; flesh of my flesh; my beautiful woman; my wife.*

"So you didn't have to make something up?" I blinked at him. "You had the heart all along?"

"Yeah, I did. You. You're the heart." He took my hands and moved them to his neck, right over his scar. "If this didn't exist. The voice. How could I tell you, Mariposa? If words no longer existed, if someone stole them, how would we communicate? Actions. Actions speak louder than words. You don't need words to make this real."

"Actions," I whispered. "Your life. You sacrificed yours for mine."

He leaned his head against mine. "*Nel mio mondo l'amore ti farà solo uccidere. Sono un uomo morto dalla notte in cui ti ho lasciato alle spalle.*"

The translation of his words was a bit loose, but his point was as sharp as a sword out to slay for love.

In my world love will only get you killed. I have been a dead man since the night I left you behind.

I pulled back to see him better, but he only pulled me closer, so close that I couldn't breathe. So close that my breath was his and his was mine.

Non servono più parole. No more words were needed, as he let me in for a peaceful swim.

26

MARIPOSA

I had somehow, *a miracle*, convinced my husband to take the day off. Not only the day, but the night, too. After Harrison's house had been sprayed with bullets, it was hard to be apart from him.

My nightmares were only getting worse.

It was the same one over and over, except the blood would increase each time. I'd look down and the slow crawl of it would inch closer and closer to my feet. I still couldn't move. Only scream out.

In reality, not dreams, he sometimes stood close to me. At other times, he did his thing. Seeking vengeance on the Scarpone family was a job to him. One he loved very much. When he admitted to me that he didn't kill them because it would be over, I understood right away.

It would end his reign of torture on them. When he fucked with them in life, playing the game, he got a thrill out of it. Once they were dead, it would all be over, and he'd be left to deal with...himself.

What worried me the most was, would he get to them first? Or would they finally succeed and end his life?

It was a game with mighty high stakes.

The life tumbling in my stomach drove the point home.

I ran a hand over my stomach. In the last week my belly seemed to explode. I wore a tight navy dress that had stretch but was form fitting, and from all angles, you could tell I was pregnant.

"Mariposa."

It took a minute for me to realize Capo had said something to me. After my doctor's appointment, where the ultrasound confirmed the baby was a boy, he took me out to eat at Mamma's Pizzeria. We sat in the front, on stools, turned to one another.

"Yeah?"

He grinned at me and then picked up the ultrasound picture I'd placed between us, leaning against a dessert menu. He flashed it at me.

"I want him to have your nose."

"Your eyes and my nose?" I grinned.

He set the picture back, ran a finger down the slope of my nose, and then kissed me on the end of it. His hands came around my stomach, cradling the bump like a ball. "It pleases me that everyone knows I did this to you."

I almost spit my drink out. "You like that everyone knows you got me pregnant?"

He leaned in even closer, keeping his hands around my stomach. My knee was close to his crotch. "No, that everyone knows it's me that fucks you."

My eyes closed and the breath escaped my mouth in a rush. "Forget the pizza. Let's go home."

"Why home? They have a backroom."

I pulled away from him, trying to gauge his face. He was dead serious.

The waitress set our salads down with a loud *clink!* against the old counter. A second later, a man with an apron tied around his waist slid our pizza between the two bowls.

"Good enough," the waitress said, and then she hustled in the opposite direction to take more orders.

Their customer service lacked finesse, but hey, the food was amazing. It was like having an asshole doctor with no bedside manners, but he was *the* best asshole doctor with no bedside manners.

My eyes went back and forth between the meal in front of me—the man—and the *actual* meal in front of me—the pizza and the salads.

He sat back, roaring with laughter. "You just busted my balls."

Not waiting around, I took a stab at my salad. Sometimes I liked to put lettuce on top of my pizza and roll it up. Mamma's had *the* best Italian dressing. "I didn't touch your balls, Capo."

"Exactly. You picked this—" he waved his hand toward the table "—over me. You wounded my balls without even touchin' 'em."

"I didn't pick one over the other." I took a bite of pizza, almost moaning. "You're dessert."

He leaned in very slow, and the bite of salad I'd just stabbed was in route to make it to my mouth. Slowly, oh so slowly, he licked my bottom lip, removing some leftover dressing. "Everything tastes better from your mouth."

It was hard for me to find excitement in the food again, but after a minute or two, when he started eating, my hunger came back even stronger. He didn't even ask. He ordered another pizza, noticing how much I was eating.

"The salad here is really good, too," I said.

He ordered another.

"That's how I met old man Gianelli." He wiped his mouth with a napkin. We still faced each other, and he reached out and wiped my face, too. "I came here for pizza."

"You bonded over pizza?"

He reached over and grabbed a standup menu. He pointed to a spot at the bottom.

"'All ingredients are locally grown or imported from Italy,'" I read aloud.

"Old man Gianelli used to supply their garlic from his garden. The old owners were friends with him. My grandfather came down from Italy, and I brought him here. They met. Hit it off. For the longest time they played correspondence chess by mail. They stopped talking after I left you with them. It wasn't safe to keep in contact."

"*Nonno* trusted Pops?"

"Yeah." He took a drink of his water. "He'd gotten to know them well. That's how I knew about all of Jocelyn's troubles. You were wanted. Maybe even needed in their lives."

I picked apart my pizza. "Do I...do I look like my mother?"

Sometimes I felt guilty about it, but my father rarely crossed my mind. I blamed him for getting my mother killed. He knew what kind of people the Scarpones were, and he still tried to take them over. Even when he was running, he was still plotting.

What hit me the hardest was the picture I found of him leaving the courthouse after the Scarpones had gotten him out of trouble, when they were still on good terms.

My mother, though—nothing came up when I searched for her.

Corrado's bad behavior made front-page news. For Maria, my mother, her goodness, her love, had landed her in a shallow grave.

Even though I couldn't remember the way she looked, I thought of her often. Especially when I touched her rosary. Even as a child she tried to teach me how to ease my anxiety with faith.

Capo stared at my face, maybe thinking back. He ran his

finger down my nose again. "Your nose. Your eyes. Even your lips belong to her. The color of your eyes..." He tilted his head. "They seem to be a mix. Her eyes were amber, like whisky in a glass right at sunset. She was a beautiful woman." He became quiet for a moment.

"Your father used to bury shit. Guns. Money. Jewelry. Papers. When I found him, he was in a bad neighborhood. The kind where people keep their heads down, eyes averted."

"I'm familiar."

He nodded once. "There was nothing in the house but ratty furniture. When he ran, he ran with very little. He wouldn't have thrown his shit away. He believed he was going to make a name for himself. He believed he was going to be the new *capo* in town."

"You think he might've buried pictures?"

"Bingo."

"I would." I swished the last of my drink around the glass. "I would love to see her. It would mean a lot to me if I had pictures of her." I touched my stomach. "Maybe I'll see some of her in him."

We became quiet as the waitress came back to refill our drinks. I only had one thing on my mind, though.

I reached out and took Capo's hand, resting it against my stomach. "Here's a twist they probably never saw coming. Two families that hated each other are now joined by one link. Love. This little boy brings them together in peace, whether they want it or not."

Even if Capo would never speak the words, this baby was created from love. Having children never even crossed my mind when I'd been struggling to survive, but when Capo gave me the choice, I'd never wanted anything more. To be able to hold my blood in my arms felt like the most amazing dream. To see someone else who maybe looked a little like me felt unreal. I craved to feel that special connection.

Capo lifted a cucumber slice from his bowl and set it in front of my stomach. Then he set another one next to it. Like my stomach had eyes. "Here's a twist. He's about the size of a mango right now, even though he's only supposed to be the size of a cucumber. He's going to be a big boy."

The grin that came to my face was slow. "Like his Papà."

Capo called the waitress over. "Let's not keep him waiting to eat then." He ordered spumoni cake and ice cream. He looked at me. "Make that double."

"*Hey!*" I started laughing, but I ate the cucumbers he had sat on my stomach. Then *he* started laughing. I stood, running a hand down my dress. "The bathroom calls before dessert."

The smile on my face lingered as I made my way through the restaurant. When I got to the back, where the bathrooms were, I noticed a room off to the side. The backroom Capo had been talking about. It smelled like garlic and tomatoes. I wondered if we could check it out after we ate our spumoni?

The bathroom trip didn't take long, and I was still wiping my hands on a paper towel when I stepped out and ran right into Capo's arm. He was standing in front of the bathroom door. Another man stood by the storage room. He was much shorter, but bull-chested. They stared at each other.

The napkin in my hand fluttered to the floor when I noticed the tattoo on his hand.

"Bobby, you got a cigarette on you?"

The man's eyes flew to mine. Then back to Capo's.

"The fuck? Vittorio?" The man's voice came out low, and a light sheen of sweat bubbled over his top lip. He was pale, his lips too red from the lack of color on his face. I wondered if the men Capo had killed, the ones who had tried to kill him, had this same reaction when they thought they saw his ghost.

Capo said nothing, but he nodded in a way that told me he wanted me behind him. I moved, but I put a hand to his side, trying to peek.

"Tell me one thing, girl." It took me a moment to realize Bobby was talking to me. "Do you see him, too?"

I didn't know what to say. Capo refused to answer, and I wasn't sure what this guy was going to do if I confirmed it was the man they all thought was dead. Would Bobby pull out a gun and kill us both? If I kept quiet and he got pissed? What then?

"See who?" I rasped out.

"The man standing in front of you. The one *you're* touching. He's supposed to be six feet under. His throat slashed."

"Did you do that to him?" I was surprised by the amount of venom in my voice aimed at this man that I didn't know but hated on principal.

Bobby shook his head, but his eyes never left Capo's. I wasn't sure if he was sizing up my husband, afraid that he was going to pounce, or was still in shock at seeing him. "Nah, that wasn't me, girl. I had no hand in his murder. At one time, we were close."

Capo laughed, but it was low. "Is that the lies we're telling these days, Bobby?"

Bobby shivered at the sound of Capo's voice, and then he raised both of his hands. "I swear on my Ma's head, Vittorio. I heard things, ya know? But that stood between Arturo and Achille. We all suspected, but you know how it is. What's done is done. We can't go against the boss, man. Achille admitted it to a few of us a few years ago—it was implied that our fate would be yours if we didn't do what we were told without question."

Capo grinned, and *I* shivered this time. "You should've never come looking for me, Bobby. You should've stayed within the protection of the pack you call *famiglia*."

Before I could even take a breath, Capo charged him, slamming his head against the wall. The scariest part was that it all took under a second and he hardly made a sound. When

Bobby went down, Capo took him by the shirt collar and started dragging him toward the storage room.

"Mariposa." Capo's voice was cut-throat. "Move."

It took me a second to focus, but once I did, I hustled to keep up. Once we were outside, he picked Bobby up and flung him over his shoulder.

"You can't kill him!"

"Consider him dead."

"But he didn't do it, Capo! He's innocent."

"You stand by and watch, I consider you guiltier than the one who uses the knife. He's a fucking poltroon. And his wife talks too much."

"The second reason is not good enough!" Besides, I didn't know what a *poltroon* was—maybe a coward?

"It's a bonus. Maybe she'll shut her mouth for five seconds, long enough to shed a fake tear."

We made the side of the building, going straight for the car parked directly in front of Mamma's.

"Someone might see!" I hissed.

"I'm dead. Let them try to find me."

As soon as Capo opened the doors, two cars came to a stop right next to our car.

"Get in, Mariposa! *Adesso!*"

I flung myself in, right as bullets pinged against the exterior of the car. I covered my stomach, afraid that one might penetrate the bulletproof layer.

Capo was inside the car a second later. He put the car in gear and peeled out, swiping the side of one of the cars as he sped off. The cars that had stopped in front of the restaurant blocked the flow of traffic. Horns blared.

"Where's Bobby?" I asked, breathless.

"He ended up being valuable in the end."

"What?"

"He took those bullets for me. We'll call it payback for not telling me that I was going to get my throat cut and then standing by and watching."

"Fair enough." I held tight to the seatbelt. "Was that them? The Scarpones?"

"Yeah, but not Arturo or Achille. Young guys. Back up for Bobby." He checked his mirror. "Hold on."

To what? I almost screamed but didn't. He weaved in and out of traffic, not even caring if there was only a breath of air between our car and the one in front or behind us.

"Did they see you?"

"They saw *you.*"

"But I thought you wanted to—*shit! Capo!*" He swerved, barely missing a biker. "I thought you wanted to make a grand entrance. Like, *'Boo, motherfuckers, I'm back!'* Then you'd serve them what they deserve."

"You're not far off the mark, but this isn't about me anymore. Your face has been seen too many times. Too many coincidences have happened for them not to mean something. The only thing they're not sure of is how Cash Kelly is involved in this. They're trying to connect you to me or figure out if you're one of his."

"Italy," I said.

"Yeah. My grandfather's funeral. If I'd be anywhere, I'd be there. That one stands out to them."

"You were." I closed my eyes, suddenly feeling motion sickness. "You knew...were you trying to get yourself killed?"

"I was ready to end it. They died. I died—again. We were all going to die." He quickly took a right and my shoulder hit the side of the car. "They didn't see me just now, though. Bobby blocked my face, and the guys in those cars are young. They wouldn't know me. Not by body alone. They were after you."

"All those men for me? Why couldn't Bobby deal with me alone?"

"What would scare you more, Mariposa? One man or a few?"

"One or a few—my scare meter would be up to here." I lifted my hand above my head.

"Bobby came in through the back, so he didn't know whether you were alone. That's another reason he called. Once he saw you, he called for backup. That was the end of his scope of knowledge before I stepped out in the open. If they find out who you really are, *Marietta*, things are going to get more dangerous. Right now, there's only a connection. Nothing else. But it's enough."

He swerved at the last second, stopping at the entrance of a garage, but it took less than an inhale of breath. As soon as he pulled in, the arm lifted and then barely missed the tail end of the car when it came down as we sped up the incline. At the very top floor—seven or eight?—he parked in the uncovered area, right in direct sunlight.

He told me to stay put until he came and got me. When he opened my door, I tried to wipe away a tear that slid down my cheek, but he noticed.

"Mariposa." He yanked me from the car, using his empty hand to slip a baseball hat over his head. My leather backpack was on his back. I had left it in the car when we'd gone into the pizzeria. He handed me a pair of sunglasses before he set a pair on. "I'm going to end this. It's time."

"The baby's picture." I barely got out. We had left it behind on the counter.

We rushed to get down the incline to the elevators. When we reached them, he handed me something from his pocket.

My tears collected inside of the glasses, almost fogging them up, but the treasure in my hand was as clear as the day. "You took it."

"I paid the bill, too."

"You did?"

"You love it there, and they have a better memory than the Scarpones when customers skip out. So I took the picture, left them two hundred bucks, and then followed you to the bathroom. Unforeseen circumstances. Make it a rule to consider all scenarios ahead of time, Mariposa."

"Was Bobby following us?"

"No. He likes to eat there, but I'm sure he called them when he saw you. He was screwing one of the waitresses. She's very quiet. He caught a glimpse of you right before you went into the bathroom. I stood hidden until right before you stepped out."

There seemed to be nothing else to say. We made the rest of the trip in silence. Once outside, in front, he opened another car and held the door for me. Before I got in, a massive explosion went off on the highest floor of the parking garage we had just left.

"They'll know we...I mean, that's your car, Capo."

"Nah." He took out a computer from the backseat and fiddled with a few things. "The paperwork states that it belongs to a guy who was killed about..." He looked at his old watch. "An hour ago. The Scarpones had a hit out on him."

"How soon?" I asked, my voice quiet. I stared at the picture of the baby in my hands. "How soon will you end this?"

"They're going to be hunting for you." He put the car in drive and pulled off. We were on a scenic ride through town, as though the last hour hadn't happened.

"Because they know you'll come for me."

"Or hoping so—if I'm still alive." He checked his rearview. "If they're hunting you, they're going after me. They already took my voice. I'll meet them in hell before they take my heart."

My wife slipped the rosary over my neck before I left.

A ritual.

A rite of passage.

A symbol of her love and sacrifice to carry with me into battle.

After the killer had made a deep enough cut that my air left my throat instead of my nose or mouth, I took out the rosary and clutched it in my hands before I went down.

Each breath was a struggle.

Each beat of my heart was fought for.

I had thought that the place where Mariposa had found her heaven—her rosary—would touch me. Because I knew where I was headed. Hell. Before my last breath, I wanted to touch the place where she found peace. To touch what the other side did before taking their final breath.

Faith.

There were only a few moments from my first life that stuck with me over the years. One of them was Mariposa's mother, Maria, before I pulled the trigger.

Maria was the first person I killed who had offered me forgiveness for what I was about to do. She told me she knew that I had no choice. She told me that what I was doing was showing her mercy. She knew the savages I was related to. What they would do to her once they found her.

In that moment, though, I'd tried to think of ways to save them both. A girl should have her mother.

In the end, we both knew it was useless. If I were going to save her daughter, the little girl she called Marietta, all ties to her original life had to be cut.

"I know where I'm going, Vittorio. I might have made mistakes in my life—I married a man who was not a man of God—but still, I am a woman of faith. I do not fear death, because I am onto a new life. Take care of my baby."

The only fear Maria showed was for her daughter. Wherever Maria felt she was going, it was to a better place. She had followed her husband through the darkest of nights, the coldest of days, and the dirtiest places her feet could've touched. When I found them, they were close to starving. They couldn't leave the filthy place they were living in. They couldn't even ask a neighbor to bring them food in fear of being found out.

We still found them.

I had killed men who cried like women, shit and pissed their pants, got on their knees and begged when death came knocking. One man even offered his wife instead of him. A life was a life. A body a body.

Not Maria. She had faith, and her faith gave her courage. Her body perished, but her soul lived on.

She had been teaching Mariposa that all along. When she was afraid, she could touch her faith to find peace. Mariposa had something that would forever comfort her.

To some it was beads on a rope. But to Maria, it was a physical representation of her unwavering belief system. No matter how close her fears came, she had something bigger on her side to conquer them.

I had wanted to die with the same peace. I wanted to taste it on my lips, feel it in my veins, have it conquer my heart before my sins came to collect me. I had felt the darkness breaking up, shattering like glass, and from it, all of the monster shadows sucking me under.

One.

Two.

Three.

No more breaths.

Then I'd woken up. Tito sat next to me. I wasn't able to speak. Still felt like I couldn't breathe. I knew I was alive, though, because I could feel. Tito wrapped the rosary around my hand and told me to hold on.

There I was, in the metaphorical sense, still holding on.

Maybe this was my last breath.

The final fourth.

It was family night at Dolce. The restaurant closed down to everyone but the Scarpones. They'd eat like kings and queens, they'd laugh like the joker had just put on the funniest show, and they'd tell their new princes tales of what their rich futures held. How powerful they'd be when they became kings.

All. Fucking. Bullshit.

"Heads up, motherfuckers," I wanted to tell Achille's sons, *"it makes the knife go in easier when the killer slices your throat. Because news flash: There can only be* one *king. Those tales? Yeah, they're pretty tall. Tall enough that only one of you will be able to reach the top."*

After the wives left, fur coats over their shoulders, jewels on their wrists, the finest shoes on undeserving feet, the men would stay behind and play poker. Achille might have one of his whores waiting to give him a kiss for luck. Only the fortunate ones got to leave the apartments he put them up in and be seen in public next to him.

Guess who's coming out to play tonight, fellas?

I'd finally be taking the seat they reserved for me one Sunday a month.

I laughed, the sound raspy and low. Yeah, how about that? They reserved a seat for me at the poker table once a month, a glass of whiskey included. I didn't even like the fucking game. Over the years, the old man's chess game had morphed into Achille's poker game. Quicker and less thinking involved. It was a sign of the times.

Three members of the staff stood inside to wait on the family. The rest were Scarpones, including the men who vowed to give their lives for the king and his joker of a son. The baby princes were there, too.

The whiz kid thought he had a handle on their security. I switched up the monitors, being *whizzier* than him. All they'd see was the restaurant, but without me standing on the side of it, chilling in the alleyway. The brightest thing about me was the rosary around my neck, but it was tucked inside my shirt.

Then my phone lit up.

I walked around to the other side of the building, out in the open, pulling up the collar of my jacket. The air still held the chill of February, even though we were in March, but the cold rarely touched me. It was more to keep me hidden until the right time.

The streets were crowded, and I got lost in the concrete jungle so I could check my phone. I stood in front of the shop that sold the little figurines my wife had wanted for our son.

Your wife: Hey, you forgot something important at home.

Me: Doubtful. Everything that's important is at home. But tell me anyway. What did I leave behind?

Your wife: Me.

A second later my phone vibrated.

Your wife: Please come home. We haven't even named him yet.

I took a deep breath, and it pushed out of my mouth in a white cloud.

Me: Saverio Lupo. Saverio means "new home." It's a cognate of Xavier or Javier. Lupo means "wolf" in Italian.

Your wife: Saverio is our new home. The wolf's new home with his *farfalla*.

Me: Yeah.

Your wife: I don't know how else to say this, and before you left, I couldn't. You found me and then left me when I was a kid. Then I found you years later. In a world filled with all of these people and all of these words, I found you. Just like you found me.

A few seconds went by. The vibration went off again.

Your wife: Don't leave me again, Capo. I had no idea what I was missing all of my life until you touched me. I wasn't starving for things. Well, I was, but it went deeper. It was you. I was starved for you. Nothing can replace you in my life.

She'd been dancing around this ever since what happened at Mamma's. Three days had gone by since then. She told me to wait a day, but another day only equaled to them having more hours to find out who she was.

I was a fucking ghost. They had already killed me. But my wife, she was the girl I saved; a girl who had a heartbeat. They'd stop at nothing to use her against me.

If they found out she was pregnant with my child—the thought alone made my blood run cold, and then it surged up hot.

Achille would rip her to pieces if he got to her first. Arturo would keep her alive long enough for her to have the baby. Then he'd kill her and raise my son as his own.

The ultimate betrayal, even over killing *his* flesh and blood, and a last *fuck you, my pretty-boy son*. If there was any peace to be found in death, he knew I'd never find it with my son in his arms.

This needed to end. There were too many unforeseen circumstances.

Slipping the phone in my pocket after I turned it off, I looked down at my watch.

It's time for the game to begin, motherfuckers.

I WALKED DOWN SOME, waiting in front of Dolce. The smell of veal *parmigiana* invaded my nostrils and tightened my throat.

Right on cue, two masked men jumped out of a waiting car, hustling to the alley.

Shouts. Gunshots. The kitchen staff was dead.

Boo. Bam. Boo. Three down.

More gunshots. The two masked men ran back out from the alley. Three men ran behind them.

The waiting car sped away with the two masked men. The three dumbfucks ran down the street to the parking garage. They were going to try to chase them down.

"Yeah," I breathed. "And how did that work out for you last time? All brawn and no brain."

I casually walked down the alley, head down. I stood to the side of the kitchen door listening. Arturo was shouting. In all his years as the King of New York, only one soul had ever tried him.

Corrado Palermo.

This was a turn of events he wasn't used to.

I laughed a little, listening to him scold Achille. After the old man retired, he'd take over. The insane joker would rule a kingdom of misfits.

Two more Scarpone men came rushing out of the door, one

at a time. When the first stopped, the other one did, and the first hit the second on the chest—a signal that meant, keep your ears and eyes open, and your mouth shut. The other guy nodded.

These men had done nothing to me except work for the family inside. So this wasn't personal. And to slit a person's throat, that was fucking personal. Without a word, I took them each out with a bullet to the back of the brain. It made a mess, but blood ran out of the kitchen anyway. The gun was quieter than the two bodies that hit the ground.

I stepped into the kitchen like I owned the place. As predicted, three bodies were down on the floor.

Looked like Cash Kelly had gotten his revenge, even if he hadn't been able to touch the main players. He'd have some clout in this town, even if his two guys ran away after.

The Scarpones had been weakened, but they were known to eat their septic paws to save the entire body. Because of that, Cash would earn some respect from the Italians, even if the Italians would be more cautious of him and his motives. In general, the Irish and Italians worked together in harmony or stayed clear of one another.

Until I started in.

Before the newly crowned princes could get the jump on me, I took Achille's two sons out. One of them fell against the wall and slid down, gun still in his hand. The other one looked shocked for a moment, his gun still raised, before he slumped over the card table.

Achille and the whiz kid son had gone to the front of the restaurant. I figured they would, to check things out.

I took a seat beside Arturo after I collected the prince's guns, my back against the wall, and set my gun on my lap. This was my honorary seat, the glass of whiskey untouched.

"Mind if I join you?" I slid a pile of cards my way, and then took a sip of my whiskey. It was in my honor, after all. I set the cards face down, looking Arturo in the eyes. "Seems like I got dealt a shitty hand. I demand a do over."

His shoulder holster held two guns, and even though he itched to use them, he waited me out. This was too good for even him to pass up. After all, what did he have to be afraid of? A ghost with a gun? A man who was outnumbered three to one?

That's right, my butterfly. The devil comes in threes.

"Walk away now." He rolled his teeth over his bottom lip. "And I'll let you live."

I leaned forward, taking more cards from the pile. I slid the shitty hand toward him. "Let me live?" I grinned. "After you were so kind to slit my throat and let me die like an animal, alone and out on the cold cement, right next to the trash."

"You double-crossed me. No one double-crosses me and lives to tell about it."

"Ah. But I did." My throat tightened and my voice came out sharp and rough. Scar tissue sometimes made my voice do funny things. "I'm telling about it." I waved a hand, taking out a card and replacing it with another in the pile. "That's all old news. It's time to put an old ghost to rest."

"What do you want, Vittorio?"

"What do I want?" I mused. "You tell me."

He looked around the room. "You've succeeded in killing most of our heirs. I know now, for sure, that you've been making war between the other families and ours. You set the Irish on us, too. You've been stealing from us. You've gotten your revenge. What else do you want?"

"You," I said, "in the Hudson. Your feet weighed down with concrete. The Joker right beside you. The Scarpones to be wiped clean from this earth. And I'm sure you're curious to know why I want you and your joker of a son at the bottom of the Hudson when next to the dumpster will do. There's trash on this earth, and then *there's* trash that needs to be buried below its surface."

He stood, towering over me. Looking down on me. Old times. Except in this moment, he was older. His black hair had turned grey around the sides. His face was weathered. His nose was bigger. His shoulders had started to sag with the burden of carrying life around for however many years he'd been on this earth. Time moves on, and it shows on the body, but some people never outgrow their roles.

Finally, I met his eyes again. When I was ready.

"Why did you disobey me, Vittorio? Why did you choose Palermo's kid over your own father? He tried to kill me! He was going to slit my throat! You had orders!"

"Your orders meant nothing in the face of an innocent child."

"Innocent child?" he breathed out. "She's the spawn of Lucifer!"

"No. I'm the spawn of the devil. How old was I when I first took a man's life at your order? When I made my bones. Fifteen? Sixteen?" I pulled the cards closer to me, tapping my finger on the top. One. Two. Three times. "Have you ever watched a child color? Or listened to the way the word 'blue' comes out as 'boo'? Or watched as she rubbed a rosary raw because she was so afraid? Afraid of every noise. Every shadow."

He was quiet for a stretch of time. I heard footsteps drawing nearer, and Achille started to say something as he entered the room, but he stopped when he noticed me sitting there. I heard the hammer of his gun click back, but Arturo raised a hand to stop him from using it. Achille always drew first and didn't worry about the fallout later.

He killed the wrong guy? *Oh fucking well. That's life.*

Arturo knew the kind of man Achille was. That was why he called him The Joker. Achille was a simple foot solider who didn't have the ability to think on his own. He had to be led. Showed. Ordered. Ruthless bones were needed to live in this world, which he had, to his core, but a strategic brain was even more important.

Violence was less than half of the battle. Strategy trumped bloodshed. If your mind was screwed on right, the bloodshed of your men could be kept to a minimum, while your adversaries took the hit.

Arturo knew this, as well, but there were more factors at play. He had me killed because I didn't kill Palermo's daughter. But he also had me murdered because he knew I beat him in all the ways that counted in *his* game. I took him move for fucking move, day after day, year after year. Patience and strategy were two of my greatest strengths.

Checkmate.

When the time was right for me, I looked over at the three of them.

Arturo's mouth morphed slowly into a grin, and then the grin grew into a smile, and then he started to laugh. He laughed so hard that he howled. The two men next to him looked between us, not sure what the fuck was going on.

After Arturo's humor died down, he wiped his eyes, sighing. "You felt sorry for Palermo's kid. Something you never felt before. Before that little bitch cast her spell on you, you had no feelings. And now you're in love with her."

He looked at Achille. "Forget sending the dogs out on the bitch we met in Italy. I know who she is. Marietta Palermo. I should've known. That fucking nose. Even those witchy eyes. She looks like her whore of a mother."

Achille smiled, but he still held his gun. "No shit?"

Vito, Achille's son, looked me over. There was no smile on his face. Nothing showed in his eyes. He was already dead inside. I understood how he felt even before my death. Nothing could touch me. Nothing existed inside.

Marietta's innocence had set me on a different path, but it took death's kiss to make me feel alive. If the knife would've never touched my throat, I would've never been able to truly feel her love.

Love. There was a new fucking concept. It was the sorest spot I'd ever had, but at the same time, even without killing these three, I was an untouchable king.

What a trip.

Still. *Back to the point.*

I kicked the chair across from me, kicking off this meeting. Arturo sat first, followed by Achille. Vito stood the longest, but after his father told him to *sit*, he did. He watched me with a void in his eyes.

"I'm not going to sit here and play a fucking game with you, Vittorio." Achille flung the cards at me. "You've been playing us all this time. Playing a fucking game as a ghost, not a man. How is that fair?"

I threw back my head and laughed. "How is that fair?"

In the span of four heartbeats, two chairs screeched, and all guns had been drawn. I was the quickest draw, and my gun was aimed at the old man's head. Arturo, Achille, and his son had their guns aimed at me.

"It doesn't matter if I die." I raked my teeth over my bottom lip. "I'm already dead."

"Marietta isn't." Arturo smiled. "Once you're dead—no second chances this time, Vittorio—we're going to find her and kill her. It won't be an easy death."

I grinned, but it was far from pleasant. "This time I don't get a front row seat to watch?"

Achille grinned, his resemblance to the joker never so strong as when his lunacy turned up a notch. "You'll get to watch, Pretty Boy Prince. This time, though, I'm the one who'll be doing the fucking. I've seen your girl. Nice ass. Nice mouth, too."

I had to keep my head on straight, keep my temper cool, or he had already won. "You didn't find her before. You'll never find her now."

"We'll find her," Arturo said. "We know what she looks like now. We know her friends."

"She's under the Faustis' protection. Kill me." I shrugged. "She'll still be safe."

"You're good at making deals with the devil, Vittorio. I'm sure that one will cost you your soul."

"It cost me nothing, since I'm the spawn of the devil," I said in Italian. The King and the Joker only had certain words. Both of them hated it when I spoke my mother's language. "But enough about me. Let's talk about Palermo."

"What about Palermo?" Arturo's thoughts worked behind his eyes. He was questioning everything he thought he knew about Corrado Palermo's death. Was he still alive?

"Ask Achille," I said.

"Achille. What is he talking about?"

Achille stared at me with such hatred that I was surprised the gun didn't go off from his heat alone. "He's talking nonsense, Pop. You going to listen to a cowardly ghost?"

None of them caught the slight movement I made, not until I slipped the paper from my pocket and set it on the table. A second later, Vito became a little too trigger-happy and pulled the trigger. The bullet grazed my arm, my coat taking the hit, and then stuck into the brick wall.

One thing about the whiz kid, he had terrible aim. There was a reason why Arturo kept him behind a computer screen. That was where he excelled in weaponry.

"What the fuck, Vito!" Achille slapped him so hard behind the head that the kid's glasses slipped down his nose.

Vito's cheeks heated, before his eyes turned even meaner— on me. I was wrong. He had one feeling going for him. Resentment.

The mishap with the gun gave Arturo the chance to read the note I'd slipped him. The look on his face fed my revenge.

Arturo lifted the paper. "You were plotting with Palermo."

"What?" Achille's face scrunched up. He went to take the paper, but Arturo held it away from him. "Let me see it, Pop."

Arturo stared at him a second longer before he handed it over. Achille's eyes scanned the page. "This is bullshit!"

"Is it?" My tone was so light and carefree. "Palermo was a hoarder. He made a habit to write everything down. He kept journal after journal. You see, he thought he was going to make it out of this life alive. Rumor had it that he was trying to become the new King of New York, but the truth was that he wasn't trying to become king, but the *new* king's most trusted advisor."

"Bullshit!" Achille roared, the gun starting to shake.

"Palermo had no reason to lie. It's all there." I nodded to the paper in his hand. "He had inside information, which you blamed Carlo, the rat playing two sides, for giving him. It was you all along. You gave Palermo the knife and ordered the hit on him." I nodded to Arturo, whose mind was *click, click, clicking*, all of the pieces falling in place.

Arturo had been so busy being blinded by my pretty-boy looks and my sharp mind that he never saw the true snake in his house.

Achille was the reason Palermo put his family in danger. He wanted to rule next to Achille, and he based his decisions on promises built from lies. Then when it all went bad for Palermo, Maria knew that she was the only living link who could shed light on the situation—and once Palermo was gone, Achille would make sure she followed behind. Her daughter, too, for good measure.

After I'd gone back to the house Palermo owned when he worked for Arturo, I started to dig. My main goal was to find a picture or two of Maria to give to Mariposa. If something were to happen to me, I wanted to make sure she had those memories.

I uncovered so much more.

It seemed like Mariposa got something from her father after all—the need to keep a journal.

Essentially, Achille had convinced Arturo that I needed to disappear after letting Marietta live. He had hammered it into Arturo that since I had saved Palermo's daughter, I'd lie to save my life. However, looking back, knowing what I did after reading Palermo's recollections, I realized that not only did Achille want me dead so he could have the entire kingdom, he wanted me dead because he had no idea what Mariposa's mother had told me before she died, or Palermo himself for that matter.

Achille didn't try another hit on Arturo because it would've been too suspicious. Arturo's trusted group was small, and his locations were not known until he had already arrived. It would've been too blunt of a move. With me gone, things were simple. All he had to do was bide his time.

We all stood with our guns drawn, waiting, Arturo's gun pointing straight at my heart. Then Arturo's hand moved, and his bullet hit Vito straight in his heart. The boy hit the wall, slid down, his glasses askew, his mouth hanging open.

Arturo turned his gun toward Achille, but with the speed of youth, Achille whipped his gun up to Arturo's head and pulled the trigger. Arturo's knees gave out and he fell to the floor. I didn't miss the look on his face before he lost the battle with death, though—anger. He was always so fucking hateful, and not even death could steal it from him.

Achille and I circled each other, our weapons still drawn.

"Even for a dead man, you lose, Vittorio." He sniffed. "You always considered me the dumb one. I might not be as smart as you, but shit happens for a reason, and I'm good at piecing things together. I had a vision while I was at the hospital earlier today, digging through the morgue, looking for my missing son. Tito Sala. He saved you that night."

"One shot, Achille," I said, sick of the game. But the mention of my uncle's name had me hesitating to pull the trigger. If he had Tito, there was no telling what kind of sick game he had in play. "One of us is going to finish this. One shot. That's all you have to kill me this time."

Achille took a step back, going for the kitchen. I moved with him, move for move. He stopped right outside of the room, where there was a closet for hanging up coats. Arturo had it put in because he didn't like anyone touching his things. After Palermo, he thought twice about what, or who, could bring him down. "Unforeseen circumstances are a bitch, Vittorio."

He opened the closet and Tito fell out. He was bound and gagged. Achille held him up with one hand, sticking the gun to his temple. Tito's glasses were gone, and his eyes blinked at me before they fully opened. Once the situation made it to his mind, he shook his head, trying to speak. I knew what he wanted without him having to use words. He was trying to tell me not to sacrifice my life for his.

I couldn't make the shot.

Unforeseen circumstances.

There was no way I'd sacrifice Tito's life for mine. The man was the angel who stood between death and me. If anyone deserved to live life, even if it was to save them, it was this man.

"Put the gun down, Vittorio," Achille ordered, pressing the gun to Tito's temple even harder. "Now. Or your good uncle is as good as dead."

Raising my hands in surrender, I let the gun fall to the floor. Tito started to fight, but it was no use. I had already surrendered.

My wife was safe. My son would be safe.

Achille would kill me, but he would never touch them.

Rocco would see to it. Especially after I sacrificed my life for Tito's.

"On your knees, Vittorio," Achille ordered. "On your knees!" he roared when I refused to move.

I kept my hands up, putting them behind my head, but I refused to kneel. He was going to kill me anyway. I'd be damned if I went down on my knees for any mere man. I only bent, broke, went down for one person on this earth—a woman, my wife.

Slowly, I took my hands down, reaching for the rosary around my neck. I pulled it out and kept it close to my heart.

The gun pressed against the back of my head, and once more, I found peace in my darkest hour.

28

MARIPOSA

Before Capo left, he had given me a blue box tied with a blue bow. He told me to open it after he left. As soon as he was out of the door, I wasted no time opening it.

The first thing I found was a note on top of blue tissue paper.

Mariposa,

That night, the night I took you to old man Gianelli and Jocelyn, you told me your favorite color was blue. Except you said boo instead of blue. It was the first time since my mother left me that I remembered smiling and feeling it. The last time will be the moment I walk out of the door to our home and think of you—you don't say boo anymore, but you still do something to me that has no word to define it.

For that, I owe you my life. It wasn't me that saved you that night, but you that saved me.

What lies beyond the surface of this box cannot bring back what you lost at my hands, but maybe that lost part of you can start to find its way back.

Capo

Under the tissue was an album full of pictures. Photographs

that I never thought I'd see. My mom. My mom holding me as a newborn. Numerous pictures of me until I was five. It seemed like she only kept her favorite ones. Photos that were important enough to bury and keep hidden.

I had texted Capo after, spilling my guts. I had been too afraid to tell him in person all of the things I needed him to know, afraid that maybe my words would jinx something, and he'd never come back to me.

He didn't tell me what he was going to do, but I knew. There was something different about him the entire day.

The way he looked at me.

Like it was the last time.

The way he kissed me.

Like it was the last time.

The way he touched me, *like it was the last time.*

More than words.

Rocco had been over, and the two of them had a meeting in Capo's office. I didn't like the way Rocco looked at me before he left. Like he might be looking at a widow he'd soon be responsible for.

Again, *more than words.*

Before Rocco left, I slipped a note into his palm. It was a natural gesture, a goodbye handshake, and that was the end of it. I had no problem using all of my words.

I couldn't keep still, though. I had given Capo my rosary to take with him, and I missed being able to rub the beads between my fingers to ease my anxiety. For the first time since I married Capo, the devil felt close on my heels again.

Slipping on a pair of tennis shoes, I crossed over to the other building, finding Giovanni in the kitchen.

"Any word from my husband?"

He shook his head. "Not since he left."

I bit my lip and nodded. "I want ice cream."

He pointed to the freezer. "It is stocked."

"No. I want vanilla. We have all other flavors but vanilla."

He watched me for a moment and then called Stefano, his second in charge, into the kitchen. "Mrs. Macchiavello would like you to run to the store for vanilla ice cream."

"I'm driving," I said, going for the keys on the hook in a room that housed most of the car keys. A password was needed to get in. The rest of the keys were on our side, in the secret firehouse. Capo thought of everything.

Capo had told Giovanni he had no problem with me going out tonight, as long as one of the men went with me. Which threw up another red flag. Why was he so sure the Scarpones wouldn't be on the hunt for me?

Giovanni nodded, and Stefano and I went into the garage. The alarm chirped on the red Ferrari and we both slid in. Before I opened the garage, I sent Capo a text.

Me: I'm going with Stefano to get ice cream. We can watch an old movie and drink root beer floats tonight. You're coming home to me, Capo.

Again, he didn't text me back. He hadn't, not since earlier. After I had poured my feelings out to him over an electronic device. All of a sudden it felt...so necessary to tell him all the things.

Truth be told, I didn't give a damn about ice cream. I was going to Dolce to see where my husband was. To make sure that my nightmare wasn't coming true—my husband bleeding out on the cement, clutching the rosary in his hands while he left me.

Stefano noticed that we were not going toward the store.

"Mrs. Macchiavello, we are going the wrong way." He pointed the other way with his finger. "The store is that way."

I ignored him. He tried again. I still ignored him. I started to go faster, a pressure inside of me that I couldn't even explain pressing my foot harder on the gas pedal. The pressure was panic.

"Mrs. Macchiavello—!"

Before I could even comprehend what was happening, the rest of the words flew out of Stefano's mouth in a sort of suspended slow motion: "—a truck!"

Those were the last words out of his mouth before a massive truck came out of nowhere and slammed into the passenger side door of the Ferrari.

It happened so fast that, while the car rolled, my mind hadn't even had time to catch up. Once it did, we were righted, but everything around me seemed distorted. Blurry. I reached up a hand and touched my head. I hissed. Blood ran along my forehead, stinging my eyes.

"Stefano," I croaked.

No answer.

I said his name again, groping for him, but there was still no answer. Then I laid a hand on my stomach, wondering if the impact had hurt the baby.

My baby.

Even though tears didn't come—maybe I was in shock— something came from a part of me that I'd never met before. That something was worry straight from the deepest depths of my heart and soul.

The thought of something happening to my baby sent me into a hollow, silent panic. Then I felt a flutter, a slight movement, and I relaxed, but didn't feel totally at ease.

The breath hissed out of me when I went to move, to try and open the door. Was my rib broken? I coughed, and it hurt even more.

Where did the truck even come from? Even though I was going fast, I was paying attention. No lights. It had no lights on. It was a demon slamming into a bright light.

The next second, my door opened and a man reached in and cut me out of the seatbelt. After he did, he yanked me out onto the street by my hair. I cried out without meaning to. My chest was on fire.

Sense finally made it to my brain. The man wasn't there to help me. He was there to kill me. The man started to fight me for the watch on my wrist. I knew it was a man because of his hairy arms.

Was he robbing me?

"Give it to me, you bitch!" He slapped me hard across the face. "You keep fighting me, I'll chop your wrist off for it!"

I froze at the sound of his voice. I focused on him, truly focused on him, and the breath left me completely. He ripped the watch off, flung it on the driver's seat of the Ferrari, and then emptied a can of gasoline all around the car. Maybe even inside of it. He walked closer to me after, his boot in my face.

He knew about the watch.

He knew that was my direct line to safety, to someone coming for me.

Capo finding me.

Saving me.

Capo...was he? I couldn't even stand the thought.

I tried to crawl away, but it was no use. The madman dragged me by the hair to his waiting truck, flinging me inside. My head spun, my eyes kept going in and out of focus, and I couldn't even call him by his name. It was on the tip of my tongue, but my mind refused to feed the words to my mouth.

He kept mumbling things, what he was going to do to me, where he was taking me, how much I'd suffer, but his voice kept going in and out of boiling water.

The last thing I remembered was seeing the Ferrari go up in flames as we drove away. The devil had finally caught me, and he was bringing me to hell with him.

A single shot rang through the air. It wasn't loud, but loud enough that I heard it. My grip on the rosary became tighter, but after a second, all I heard was a body hit the floor.

My eyes shifted to the left, then to the right.

It wasn't my body.

I was still upright, the rosary cutting into my palm.

"Amadeo," Rocco said, "help me untie this damsel in distress before he gets the vapors."

It took me a moment to comprehend what had happened. Rocco was untying Tito. Achille lay on the floor behind me, blood pooling around his head. He was dead.

Death was all around me. And even though their deaths satisfied me because they wouldn't be bothering mine anymore, that was all it was, relief that they couldn't hurt my family.

"You!" Tito roared after Rocco tore the tape off his mouth. "I am going to hurt *you* when Rocco unbinds these hands." He wiggled them, like he couldn't wait to put them around my neck.

Rocco grinned at me. "Should we put the tape back on?"

"Do not dare!" Tito growled. "I will castrate you both!"

"Uncle," Rocco said. "Shouldn't you have done that to—" he nodded toward Achille "—before you allowed him to abduct you?"

"I was tired! I had a very unstable patient at the hospital. Achille came out of nowhere in the parking garage. When I wouldn't tell him anything, he hit me on the head and then tied me up! It just so happened that he abducted me on the evening you sought your revenge!"

"Rocco." My voice came out tight, urging him to explain the reason why he was here.

Under no circumstances did I want the Faustis getting involved in my affairs. When this night happened, it was on my terms. If one of the Scarpones had come out on top, that was the way the dice would've rolled.

Games. So many fucking games. All of them ended.

I'd had this conversation with Rocco on many occasions. I had brought it up again after he'd given me his word that the Faustis would take my wife in if something were to happen to me. Mariposa didn't know this, but even before she had agreed to marry me, I had asked him to take care of her. She was the sole heir to anything that belonged to me.

Rocco stopped struggling with Tito and focused on me. He dug in his pocket, pulling out a sheet of paper. It had been torn out of a journal. He handed it to me.

Dolce. Tonight. Don't do it as a favor to me, do it as favor to love. I won't owe you one, but love will.

Mariposa. My wife. I could recognize her handwriting anywhere, especially after reading her journal from front to back. I lifted the paper.

Rocco nodded. "Your wife. She slipped it in my palm before I left your place earlier." He shrugged. "She spoke to the romantic in me."

"Release me, nephew!"

We both looked at Tito, who struggled to free himself the rest of the way. We had no time, though. Sirens wailed in the distance. We each took an arm and lifted him up, carrying him out with his feet lifted off the floor. He cursed the entire way but became quiet when we set him in the car. Then he just *hmphed* and looked out the window, like he refused to speak to either of us.

I took out my computer, making sure all of the precautions I'd put in place were still there. The camera had recorded only a few snippets from the night.

What it did show from inside was the masked men running in and killing the kitchen staff, the Scarpone men running after them, Arturo killing Vito, and then Achille killing Arturo. The note from Corrado Palermo was still with Arturo.

The police would never see footage, so they would have to take a wild guess when it came to Achille. The list of his enemies couldn't be contained to one page. I doubted the law would put much effort into finding Achille's killer. Rocco had done them a favor.

"Old man," I said, still looking over my computer, speaking to Tito. "You saved my life once. You gave me a second chance. My life for yours was the least I could do."

He slapped me on the back of my head. Hard. From the corner of my eye, I saw Rocco grin.

"Exactly! I am an old man compared to you! Your wife! What of her?"

"I wouldn't have a wife if it wasn't for you."

"Your son? Who would have raised him?"

"You," I said. "And again, without you, I'd have no son."

He started to curse in Italian. Even though he was pissed at me for what I'd been willing to sacrifice for him, I really thought he was pissed at himself for getting abducted by a dumbass like Achille. The men would probably start calling him Tied Up Tito or some shit to give him a hard time. No way was Rocco going to let him live it down.

Then my phone rang. *Giovanni.*

"Mac." He was breathless, as though he'd been running. He was a big dude, and his voice was naturally deep.

"Talk to me, G."

"It's." He took a deep breath. "Your wife." He started to ramble off words. *Left with Stefano. The store. Vanilla ice cream. Taking too long. Couldn't get a signal on either Stefano or your wife. Went out to look for them. Glass in the street. Ferrari. Burnt to a crisp. A body in it. Passenger side. Not sure who. Couldn't tell if it was a man or woman. Firemen and police on the scene.*

Without a word to him, I hung up and dug out my phone from my pocket and turned it on.

New text.

Your wife: I'm going with Stefano to get ice cream. We can watch an old movie and drink root beer floats tonight. You're coming home to me, Capo.

"Fucking bullshit," I said. "She was going the wrong way. Going toward Dolce. She was coming to check on me." Then I told Rocco to stop the car. As I pulled up a different program on my computer that I'd designed, I gave them the gist of the situation. My voice came out calm, controlled, maybe even cold, but on the inside, Mount Vesuvius had gone off.

Giovanni was right. Her watch showed no signal, and neither did Stefano's work phone. I even traced his personal device, and it couldn't be located either. Neither could Mariposa's phone.

"Come on, my little butterfly," I whispered. I switched gears, checking my last resort—it was the way I'd always tracked her. Even to Harry Boy's house.

Her wedding ring.

She never took it off. There was a device located in the metal behind the diamond. Her band, too, if she ever decided to wear one without the other. If whoever did this wasn't doing it to rob her, he wouldn't have thought of taking her ring. Her watch. Yeah. Her car. Yeah. But her ring? It was inconspicuous as a device.

As soon as the heart started beating on the screen, I closed my eyes and squeezed the rosary around my neck. Stefano. Stefano had been killed. But then a cold hand touched my neck and my voice was low and tight when I spoke. "Rocco. Bring me to the Hudson." I told him the area. "As fast as you fucking can. And on the way, call Brando."

Brando Fausti had once been in the Coast Guard. He had been a rescue diver in Alaska. He was the best of the best. The motherfucker was like a shark in the water. He had all of the right equipment and could see in almost blind conditions.

The second man needed, the doctor, was already in the backseat, sitting forward, listening. He mumbled things, medical things.

Whoever took my wife was taking her to the Hudson River. I could see the heart on the screen, making its way closer and closer to the water. Whoever took my wife, the dead man, was going to drown her.

30

MARIPOSA

Sicily. I kept think about my time in the water there. Going under just to pop right back up. My head breaking the surface before sound made it fully to my ears.

My head. It was doing the same thing.

Hands groped for me. I fought them the best I could. I clawed and bit and screamed. I wasn't sure if the screaming was loud enough. I was under and everything was distorted.

Would anyone hear me?

If not for my baby, I would've given in, given up. The devil had caught me, and my husband was probably dead.

I was done for. I was sick and tired of the fight, of the chase.

My will to live had burnt out.

I had been so tired when I found Capo. And after he took me in, gave me shelter and food and protection, not to mention what I'd been missing for so long—love and security—I slept. I took refuge. But my will to live was still tired, still aching for sleep, for rest in a safe house, a comfortable bed, and to be held in strong arms.

It wasn't only me that I fought for, though. He deserved a

chance to live a life he hadn't even tasted yet. Not to merely survive but to live. A life I'd been willing to sell my body to have.

Turned out, I'd given it instead.

Capo. My baby. Saverio. I hadn't even told Capo how much I loved the name and the meaning behind it. *New home.* Saverio was the home we'd always share. He was our blood vow in physical form.

I clawed even harder. I hoped my teeth felt even sharper. And my scream—even if it came out hoarse, maybe someone would still hear me.

My back slammed against something hard, the breath escaping my mouth in a *whoosh*. I lost even more focus, even more control over my limbs. My entire body was on fire.

Mumbling. There was so much mumbling.

Shut up! I wanted to shout. My voice was muted, but his wasn't. It was right in my ear, screaming inside of my broken skull. It seemed to bounce from one side to the other, making my head ache even more.

I felt sick. Nauseated.

The burning was so hot.

My feet. I couldn't move my feet. My hands. I couldn't move those, either.

I had nothing, absolutely nothing to fight him with.

The fire came closer, licking every inch of my skin, and then there was a free fall into nothing, a hard slap of frigid water against scorching flesh, and then it took me under. Sucking me down, down, down, faster than I could take a breath.

The pressure was immense. All-consuming. It put out the fire but sent me in another spiral.

Frozen arms held me tight, and thousands of hands stabbed me with hundreds of sharp, cold daggers. Then the water ran into my mouth, invaded my nose, and consumed my lungs. A different kind of burn, but still a burn, one that seized instead of charred.

There was no use fighting it. I was bound. Being dragged to hell through a watery grave. Fast. It was worse than when Capo pushed the speedometer in one of his cars, almost like we were flying instead of cruising.

I wondered if touching hell would bring me to a pathway to heaven?

It had to be easier than this, more peaceful. *Maybe that's why death is so hard.* We had to pay for our sins before we were given complete peace.

I thought of the rosary, the safety I found in stroking the pearls between my fingers, and then I let go, giving over to something greater than me.

31

CAPO

Before the car came to a complete stop, I jumped out, running toward the pier that stretched to a platform with construction equipment.

The water was dark, and I couldn't see past the surface. A small light lit the platform, but a bigger light was centered on a specific area of the river. A man stood next to a ladder that had been clipped to the pier and touched the tip of the Hudson.

Romeo waited on his brother. Brando had already taken the plunge. Diving equipment was laid out on the pier next to Romeo, along with emergency apparatus.

Romeo's head snapped up when he heard me. He held out his hand, and when we connected, he drew me in. "Amadeo." He stood back, his dark eyes solid on mine. "My *fratello* went in after *tua moglie*. We heard the splash as we rushed up. Brando was able to see where Mariposa went under. That is a good thing. A few seconds later and he would have had to search the entire area."

Rocco and Tito caught up to us. Tito stared down at the water for a minute before he went over to dig through the stuff Brando and Romeo had brought.

Rocco stared beyond Romeo at a man sitting on the pier. His hands and legs were tied up. His mouth was full of blood, white specks on his legs. His teeth. The area around him was littered with cement blocks, lines of rope, knives, scissors, packets of cement, molds, and tape.

He was going to make specific molds to fit my wife's feet, set her in them, and then make sure no one was able to pull her up. Time. He ran out of fucking time.

Bruno. That motherfucker had slammed into my wife with a truck, abducted her, did who knows what to her on the way, and then threw her in the Hudson with cement blocks tied to her legs. And he had killed a good man. Stefano.

Romeo nodded. "I am sure you have plans for him. I was able to stop him before he disappeared. Unless he wanted to jump into the water, he had no other choice but to face me. He was too much of a coward to take the leap. Therefore." He rolled his shoulders. "He got me."

I rolled my teeth over my bottom lip. "The water would have been the kinder choice," I said in Italian.

Romeo agreed. "He shall suffer for this."

Then we said no more as we turned and waited for Brando to break the surface with my wife. Tito came to stand next to me, putting a hand on my shoulder, squeezing. I hadn't realized how hard I trembled until he touched me. His was a steady hand in a tilting world. Each second felt worse than getting my throat slit a thousand times. My heart felt like it was going to burst from my chest.

Any second now, Fausti, any second now, I chanted underneath my breath. The longer she stayed under, the less of a chance she had to—

I refused to entertain the vicious thoughts attacking my worn-down sanity. All of a sudden, my knees gave out and I landed on them, the pier taking my weight. I closed my eyes, clutching the rosary around my neck, wondering if this was payback for my sins. The cost of living in a body that had a soul made of hate and revenge.

Until she came along.

She set me on a different path, and when we collided, we both shattered into a million pieces from the impact. She snuck in through my cracks and ran over every strip of lead I'd put down to keep myself together. Her colors bled with mine, and the stained glass no longer showed a solitary figure, but one with a butterfly on its shoulder, its heart on its sleeve.

No longer able to bend or I'd fucking break, I stood, kicking my boots off.

Any fucking second turned into *now*. I refused to wait a second longer to bring my wife home. *Back to me.* Even if it meant that I drowned at the bottom of the Hudson with her. That was my fate. It had been meant for me. We'd share it. She'd be my Juliette, and I'd be her Romeo.

Rocco put a hand to my shoulder, Romeo the other, and they held me back while Tito came to stand in front of me.

"Nephew." His voice was as serious as when he'd been saving my life. "You will do your wife no favors if you go in after her and we have to get *you* out."

"I'm not Brando Fausti," I said, "but I can fucking swim." I hit my chest. "I refuse to stand here and wait for him to bring my wife back to me."

"You are as close to me as a brother." Rocco squeezed my shoulder. "So trust me when I say this. Brando will bring her up. He will retrieve her. He is the best there is. Let him do his job."

His job. *My wife.*

As soon as the thought came to me, the most beautiful sound I'd ever heard seemed to explode around me. Brando broke the surface with my wife in his arms. He seemed to move quicker than a shark in the water. Once he carried her up the ladder, he set her on the pier.

Tito went straight for her. Brando flung his mask off, and after Romeo helped him with his tank, he went straight to Tito, and they both started working.

"Hypothermic," Tito muttered while he checked her pulse. "We must be very careful. Brando. Cut her out of these clothes. Then get the warming blankets on her. Now!"

My wife was lifeless on the pier. Her skin had no color. Her lips were blue. She had a gash on her forehead. It was deep and red, but there was no blood.

I crawled to her side, taking her wrist in my hand, checking myself. "Uncle." My voice was tight, raw, low. "She doesn't have a pulse."

Tito watched my face while Brando stripped her down to her bra and underwear and then covered her in blankets. "The water—we had a hard winter—it's too cold. She's too cold. We need to get her body temperature up."

"CPR," I said, clearing my throat. "Chest compressions. Do them—"

"I will start CPR, but not until the ambulance gets here. I need to continue once I begin. There will be no stopping until I can bring her back. Right now, her pulse is too low to detect. But that does not mean we cannot get her back."

Sirens wailed in the distance. An ambulance was on its way. But if Tito couldn't save her, I knew no one could.

Romeo walked Bruno to his car before the police arrived. Our eyes met as he passed. He smiled at me, no more teeth in his mouth, but nothing but satisfaction on his face. I'd skin him alive, from head to toe, and then fit him for cement blocks. Then he'd take a ride to the bowels of the Hudson River. The crabs could feast on his insides. They wouldn't have to worry about his skin. They'd get a peeled snack.

"Nephew!" Tito roared.

It took me a minute to turn to him, to focus on anything but my anger. My desire to kill tasted like blood in my mouth, and I was a starved animal. The dead man's cry when his skin peeled back, inch by inch, would represent what was happening to my heart and soul.

"Keep your focus here!" Tito nodded toward my wife. "Talk to her!"

Talk to her.

My wife.

She had no pulse, but I was the dead man.

I didn't want to think about why Tito had ordered me to talk to her.

I refused to.

But if this was it, the end, it was final, for the both of us.

I'd never see her again.

She'd be in heaven. I'd be in hell.

We were never meant to be longer than we were on this earth.

I lifted her hand to my mouth, blowing warm air on it, my lips close. "Mariposa." My voice cracked. "You left something important behind, Butterfly. You left me behind to die the worst death. You being away from me is the worst death. It's more painful than anything I've ever known. But words are useless. *Hear* me, Mariposa."

There was a time when I didn't know if I'd ever be able to speak, the knife had cut me so deep. I knew then how useless words were. I demanded more than words, and that was what I vowed to give to her.

Feel my pain and let it bring you back to me. You're the only one who can save me from it. My life and my death. My dash in between—

Brando's voice cut through my thoughts, a jumble of words standing out: *Temperature. Water. In too long. Rope. Cut to release her from cement blocks. Hypothermia. No pulse. Pregnant.*

The words slipped into my mind, pushing out everything

else, poisoning my soul, as the men discussed my wife and her current state of life.

No life.

She had no life.

All that she had left to do on this earth assaulted me. All that she had missed out on stabbed me like a thousand knives. All the days and nights she suffered. She'd told me that she'd never touched true peace until we were married. For the first time in her life, she could sleep, she could rest, and it wasn't only physical. The devil on her heels was too far behind to catch her—her shoes finally fit and kept her steady.

She had struggled so damn much with life. Struggled to change from surviving to living. And she was gone. My butterfly was gone after getting her wings.

As the men drew closer, I pulled her closer, not realizing I had her pressed against my chest, rocking her.

I refused to give her up.

I refused to allow them to take her from me. I'd rip their hands off with my teeth.

She was so cold. I could feel the iciness of the water seeping into my shirt. Her skin felt even colder, as though all of her blood had been drained.

Our son. He had no life if she didn't.

My all gone in the matter of minutes.

An unforeseen circumstance. A man out for revenge.

My own revenge had me *there* when she needed me *here*.

"Nephew." Tito leaned down, looking me in the eye. "Give her to me. I will take care of her. Trust me." He hit his heart.

I allowed the EMTs to take her, while Tito directed them every step of the way.

"I am the doctor! You listen *to me!*"

Tito kept saying that there was a chance her pulse was too low to detect. If she warmed up enough, there was a chance she could still live.

Chance. Chance. Chance. My wife's life, *mine*, depended on a fucking *chance*.

The EMTs didn't argue, but they'd already pronounced her dead in their heads.

They watched me warily, one of them eying my tattoo, as I kept up with them to the waiting ambulance. I refused to leave her. They hooked her up to monitors once inside and...nothing. Nothing but a flat line, and the sound of a machine alarm.

Controlled chaos ensued.

Tito barked out orders like a solider on a battlefield. They were doing chest compressions while they used another warming blanket to try to get her temperature up.

"Nothing," one of the EMTs said, checking the monitors and then looking at Tito. "Still no pulse."

"We keep going!" Tito snapped. "Mariposa. Come on, butterfly. Come on. Breathe for me."

I looked away, my newly beating heart dying a thousand separate deaths at the sight of it. The sound of the machine going off in panic because it couldn't detect life seemed to echo the unrest in my soul.

"Mariposa," Tito whispered.

The sound of his voice ripped the last shred of hope from my chest.

"Tell me," I said. I refused to look at him, because I wasn't sure what I was going to do when I met his pitiful stare. The tone of his voice confirmed my worst nightmare. My butterfly was gone.

"*Farfalla*," Tito said a little louder. A second or two went by. "I have it!" he almost shouted. "A pulse!"

My eyes swung up. The EMT started frantically fooling with his machinery, and like watching the peak of a mountain break through tough ground, the lines started to go up, up, up. Her pulse was picking up. Even the cut on her head started to bleed.

She moaned, and a second later, when we hit a pothole, she cried out in pain. Then, without opening her eyes, she squeezed my hand, and like that, I lived to tell about a thousand deaths—and the one life I still had left to live. With her.

32

CAPO

5 Months Later

My son was only a few hours old, but he ruled our worlds already.

He was what Tito called a miracle baby. He had survived despite the circumstances. He took after his mamma. She said he took after me, too.

He had thick black hair, brown eyes that seemed light enough to maybe turn amber someday, and almond-colored skin. His shoulders were wide, and his arms and legs long. He was a big boy.

Mariposa said he had the features of my face and my build, but he didn't have her nose or my eyes, the two things we had both wished for him to have. But between the importance of getting certain features or having the strength to survive this cruel world, I was thankful he took the latter over the first.

A wise man once told me that we often get not what we want, but what we need.

I had once wished to be king. I had once wished to rule it all. Not wished, but demanded.

I got both of those things, but in ways that I never knew I needed. I was the king of my wife's heart and the ruler of this world we had created together. If it were in my power, my son would have all that he ever needed.

Carrying him over to the window, opening it up, letting the Milano sun shine on his face, I allowed the world to take their first glimpse of this newly born prince.

My son.

Saverio Lupo Macchiavello.

He was the new prince, but the prince of our world. He wouldn't have to prove his ruthlessness to rule. He just did. Regardless of his footsteps, the paths he would take, the choices he'd make, he would always have a kingdom to return to. A safe place to escape to when the devil was on his heels.

"He's just as beautiful as his papà."

I turned to find my wife staring at us. She had been sleeping, but for eleven hours of labor, she looked...brand new. Someone I had never met before. She was soft on the outside, pliable enough to deliver a son into the world, but her soul was a warrior queen. She was a woman who had found unbreakable faith, a strength not known to the strongest man on earth. Her flesh and bone could bend, could break, but her soul was unbendable, unbreakable.

It took this woman to show me how much of a man I was. Sweat still coated my skin and clothes from the intensity of it all.

"He's going to be as big as his Papà, too." She winced. "He seriously hurt my oonie."

I laughed and my son blinked at me, yawning after. "Save the memory for later, when he's older, when you don't want him to do something." I shrugged. "Guilt trip."

She smiled a tired smile, but the sun lit up her entire face. She looked so healthy. Alive. She patted the bed and then opened her arms. "Closer. I want you both closer."

The nurses kept coming in, wanting to take him, but we both refused to let them. After what had happened to my wife, I wanted my family as close to me as possible. The *chance* of letting him go for a few hours wasn't worth it.

Mariposa took Saverio from me, bringing him close to her chest, inhaling his hair like air. He had so much of it that we could comb it. I grinned as I ran my hands through it, making it stand up.

"Capo," she whispered.

It took me a moment to look at her. It was hard not to keep staring at him. I wondered if I'd ever be able to stop.

"Mariposa." I leaned in and kissed her forehead. She closed her eyes, but her face wasn't entirely at peace. She had something on her mind. "Use all of the words."

She nodded. Opened her eyes. Fiddled with his blanket. "I was going to forgive him, you know? Bruno. Right before I went under. I felt that I should. But I couldn't. Right before I took my last breath...I couldn't. I could forgive him for killing me, but not him." She pressed Saverio closer to her chest, resting her lips on his head. "I couldn't forgive him for killing my baby."

Her words were firm, but to my ears, eerie, as if her mother had spoken through her. Maria had forgiven me, but she wouldn't have if I had hurt her daughter. It hadn't been my intention to hurt Mariposa—I was determined to save her. Therefore, Maria forgave me for taking her life without a tremble in her voice.

I stroked the side of Mariposa's face with my thumb. "You were meant for this. For him. You'd kill for him. Die for him."

"I was meant for you, too." Her voice was soft, and she refused to look at me. She fixed his hair. "You died for me. You killed for me. You love me, us, *this*, beyond what you can understand. That's why he's here, why he's ours, because you loved us enough to sacrifice everything for this moment."

She looked up at me, met my eyes, and touched my throat.

"I love you, Capo. I'll always love you. You're stuck with me forever."

I took her hand and brought it to my mouth, kissing her pulse longer than usual.

She grinned. "*Più delle parole, mio marito,*" she whispered in Italian. *More than words, my husband.* Then she started to hum while she stared at our son.

A knock came at the door. Mariposa didn't even bother to look up. She was beyond tired and well past in love with the baby in her arms—she was deliriously high on life.

Not long after Saverio had been born, I sent our family out the door. Mariposa needed rest, and I wanted time to study his features without having to share him when one of the women got grabby hands. So I had no idea who it could be—maybe it was one of the nurses, but they usually knocked and then came in.

Keely, Cash Kelly, and Harry Boy stood on the other side of the door. Keely had gifts in her arms.

I narrowed my eyes at the two men after Keely barreled past me, going straight for Mariposa and Saverio.

Harry Boy nodded at me. "Do you mind if—" He nodded toward my wife.

Mariposa glanced up when he asked. Keely had already taken Saverio in her arms, making faces at him, but she looked up, too. All eyes were on me.

I nodded once but said nothing. He thought we were cool after I saved his sister, but he'd always be on thin ice with me. He was still in love with my wife, even after he showed some interest in my cousin, Gigi.

Cash stood at the door, not entering. "You got a minute to spare, Macchiavello?"

I turned to Mariposa. She was biting her lip, squeezing the blankets covering her legs, her eyes wary. She didn't like that Cash was here.

"A minute," I said to her.

She nodded once but said nothing. Keely said something to her, but she didn't look away from me until she knew her point had been caught and taken to heart—*don't commit to anything that would take you away from us.*

After shutting the door, we stood out in the hallway, my back to the wall. Cash stood next to me.

"Congratulations," he said, sticking his hands in his pockets. "Your wife did a fine job. Your son is a big, healthy boy."

He didn't have a hard Irish accent, but the lilt was there.

I nodded. "You came all this way to chit chat about my family? Doubtful. Let's discuss business."

He sighed. "Tell me where I stand with the new King of New York. I've heard rumors. After Arturo and Achille were killed, no sons left to claim the throne, rumor has it that you're the man who's stepped into the role of king. We don't usually run in the same circles." He grinned. "But unforeseen circumstances, gravity, perhaps, has sucked us into this gray area at the same time."

"You stand right where you are. I stand here. We're neither friend nor foe. I did you one. You did me one. We're square now. But I'm not taking over the Scarpone family. That legacy has died with the men who made it into what it was. What it was? Depends on who you ask, but if you ask me, here's my answer. It was something I want no part of. I've made my own life. I'll rule it the way I see fit. I work for one family beside my own—the Faustis. Other than that...." I shrugged.

I had my investments, my businesses, plenty for me and mine to live comfortably on for the rest of our lives.

It had been my intention to be the new King of New York, the new King Wolf, but unforeseen circumstances—my wife, my son—had changed the direction of my footsteps. And those footsteps led me back to the door where, beyond it, my kingdom waited for me to return.

EPILOGUE
MARIPOSA

10 Years Later

"Peeeeeassse. *Mamma, peeeassse!*"

My entire body tilted to the left, my arm being yanked, my shoulder shaking up and down. "Evelina, child, calm yourself." I smiled at my spunky five-year old. She was our third child out of four, and our only girl. To say she was the apple of her Papa's eyes would be a lie—she was the entire pie. And the poor thing had my nose. At least she had her Papa's eyes.

She stopped shaking me, and I saw the thoughts move behind her sapphire eyes like honey. Her black hair made them pop against her tan skin. Her lips were full and pink, and she puckered them just right. She learned early on that it took sugar to catch butterflies, not salt.

"Mamma." Her voice was so soft, so sweet, and she put my hand to her mouth, placing a tender kiss on my finger. "Can I *peeeeeeassse* see dis wing?" She lifted the hand she held, showing it to me.

She wanted to try on my wedding rings. She had gotten into

a stage where she loved princesses, and if it was shiny, like something they wore, she wanted it, or to at least try it on.

I rarely took my rings off. The last time was when I made meatballs, but only so the meat wouldn't get stuck between the facets. I put it in a special place until my hands were washed. It took ten minutes, tops, and they were back on. Sometimes I even left my wedding band on and just used a brush to scrub the ring after.

For our ninth anniversary, Capo had given me a diamond band to wear on my right hand, third finger, and I never took that one off either. Four butterflies circled around my finger, as they would forever circle around my heart. Each butterfly represented one of our children.

Evelina often asked to wear that one, but this was the first time she asked to wear my wedding rings. They were symbols I'd never get tired of.

Him. Us. Spending this life together. Living it.

"I give 'em right back." She batted her thick lashes at me. "Pweety *peeeeeeassse.*"

I laughed at how sweet she was being. Miss Subtle. That was our daughter—Evelina Noemi Maria. "All right." I sighed. "But you have to sit at the kitchen table. And you can only wear them for a second. These rings are like important clothes to mamma. I need them to feel dressed and ready for the day."

She giggled, taking my hand and leading me to the table. I picked her up before she could climb up, and she went *weee!* as I sat her chunky little bottom down on the chair.

We were at the villa on the outskirts of Modica. It wasn't a large house, but we had made it comfortable for our family. We made it into a home. The kitchen was my favorite room. We spent most of our time there.

I took both rings off and slid them on her finger. They were so big that they almost slid off, but she held them together. I kissed her hand before I stood, watching her eyes shine at how pretty they were.

"Dese are so pweety, mamma," she breathed out. "I luv dem." Then she hugged herself, like she couldn't get any happier than she was in that moment.

The timer went off on the oven, and I turned for a second, remembering that I had to take the red pepper tart out. Family was coming over to have dinner in our garden for our anniversary.

"Evelina." My voice was sharp with warning. "Sit right there and don't move. Do you hear, Mamma? I'm just going to take the tart out of the oven."

She nodded her head frantically, excited that I was going to let her wear the rings for a second longer. I hurriedly took out the tart, placing it on the stove, mentally calculating what else I had to do.

"What dis says?" Evelina asked.

I turned to find her staring at my engagement ring. She had taken it off and was holding it up to the light.

"Here." I held my hand out, giving her my left finger. "Time to put them back on. I can't go without pants, can I?"

She giggled, like it was the funniest thing in the world, kissing me on the nose when I bent down for her to slide the rings back on. She put my band on first, but before she slid the engagement ring back on, she showed me the metal.

"What dis says?" she asked again. Her little eyes were narrowed on whatever she saw, her eyebrows furrowed. When she did that, I could've sworn Capo possessed her.

She couldn't read, but she recognized words. I wasn't sure what she was talking about, though. "It doesn't say—"

Anything, I was going to say, but stopped when I noticed what she had pointed out.

For the first time in ten years, I noticed an inscription on the inside of my engagement ring.

"Fucka me," I breathed.

"Wat that, Mamma?"

"Ah." I realized what I'd said. "Fudge *me*."

"I luv fudge!"

I gave her loud smooches on her cheeks, trying to play off my sudden mood. "I know you do, baby girl! How about this? How about we find Papà and your brothers? I bet you'll see a butterfly in the garden!"

She had refused to stay outside with the boys because she wanted to help me cook. She loved to get her hands dirty in the kitchen, but it was more than that. She wanted the first jump on the sweets.

"Ooh!" she said excitedly, jumping down from the chair before I could stop her. She took off toward the door, only stopping when Capo opened it and lifted her up, turning her upside down, making her squeal with delight.

"Say it, Evelina. Say the magic word."

"Boo!" This was what she said instead of blue. It was her favorite color at the moment. "Boo, Papà, *boo!*"

Capo righted her, and she pulled his face closer to hers, squeezing him so tight that her eyes scrunched.

Anytime I took my rings off, he made an appearance not long after. It was strange, like he was waiting for me to lose them so he could give them back.

"Where are the boys?" I asked.

Saverio was our oldest. Salvatore was our second. Evelina was our third. And coming up as the caboose was our baby, Renzo. He was three, and if anyone called him a baby out loud, he furrowed his eyebrows and pulled Capo's *I'm severely pissed* face.

Capo narrowed his eyes at me, noticing how breathless I sounded, before he glanced down at my hands. "Saverio took Salvatore and Renzo to meet the Faustis. The *Zie* walked with them." He watched me for a second longer before he nodded behind him, wordlessly telling me to follow him out.

Over the years, the need for words between us became less and less, because sometimes his voice became lower and lower. His actions were always louder than his words.

He took my hand when I was close enough, pulling my wrist up to his mouth, setting his lips over my pulse. He glanced down at my rings again. This time it seemed like he was checking to make sure that their positions were right. Again, *strange.*

"Kiss me dere, too." Evelina gave him her wrist, more like set it against his mouth, and he planted a loud smooch over her pulse. "I your princess, Papà."

"You are my princess. *Per sempre.*"

As soon as we were out in the garden, he set Evelina down, letting her run free. She went straight to one of the sugar-water stations we'd set up, watching as a few butterflies stretched their wings in the evening air, soaking up the nectar and the golden sunlight. Even though Evelina was a zealous child in general, around the butterflies, she'd been taught to be quiet, to be kind, to respect them.

I stood back and admired all that my boys had done.

Butterfly lights were strung up over the table, from lemon tree to lemon tree, set and ready for over twenty people, and soft music played in the background—what Saverio called "old people" music. How the times had changed. If I was old, my husband was ancient, and he didn't like it any more than I did when our children called us out on it.

The garden we'd planted with *Nonno* was never as beautiful as it was in that moment. The colors exploded in the evening light, and butterflies were in constant motion, enjoying all of the safe places.

Roots. They had roots here. Just like I did. And whenever the chance presented itself, we told our children stories of the man who had showed us how to plant and nurture them. Each of our children knew the story of the wolf and the butterfly better than we did.

I fiddled with my wedding rings, wishing, hoping the Faustis took their time getting to our area of the land. I had a hard time focusing on anyone, anything, other than my husband.

Time had been sweet to him. He had only grown more attractive over the years. He was as fit as ever, not an ounce of fat on his body, and any lines he gained only upped his "fine-ass mature man" factor. A few lines of gray streaked the sides of his black hair, a few streaks in his stubble caught the light and sparked silver, but it only made him seem wiser.

He still had his shit together.

He still made me feel safe.

He still made me breathless.

He still made my heart do wicked things and the butterflies in my stomach flutter madly.

He still made me want him, crave him, feel starved for him —every day, every night, sometimes every second of my life. The empty space he filled was never truly filled. The space only grew to accommodate a greater hunger. Satisfied but not fully satiated.

I still loved him, but it was not the same. I loved him even more, in all the different ways. My best friend. My lover. My heart. The father of my children. My king wolf. My boss. My everything.

With each passing day, our love only grew. Like the garden around us, our roots went deeper and deeper into a soil that would always welcome us home. Whatever it took, we did, to make *us* right.

"If this isn't what you want." He took a step closer to me, and my breath caught in my throat. The lowering sun hit his eyes just right and reminded me of naked swims in the sea in summer, just the two of us, body sliding against body. "Speak now or forever hold your peace, Butterfly."

"A little too late for regrets, isn't it, Capo?" I took a step closer to him, running my hand along his chest, stopping at the scar around his throat.

"You got any of those, Esquire?"

He sometimes called me that. After Saverio was born, I went back to school and became a lawyer. I worked with Rocco, handling family business from time to time. I also donated my time to kids who were like I had been—needing help when the system failed them. I mostly wanted to take care of my children, but it was nice to have something for me on the outside, too.

"Regrets?" I shook my head. "Not a fucking one."

We both turned to look. Evelina was in her own world. She was playing with her little outside fairy world. She whispered things to the fairies, not wanting to disturb the butterflies flittering around.

Capo grinned, but before he could speak, I pulled myself up by his shoulders and slammed my mouth against his, wanting him so bad that I ached. I needed him inside of me, not giving me a chance to escape his intensity.

When he broke the kiss, I kept my eyes closed, leaning my head against his chest. His heart beat slowly in my ear. "*Ti amo,*" I breathed out, holding his shirt in my hands, refusing to ever let him go. Two words that meant life or death to me—the two words he had engraved on my engagement ring.

He pulled back, studying my face. "After ten years." He shook his head. "You finally read it."

"Ten years?" I blinked up at him. "You had the words engraved before we were married?"

"Since I had the ring made for you."

The laughter that escaped my mouth came out soft—the awe for him thickening it. "Better late than never."

He was a patient man—in revenge and in love.

"'Bout fucking time." And he slammed his mouth against mine, returning all of the things I'd shared with him without using any words. "If I couldn't tattoo the words across the heart in my chest, I did the second best thing. I had it inscribed on your ring and then put it around your finger—lock down. You take my ring off, even after ten years, I know."

"What about your body?" I raised my eyebrows. "Shouldn't I be there, too, Capo?"

He grinned and set his hand around my neck, right over the frantic pulse. "We both know that's a done deal, Mariposa. You're on me, in me, in all the ways. You're mine. Today. Tomorrow. *Per sempre.*"

He had gotten a small blue butterfly tattooed on his hand, right above the wolf's head. It was as electric as the color of the animal's eyes. But if the scar around his throat wasn't enough of a marking, I wasn't sure what was. He acted like the tattoo was a bigger deal, though, like the cost of saving me hadn't been the highest of his life.

Something dawned on me then. I knew him well enough to put two and two together after the big ring inscription reveal. "Our arrangement." I let those two words hang between us for a second. "If you knew you loved me before then…"

A wolfish grin appeared on his face. "The other women?" He shrugged. "Yeah, it would have been an arrangement, nothing more. The terms would've been set, and there was no moving them. The only reason I made an arrangement with you—" He watched me for a minute or two, drawing out the moment, before he exhaled. "—I needed to work around your aversion to kindness. What better way than with terms? It was real in a sense—you'd get everything if I died—but other than that, it meant nothing. Agreement or not, that ring was on your finger for good."

He had been, all along, my *"for good."*

"Do you remember when we played twenty questions after our wedding?"

"There is no little man running around with a tab jar," he mocked my voice.

"Yeah," I said, not at all surprised by his memory. "I asked you then if you'd ever been in love."

"I told you no."

"*Next question*," I said, remembering what he had said.

"You didn't ask me if I *was* in love, you asked me if I'd ever been in love. I hadn't. Not before you. Words, Mariposa, have to be used wisely."

"Fucka me," I whispered, and then a laugh exploded out of my mouth.

Evelina hushed me with a finger to her lips. "You just scared a boo buttafly, mamma!"

Capo and I moved even closer to each other, laughing quietly. Each year around the sun with him only got better. I couldn't wait to go a hundred more.

"Mia!" Evelina whisper-shouted, rushing over to meet the little girl. Saverio walked next to her. She was the same age as Evelina.

We didn't move until the group was close enough for me to hug and for Capo to shake hands. Our group, our *famiglia*, had grown over the years, not only our family tripling in size. We were a built-in party.

Where I found myself in life was more than I could've ever wished for. It went beyond what I ever dared to hope for. More than I ever dreamed I wanted. It was, all along, what I'd always needed.

There were times in my life that I didn't think I'd survive another ten minutes, much less ten years.

A million years with my *capo* and our children wouldn't do, only forever, as long as I lived it with them.

THE END

CAPO

Now you know—
Her love of living life.
Her wild laughter that can't be caged.
Her infectious smile.
Her regal nose.
Her pillow-soft lips.
Her irresistible scent.
Her fierce passion.
Her *lasagne al forno* and her root beer floats.
Her love of old movies.
Her love of kiddie coloring books.
Her love of journals, of collecting words.
Her love of old songs and new.
Her voice when she sings to our children.
Her touch—more than words.
Her legs when they're wrapped around me and she's screaming out my name as I bury myself deep inside of her.
Her.
My wife.
My lover.

My best friend.

My ride or die.

My queen.

My most trusted advisor and confidante.

My heart.

My rosary.

My stained glass, my mosaic.

My butterfly, *mia farfalla*, my Mariposa.

My everything.

I love her.

The mother of my children.

I love her.

You tell anyone our secret, I'll fucking hunt you down.

I hope you enjoyed Machiavellian. If you did, would you please consider leaving a review for Mac on Amazon, Goodreads, or BookBub?

Thank you so much!

ABOUT THE AUTHOR

Bella Di Corte has been writing romance for seven years, even longer if you count the stories in her head that were never written down, but she didn't realize how much she enjoyed writing alphas until recently. Tough guys who walk the line between irredeemable and savable, and the strong women who force them to feel, inspire her to keep putting words to the page.

Apart from writing, Bella loves to spend time with her husband, daughter, and family. She also loves to read, listen to music, cook meals that were passed down to her, and take photographs. She mostly takes pictures of her family (when they let her) and her three dogs.

Bella grew up in New Orleans, a place she considers a creative playground.

ALSO BY BELLA DI CORTE

ACKNOWLEDGMENTS

Saying **thank you** is not nearly good enough, but here goes...

My Family:

None of this would be possible without you. From my husband cooking dinner, to my daughter helping me with social media issues, to my mom answering medical questions, to my brother always reminding me to take a break, to inspiration that comes straight from the vault of my huge, beautiful family, none of this would be possible without ya'll. My success is your success. Anything I'm able do in this life, I do because you love me.

Alisa Carter, my editor:
    You will always be my BEFL. Thank you for always polishing my diamond in the rough.

Stephanie Phillips, my agent (SBR Media):

Thank you for taking me on! I appreciate all that you do for me!

Buoni Amici Press (Drue & Debra):

What a team you two make! The marketing side of the book world can be very overwhelming, but ya'll have made such a difference in that part of my life. I'm thankful for all that you two do for me on a daily basis.

Bella's Beautiful Betas
    Stephanie, Lashell, Anna, Malia, Pam:

Every writer deserves betas as special as the five of you. You love my stories as much as I do, and your feedback is worth more than gold. *Grazie, Bellas!*

Najla & Team over at Qamber Designs:

I still don't have the words to express how much I love Mac's cover. When I look at this cover, today & forever, I *see* Mac, and for someone who works entirely with words, there's something so special about the moment your book comes to life through the cover. It's magical. Thank you for sharing your magic with me.

All of My Reader Friends:

You're the best! Thank you for letting my stories (and me) into your world for a little while. Like the body needs a heart, a writer needs readers. You're the beat that keeps me putting words to the page. Keep being amazing!

———

I'd also like to take a moment to thank **New York** and **Italy** for being such inspirations while I was writing Machiavellian. Both places, along with my home state of **Louisiana**, have really taken a beating over the last few weeks. This virus, this invisible foe, has come in and changed so many lives, our entire world. *This too shall pass.* Until then...I'm sending prayers and love.

Printed in Great Britain
by Amazon